Myrtle Beach

Bedside Books
An imprint of American Book Publishing
5442 So. 900 East, #146
Salt Lake City, UT 84117-7204
www.american-book.com
Printed in the United States of America on acid-free paper.

Myrtle Beach

Designed by Acharya D. Hargreaves, design@american-book.com

ISBN-13: 978-1-58982-582-6
ISBN-10: 1-58982-582-9

Knight, Luther, Myrtle Beach

Special Sales

These books are available at special discounts for bulk purchases. Special editions, including personalized covers, excerpts of existing books, and corporate imprints, can be created in large quantities for special needs. For more information e-mail info@american-book.com.

Myrtle Beach
Luther Knight

Luther Knight

Vardaman

November 1, 2014

Dedication

This book is dedicated to my loving wife, Janis.

CHAPTER 1

United States Veterans Administration Hospital
Gulfport, Mississippi
Summer, 2004

An old man with half closed, watery eyes sat slouched alone, seemingly immune to the activities going on around him. Behind him stood a dull yellow brick building that had been his home for the past fifteen years. To his front, a well-manicured centipede lawn punctuated with huge grayish-white Spanish moss-draped live oaks sloped gradually to U.S. Highway 90. Beyond the highway, the flat brown waters of the Mississippi Sound stretched monotonously toward distant barrier islands. A flight of brown pelicans skimmed the velvet water just off shore, following in unison the subtle declivities of the water's surface. A small gray tern played games with the incoming tide, racing just out of reach of the brackish waters. In the distance toward the east, the vulgar scream of a pair of F-16 jet fighters leaving Keesler Field shattered the serenity of the old man's dreams, causing him to stare skyward.

A passing orderly paused momentarily, started to speak and then, thinking better, shook his head and continued on to the main entrance of the United States Veterans Retirement Facility, eager to finish out another boring day before heading home to more pleasant surroundings.

Annoyed, the old man glanced at the retreating orderly and, with a thin smile, drifted silently back into the dream world he escaped to when he wanted to be left alone. During these soft summer days, he often spent his time sitting there gazing at nothing, remembering, waiting to die. Closing his tired old eyes, Chief Master Sergeant Lucas Mackley sat placidly, having forgotten the orderly's interruption, while the images of his youth formed again a blurred dream world.

Frequently now, those long ago memories crept back as he whiled away his few remaining years. She was seventeen, a lovely wisp of a girl, when he first saw her that night at the Normans' small apartment in downtown Myrtle Beach, South Carolina. He hadn't even noticed when she first came in, and only as she approached where he and Joel sat talking did he look up. Golden blond hair fell about thin pale shoulders, and a shy smile touched lips that could beguile any man. As Betty Norman introduced her, Lucas had quickly pushed the warm beer aside and stood, suddenly tongue-tied, trying to say something witty. Her laughing blue eyes dared him to speak as her enticing smile broadened, revealing even white teeth.

The old man's mood suddenly turned dour, and as the compelling image of the girl faded, the sweltering Mississippi Gulf Coast of 1951 took its place, as often happened now that he was in the waning years of his life. Too often, thoughts drifted back to those younger, wilder years when he first joined the United States Air Force, searching for his place in life.

Fact was, Mackley hadn't intended to join the Air Force. More than likely, he would have remained in small-town Arkansas scraping out a meager living working at some mindless job had it not been for Jack Lowe. Jack had been a classmate. They knew one another only casually but, like Lucas, Jack was at loose ends after leaving high school the previous May.

Nineteen-year-old Lucas Mackley was born and raised in the small town of Dumas in the rice belt of Eastern Arkansas, and growing up in rural Arkansas hadn't exposed him to the realities of life. This came somewhat to an abrupt end during the autumn of 1948. Peer pressure dictated that all boys participate in sports in high school, if for no other reason than to satisfy the vicarious need of the men of the community to re-live their macho dreams through their sons, or someone else's sons. Unrelenting pressure, applied equally by Lucas and the coach, eventually gained Mr. Mackley's reluctant permission for his boy to try out for the varsity football team. The coach was happy, and Lucas wallowed in the privilege of being on the team with all of its social benefits. The jubilation lasted until Lucas was in his senior year and last year of eligibility, then his life changed forever.

Until enlisting in the Air Force on January 19, 1950, the farthest he had been from home was Memphis, Tennessee. Even then, that trip had not been one of his choosing. He was beginning his senior year in high school, and was in his third year as a member of the varsity football team. In the middle of the week during night practice, he suffered a severe injury to his right leg. Although he said nothing to the coach and attempted to play in the next two games, it became evident that broken capillaries in his thigh meant an abrupt end to his football playing days. To be on the safe side, and to prevent possible litigation, the school superintendent personally took Lucas to Campbell Clinic in Memphis for treatment.

The memory still disturbed him. Lucas had not wanted sympathy, but had naively expected to be treated with a bit more respect than the coach was willing to give. That was one of his first disappointments in his life. Once the ability to play football for the old alma mater was gone, Lucas became an insignificant member of the common herd, just another high school student struggling through a final year, scared of what the future would bring.

Although the examining physician in Memphis assured Lucas that he would never be drafted into military service, six months later he was glad to be accepted for a four-year tour of duty in the U.S. Air Force.

Lucas weighed one hundred sixty pounds and was not quite five feet ten inches tall. He was of average build and sported black hair that required frequent cutting. From the time he was in junior high school he had shaved regularly. His hairy chin made him look older but, since he joined the military, had plagued him considerably.

Now that he was in the service, earlier doubts about the future continued to bother him. Had he made a mistake by enlisting? No. The military was the only way out for him. What had really convinced him to join up was what happened during the Christmas of 1949. When everyone around seemed to be smiling and looking forward to the holidays, Lucas felt dread, wishing he could by-pass that time of year. For as long as he could remember, even as a small boy, Christmas season was an unhappy time for him. He could never say exactly why, but while others were gay and cheerful, he seemed to have a cloud of hopelessness hanging dismally over him. In the past, he had made some effort at making the season joyous but, this time, when he was nearly a man, Christmas Day brought with its arrival another depressing dose of the same hopelessness. With those feelings nagging at him, Lucas headed to Little Rock to the recruiting office with Jack, and didn't look back.

Lucas had been hanging around Preacher's Pool Hall watching the hustlers taking the suckers at eight ball when Jack Lowe sauntered in, looking down at the mouth. They were on their third game of straight pool when Jack suddenly stepped over to the side, put his cue back in the rack, turned around, and challenged Lucas to enlist in the Air Force with him. Lucas considered momentarily, then agreed, thinking, *Why the hell not?* Three days later, Lucas was in Lackland Air Force Base near San Antonio, Texas, looking at a four-year hitch, and Jack was back home, having failed to meet minimum requirements for enlistment.

June of 1950 found a bewildered Pfc Lucas Mackley at sprawling Keesler Air Force Base adjacent to Biloxi, Mississippi, awaiting assignment to radar maintenance school.

Shortly after 4:30 p.m. a couple of days before, the Greyhound bus had pulled away from the bus station in sleepy downtown Dumas, turning noisily onto Highway 67 and heading south toward New Orleans. Only six other passengers were on board. An elderly man in a rumpled gray suit with old-man unhappiness etched in the tight lines around his thin-lipped mouth sat immediately behind the driver. A tired young mother with two fussy tots had claimed the last seat at the rear of the bus. A stringy-haired teenage girl sat three rows back from the front of the bus with a pimple-faced young man of about nineteen. The two were entangled, he with his head on her shoulder, oblivious to the rest of the world. Lucas threw his small carryon bag onto the rack above the seat and settled into a comfortable position, eager to get the long trip to Biloxi underway.

CHAPTER 2

Assignment to Keesler AFB
Biloxi, Mississippi
June, 1950

Several hours later, the countryside changed from hazy dusk to darkness as the bus rumbled down the winding highway, eventually leaving the flat Arkansas cotton fields behind in the gathering darkness. By now the young mother and her babies were asleep, and the young hippies had paused in their endless petting and caressing. The grumpy old man had gotten off the bus during a rest stop in Lake Village earlier, and had returned immediately with a brown paper bag sprouting from his pocket. Just before they entered Louisiana, he snuck a long drink from the concealed bottle. Lucas grinned, hoping the nip of whiskey would loosen the old codger up a little. In the quiet of the early hours of darkness Lucas nodded, finally letting the lethargy of the tedious ride lull him to sleep.

He awakened with a start when the bus swung wide left onto U.S. 61 north of New Orleans. Dragging a forearm across his bleary eyes he struggled, trying to remember where he was. The young couple, exhausted from a long night of petting, shifted slightly in their seats then, with matching sighs, drifted off to sleep again. Lucas stared, slightly envious, at the couple for a brief moment then, embarrassed for intruding, quickly averted his gaze. The old man in the wrinkled suit with his head against the window snored noisily, his mouth open and smelling of liquor. The young mother sat wide-eyed in the back of the bus, her children sleeping peacefully.

With the breaking of dawn, the bus rolled into the outskirts of New Orleans, skirting the edge of the city, its driver eager to reach the terminal downtown and end his long, dreary shift. The old drunk snorted audibly, his troubled sleep disturbed by the turning of the bus onto Canal Street. Irritated, Lucas turned his attention from the passing panorama of New Orleans and glared at the snoring man, grimacing at the spittle hanging from the corner of the age-worn mouth. Lucas shook his head in disgust, allowing his thoughts to once again return to perceived glamour of exotic adventure in the French Quarter of this historic Mississippi River town. Back at Lackland, when he had learned of his assignment at Keesler, Lucas had promised himself a jaunt to that fabled place.

The bus pulled into the station and the weary driver got up, stretched, and in a raspy voice announced that there would be a two-hour layover and that all passengers would need to claim their baggage in order to change buses for the final leg of the trip to Biloxi.

With two hours to wait, Lucas crammed his bags into a locker in the waiting room, pushed the door closed, and shoved a quarter into the slot. Contented that his belongings were secure, he pocketed the key and pushed his way into the men's room. Then, standing for a time before the urinal, he savored the relief as the long pent-up fluid flowed from his taut bladder, splattering noisily onto the porcelain. Satisfied, he tentatively washed up at the dirty basin, trying to touch only what couldn't be avoided. A quick swipe with his comb through tousled hair and a final glance in the cracked mirror showed him the need to get onto the street away from the smelly restroom into the less noxious air of New Orleans.

With time to kill, Lucas strolled casually down Canal Street toward the river, aimlessly looking into store windows of businesses not yet open this early in the morning. Already, the humid New Orleans air, pregnant with the decadent smells of the crowded big city, hung oppressively about him. Even in his languid walk, sweat had begun trickling down his back, and the once meticulously pressed uniform of yesterday became dank and wrinkled. *Hell of a way to report to a new assignment,* he thought. But then, what could he do about it?

Soon after, a street marker just past Woolworth's with Bourbon Street emblazoned on it in cursive letters came into view. Lucas picked up the pace despite the increasing heat, recalling what some of the men at Lackland had said, and hurried to the French Quarter. Disappointment played across his face and brought Lucas to a stop as he looked about, glancing along the narrow street. Dirty sidewalks melded into even dirtier gutters and rough pavement. Dull, almost dilapidated balconied buildings crowded the sidewalk, striving for prominence. All were shuttered and silent in the early morning humidity of the Quarter. Only the peeling signs and unlit neon beacons extolled hidden pleasures within, giving hint of what the street must be like after dark. But here in the glare of daylight, all was silent with only the occasional passage of some streetcar on nearby Canal Street disturbing the stillness.

"Well, hell's bells," grumbled Lucas half aloud, "so this is that hot spot them guys back in basic was telling me about. May have to change my plans about coming over here." He glanced at his watch, shaking his head in disappointment, then turned and sauntered back to the bus station, resigned to having to kill another hour.

The Greyhound bus slowed to a stop in front of the station in Biloxi, Mississippi shortly after noon that Friday in June, its air brakes hissing loudly as it halted. Without waiting for the bus to completely stop, Mackley retrieved his carryon bag from the overhead rack and then hurried down the steps to the scorching pavement. Outside, he waited to claim his duffle bag as the driver and an old black porter shifted through the baggage stored in the separate compartment beneath the passenger section.

Lucas grabbed his duffle, wondering what to do next, and moved over in the shade beside the station. Already he could feel the oppressive coastal heat coming off the Gulf of Mexico. Though he had just been off the bus for a couple of minutes, sweat had begun beading on his back, rapidly darkening his shirt around the armpits. Uncertainty clouded his face as he looked about, orienting himself. Dragging a hand along a grimy face, he felt the day's growth of stubble and considered whether or not he should grab a quick shave in the bus station restroom before continuing on to the base. He swiftly dismissed the notion and instead reached for his gear when his thoughts were interrupted by a short, over-weight and red-faced staff sergeant holding a clipboard in a pudgy left hand. Waddling over, the sergeant growled, "What in hell you gawking at, airman?" Then, without waiting for Lucas to reply, he asked belligerently, "Your name Mackley, Lucas A, AF18386881?"

Mackley eyed him momentarily before replying sharply, "Yeah, you got it right, Sarge."

"Then, move it! Get your gold-bricking ass in that jeep over yonder. I ain't got all day to wait around here for shitheads like you," he shot back over his shoulder while heading for the dull blue vehicle parked at the curb in the blistering Mississippi sun with USAF and squadron numbers stenciled on its sides and bumper, identifying it.

Lucas Mackley grinned resignedly, thinking things hadn't changed much from Lackland. Then apathetically fetching the bag and duffle, he dutifully followed the sergeant. That was his first encounter with Staff Sergeant Wilbert Burnham Webber, duty sergeant of the 3384th Air Training Squadron at Keesler AFB in Biloxi, Mississippi. It wouldn't be his last.

Lucas Mackley's encounter with Webber at the bus station was incidental when compared to the trouble he would have during the next few months. It was the usual procedure that incoming airmen were assigned to school within seven days after arrival. Newcomers were indoctrinated, assigned quarters, and allowed a day off to get settled in before beginning formal classes. Since he checked into the squadron near the end of the workday on Friday, it was assumed, at least by Lucas, that the weekend would be free time.

At 0600 the next morning, a bellicose Sergeant Webber stormed through the barracks bay, pointing at a half dozen bleary-eyed airmen, including Mackley, and bellowed, "Get your asses down to the mess hall in five minutes!" Enjoying their puzzled looks, he smirked, adding "You people are on KP." Whirling about, he then stomped out of the barracks.

Several bunks down from Lucas someone, getting up and dragging his fatigue pants on, said angrily, "Wouldn't you know it! Bastard caught me agin. Third time since I been here in this damned hell hole of a place."

One of the ones lucky enough not to be selected laughed, saying patronizingly, "Well, Becket, you learn to play it cool like me, you won't get caught on all them shit details. Gotta play old lard-ass smart, my man. Gotta be a step ahead of him."

"Up yours," responded Becket sarcastically.

During the exchange between the two, Lucas realized that since Webber had only seen him once the day before it was doubtful the man would even remember his name. It was also more unlikely that he would remember how many potential kitchen police he had pointed out. With that working in his favor, Lucas sneaked out of the barracks, staying out of the sergeant's sight for the rest of the weekend, hoping Webber would never know. He was to learn later that Webber suspected Lucas had pulled a fast one on him, although he couldn't prove it. Not deterred by any formalities of fairness, Webber set out to make Lucas's life miserable for the next ten months. Lucas resisted the treatment at first, then, realizing that protesting only made matters worse, stoically accepted whatever punishment he got, determined that someday the sergeant would be amply repaid.

It has been said that true leaders lead by example, but Staff Sergeant Wilbert Burnham Webber was from the old school, relying on harsh, unyielding obedience rather than soldierly leadership in commanding troops. Webber's history of maltreatment of those under him was reflected in tiny pig eyes perpetually squinting as if he was overly sensitive to the harsh Mississippi sunlight, making them even less obtrusive than normal in his florid face. His tightly compressed lips described a thin horizontal line reminiscent of the Greek letter sigma. The left corner turned upward, misleadingly suggestive of a benign smile, while the right juncture of his mouth abruptly curved downward in a perpetual grimace. Tiny ears pressed flat against his head tried in vain to hide in the folds of flab and would have succeeded had it not been for the close cropping of hair. His neck seemed to be lacking. His total appearance was in direct conflict with the trim athletic concept of a United States Air Force noncommissioned officer.

As the duty sergeant for 3384th Electronics Training Squadron at Keesler, he was one of the most despised NCOs ever to serve in the squadron or, for that matter, at Keesler. Whether it was a point of pride or plain foolishness one could not determine, but to push Webber to the point just beyond which common sense dictated seemed to be the game played by the majority of the 3384th's student cadre. To a man, they hated the sergeant with passion.

Immediately upon arriving at Keesler AFB in 1946, Webber began cruising the seedier sections of Biloxi, soon finding one of the numerous local dives on Back Bay to become his chosen watering-hole, and it was there that he spent most of his leisure time alone, brooding. On his first visit to the bar called the Bayside, the bartender attempted to strike up a conversation, but the look of contempt from Webber stopped the effort in mid-sentence. Word spread, and eventually everyone left the morose airman alone, going about their business and ignoring him.

CHAPTER 3

Biloxi, Mississippi
Late February, 1951

Late one chilly night, sometime near the end of February 1951, Mattie Lou Simpson wandered into the bar. Mattie Lou, from Wool Market north of Biloxi, hadn't been in the Bayside Bar before, but that night she was on her way home after usual visits to several of her other favorite hangouts along the bay. A bit tipsy from bar-hopping, she found herself in the Bayside, trying to make the lonely night pass.

With her overindulgence in nightlife and her push on forty, she looked older, although she still retained a certain sultry attractiveness. She still had her slender figure and appeared pretty to any half-drunk airman from Keesler if he didn't look too closely at the lines creasing the corners of her mouth and if he'd had enough booze to muddle his common sense. Harsh manual labor where she worked at Gallataine Shrimp Industries kept her trim despite the evening indulgences. Considering her environment, she was not unattractive despite the hard life dealt her.

The telegram had arrived only days before the war in the Pacific ended, and even before opening it Mattie instinctively knew that

Private Samuel Simpson wasn't coming back to Mississippi. Her faith in God that had sustained her while he lived quickly became hollow, shattered by his death. Unable to cope with the reality that he was never coming home, she turned to alcohol. Within a few months, her drinking, and resulting inability to carry out her responsibilities as executive secretary to one of Biloxi's most prominent lawyers, resulted in Mattie's dismissal. After several weeks of steadily drinking instead of steadily working, she had reached bottom in a quagmire from which there was no escape. Eventually, she persuaded the personnel officer at Gallataine to take her on in one of the cheap-labor jobs usually reserved for the down-and-out. Pay was five dollars per day with little chance for advancement. This suited Mattie because now the tiring mind-dulling work kept her from self-pity. It was only after the sun went down that she remembered and fell back into the terrible depression of her loss.

On that night Webber was the only other patron in the bar. He had gone through six beers and was thinking about returning to the base when Mattie came in. The odor of stale tobacco smoke mixed with the sour smell of beer hung heavy in the confined space of the lounge, assailing Mattie's senses as she pushed the heavy entrance door open and entered. Against the wall to the left, a jukebox was changing records, its mechanical insides protesting, mimicking the apathy Mattie felt deep within. The bar, facing the front of the room, had behind it a large mirror that reflected the lounge, giving the patron an illusion of spaciousness. In front of the mirror partway to the ceiling were rows of glassware seldom used by the beer-drinking crowd that frequented the barroom. The single window to the right of the front entrance with its glaring neon sign bespoke a false sanctuary for the lonely. The only other person in the lounge was the middle-aged bartender, Mike, a former part-time roustabout from the Gulf oil rigs south of the barrier islands.

Webber looked up sullenly from the water-beaded amber bottle he had been toying with, momentarily perturbed at being distracted from his drinking. His leering eyes compelled Mattie Lou to the bar, but once she was seated, his attention returned to the drink he had been nursing for over an hour, her passing merely a brief interruption.

She sat at the bar two stools from Webber and, brushing a stray strand of hair back, ordered a Bloody Mary. A few small sips and a couple of cigarettes later, trying unsuccessfully not to be obvious, she glanced in his direction and let her bleary, alcohol-dulled eyes linger for a moment on his sullen face. *Ugly bastard*, she thought. *Undressed me all the way across the room. I wouldn't shack up with that fat pig even if he was the last man on earth.* Hormones, stirred by Webber's apparent disinterest, made her uncomfortable. *Damn him, he won't even look this way. I'll be damned if I let him know I'm interested.*

With the smoke-dimmed barroom and two more Bloody Marys numbing her mind, Mattie hummed the lost love tune playing soulful on the jukebox and moved brazenly over to sit by Webber. "You look lonesome tonight, Sergeant, and...well, I'm... I'm a real friendly sort. Want some company?" Mattie whispered suggestively as she sat next to him.

Webber snorted and looked disdainfully at Mattie, saying, "I ain't that bad off yet, sweetheart. Least not enough to mess with no damn whore like you. So beat it."

Embarrassed even in her drunken state, Mattie quickly moved to the end of the bar, flashing her dark eyes angrily, and snapped, "Well, the hell with you, sport!"

Webber squinted viciously at the retreating woman, drained his beer and signaled for another by tapping the counter top with the empty bottle. After chug-a-lugging the next, Webber plopped the bottle onto the bar, raked his change into his left hand, pocketed it, and then bulled his way out of the Bayside, scowling. He stopped only long enough outside to empty his bladder against the side of the concrete block lounge then jerked the car door open and slid behind the wheel.

A short while later a drunken Mattie Lou Simpson left the Bayside Bar, mumbling incoherently to herself, and staggered toward the sidewalk heading nowhere in particular. Mike swiped at the bar top with his ever present rag and shook his head at another wasted life.

Waiting outside in his car like a raptor in the shadows at the far edge of the parking lot, Webber motioned her over. When she obeyed, he growled dourly, "Get in, bitch, me and you are gonna have some fun."

Shrugging drunkenly, Mattie stumbled around to the passenger's side, opened the door and slid over against the ill-tempered sergeant as they squealed away into the dark night.

Three days later the shrimper, Lucky Lady, pulled away from her mooring in Back Bay. Holds empty, she rode high in the water and headed to the open waters of the Gulf. The boat cleared the bay, steering south when an alert crewman noticed an object floating on the seaward side of the middle pier of the U.S. Highway 90 bridge. The Lucky Lady's captain, slowing only long enough to verify that the object was the body of a woman, radioed the Biloxi Police Department before throttling up again to normal speed and continuing out to sea, unwilling to waste any more trawling time.

Detective Larry Laplace investigated, recovering the body and identifying Mattie Lou based on fingerprints and a driver's license. Finding no visible marks on the body and knowing her history of depression and alcoholism, the coroner ruled the death a suicide.

When Webber learned that the body had been found, he celebrated in his own perverse way by going to the Noncommissioned Officers Club to spend the afternoon sullenly drinking.

CHAPTER 4

Keesler AFB, Mississippi
Friday, 2 March 1951

Mackley had rolled over just as the sun, a blood red ball, was breaking through the haze obscuring the horizon over Back Bay east of the base. Shaking the cobwebs of fitful sleep from his gritty eyes, he dropped his bare feet over the edge of the olive drab metal cot, letting them touch the rough barracks floor. As he ran his tongue over crud-caked teeth, memories of last night resurfaced while his mind cleared with the increasing morning light.

Even this early the overcrowded barracks was already heating up to its usual stifling, oven-like condition, which was abetted by the metabolism of the sleeping bodies in the confined space of the building. A sticky hot breeze wafted briefly through the open door at the end of the bay, lingering only long enough to tantalize.

Sighing, Lucas scrubbed a hand across his eyes then got to his feet and fumbled in the metal foot locker at the foot of the cot for the shaving kit meticulously stowed in the corner of the tray. Then, stumbling dizzily toward the latrine, he stopped only long enough to kick Charlie's bunk, feeling better as Charlie Kesterman growled, "Mackley, you half-wit."

Flipping him a finger, Lucas continued on to the latrine.

Today was to be his last day at Keesler, and yesterday he, JJ, and Charlie had wasted most of the night cruising the joints and dives along Back Bay Drive, trying to get in one last fling before shipping out. Around midnight, they staggered into the Bayside Bar and flopped down at a table near the jukebox. A man of about sixty dressed like a salesman was talking intently to a much younger woman seated next to him. The young woman nodded now and then but otherwise appeared disinterested in the one-sided conversation.

Charlie led the way into the lounge and as they headed toward a table, the girl looked up, curious. Charlie winked, giving her a lopsided grin, while nudging Lucas and saying. "She's mine, so don't try cuttin' me out, good buddy."

"Hell, Charlie, you can have her, but looks like to me that old man done beat you to her," Lucas had responded, moving over to sit at the nearby table.

"Well, just so you understand, an' don't worry yourself about that old coot. If I can't take her away from him, I don't deserve her," he retorted and then joined Lucas at the table along with JJ.

The bartender, Mike, glanced their way. A grinning Charlie held up three fingers and mouthed Pabst Blue Ribbon. The bartender then reached gingerly into the cooler and retrieved three ice cold bottles and popped their caps on the rusty opener attached to the side of the cooler. Then, with a dirty bar rag draped over his left forearm, he angled across the room and set a beer in front of each man.

As he was turning to walk back to the bar, Charlie tapped the grizzled bartender and stopped him with an inquisitive look. "Say, buddy, ain't this the joint where that stinkin' whore they pulled outta the bay was last seen a couple weeks ago?"

Mike, a big muscular man with a boxer's stance, stared intently at Charlie, trying to place the young airman's face before answering. Charlie started to say something, but the bartender silenced him with an outstretched hand. "I'll let what you just said about her bein' a whore slide, mainly 'cause you look too green to understand about things," he replied angrily. "She wasn't no whore, so get that damn thought out of your dumb mind. She was just some lonesome woman lookin' for a little kindness. I didn't know her too well, but she wasn't no whore. Come in here just that one time to have a drink. That's all. Didn't cause no trouble. Then some sorry bastard hadda up and kill her for no reason. So what's it to you anyway?"

"Didn't mean to piss you off," Charlie replied, visibly shaken. He glanced uneasily at Lucas before continuing. "Just wondering about it. Understand they ain't found her killer yet—that right?"

"Yeah, that's the way it goes. Had she been some rich up-town gal, things woulda been different. Tried to tell 'em who done it. Police wouldn't listen though, and that's what gives me the red ass," spat the bartender. "Tried to tell 'em, but they wouldn't listen."

His interest piqued, Lucas asked, "Mind saying who you think it was?"

"Hell no, I don't mind. son of a bitch useta come in here two to three times a week. Set around, lookin' like he wanted trouble. Ain't seem him since that night, neither. Now, ain't that strange?"

"He got a name?" Charlie asked, returning to the conversation and looking closely at the other man's face.

"That's the damn problem, buddy. I try to keep my nose outta people's business, so I never asked, and he never volunteered. Fat pig of a devil just always set right over there at the bar looking pissed off. Guess, 'cause I couldn't put a name on him the cops figured I didn't know what I was talking about."

"Couldn't you pin it down a little for them—like giving a description of what he looked like?" Charlie persisted, drawing a frown from both the bartender and Lucas.

"Sure I did," Mike replied. "Told 'em he was a fat-assed staff sergeant from out at the base."

Startled, Lucas sat up straight now, stone-cold sober, as Charlie continued questioning the bartender. "You talkin' about a guy weighing around two hundred thirty-five and a little over five feet-eight. Got little squinty pig eyes and a real red face. Face like it was sunburned. Real ugly?"

"Yeah, that's the one. One mean lookin' son of a bitch, if I ever seen one," the barkeep replied as he turned, then walked quickly back behind the bar to serve cold beers to a couple of drunk local shrimpers yelling for service.

The night gone sour, the three airmen sat there breathing in the rank odors and listened to the raucous jukebox while nursing tepid beers. All the time JJ hadn't said anything, but now he broke the silence that had come over them. "You know, men, right about now I don't feel so damned good. If it's who I think it is, maybe we ought to do something," he said soberly.

"Like what, stupid?" Lucas fired back. "We're shipping outta this place tomorrow night, and we go hollering to anyone, all it'll do is get us delayed getting outta this here stinking place. And besides that, there's no way we can be sure it's him."

"It's Webber, awright," Charlie stated emphatically. "Knowing him like we do, I betcha it was Webber that killed her. But hell, it ain't no hair off my ass. I ain't getting involved over no whore. She…"

Quickly interrupting him, Lucas hissed, "Shut up, Charlie, before that bad-assed bartender hears you. C'mon let's get outta here."

With the night ending as it did with the bartender at the Bayside all but naming Webber as a killer, the mood Lucas had been in for the past several days was only more reinforced. As the time to ship out after finishing radar technician school neared, he worried about leaving familiar surroundings. Keesler was a miserable place, and Biloxi was even worse. But starting on a new assignment somewhere else was almost worse than staying.

A quick glance at the luminous dial of his watch told him it was already past midnight. Graduation and shipping out day, 2 March 1951, had arrived. If things continued as they had for the past few hours, this day would be as bad as yesterday, he mused. Well, he'd be on his way with JJ and Charlie later tonight, and if there was any redemption, it had to be that Webber would be off his back. That is unless by some turn of luck the sergeant also got transferred.

Graduation exercises were held on the tarmac outside the classroom hangar immediately following the final class session that morning.

Airman Third Class Lucas Mackley stood proudly at attention in the stifling heat of the brightly burning Mississippi sun, wishing he'd had sense enough to wait to be drafted rather than volunteer. Sweat trickled slowly into the corner of his left eye as he waited. He blinked to no avail, trying to will the annoyance away.

They'd been there for nearly an hour, and now their once starched and pressed uniforms were wilted while they waited for the presiding lifer colonel to arrive. Then suddenly a flight of F-80's roared overhead across the Gulf and circled wide toward the barrier islands. After lowering their landing gear and turning back toward shore, they landed on the runway directly behind the assembled troops. The lead jet taxied over to the flight line, and Lucas listened as its engine wound down and stopped. Out of the corner of his eye, he saw the colonel, still in flight suit, jogging over to the formation. *Man, I hope he makes this quick*, thought Lucas, who now needed to take a leak from all the beer he had drunk the night before.

After they were dismissed following the graduation ceremony, Lucas walked back to the barracks with a diploma and orders in hand assigning him to Pope AFB in central North Carolina. He was uptight about transferring to Pope, feeling much as he had during his senior year in high school. It was not so much a lack of confidence now, but more a feeling of uneasiness at having to get used to new surroundings. Right out of basic training at Lackland

AFB in Texas, he had arrived at Keesler last May, eager to get through school and out on line. He had spent an intensive thirteen weeks of basic training at Lackland where every waking moment was programmed. Here life was more relaxed. But still, as an airman with only one stripe waiting to be assigned to a class, his activities were still closely regulated, always with Webber on his back.

Once at Keesler, he had assumed he would begin radar maintenance training immediately and would soon be through the school and out on the line working. But, his start to classes had been delayed through some bureaucratic bungling, leaving him in limbo, and for the next several weeks he had pulled all sorts of squadron and base duties, anything Webber could come up with anything that would punish Lucas for that first day at Keesler when he slipped away from KP.

With his patience worn thin, he had gone to the squadron's commanding officer when he learned of his deployment to the Far East, possibly to Korea, and complained that he was apparently not going to school. The complaint got the desired results, and within a day or two he was enrolled in class, and Korea was momentarily forgotten.

That was over nine months ago, and during that time he had become used to Keesler, at least enough to tolerate the sultry Mississippi Gulf Coast and the adverse conditions associated with being a student airman. Now that it was time to ship out, he was nervous about leaving things familiar for the unknown. The Gulf Coast was not exactly the most ideal post, but he had no other option if he wanted to become an electronics technician. The good side was that he would be transferring with two of his best buddies, Charlie Kesterman and JJ Phelps. That was much better than jumping off to a new location alone.

Keesler AFB Airman's Club
1730 hours

Three airmen sat on the patio near the south entrance of the Airman's Club at one of the rusting metal tables sipping beer and trying to catch a little of the breeze from the Gulf.

The sun, a sickly haze-dimmed candle, hung defiantly just above the horizon in the western sky. The odor of salt permeated the sultry air that threatened to stifle what little animation remained. Even the ever-present biting gnats or no-seeums seemed to have given up to hide out in the ghost-like shrouds of Spanish moss draping from the drooping limbs of the few giant live oaks left on base. A lone fly, more energetic than its compatriots, landed near a droplet of beer on the table and extended its proboscis into the droplet to draw its fill of the tepid liquid. Sated, it rose effortlessly into the air to buzz about Lucas's head.

Charlie Kesterman, always looking for some way to nettle Lucas, remarked with a smirk, "You know them flies always seem to know exactly where the biggest pile of crap is located, don't they, Lucas?"

Ignoring Charlie, Lucas winked at JJ Phelps and tilted the mug to down a hefty slug then swiped a fatigue sleeve across his mouth before placing the mug back in exactly the same condensation ring formed on the metal tabletop. Tracing the wet outline by rotating the mug and watching the circle widen as it was disturbed, he stayed silent, refusing to be drawn in by Charlie.

Airman Third Class Charles L. Kesterman grew up in the dusty delta town of Leland, Mississippi, the elder of two sons of a divorced mother. When Charlie was seven or eight, she remarried a deckhand on a towboat, The Sanford E. Hutson, operating on the Mississippi River out of Vicksburg. He resented the replacement of his real father by another man and left home when he was sixteen to live with an aunt. Charlie's younger brother, James, however, accepted the stepfather without reservation, which added to the resentment Charlie already felt.

It may have been the hurt of losing his father, or it may have been the belief that the stepfather abused his mother. Whatever the cause, Charlie seemed to constantly be in trouble. And, instead of his mother disciplining him, something that could've been accepted, it seemed that the stepfather always took it on himself to correct the boy as his right. Charlie seldom spoke about his childhood to Lucas but on occasion when there had been a bit too much drinking, let slip some repressed feelings.

When he graduated high school, Kesterman tried a number of dead-end jobs including short stints as a service station attendant, short order cook, laborer, and deck hand on the Hutson. It was the job on the Hutson that allowed him to save enough money to buy a car, a 1947 maroon Fleetmaster Chevrolet sedan, a possession of which he was overly proud.

Charlie stood about five feet, ten inches tall and weighed one hundred fifty-five pounds. Since high school, he kept his reddish-brown hair cropped close in a crew cut. From the demanding job as a deckhand on the Hutson, he quickly developed upper body muscle to where he eventually measured forty-four inches around the chest. Perhaps he was even prouder of his large biceps, again a legacy of hard physical work and favorable genes.

The great disappointment in Kesterman's life was the meeting with, dating of, engagement to, and eventual loss of Margaret Anne Debreau. Maggie, the youngest daughter of one of the stockholders of the barge line where Charlie worked, was seventeen and a junior in Saint James Academy at Vicksburg. Why she was attracted to someone as rough mannered as Charlie Kesterman was anybody's guess. Perhaps the attraction was in sampling something frowned upon by the upper-crust, closed social order she belonged to. Or it may have been merely a matter of teenage rebellion. Maggie had dated a few boys her age, but even then, never got serious about any of them.

She could have had her choice of any number of beaus but, for reasons known only to her, fell for Charlie. She had seen Kesterman one afternoon after school when she and her best friend, Sylvia Arnold, had gone down to the waterfront looking for Mr. Debreau. Charlie was stripped to the waist in the hot afternoon heat, busy hosing down one of the Hutson's decks. As the girls approached, Charlie shut the water off, reached into the pocket of the shirt he had hung on the boat rail, and pulled out a crumpled pack of Camels. Lighting one he leaned against the railing and sucked in a long drag then exhaled a blue cloud of smoke at the sky and watched the girls out of the corner of his eye.

Maggie knew she was staring and that proper young ladies simply didn't stare, especially at strange men, but she was unable to stop. "Huh?" she said, flustered as Sylvia's voice penetrated her consciousness. Embarrassed at being caught, she turned toward her friend, blushing.

Sylvia was laughing impishly. "That's a boy, Maggie," she said, patting Maggie's arm. "And from the way you were staring, it would seem that he's the first one you've ever seen."

"I'll tell you this, Miss Smartass, I intend to find out who he is, and if he doesn't watch out, I'm going to have him," Maggie declared, nonplused. "And for your information that is a man, not some little boy like you would chase after."

"Your daddy will purely have a fit and your mom will have another one of her famous nervous sinking spells," Sylvia said smugly. "I just hope I'm around when you bring him home to meet them, that is, if you think you can. That would be a show worth paying admission for."

After giving her a warning look, Maggie turned back smiling toward Charlie where he still leaned casually against the rail smoking and pretending to be unaware of the girls. "He knows we're talking about him and is trying to act like he doesn't see us. He's playing games with us pretending he's not watching us. But, Syl, whether he knows it or not, that boy's gonna be mine."

Sylvia looked into Maggie's calculating eyes, then to Charlie, and then back to Maggie. Seeing the determination in Maggie's face, she shook her head and smiled, unwilling to argue with the headstrong girl.

Charlie had not intended that it happen in the way that it did. He had seen Maggie as another pretty, young, somewhat pretentious girl to seduce and then drop. That, as in most similar cases, wasn't what happened. Before he realized how deeply he was committed, the romance blossomed into a full-blown love affair. When Mrs. Debreau found out Kesterman was from a blue-collar background, she confronted the lovers and demanded that Charlie stay away from her daughter. But to her consternation, the young couple surreptitiously continued the affair. Outraged Mrs. Debreau demanded that her husband intervene. To keep peace in the family, Debreau had no choice but to call in a marker from the owner of the barge company and have Charlie fired. Unable to find another job, Charlie moped around, drinking heavily and picking fights with anyone willing to accommodate him. After several days, Maggie pressured her former lover to defy Mrs. Debreau and resume the relationship in trysts, an arrangement with its aura of mystery suiting Charlie just fine. However, when Mrs. Debreau became aware of what the two young lovers were up to, she set up strict monitoring of Maggie's every waking hour. Weighing the benefits of continuing with Charlie or returning to her own social level, Maggie dropped Charlie and was soon seen being escorted about town by one of several young men in the mother's estimation as more suitable beaus for a Debreau daughter.

A couple of weeks passed with no progress being made toward getting back with Maggie when an event occurred that changed Charlie's direction.

He was playing pool with Red Holman in the Ace Pool Hall downtown when Red casually asked how his love life with that uppity hot-tailed little blond was going. Although Red had meant no disrespect, Charlie slashed him across the temple with a pool cue, knocking him unconscious. Thirty minutes later down at the police station, Kesterman was sitting in Chief Will Allen's office listening to some fatherly advice from the chief. Immediately after the one-sided session, a hangdog Charlie headed to the United States Air Force recruiting office in downtown Vicksburg with his tail between his legs and enlisted for a four year tour of duty and left town without even saying goodbye to Maggie.

Sitting there with these two good pals would have been beyond Mackley's comprehension just a few short months ago. But now, he had successfully completed several intensive months of training and would soon be out on the line. He felt confident that, once there, long overdue promotions would be his and the pressures of technical school would be only a distant memory.

"Hadn't been for you two," Lucas nodded accusingly at his companions, "we coulda been halfway to Memphis by now instead of sitting around this dump sweatin' and drinkin' this god awful brew. All the damn stuff does is make you wanta pee."

"Hell, don't blame us. Wasn't us pissed old Webber off," Charlie replied sharply. "Seems to me it was you who talked us into sneaking out of squadron duty this morning," he continued fussing, giving Lucas and JJ a lopsided grin. "To tell the truth, Lucas, you act like you get your jollies pissin' Webber off. Be damned lucky if he don't make us hang around till 2400 hours before he lets us sign out now."

Airman Third Class James J (JJ) Phelps, agreeing with Charlie, slumped further down in his chair. He towered over his friends at six feet four inches tall, carrying one hundred sixty-two pounds of muscle and sinew. His long gangly frame made it appear that he was sitting on his spine as he slouched lazily in the hard metal chair.

JJ had grown up in Kennett in the bootheel of Missouri, the part of the state that juts southward into northeast Arkansas and probably should have been a part of Arkansas. After graduating high school in 1949, he enrolled the following fall in Southeast Missouri State College in Cape Girardeau with plans to become an electrical engineer. In his first and only semester, JJ unfortunately had his plans and life irrevocably changed by an incident in freshman Calculus class one day mid-way through the term.

The instructor, Burton Beavis, customarily called individual students to come to the board and write the solutions to problems. In this instance, JJ was not quite rapid enough or, for that matter, smart enough to suit the old man.

Beavis yelled hysterically in his high squeaky voice, "Boy, I have a no-good dog who has more sense than you! Who ever told you that you were college material, anyway?"

JJ grabbed the old man and, after shaking him thoroughly like the old man's dog would have worried a bone, dragged him over to the window and threatened to pitch him out. With the old man begging for help, JJ dropped his hands to his sides, shook his head in disgust and stalked out of the classroom.

Over a pitcher of beer one night at the Airman's Club, JJ said kind of sadly that when Beavis pleaded so pitifully, he just couldn't throw him out, no matter how much he wanted to. Furthermore, he said that a college education was just not worth the bother he would have had to contend with. Two days later he enlisted in the USAF, never denying that maybe old Beavis might have been right about that dog being smarter than he was.

CHAPTER 5

Keesler AFB, Mississippi
3384th Electronics Tng Sq, Barracks B
Saturday, 3 March 1951
2128 hours

Lucas and JJ were busy giving their black GI brogans a final spit shine before checking out, wondering how to speed up their departure time from the base.

Charlie called from the end of the barracks, "C'mon, let's go back down to the club, and have a couple uh cold ones for the road. We still got two or three hours before they'll let us sign out anyway, an' we should make good use of it. That is doing nothing requiring work."

"You guys go on, and I'll meet you there in a little while," JJ grunted, pausing long enough to spit on the toe of his boot before buffing it some more.

"C'mon, Lucas," Charlie said, heading for the door, then stopping and looking back, asked JJ, "You want us to come back and pick you up on the way off base?"

"Naw. Let me throw my stuff in the car, and I'll walk on down later. And remember, Charlie, you damned bum, you owe me a couple beers from yesterday afternoon. So look for me after a little while."

Lucas grabbed JJ's duffel bag, slung it over his shoulder and followed Charlie who had just flipped JJ the bird before picking up his buddy's B-4 bag.

"See you later," laughed Charlie, following Lucas outside.

"You know," Lucas said when they were out of the barracks, "if I didn't know better, I'd swear that JJ is just a bit reluctant to leave here. You reckon he has himself a gal friend stashed away that we don't know about or is he afraid to get out on the line where he'll have to show if he learned anything about radar or not?"

"Beats me," Charlie replied, noncommittally. "You know him 'bout as well as I do. Hell, he's about as moody as anybody I ever knew. Still a good man to work with—at least most of the time, anyway."

"Whatta you mean by that?" Lucas asked, eyebrows raised.

"Nothing. Nothing at all. Just talkin'," Charlie answered solemnly.

"Well, hell, I figured he'd want to down a couple of cold ones just to celebrate the fact we're leaving this place, especially since it lets us get away from your buddy, that no-neck worthless bum, Webber. Don't think anyone of us could take much more of the bastard. Know I can't," Lucas said, frowning, remembering how many times he had had run-ins with the sergeant.

"Yeah, I guess all of us have pretty well got a belly full of him," responded Charlie, his eyes momentarily flashing. Then his mood shifted quickly and he said, "C'mon, I'm buying the first round."

Orderly Room, 3384th Tng Sq
Sunday, 4 March 1951
0010 hours

"Hey, Sarge, you got our orders ready? We're more than eager to leave this here lovely paradise of yours forever," Charlie jokingly informed Master Sergeant Shuguro Iwo, the Charge of Quarters for the night. "We done graced this place long enough. It'll trouble me real bad knowing I'm going and won't never be coming back, but I'll try not to cry now that I'm actually leaving. So," he continued, waving his hand, encompassing the orderly room, "it's so long, adios, goodbye and we're outta here."

"Don't sweat it, men," Iwo said, grinning. "You boys ain't any happier to ship out than I am to get rid of you three screw-ups. And, Kesterman," he nodded toward Charlie, "I'm sure you'll cause trouble no matter where you go."

"Why, Sarge, I didn't know you loved us so much," Charlie said, raising his eyebrows in mock disbelief. "You really seem like you hate to see us go, don't you, Sarge?"

"In your wildest dreams," snorted Iwo, getting up from his desk and handing each man a copy of his orders. "Now if you men will sign on the dotted line, I'll be rid of you."

"By the way, Sarge, where's our good buddy, Sergeant Webber? Thought he was supposed to sign off on us so we could get outta this place," JJ asked, grinning.

With creases forming across his forehead, Iwo replied, "Don't know for sure, JJ, but my guess would be he's hanging out at some joint on Back Bay. Not like him, though, not to be here, especially the way he enjoys hassling people."

The three young airmen laughed because they knew the sergeant was all business and, much like themselves, cared little for Sergeant Webber. Iwo was one of the few NCOs who treated student airmen fairly, looking after their interests more like a father than a superior.

When the necessary papers were signed and pay vouchers issued, the men solemnly shook Iwo's offered hand, feeling a sense of apprehension. Turning to leave, they looked back as Iwo nodded and tossed them a sloppy salute. "I don't usually salute eight balls, but I'll make an exception with the three of you," he said more soberly. "Good luck, fellows."

They gave him an exaggerated salute in return, grinned self-consciously as they left, and closed the door on a part of their lives.

After showing their orders to the guard at the main gate, Charlie slipped the Chevy into low, easing on to Beach Drive and heading west along Mississippi's "redneck Riviera." Passing the bawdy clubs, sleazy beer joints, and tourist traps, they rode toward Gulfport as Biloxi faded into a blur of lights behind them. Glancing into the rearview mirror, Charlie sanguinely observed, "You know, men, next to sex with a good looking woman, or for that matter an ugly one, there ain't nothing I can think of as fine as seeing that armpit of a place disappear behind us. I'd rather eat day-old dog doo with a rusty spoon than have to stay here one minute longer. I just hope I never get sent back here. Not ever." Neither of his companions responded, and Charlie turned to Lucas and prodded, "Well, hell, ain't either of you gonna say anything?"

Already lost in their own thoughts, neither man wanted to comment on the obvious. They were friends of a common mind when it came to thoughts of the Gulf Coast, the long hard hours of school and the poor treatment they had received from both the superiors and civilians. After nearly a year of tedious, never-ending studying with little leisure time and low pay, the idea of shipping out and never returning was more than appealing. It was something they had eagerly looked forward to for months.

JJ, alone in the back seat, was unusually quiet. When they had waited at the beer garden for sign-out time he had sat slouched at the table sipping beer silently and scowling almost belligerently. Now he crawled back into his shell of silence. Charlie, on the other hand, had chattered on incessantly, making light of their leaving. Lucas rode in the passenger seat feeling somewhere between relief and dejection. There was the elation of finishing school and leaving Biloxi but, at the same time, a let-down feeling. But also, there was the hint of uneasiness at having to start over at a new station. He wondered if JJ and Charlie felt the same way.

"Ain't you talking to us common folks tonight, JJ?" Lucas

asked, looking back at their strangely quiet companion. "You ain't said two words since you finally made it to the beer garden. Me an' Charlie just about gave up on you showing up at all. You sure something ain't wrong?" Glancing from the road to Charlie and back to the road, he continued, squinting at the lights of an approaching car, "You reckon he's missing good old 3384 already?"

Trying to see the edge of the pavement in the glare of the oncoming car's lights, Charlie quipped, "Hell, the bastard's drunk on all that beer we done bought him, that's all: just plain shit-faced. Why, Mackley, you seen him. Soaked the stuff up like he was a damned sponge. Tell you what, if he needs to pee on down the road, he'll just have to wet his pants or fling it out the window, because I ain't stopping till we hit Jackson town."

"Aw, go to hell," JJ muttered, trying to hide his feelings about leaving Keesler. The thought of leaving familiar surroundings worried him now that the time for shipping out had come. He had never let on to either one of them, but going to Lackland was the first time he had ever been away from home overnight. For the first few days, homesickness was shattering to the point that faking being mentally unfit to get out of the Air Force was a serious consideration. By determination he had never used before, he managed to survive the first few days before realizing quitting was not an option. He had struggled through basic training and then struggled again to get used to the routine of school at Keesler. Now, like before, he was being forced to leave familiar surroundings for a place he had only heard about. *I wonder if Lucas and Charlie feel like I do or if they really want to leave here as much as they pretend.*

After a short stop at an all-night gas station in Jackson, then north on Highway 51 for six hours, they found themselves pulling into the West Memphis Greyhound bus station at mid-morning. Here they separated, each going separate ways after agreeing to meet back at the bus station in eight days, following their furloughs.

CHAPTER 6

Keesler AFB, Mississippi
3384th Squadron Recreation Room
Sunday, 4 March 1951
0123 hours

The 3384th recreation room was sparsely furnished with only the barest items haphazardly scattered about the small space. Gray walls were free of any adornment, and only one non-curtained window allowed a minimum of outside light. A couple of couches, along with a half dozen metal folding chairs, were arranged in front of a small black and white television set to the left of the entrance. A frayed felt pool table occupied a prominent position in the center of the room. In the far corner to the right of the doorway was a scarred jukebox. A cold drink box and a small table holding a beat-up coffee pot, complemented by a sleeve of paper cups, completed the room's accouterments. That is, until an early Sunday in March 1951 when Staff Sergeant Webber's body was discovered.

"Looks like somebody finally took care of that sorry loser," Master Sergeant Shuguro Iwo commented unemotionally to the ashen faced Officer of the Day as he nodded toward the bloodied body.

Staff Sergeant Wilbert Burnham Webber lay in a pool of his own blood. His body, wedged in a fetal position, lay on its right side between the jukebox and the wall, indicating futile attempts at protecting himself by crawling as far into the corner as possible. Jammed against the intersecting walls, arms and hands shielding his head, legs bending with the knees against the wall, back pressed against the jukebox, he had met his fate. Copious coagulating, darkened blood covered his head and shoulders, evidence of the brutal beating and elapsed time endured before death. The gore-covered left sleeve of his fatigue shirt was ripped at the shoulder. Blood had collected in his right eye, while the left one stared vacantly. It appeared that Webber had been dead for at least a couple of hours. The officer and NCO studied his body, being careful not to disturb anything.

"Yeah, Sarge, and I can't say this comes as a surprise," the OD replied, struggling to keep from vomiting. With bile rising in his throat, First Lieutenant J. D. Valic, the 3384th's Executive Officer, swallowed hard and with shear willpower forced the contents of his stomach to stay down. "Way he's crapped on his men, I guess it was just a matter of time until someone got enough of him and hit back," he added, shrugging and turning away, wishing this had happened on someone else's duty. "APs will want to talk to some of the men, but don't wake the colonel. Hell, just as well he finds out in the morning," he continued, speaking softly as if not to disturb the dead man, not realizing it was already morning.

"Yessir," Iwo replied, glancing curiously around the room and wondering if the killer had slipped up anywhere. "I'll get the men mustered right away, but I doubt it'll do a helluva lot of good. Nobody's gonna tell us anything, anyway, even if they knew what happened. Hell, Lieutenant, I've had a mind to kill that bastard more than once myself."

"Yeah, Sarge, I know, but we have to go through the motions anyway," Valic responded with a wan smile touching his chalk-dried lips, still wishing this had happened under someone else's watch.

Iwo followed the lieutenant outside and waited while the young officer leaned against the iron railing along the recreation room steps.

Settling his thoughts still seeing the grizzly scene vividly imprinted in his mind, Valic tried to decide his next step. Finally, he cleared his throat and spit quickly into the shrubbery that bordered the building. Then gesturing nervously with his hand, he ordered, "Might as well send for the APs, and let them get started, Sarge. And while you're at it, seal off this area. Don't let anyone in until the APs get here. Like I said," Valic repeated, forgetting he'd already ordered Iwo to assemble the squadron, "I guess we also need to turn all troops out in formation. They're not gonna like it, but do it anyway. And, don't let on what's happened until we get them assembled; then the APs can handle it."

Two weeks later, a directive from the investigating officer, a Major John S. Croft, of the Judge Advocate General's office, was delivered to the Commanding Officer of the 3384th Training Squadron. It stated in the text that after all leads had been exhausted, the investigation involving the death of Staff Sergeant Wilbert Burnham Webber be placed on hold as a cold case until such time that additional evidence should be found. The CO forwarded the directive to Lieutenant Valic who, after glancing briefly at it, shrugged indifferently and passed it on to the orderly room clerk for filing.

CHAPTER 7

West Memphis, Arkansas, Greyhound Bus Station
Monday, 12 March 1951
1045 hours

Lucas and JJ arrived under slate-gray skies pregnant with snow at the busy Greyhound bus station around the same time on the morning of 12 March 1951. They were having a cup of coffee in the station restaurant when Charlie came hustling in, fully expecting one or both of his friends to be late.

Before Charlie could speak, JJ commented sarcastically, "Well, Lucas, look who's late this time. Told us we had better be on time, and now old Charlie's running behind time as usual."

Grinning his crooked grin, Charlie thought fast and responded smugly, "Figured I didn't need to hurry. Way the weather looks, we ain't gonna be able to drive very far today anyway. All we can do is drive as far as we can, and then hole up for the night."

"Yeah, but won't that be cutting it pretty damn close getting to Pope on time?" asked JJ with concern slipping into his voice as he sipped his hot coffee. "Sure don't wanta be late right off the bat on our first real assignment."

"I guess we will be running pretty thin at that," Charlie admitted, shrugging, "but if we're late, well, hell, it just can't be helped. At least in this weather we'll be a helluva lot better off being late than upside down in one of them ditches. Never seen it like this at this time of the year, and if it snows, the road's gonna be too slippery to travel on."

Each had been given a ten-day delay en route to their new assignments at Pope AFB near Fayetteville, North Carolina. Lucas had spent his time in Dumas while JJ went on to his home in Kennett. Pretentious Charlie, on the other hand, didn't go home, but instead had gone to the small hill town of Oil Trough over in central Arkansas and spent the entire time visiting his most recent girlfriend, Lila Settles, to the envy of JJ and Lucas, who had been informed of his intentions earlier.

In a hurry to get started, Lucas and JJ loaded their gear into Charlie's car. Lucas slid into the front passenger seat while JJ piled unceremoniously into the backseat among the bags and gear. The car rolled out of the bus station parking lot at 1100 hours and headed south to the bridge spanning the Mississippi River between West Memphis, Arkansas and Memphis, Tennessee. It was almost noon, 12 March 1951.

Sometime around mid-afternoon, they pulled into Savannah, Tennessee, with freezing rain slanting like glancing birdshot against the fogged up windshield. The rain, now full fledged sleet, changed to huge, wet flakes of snow a few miles down the road. As they drove eastward visibility became poorer and poorer; the burdened windshield wipers were no longer able to keep the glass clear.

As long as daylight held, Charlie didn't have much difficulty with the icy road. There were patches of deadly black ice occasionally along the highway, especially on the bridges, but for the most part, normal traffic kept the two lanes relatively clear. Well past dark, the lights of Lawrenceville appeared faintly through the swirling snow, promising refuge from the storm if they were willing to chance arriving at Pope late. Braking for a stoplight, the Chevy swerved into a skidding fishtail. Charlie, reacting instinctively by turning the wheels into the skid, brought the car to a sliding stop partway through the intersection just as a beat up pickup truck sped by, barely avoiding a collision. Without breaking speed, it shot through the intersection, its tail lights quickly fading into the swirling gray curtain of snow.

"Whew! Didja see that son of a bitch? Damned near hit us! Tell you for sure, that does it for me!" Charlie blurted, white-knuckled, firmly gripping the steering wheel. "I say we get off this slick-assed road first chance we get before we all get killed. I'm gonna try to drive on, so keep a lookout for a motel or someplace we can stop." With visibility virtually zero, he shifted into low and eased through the intersection, still shaking over the near accident.

Red and blue neon lights ahead announced the Dixie Starlite Motel, a welcome haven to the road-worn traveler. The sign in the office window, missing the letter "N," boldly beckoned with a single word, "VACA CY."

Charlie Kesterman's true mischievous nature revealed itself when the sign came into view. Looking back, he said, "Phelps, you crawl your butt under them bags, and Lucas, you throw one of them blankets on top of him so he'll be out of sight."

"What the hell for?" JJ asked indignantly. "I ain't about to crawl nowhere, especially under no blanket." But then, waiting only momentarily, he laughingly said, "Now on second thought, Charlie, had you brought Lila, that old gal friend of yours, along, then I just might consider gittin' under there real cozy with her."

"Goddammit, JJ, do like I say! Now, both of you listen up. I'll stop a ways away from the office near one of them rooms at the end and check me and Lucas in. They won't know but what there's only two of us, and that way we'll save us some pocket money," Charlie explained irritably.

Frowning, Lucas complained, "Charlie, you bum, you and another one of your hair-brained schemes, again! Is that all you ever do, try cheating someone. If you spent half as much time chasing women as you do trying to screw over people, you'd be plumb whipped to death in half a day."

"Look, you guys. It'll work. I know it will. Me and my brother done tried it before," Charlie argued persuasively, not bothered by Lucas's criticism. "Once I get Lucas and me registered, I'll open the office door as a signal, then Lucas can make a big play of getting our stuff outta the car on the side toward the office, and while he's doing that, JJ can slip outta the other side and into the room."

The battered roadside inn was a series of a dozen adjoining clapboard-sided rooms facing the highway with just enough space in front of each unit to park a car. A trash-strewn alley by the side of the building led to the rear, where a rusting 1941 Ford Coupe was parked, barely visible. The office, located midway in the single row of rooms, was bathed in a sickly yellow glow from a lone street light. The office extended about six feet closer to the road than the rooms, so the desk clerk could easily see the front of each of the rooms without having to go outside. A hand drawn sign with the word "OPEN" hung from the inside of the small window in the door. The only concession to modern technology was the gaudy neon sign with its burned out letter.

Charlie swung the car into the slot in front of the third room from the left end of the row then switched the engine off, got out, and swaggered nonchalantly to the office. Returning almost immediately with a smug grin, he tossed the room key to Lucas and hand-signaled him to start unloading the bags. In the back seat, a hunkered down JJ opened the left rear door and, bending low, slid out onto the icy ground, keeping the car between him and the office. Just as he stepped past the front of the car the motel night clerk, a large, rawboned woman of about fifty, looked up and saw him. Realizing what they were up to, she threw the office door open with the force of a Texas tornado and, like a Texas tornado, stormed out into the cold Tennessee night, not bothering to even put her coat on.

She reached Charlie before he could move and grabbed him by

the arm, spinning him around and vehemently spitting, "You damned little sawed off crook, what in hell you trying to pull on me? You registered and paid for two people, an'...an'...and there're three of you! Answer me, you little bastard!"

Quickly regaining his composure, Charlie grinned boyishly and replied patronizingly, "Why, no, ma'am, you must be mistaken. Why, I plainly remember telling you there'd be three of us. You just apparently didn't hear right."

Lucas and JJ were taken by surprise initially. Then when they realized what had happened waited to see how Charlie was going to talk his way out of this dilemma. Smirking, JJ leaned back against the car while Lucas stood rooted at the door to the room and held it open. Seeing that Charlie had been found out, they grinned expectantly and watched him squirm.

The clerk placed huge mannish hands against Charlie's chest, forcing him back, and glared menacingly at Mackley and Phelps. Then with a venomous smile, she said, "You two punks are in this up to your asses, too, and you better wipe them silly grins off them faces. I'm fixin' to call Chief Willard down at city hall and tell him what you are trying to do to me. Think I won't sign a complaint and let the three of you spend the night in jail, you better think agin, and you can betcha your puny little asses I will. The very idea, tryin' to pull that stuff on a poor old widder woman like me."

"Look, you old heifer, you better take your hands offa me!" Charlie shouted, enraged, but then the angry woman shoved harder until he was pinned against the Chevy. The look on Charlie's face told his buddies that he now knew she would carry out her threat.

Seeing he had gone too far, Charlie knew that it was time to try to sweet talk his way out of a difficult situation. Taking a deep breath, he exhaled audibly, trying to play on her sympathy. Keeping his head down, he mumbled contritely, "Yes, ma'am, you are absolutely right. I did try to cheat you, and I truly am sorry, but we had a good reason, and I'm sorry I called you a ol' heifer. You see, ma'am, we've been on leave, an'...and are on our way to Pope Air

Force Base in North Carolina and from there," Charlie's lower lip quivered, "it looks certain we'll be shipping out for Korea in a few days. And, ma'am, more than likely one, or maybe all three of us, may not get back. Well, anyway, we're all three broke and, as cold as it is tonight, were just too tired to drive any further."

Charlie was at his finest. Even knowing that all of this was pure fabrication, Lucas and JJ could almost believe Charlie's impassioned plea. They could almost imagine tears welling up in his eyes.

The woman looked from Charlie to the others then back to Charlie, and finally relented, saying, "Well, I had me a son in World War II, so I guess I sorta understand. I won't press no charges if you'll git back in your car, and haul ass outta here. Now, go on and git before I change my mind." As she spoke her face took on a softer, gentler, more motherly look.

Not willing to let well enough alone, Charlie said forcefully, "Awright, ma'am, but you need to gimme my ten bucks back."

"Why you smart-assed little bastard!" she exploded indignantly, "I'm a doin' you a favor letting you go, but you ain't getting no damn refund. Now like I told you, get the hell outta here, or spend the night in Willard's nice, cozy jailhouse."

Charlie, livid at her refusal, had to be dragged bodily to the car by his buddies.

"Charlie, get your stupid butt in the car and let's get outta here. That crazy old bitch means what she says!" Lucas shouted adamantly.

"Lucas is right," JJ added, pushing Charlie into the driver's seat. Then getting into the back, JJ slammed the door and said, "C'mon! Let's get the hell outta here while we still can."

Still fussing about the money, Charlie cranked the car, backed onto the icy street and turned east, muttering. As he drove away, the humor in the situation suddenly struck him. Sneaking a peek behind them, he saw the woman rooted in place in front of the neon sign with its broken letter. Arms folded and legs akimbo, she stood daring them to defy her.

Turning his attention back to the road, Charlie grinned his crooked grin and said sardonically, "You know, I do believe that old biddy coulda whipped my ass."

"You danged well better believe she could! You danged near got us in deep trouble with your big mouth, didn't you, old buddy?" said JJ, his eyes angrily flashing. Leaning against the car cushion, he closed his eyes, wondering why he was short-tempered with Charlie. *I can't believe Kesterman cheating that old woman back there at that motel like he done. And me helping!*

"Naw, that old heifer wasn't gonna do nothing," he responded to a disgusted JJ. "You saw how the old master handled her, didn't you? Had her eating right outta my hand."

"Hell, Charlie. She wasn't eating out of it, she was damn near ready to bite it off, and your stupid head, too," Lucas responded unsmiling. "We're lucky we got outta there with our asses in one piece, no thanks to you and your crooked schemes."

Winchester, Tennessee, U.S. Highway 64 E.
Monday, 12 March 1951
2116 hours

"Okay, smartass, what do you suggest we do now that you got us throwed out of that motel?" asked JJ, spitting the words at Charlie. "Next closest place from here is Monte Eagle, and in this mess, we ain't going to be able to go much further." Outside, the dull white cold of Tennessee seemed to close in on them, forcing what little security the car offered to become even more fragile.

"Look, guys. I'm sorry," Charlie said apologetically, seeing their predicament. "All I know to do is to go on until we can't, then pull over somewhere and try to sleep in the car. If we git too cold, we can run the engine ever now and then to knock the worst of the chill off."

"Probably, we woulda been better off spending the night with old Chief Willard. At least we wouldn't freeze to death tonight," JJ fussed, wiping the frost from the window on his side of the car and looking out at the thickening, swirling snow.

Realizing that arguing further would do little good, JJ and Lucas silently agreed to do as Charlie suggested. In less than a mile, Charlie turned onto the parking area of a small roadside country store, unable to go further. He switched the engine off, kicked the shift into neutral, and set the emergency brake. "I'll leave the keys in so whoever gits cold can reach over and crank her up for a few minutes." And with that, he turned his face toward the door and within a few moments was snoring.

It continued snowing heavily until well after midnight as they huddled miserably in the frigid car. Around 0200 hours, Lucas awakened to the sound of wind whistling through the leafless trees across the road and shivered involuntarily. The tin awning strained to remain in place to shelter the barren storefront while a single light in the back of the store provided meager light. Outside the skies had cleared, and the new moon gave an eerie, fairyland cast to the snow-covered landscape.

After dozing fitfully throughout the long taxing night, Lucas took a moment to remember where he was. Bone-breaking cold crept steadily into the car through every crevice, and he shivered again despite himself. The Chevy creaked and groaned, buffeted by the wintry gale. Rousing in the pre-dawn darkness, JJ reached across the back of the seat and tapped Lucas lightly on the shoulder. Then seeing that he was awake, JJ said with chattering teeth, "How about cranking up, I'm damned near froze to death back here."

Behind the wheel, Charlie slept soundly, a muted snort escaping him as the interior warmed up.

At dawn Charlie awoke suddenly, stretched, groaned and stepped out of the car to urinate, trying to sign his name in the snow. Shaking his head, Lucas grinned. When he finished, Charlie got back into the semi-warmth of the car and said decisively, "Well, men, this is the way it is. You need to pee, you better get 'er done, 'cause we're just about to be on our way to Caroline."

Snow, not yet beaten off by the few early morning vehicles on the move, still covered the road. From the parking lot where they had spent the night they could see the distant skyline of Monte Eagle, distinct against a cobalt sky. Already the brightness of the early morning promised a much better day than yesterday. With renewed optimism, Charlie stepped on the starter, goosing the gas pedal a couple of times and listened to the roar of the engine before pulling onto the highway.

After they reached the Piedmont of North Carolina later that day, their worries about reporting late diminished with each mile. By pushing the speed limit they managed to reach the main gate of Fort Bragg at 1800 hours, well ahead of check-in time.

Pope AFB, located on the larger U.S. Army installation, served as the flight base for the 82nd Airborne, one of two elite paratroop divisions of the U.S. Army. Once they had been cleared onto Fort Bragg, it was only a short drive to the 507th Tactical Control Group where they would be on their first assignment as radar mechanics with the 726th Air Craft Control and Warning Squadron.

CHAPTER 8

Post Exchange, Pope AFB
Wednesday, 18 April 1951
0900 hours

Lucas was having serious doubts about staying in the Air Force. With nearly three years more to go on his hitch, however, there was little he could do about it at the moment but serve the rest of his time. Still he had his doubts.

They had surfaced back at Keesler, but now misgivings about strict regimentation of military life were more worrisome with conditions in Korea deteriorating. Talk of going to Korea was a common subject of barracks gossip. Lucas didn't think of himself as a coward, but the fear of being in some fire-fight still tortured him. It seemed, even this early in the Korean intervention, that the country was into more than just a police action. Yet, that was what it was called—a police action. The United States had only recently gotten back to peaceful times after WWII, and now there was fighting and dying in some godforsaken place he had never heard of to prevent some undefined danger from happening. It already seemed that the United States forces and their allies were expected to win a war where unreasonable limits were imposed on the young men and women charged with fighting it. The question that bothered him most was: Why sacrifice him and other young Americans to save people in some far-away place he knew little about and cared even less about? What was the purpose? Was it to save them from their own country or from themselves?

It boiled down to the fact that it wasn't smart to get drafted since it was draftees who got sent to Korea. He just wanted his four years to hurry up and end. The duty he had at Pope was not dangerous, but it was causing him to regret ever enlisting. He should have played it smart and let them draft him, or maybe he could have used his bad leg to stay out. Who knows, he might have gotten lucky on the draft lottery.

The work here at Pope wasn't difficult, but each afternoon at 1600 hours he reported to the maintenance noncommissioned officer in charge, and two hours later found them atop the radar tower going over the checklist for the radar system. Even though it was early spring, working thirty feet high on the tower by nightfall without adequate shelter was difficult. Cold hands dropped tools, and numb fingers made fine-tuning of the set tedious. To compound his gloomy attitude, the harsh shift prevented Lucas from leaving base except for an occasional trip into the nearby seedy town of Fayetteville.

Lucas straightened up, secured his fatigue collar snug about his neck and pulled his cap down tighter on his head. Cold rain, which had steadily fallen since noon, seemed to slow the dreary day to a crawl, and now with darkness approaching, the wind picked up out of the north to a brisk chilling pace, making the day even more dreary. Even the usually bustling flightline seemed to have slowed down.

Lucas blew on his hands while rubbing them together to restore a little flexibility to his cold-numbed fingers. With his circulation partially renewed, he turned back to the task of finishing the last of the preventive maintenance procedures. As he attempted to fit the small screwdriver into the slot on the rheostat it slipped, clattering loudly through the steel grating to the ground thirty feet below, its passage echoing metallically as it fell, clanging on the steel girders of the tower.

"Shit fuzzy!" he shouted to no one in particular while rummaging in the tool kit for a replacement.

"Now I know where all my tools have been going," said Staff Sergeant John Charles Burkhalter accusingly. "Here. Try this one. It ain't as small as the one you dropped, but I expect it'll work."

"Thanks, Sarge," Lucas responded, reaching stiffly for the tool. "I get this tuner set and that should finish us up here. We'll need to check the PPI scope in operations, and that should do it for the night."

If I have to spend the rest of my tour freezing my ass off like I am tonight, I don't think they can talk this old boy into re-upping. Lucas was already disillusioned with his new assignment, even though he had only been at Pope for a couple of weeks. Living at Keesler was difficult enough, but at least it was warm. Here, all he had seen was cold wet weather that never seemed to improve. Since arriving at Pope, he had spent some serious time thinking about his future. Overall, he liked being in the Air Force, and if a chance to move to a new assignment came up, his attitude about re-enlisting could change. Even here at Pope, if he could be placed on a better duty shift until he could become adjusted to his new job, he might be more at ease with the Air Force.

He'd found out that the CO was looking for people to go to Shaw AFB in South Carolina, but being new at Pope had dismissed the idea of volunteering. *Cold as I am right now*, he reflected, rubbing cold stiffened hands together, *a transfer south looks good. Hell, just the word, south, sounds warm.* Shivering, he made the final adjustment and stiffly climbed down from the tower to the jeep where Burkhalter waited. Next morning Lucas, without saying anything to Charlie and JJ, went down to the orderly room and put his name on the list to transfer.

A few days later, Staff Sergeant Burkhalter noticed Lucas waiting in the checkout line in the Post Exchange and, purposefully walking over, held out his hand and said, "How are you doing, Mackley?" But before Lucas could respond, he continued. "Let me see, you been working with me for how long now? Something like a month, maybe?"

Burkhalter had been a fighter pilot in World War II, flying a P-51 in the Pacific theater of operations. During that time he had achieved the rank of first lieutenant but, as happened to a large number of junior grade reserve officers, was reduced to his permanent rank of staff sergeant after the war ended. Since then, he had finished radar school easily at Keesler and then was immediately assigned to Pope AFB. "I guess you know when you agreed to transfer to Shaw that you lost a promotion to airman second." Burkhalter reminded him. "I recommended you, and the captain endorsed the promotion request, but when you volunteered for Shaw you blew the chance."

"Yeah, I had heard about that," replied Lucas, shrugging. "I appreciate your effort for me anyway, even though I won't git it now for a while longer. To tell you the truth, though, I just don't think I can handle that early night shift on that cold tower anymore. I thought Mississippi was miserably hot, but honestly, I could stand some of that Gulf Coast heat right about now."

With a nod, Burkhalter replied philosophically, "Yeah, it's a shitty world, but we ain't gonna change it, I guess. You gotta go where the brass sends you, but it's your decision this time. To tell you the truth, I like your work and would have liked for you to stay, but the old man wants some men to start that new team at Shaw. So a man has to do what he thinks is best."

Lucas was to find later that Burkhalter was right in his assessment about the condition of their world, and that he would find that it was an unfair world, where he was concerned, for the rest of his time in the service. What he didn't know now was how deeply he would become involved in a situation from which there appeared no escape—one that would challenge his faith. Right now, though, he was pleased to be leaving Pope and heading for Shaw.

726th AC&W Sq Orderly Room
Pope AFB
Thursday, 19 April 1951
0800 hours

Next morning Lucas picked up his orders and signed out of the 726th at the orderly room. Airman First Class Al Thurston was waiting for him outside in the squadron jeep.

"Hop in and I'll run you down to the flightline," Thurston said, looking around to see if anyone was watching as he flipped a half finished cigarette into the gutter without bothering to field strip it. Seeing Lucas's questioning look, he muttered, "Been wanting to do that ever since I got outta basic—just never had the guts to do it before."

Laughing, Lucas replied, "Yeah, me too, but it'd be my luck for some fresh-outta-OCS second john to catch me. Anyway, thanks, Al," he added and, throwing his gear into the backseat of the jeep, climbed into the passenger's side.

"You ever been to Shaw?" Thurston asked not really interested in knowing but feeling he needed to say something.

Lucas settled into his seat before he answered, shaking his head. "No. Actually, I never even heard of it until a couple of days ago when Burkhalter was asking for volunteers."

"And you volunteered? Didn't your daddy ever tell you that you never volunteer for anything in this man's Air Force?"

"Yeah, I know, but hell, it got to the point where I don't think I coulda stood working on that cold tower another night," Lucas replied, remembering how the night winds whistled chillingly through the tower superstructure. "And besides, that piss-ant night shift was cutting into my social life."

"Well, you got nobody but yourself to blame if you get down

there in South Carolina and find it's not the paradise you thought it was," Al responded, starting the jeep.

"That's right, Thurston, but don't let it bother you," Lucas snapped, testy over constantly being reminded of what he was missing by leaving. "I'll make out all right. So, like I told Burkhalter, don't let it bother you, Al."

Thurston glanced around at Lucas as he pulled away from the orderly room and started to speak but instead shrugged and remained silent.

Ten minutes later Thurston parked on the tarmac near a waiting C-47 where Lucas hopped out and retrieved his gear from the back of the jeep. "Thanks again, Al. You ever make it down to Shaw look me up, and the beer's on me," he said, trying to make amends for the sharp retort earlier. After shaking Thurston's hand, he trotted out to the airplane.

A technical sergeant standing by the plane checked Lucas's name off a list and instructed him to pick up a parachute and board. Minutes later, the airplane roared to life as the pilot prepared to run through his checklist prior to takeoff. Taxiing to the end of the runway and stopping, he revved the engines up a final time, received clearance and accelerated, hitting liftoff speed well before reaching the end of the runway.

As the airplane gained altitude and banked right to a southerly heading, Lucas realized that another phase of his life was at an end. He would be a part of a newly formed outfit, a number of whose members would be friends from Keesler, and in fact, he had learned through the grapevine his best buddies, Charlie Kesterman and JJ Phelps, would follow him to Shaw in less than a month. At Shaw, they would organize a team capable of operating along the South Carolina coast monitoring air traffic while training for eventual overseas duty.

During the bumpy flight, Lucas had time to think about his new assignment and began feeling a little edgy. Even though he had gained a little on-line experience at Pope, the thought of starting over was a bit frightening, but he had made his choice and would have to live with it. He leaned back against the bulkhead of the fuselage, feeling the vibration of the engines as the plane cut through scattered clouds toward Shaw. With the parachute helping pad the sharp edges of the bulkhead, he dozed fitfully with the roar of the airplane shutting out all but his own thoughts.

A little over an hour later, the airplane circled Shaw AFB, arousing Lucas. Shaking the cobwebs of sleep from his mind, he felt the plane shudder spasmodically as the landing gear lowered and locked into place. The C-47 banked slightly to the left as the pilot lined up with the runway, and Lucas could see the base geometrically laid out to the east. Adjacent to the tarmac a series of hangars stood with huge doors looming open, waiting to devour incoming planes for maintenance. A flight of two F-80's waited at the end of the taxi strip for their turns to take off. Beyond the hangars and maintenance shops lay neat rows of wooden barracks. He wondered which of these would be his and if Shaw would be his home base from now on, or if he would be going somewhere else before long. The C-47 touched down with a puff of smoke and the squeal of tires on the skid-marked runway. Suddenly, everything was quiet as the plane slowly taxied to the apron.

CHAPTER 9

Veterans Administration Hospital
Gulfport, MS
Spring, 2005

"Sergeant Mackley?" the soft feminine voice drifted through the pathways of his memories, breaking into his innermost thoughts. For a moment he had been back in South Carolina over fifty years ago, reliving those early days as a young man venturing out of rural Arkansas. Slowly, he turned at the sound, annoyed at the intrusion. Then, recognizing the speaker, he lifted a palsied hand and smiled wanly at the comely young woman in the starched white nurse's uniform.

She had come to work at the retirement facility a little over a year before. Lucas had been sitting alone in his drab room, waiting patiently for another day to pass, when she had entered the room briskly with an official looking clipboard clasped against her chest. She had marched straight to him, reaching out and grasping his gnarled hand in her small but surprisingly strong one. He knew he was staring rudely but couldn't help himself. Confused, he had blurted, "Em?"

The lilting voice had said soothingly, "No, I'm not Em. I'm

Marty Judson, Sergeant. I'm sorry I startled you."

"I...I...I thought..." he had responded then, remembering where he was. "I'm sorry. I must have been doin' a little woolgathering." *God,* he had thought, *this is Em.*

Looking quizzically, she had said, "Oh?" Then smiling radiantly, she had explained that she hadn't meant to disturb him, but since she was new on the job wanted to visit and get acquainted with the residents she would be working with. "I don't mean to pry," she had said, "but you seemed to be puzzling over something, and I would like to help, if I may."

"No," he had responded rather curtly. "I prefer to be left alone."

She had then turned abruptly away and, without further comment, hurried out of the room. "Dammit, why did I run her off like that? She didn't mean to intrude. Just doing her job and I acted like an immature fool," he chided himself.

That was over a year ago, and since then, Lucas eagerly looked forward to Marty's visits. Once or twice she had attempted to steer their conversations to that initial meeting, interested in why he called her Em then attempted to cover up the slip. Each time it came up, Lucas quickly changed the subject.

She had shared lunch with him, and the matter had come up again. *I can't tell her about Em,* he had reminded himself. *There are some things that shouldn't be shared, and thinking of Em brings back too many sorrows. Maybe someday I'll get the nerve to tell her, but not now.* They talked small talk then. After eating, she walked with him to his favorite spot overlooking the Gulf. As so often happened in the past few months, he sat alone, re-living those days at Myrtle Beach. At first, there was resentment when Marty seemingly tried to get into his mind, making those distant memories fade. That he didn't want. Rather, it was those very memories that sustained what little life remained. Still, Lucas had to admit, Marty was a ray of sunlight that brightened an otherwise dull existence.

The disturbing thing about the pretty young nurse was her uncanny resemblance to Emily. The same blond hair, the fathomless blue eyes coupled with her little-girlish short-tempered manner when she showed displeasure. She was the exact image of the young Emily he had loved. The hurt of losing Emily was strong but not strong enough to cause Lucas not to treasure the brief visits from Marty.

Bubbling with the exuberance of youth, Marty had visited much longer than intended. A quick glance at the oversized nurse's watch on her slender wrist, and she was tenderly touching his arm before hurrying off toward the main building. Left alone so abruptly, he felt the sadness slip in uninvited, and his mind shut out the present and traveled back to those earlier days of more innocent times. *It's been such a long time, but Em, girl, you're still on my mind.*

CHAPTER 10

Shaw AFB, South Carolina, 707th AC&W Sq
Monday, 21 April 1952
1045 hours

Lucas had visited Myrtle Beach briefly nearly a year ago shortly after being transferred to the 707th at Shaw AFB. At the time, Captain Kenneth R. Cook, Technical Sergeant James W. Jackson and he had spent several days in the low country of South Carolina reconnoitering the coastal area for possible future radar installations for maneuvers and possibly permanent sites. One particular location showing promise was the de-activated air base south of Myrtle Beach.

All that remained of the old base, their primary site, were a few bachelor officer quarters and the decrepit old guard house, now one of the few remaining serviceable buildings. Structurally, it was still in reasonably good shape, although repairs would be required before it would be suitable for habitation. Even in its present neglected condition, the base seemed suited for anticipated radar surveillance activities.

At the time of the planned shakedown maneuvers to Myrtle

Beach, the police action in Korea was beginning to wind down with the promise that hostilities would be over before the end of the year. The implication was not that the United States was winning the conflict but more that public pressure was building up to where prolonging the effort for a full military victory didn't seem politically favorable in Washington. Negotiations had already been underway between the antagonists for several weeks, and the prospects for some sort of mutually satisfactory settlement seemed within reach. With the leadership of both Koreas and their respective allies and uncertain support back home, it was anyone's guess if all the problems would actually be resolved and peace achieved.

Radar emits and focuses a powerful scanning beam of ultra high frequency electromagnetic waves that establish through timing and reception of reflected waves the distance, direction of motion, and altitude of any object in the path of the beam. Radar works along a line of transmission to the horizon beyond visual sight. Beyond the earth's curvature, ground radar is quite inefficient. Additionally, at the extreme fringes of coverage, early radar types were limited. Primary among these limitations were the blank spots due to cancellation effects caused by reflected waves or by blockage from terrain and buildings. To compensate, smaller, easily transportable, lightweight units, such as the TPS-1B, were used for these blacked out areas. To fulfill the mission of surveillance of such blank areas, these units were deployed when it was determined that a gap in coverage existed.

The 707th consisted of a permanent installation at Shaw AFB ten miles west of Sumter. Additionally, there were two or three of the smaller mobile lightweight TPS-1B units to fill in the gaps in coverage patterns of the larger set. Such units typically were moved out from the base 150 to 180 miles and operated for a period of a few days to as long as a year or more.

Each of the mobile units was designed for rapid deployment, and even when it was necessary to traverse rough terrain, all the necessary equipment could be transported by the troops on the team. A full team included two commissioned officers and thirty enlisted men. Personnel included at a minimum one or two radar mechanics, twelve radar operators, two automotive mechanics supporting radio repairmen and operators, an enlisted medic, a cook and mess personnel. Captain Kenneth R. Cook commanded Radar Team 1 and had as his Executive Officer a young second lieutenant named Quinton A. Walton.

Shaw AFB, Mississippi
0530 hours

The convoy had formed up the preceding night. The next morning, 22 April 1952, an hour before dawn, the line of vehicles moved out through the main gate and turned east on U.S. 378 with Captain Cook driving the lead jeep while his driver sat in the back. By 0617 hours, the last of the convoy had passed through Sumter with all the vehicles evenly spaced, traveling along at 45 mph in the early morning traffic. Each vehicle, a two and one half ton truck commonly called a six by six or two and a half duce, carried two drivers with the remaining team members riding in the team's two utility vehicles.

Lucas's gut told him the practice maneuver was headed for trouble. Talk around the barracks was that they were being given busy work to keep them out of mischief in the nearby bars and whorehouses of Sumter and Columbia. If that was the only reason, the exercises would not accomplish much except to kill a few days. If the men wanted to get into trouble, they would find a way no matter where they were. Ever since it had been announced that the team would deploy to Myrtle Beach, set up the radar and support equipment, operate for five days and then return to Shaw, he had felt that the exercise was not needed. With as many inexperienced men on the team it seemed to Lucas that a site closer to Shaw, or even Shaw itself, should have been chosen for the shakedown run. He saw no reason to go all the way to the coast just for practice.

Nevertheless, the decision had been made, and the team was on its way.

The convoy passed through the outskirts of Sumter shortly after 0615, moving snail-paced directly into the early morning sunshine, heading toward Lake City. Already day hands were working in the cotton and tobacco fields along the highway, pausing only long enough in their labor to watch the line of vehicles crawling by. This early in spring there was still a chill in the air. Dew was heavy on the roadside grass, and along fencerows spider webs, laboriously spun during the night, glistened as their makers awaited errant insects to be trapped. An occasional meadowlark perched singing on the telephone lines along the road, its bright yellow breast vivid in the breaking dawn.

Rumbling along the highway, diesel trucks emitted fumes that dulled Lucas's mind. His thoughts wandered back to his home in Arkansas and the many times he had witnessed similar scenes along the gravel back roads and fields around Dumas. He turned to Charlie and asked, "Do you ever miss not being back home?"

Charlie considered for a moment before replying, "Nah, I can't say that I do. I left things back there that I would just as soon forget about."

"Like what?" Lucas asked curiously.

"I'd rather not say now, Mackley. Maybe someday, though, but right now, I don't even want to think about it."

At about 1100 hours, near Lake City, Cook halted the convoy for a short break to eat the sack lunches provided for each man. At his signal each vehicle pulled onto the shoulder of the highway, leaving four or five feet distance between vehicles. Before eating, each driver was required to make routine checks of his vehicle. Once finished with these duties, the driver had a few minutes to relax before the convoy moved on toward its destination.

Before the trip had begun, Airman First Class J. C. Cagle, a radar operator fairly new to the team, had spent most of the night in the honky-tonks around Sumter when he should have been at home with his family.

He was confronted by a very angry young wife after arriving home well after midnight, and harsh words were exchanged. The chastised airman returned to the base barely in time to prepare to move out with the convoy. In no condition to drive, he soon found himself nodding sleepily as the trucks droned monotonously down the arrow-straight highway toward their destination on the coast. Rolling since well before daylight, the constant sameness of the truck directly ahead and the unnerving confrontation with his wife had blunted Cagle's reflexes. Staring at the olive green truck, his eyes glazed over, and in this state of mind, Cagle narrowly missed plowing into the leading vehicle when the signal to pull over was given. Lethargically dismounting, he halfheartedly began checking the truck while his co-driver carried his lunch to the shade of one of the vehicles where others were preparing to eat.

CHAPTER 11

Lake City, South Carolina
A Tobacco Farm 15 Miles East of Lake City
Tuesday, April 22, 1952
5:00 A.M.

Sarah Moorland reached over to playfully nudge her husband, Roscoe, in the left side and said, "Ain't it about time you was gettin' up if you're goin' to Sumter this mornin' with that load of tobacco?"

He shook the dregs of sleep from his mind, grunting as the woman jabbed him again, harder this time. "Lemme alone, dammit, woman, I'm awake. I been awake for the past hour," he groused, knowing that she knew he was lying, and knowing also that this was the same game they played every morning.

"Sure you was. And hogs fly, don't they?" she responded, giving him a playful pinch on the loose skin about his middle, letting her hand slide down his hip.

Rolling over to face the woman lying in bed beside him and letting her woman smell overpower him, Roscoe squinted through slit eyelids and said languidly, "Mess around like that, woman, you gonna cause things to happen that no tellin' if you can handle or not."

"Look, Roscoe, you ain't seen the day you could wear me down." She giggled suggestively as she snuggled against him, her bare breasts rubbing tantalizingly against his chest.

She sure knows me, he realized. *Ever time she wants her way she rubs them tits agin me like that and I can't say no, even if I wanted to. Damn woman. Can't live with her, and can't live without her.* Placing his hands on her shoulders, Roscoe pushed her away and then grabbed a breast in each hand. Sarah squealed with delight and pulled his head to her bosom.

Sarah wasn't all that good looking, but still often received second looks from both men and women when she walked down the street. A chipped tooth showed in her smile, and there was a decided bounce in her gait, a kind of cotton-row hop that made her hips jiggle a bit more. These flaws, if they were truly flaws, enhanced her appeal. There was something about her that made Sarah stand out from the other women around Lake City. Men admired her unique prettiness, and women were a bit envious. Even at thirty-two, her tall, willowy stature, emphasized by well-formed breasts and proud appearance, drew attention. Not only was she reasonably attractive in a coarse sort of way, she had the personality that led people to like her and want her company. The startling thing was no one around Lake City ever believed Sarah would fall for such a plain man.

Moorland could hardly believe his good fortune at winning the love of Sarah. He was well aware he lacked the abilities to provide for her as well as some of the other more successful men pursuing her. And he knew also that he was not at all a good-looking man. He made up for these shortcomings, however, by devoting all his efforts to pleasing Sarah. What he never knew was that Sarah was unconcerned with looks but was sure that she had found in him a man with depth of character who loved her deeply.

Roscoe, tall and pinched-faced, possessed both a prominent nose and Adam's apple and could be considered homely. It was even doubtful that with sufficient money and advice he could have improved. He was simply one of those individuals whose genes, through the vagaries of gene distribution, precluded his ever being a handsome man. His few friends considered him an extremely lucky man to have Sarah.

Since they married six years before, she had looked after him, making him a fine wife. Like Roscoe, she was uneducated, but many folks around Lake City thought that she could have done better in her choice of a husband. He had met her one night in 1945 in the Pines Lounge south of Lake City. This had been a couple of months after he had been released from the infantry not long after Japan surrendered, ending World War II.

After he returned to the Lake City area, Roscoe had been more or less at loose ends, drinking up what little money he had saved from service allotments and mustering out pay as a veteran, and generally drinking himself to death. Nobody could say what Sarah saw in Roscoe, but one special night in the Pines something clicked between them, and within the month, the two became husband and wife.

Roscoe even quit drinking after the marriage, except for an occasional beer, settling down to the rigid routine of tobacco farming. He and Sarah planned on having several children to help in the tobacco fields, but try as they may, Sarah just couldn't conceive. The desire for a family may have influenced the frequency of their frenzied coupling, or it may have been that they just enjoyed the sheer sexual pleasure of each other. Who knows, but in any event, neither let an opportunity to procreate go by.

Their lovemaking took the better part of the next three blissful hours before Roscoe finally left the house at 9:30, leaving Sarah standing on the front porch, watching him with dreamy eyes as he drove out of sight toward Lake City. Little did they know their lives were soon to be changed forever.

CHAPTER 12

East of Lake City, South Carolina, U.S. Highway 378
Tuesday, 22 April 1952
1115 hours

In his haste to finish and go about the business of eating lunch, Airman Cagle, still hung over from the night before, stepped backward from the fender of the truck onto the highway, unaware that Roscoe Moorland's old pickup truck was fast approaching. Misjudging the distance from the truck to the pavement, Cagle reeled off balance. Another driver, seeing what was about to happen, yelled a warning, but Cagle stumbled and fell backward, panic stricken and staring wild-eyed at the battered, mud encrusted grill of the ancient Ford pickup bearing down.

Roscoe had been idly watching the men milling about the convoy as they went about their duties but didn't slow down as he approached the parked trucks. Gasping involuntarily as Cagle fell, he realized that the man was directly in the pickup's path. Reacting instinctively in an attempt to avoid running over the stumbling man, he braked, trying his best to swerve away from Cagle. With brakes locked, the pickup, now out of control, slued sideways toward the hapless airman while Roscoe helplessly braced for the impact. Slow-motion moments later, the skidding truck straightened out and plowed into a screaming Cagle, knocking him back toward the larger military truck.

Feeling the body's sickening impact, Roscoe slammed his eyes shut, trying to blot out the horrific scene before him. Now out of control, the pickup continued on its deadly path, crashing into the six-by-six immediately in front of Cagle's truck. Careening off the second vehicle, the doomed pickup rolled to the left onto the blacktop, barely missing a swerving oncoming car. Coming to rest in the weed-choked ditch opposite the convoy with sparks from the disintegrating truck igniting the ruptured gas tank, the entire vehicle erupted into a fiery inferno. Moorland, trapped, fought desperately to escape, screaming frantically as the conflagration enveloped the truck.

Two passenger cars traveling a short distance behind Moorland quickly pulled off the road and skidded to a stop. Both drivers rushed toward the wreck, urged on by Roscoe's screams. Those airmen closest to the accident site stood stunned before reacting but quickly recovered and ran to help.

Roscoe Moorland died in the gasoline-fed inferno of his burning truck, pleading as would-be rescuers tried desperately to reach him.

Airman Cagle's body bounced off the side of the six-by-six with enough force to snap his neck and then slid facedown in the gravel between the pavement and truck, leaving no doubt that he was dead from the moment of impact. Once the initial shock was over, several of the men nearest the accident ran toward the body. Lucas, having seen the incident and knowing what to expect, quietly stood back as Staff Sergeant George Williams, the team medic, double-timed from the front of the convoy with his medical kit.

Choking back bitter bile that rose in his throat, Captain Cook quickly posted guards to direct traffic around the gory scene until local authorities could be called to take charge.

Stunned, Lucas sat with Charlie under their truck's bed, no

longer hungry.

"You know, Lucas, I had me a bad feeling about this damned trip all along. We should have just gone ahead and set up permanently without going down to check out the beach first, or whatever the hell it was Cook wanted us to do," Charlie said, shaking his head.

Lucas sat, still in shock, trying to comprehend the abruptness by which a human life could end. Only moments before Cagle had been alive, eager to finish the shakedown and return to his family in Sumter to make amends for his night on the town. Now there he lay, a bloody broken mess on the side of a highway, his life snuffed out much too soon.

"Know what you mean. Hell of a thing to happen to a man," a thoroughly shaken Lucas finally responded. "Damn! You never know when your number's gonna come up, do you?"

"You got that right, buddy, and I'll tell you something else, if that poor bastard in that burning pickup over there had a wife and kids, then there's gonna be some more people sad today," Charlie replied, nodding toward the burning truck and rubbing his nose to try to quell the stench of burning flesh mixed with gasoline and melting truck parts floating in the acrid air.

Lucas sat quietly watching the gawking crowd milling around and wished he could help but didn't know what to do. Several motorists, morbidly curious at the death scene, slowed to stare before several airmen directing traffic urged them on their way. Finally registering what Charlie had said, Lucas replied earnestly, "Yeah, Charlie, you're right. It might not be so bad to die, but I'd hate to think what it would do to my family. Like being in the service, I guess."

"Whatta you mean by that?" Charlie asked, shifting around where he could lean against the truck tire.

Lucas answered slowly, trying to pick the right words, "I joined the Air Force so I could get away from home. Hell, Charlie, my old man wouldn't have kicked my ass out, and anyway, if he had,

Momma would've been on him in a minute, but I knew they couldn't support me. Hell, Charlie, I had to get out on my own. At the time, I didn't even think about maybe dying. Thing is, I didn't know someone would start a damned war like that Korean crap, which means I could get killed, and so could you, Charlie. Oh, hell, I don't know what I'm saying." He suddenly realized he was letting his feelings show and backed off, saying in a low mumble instead, "Guess I got no real complaints, though. Hell, I volunteered for the Air Force just like you did, so it looks like we gotta take the bad with the good."

"So what has that got to do with Cagle getting killed and that guy in that pickup turning to burnt toast?" Charlie asked, sneering in a macho manner like he had hardened to things like this in a matter-of-fact manner over the years.

Ignoring the flippancy in Charlie's question, Lucas mused, "I don't really know, Charlie, but it still bothers me that we didn't even try to help either one of them men. Looks like we coulda done something."

"Hell, Lucas. What could we have done? No way in hell was anybody gonna get that fella out of that pickup, and it was plain that Cagle was dead by the time he hit the ground. And I sure as hell didn't aim to get myself killed trying to be a hero." Charlie gestured toward Cagle. "All I can say is better him than me."

"Damn!" exclaimed Lucas, shivering. "That guy hollering like that. That's got to be one hell of a way to go. Trapped like that, knowing you're gonna die. And that fire burning like it was. Don't think I'll ever git over the smell of him and that load of tobacco burning. Damn!"

"You act like you ain't never seen nobody dead before," Charlie fired back angrily, a smirk crossing his beet-red face.

Still looking at the burning truck, Lucas turned at Charlie's comment and solemnly said, "No, I ain't, Charlie, not like that anyway. I've seen dead people before, like my Uncle Jessie, but he was an old man. But for sure, I ain't never seen nobody killed like this. Have you?"

"I have, old buddy. One time, couple years ago when I was working on the river a clumsy, four-footed deckhand named Eddie Whitten fell between two barges we was tying off, and before he hit the water them barges slammed back together like you'd clap your hands. Mashed him clean through at the hips. Took ol' Eddie more than four hours to die." He paused to let Lucas consider what he just said. "Well, you'll get over this—just like I done that one."

Lucas asked sharply, "Don't you ever think about it?"

"Yeah, I thought about it for awhile," he responded, becoming angry. "What I ain't told you was they tried to blame me for what happened. He slipped on some loose cable and fell, but I didn't make him slip. Him falling was his own fault, but them bastards fired me anyhow."

"Aw shit, Charlie. I'm sorry," Lucas responded contritely.

The sound of sirens off toward Lake City brought them back to the current tragedy. They stood watching the first of several police cars as it slowed to a stop, lights flashing, closely followed by a racing ambulance, its siren wailing. Hurriedly, two officers got out of the cruiser and trotted over to Cagle's body, giving it a cursory glance before turning their attention to the burning pickup truck. The younger of the policemen, seeing Roscoe's still smoldering body, turned away vomiting. The more hardened older officer stared briefly, hands on his hips, and then turned aside to lead his partner away, mumbling to him.

Airman Ben Swindell of the motor pool examined the two damaged military vehicles, one of which was too badly wrecked to go on to Myrtle Beach. Then, seeing Captain Cook look his way, he walked over and asked for permission to call Shaw for someone to come and tow it. The other one appeared capable of continuing the trip to where it could be repaired on site, so its cargo was offloaded and distributed among the other vehicles just to be on the safe side.

Lucas and Charlie watched silently as Cagle's body and what remained of Roscoe Moorland's were placed into the ambulance as the police cleared the accident site. Once the bodies were seen to, Captain Cook spoke briefly with one of the police officers then nodded and turned to motion at Sergeant Jackson that he should have the men mount their trucks and prepare to get under way.

Lucas walked back to their vehicle with Charlie, shaken by what they had just witnessed. Charlie pulled his fatigue pants away from his crotch and climbed into the driver's seat while Lucas walked around in front of the truck and settled himself into the passenger's seat.

Glancing toward the front of the convoy, Charlie turned the ignition on and stepped on the starter. The truck roared to life synchronously with the rest of the vehicles in the convoy, each waiting for Cook's signal, straining readily to follow the one in front as if they too were as eager as Lucas and Charlie to leave the accident scene and get this exercise finished.

Captain Cook returned to the lead jeep and pumped his fisted hand to signal the convoy to move out and then pulled onto the highway. Charlie revved the engine of his truck, causing it to belch black diesel smoke, then, shifting into low, followed the truck in front of him onto the pavement.

"Goddammit!" Lucas shouted to no one in particular. "Life's just a plain lousy deal when you see stuff like this happen."

Charlie shrugged and, double-clutching, shifted into second gear as the truck strained to keep its proper place in the convoy.

Once the shock of the accident had sunk deeply into his subconscious, Lucas let Charlie's comment resurface in his mind. Here was a fellow team member whose life had abruptly been obliterated. The tragedy would have been difficult enough to accept if only Cagle had been affected, but he had left behind a young wife and baby back in Sumter. *Where was it they came from?* Seems he remembered that J.C. was from somewhere in west Nevada, so it would appear that his wife would be from there also. Lucas surmised that would be where she would return. He was really not that close to Cagle, but the death of anyone you know, even if only casually, touches home if you have any feelings at all.

That was what was so troublesome about Kesterman saying *better him than me*. Lucas silently mused that he knew Kesterman fairly well, but this seemed out of character to say the least. Yet, the more he reflected on Charlie's attitude, the more troubled his feelings about death became. Maybe if that comment had been only about the tobacco farmer's death, he could possibly understand. The farmer was a stranger, and although the death would always be remembered, it could be hidden and forgotten in the mind's recesses. But to dismiss an acquaintance's death as cavalierly as Charlie had was too unfeeling for Lucas.

He thought back to younger days with his distrust of organized religious types and hyped-up preachers just trying to make a fast buck off the ignorant masses. *Heck, I don't know much about* all *that preacher mumbo-jumbo about sin and such*, he considered. *Seems to me far back as I can remember, they been condemning me for sins I ain't even done, and then saying they can get 'em forgiven 'cause they got a hotline to God to keep my ass off the hot seat of hell. Don't understand what's happening. Seems like the more I try to figure all this out, the more messed up it gets. I know I can't blame God, but what can a man do when he may get sent someplace to get killed and there ain't a damned thing he can do about it? Just like old Cagle, a man don't know when his number's comin' up.*

CHAPTER 13

Myrtle Beach, South Carolina, Old Myrtle Beach AFB
Tuesday, 22 April 1952
1610 hours

Myrtle Beach AFB, South Carolina, had been an integral part of the national defense system on the eastern United States seaboard during World War II. Now the base lay abandoned, another reminder of a brutal war. The stage was set for another conflict, a police action that would cost thousands of lives but would generally be ignored by a war-weary world.

With downsizing of the military and shifting of forces in Europe and Asia, the outbreak in Korea required the immediate reclamation of many once busy facilities. Left to the elements, most of the temporary buildings at Myrtle Beach AFB had deteriorated, leaving only the more substantial ones remaining. All of the flightline structures had been razed and salvageable materials sold off at ridiculously low prices. Besides half a dozen small one-room bachelor officer quarters facilities, the only usable building remaining was a base guardhouse. It consisted of one large room suitable as a barracks for the enlisted personnel, two additional smaller rooms that could house senior NCOs, one common latrine, and a small bathroom with a shower that was available for the NCO quarters should extended maneuvers be initiated at some future date.

The team arrived on the defunct base around 1400 hours that windy afternoon in the spring of 1952 and used the next couple of hours half-heartedly setting up the equipment and squad tents, just going through the routine to make the site operational.

"Captain," Sergeant Jackson said, approaching Cook. "I think we got us one major morale problem with the men. Ain't a one of them seems to be doing more than going through the motions."

"You're right, Sergeant," Cook agreed. "I guess what they saw this morning was the first time most of them ever saw a dead body. Scares the hell out of me what happens if this bunch goes overseas to where the real fighting is." Briefly pausing, he looked around at the men mechanically going about their duties and added, "Probably best that you keep them busy so that they don't have much time to think about it."

"Yes, sir, I'll try, and if I have to, I'll work them right on until dark."

Lieutenant Quinton Walton approached the two men and, with a sly grin, said, "That may not be necessary, Sarge. Captain Cook asked me to run an errand to town for him—sort of a reconnoitering mission—that may have solved our problem, at least for the time being."

Noticing that the three had been conversing animatedly for several minutes, Lucas reached for a screwdriver when Jackson detaching himself from the officers and came walking toward the radar truck, motioning for Lucas. When Lucas looked up, Jackson said, "Mackley, this ain't been a very good day. No two ways about it. I see you've about got the system set up, an' I guess that you have it aligned an' ready to go on the air." The last part of the comment was more a question than an observation.

"Yeah, Sarge, got 'er finished about half an hour ago. You want us to go for real now, or should we wait till tomorrow?"

"We'll crank up tomorrow morning early. But right now, just make sure your equipment is in top shape. We blow this chance, and the old man may send us over to Congaree or some other god-awful place instead of here. With that wreck this morning, Captain Cook's gonna have one hell of a time convincing the colonel that we should come back here."

"You want me to check with Martin to see if he's ready with the radio setup? And what about the motor pool? Want me to see about that, too?"

"Yeah. If you would, why don't you see to all the units for me? Tell all the other NCOICs to be ready to begin operations at 0800 in the morning."

Mackley had been in South Carolina for only a short time but already liked the place. It reminded him of back home in Eastern Arkansas where the land was relatively flat and where one could see for great distances over cotton and soybean fields clear to the horizon. The difference here in Carolina was a good bit of the land was taken up in tobacco farming. He had noticed earlier that morning near Sumter the numerous tall, gray, wooden sheds scattered along the fence-lines at the edges of the fields and had asked about them. Sergeant Williams had explained to him they were curing sheds, and later in the summer, carefully selected tobacco leaves were harvested and hung there to cure and dry. Flying down from Pope, he had not had the opportunity to see much of the terrain but later had driven toward Greenville in the hilly northwestern portion of the state. Now he was getting his first look at the coastal area of South Carolina, locally known as the low country.

South Carolina rises gradually from the Atlantic Ocean to the Piedmont Plateau and Blue Ridge Mountains to the northwest corner of the state. The Blue Ridge and Piedmont form the upcountry while the remaining two-thirds below the fall line of rivers is known as the low country or Coastal Plain.

The small resort town of Myrtle Beach is strung out along U.S.

Highway 17 and Ocean Drive for a distance of four or five miles in the coastal plain. The nearness of the Atlantic Ocean is apparent from the stringent odor of salty air. Swaying sea oats grow sparsely beyond the tan sand dunes set against a background of dark-green palmettos and scrubby salt-stunted shrubs while, a short distance inland, vegetation grades into stately pine and hardwood trees. Beyond the tidal marshes, freshwater wetlands dominate, and farther south toward Charleston, Spanish moss clings shroud-like to huge, majestic, live oaks.

The beach itself is neither the most beautiful, nor the ugliest, beach along the eastern seaboard from Maine to the Florida Keys. For the most part, the ecru sands are fairly firmly packed and, like the sugar-white sands along the coast of Florida, are fine grained. In low tide the beach extends from the high water mark, delineated by a ridge populated by meager bands of golden sea oats and salt spray, stunted shrubs to about seventy-five feet at the water's edge. During high tides, waves may wash nearly against the shoreward boundary, and at times, errant breakers may spill over the low sandy berms onto the dunes beyond.

Ghost crabs scurry back and forth with each encroaching wave, seeking tidbits of food. Hosts of tiny clams and scuds and a myriad of other crustaceans inhabit the intertidal strip between the beach and the water's edge. Plovers and terns race shoreward, avoiding the incoming waves and then turn to chase the receding waters back to the sea.

On either side of Ocean Drive, houses, condos, and apartments crowd together like so many purple martins lined up on the utility lines, supplying the temporary inhabitants of the town. At precise intervals, lateral streets and lanes extend eastward, terminating at the beach. Paralleling the beach along the extent of the downtown business district is a boardwalk of weathered, sea-battered timbers to accommodate the multitude of tourists who descend on the town in the summer. To the west, and pushing a few blocks inland, less expensive summer cottages along with homes of many of the resort's permanent residents crowd the town, trying to conform to the ever-burgeoning tourist accommodations located east along the ocean's shore. During the winter in the 1950's, Myrtle Beach's population numbered no more than 4,500 to 5,000 souls, those individuals who called the small seaside town home. Summer, however, saw an influx of well over 60,000 visitors migrating like locusts from the western Carolinas, Georgia, and as far as Virginia to the north.

To the north along the Atlantic coast, occasional beach communities are scattered all the way to the North Carolina line. About twenty-five miles to the west is the small city of Conway, the county seat of Horry County, and along the coast to the south, the small fishing village of Murrells Inlet lies sleeping among the dunes. Nearby, the Intracoastal Waterway runs more or less along the ocean to the west of Highway 17.

CHAPTER 14

Radar Team 1, Command Van
Wednesday, 23 April 1952
0932 hours

Captain Cook, Lieutenant Walton, and Sergeants Jackson and Wilson Anderson were discussing the feasibility and advisability of moving the team to Myrtle Beach for an extended period beginning in April 1953. Cook felt strongly that it would take about that time to fully assemble and train the team into a well-functioning unit. Of course, opinion was divided among the enlisted men, and Cook, eager to settle the matter, had asked Walton and the sergeants for their professional input.

Knowing the final word would be his, Cook commented rather patronizingly, "Give me your views, including some solid reasons. The old man is already on my case thinking we're dragging our feet."

"Sir, I don't know that we'll need that much time," Jackson spoke up, ignoring protocol, before Lieutenant Walton could speak. "Over half the men have had some experience at Pope, and the ones just out of Keesler should be able to pick up enough know-how until they get on-the-job training. Matter of fact, Captain, we got a couple of pretty good radar people, Mackley and Kesterman, who just got their MOS upgraded to 7, so I believe we're in good shape with our personnel as far as on-the-job training is concerned."

"You may be right, Sergeant," he replied, slapping at an annoying gnat buzzing in front of his face. Then, nodding toward Walton who stood quietly listening, he asked, "What do you think, Lieutenant?"

Uncertain of what to say, Walton hesitated noticeably before answering. Fresh out of the Citadel, his golden lieutenant bars still brand new, he didn't want to mess up on his first field assignment. Showing bravado he didn't feel, he looked toward the men working setting up the site then glanced at Jackson, hoping for some sort of support before he said, "I…I'm inclined to agree with Sergeant Jackson, Captain. Hell, the war will be over before then. Why…?"

Why the hell did I ask? Walton's never had an original thought in his life, Cook reflected. Then, interrupting the young officer with a shake of his head, he turned to Anderson. "You got anything to add, Sergeant?"

Staff Sergeant Wilson Anderson, NCOIC for Radar Operations, replied quickly, "Yes, sir. I think Jackson is living in a dream world. Them boys ain't had near enough training. They may know how to operate them weapons, but you get 'em in battle and half of 'em'll be killed before we get set up." Anderson looked hard at Jackson, silently daring him to argue.

Grinning crookedly, Jackson shrugged and responded, "Sir. You have my opinion. There are the lucky living and the walking dead among us, so take your pick."

Cook considered what Jackson said, wondering what he should do. *They tell me I gotta get this bunch battle-ready and proficient, and then give me inexperienced people like Walton and a loser like Anderson. Knew all along I shoulda decided on my own.* "Okay, men, that's all. Jackson, you stay."

When Walton and Anderson were out of earshot, Cook blurted,

"Dammit, Jim, what's happened to all the seasoned NCOs? The colonel may not like what I'm gonna do but, hell, he'll just have to get his drawers pulled up and get over it. We're gonna abort this little exercise, so have the men start breaking down at 1500 tomorrow afternoon, and be ready to move out at 0500 next day. And, by the way, Jim, tell the men what Lieutenant Walton has been doing moseying around town. Assure them that real girls from a couple of those cotton mills will be in the Beach House Bar tonight. I'm confident that they'll be there on time." When Jackson looked past him, Cook turned and, seeing Walton approach, muttered, "Now what?"

With a quick salute and a cheeky grin, Jackson left them.

Walton looked hard at Cook. "Ken, uh. Captain Cook, you think this is a good idea?"

"What do you mean? We got most of the kinks worked out, so I don't see a problem. And you got to admit we have worked the men pretty hard, so it's time to loosen up on them a bit." Cook laughed, knowing full well what Walton meant. "Actually, though, what really bothers me is that I'm concerned with the effect that Cagle's death may have on morale. The men have had time to think about it, and we may lose them."

"Nope, what I mean is if we turn that bunch loose down town, there's no telling what trouble they'll cause. I'm telling you, Ken, Kesterman and his two cronies can stir up trouble in a convent by just walking through the door."

Smiling at the analogy, Cook said, "Quinton, the trouble with you is you worry too much. Both of us should take a tip from those three and enjoy life for once."

Myrtle Beach, South Carolina
Old Myrtle Beach AFB
Wednesday, 23 April 1952

Most of the men lazed around the operations tent while Lucas and a few others finished up last minute details when Captain Cook came out, dressed in summer uniform. The radar and radio sets had been assembled and checked out and were operating as expected.

Lucas and his crew of mechanics aimed the antenna at a smoke-stack off in the distance toward Myrtle Beach. Using a compass and gridded map, they had triangulated the exact location of the structure for now, as well as the future alignment. After setting the azimuth, the ring on the PPI scope was rotated to correspond with the antenna setting. With that accomplished, Lucas had Charlie tweak the cat hair crystal in the receiver module to obtain the maximum return from the smoke stack target while compensating for local ground clutter. At the same time, the radio mechanics and operators were performing their set-up procedures in preparation for tomorrow's actual operation.

"Wonder what the crap Jackson wants now?" JJ whispered out of the corner of his mouth.

"Now just how in hell should I know? I ain't his confidant or his mother. You're always sucking up to him, JJ, so you should know without asking me," responded Charlie sarcastically. "You need to know, I suggest you go ask him."

"Hell, I believe I'll just do that," JJ spoke over his shoulder as he turned and walked over to where the sergeant was standing. "Hey, Sarge, what's up? You find us another shit detail or something equally pleasant?"

Jackson pinned him with hard eyes and growled, "Tell you what, smartass, I just might be able to do exactly that. So keep pushing. Now get them other goof-off friends of yours and fall in over here."

"Awright. Awright. Don't get your bowels in an uproar, Sarge." JJ acknowledged, motioning for Lucas and Charlie to come over.

"What did he say?" Charlie asked.

"Said get your asses over here and fall in," JJ replied nonchalantly.

When the troops had assembled a couple of minutes later, Jackson shouted, "Ten'hut!" then turned to Captain Cook, came to attention himself, saluted and reported, "All troops present or accounted for, sir."

"Thank you, Sergeant Jackson," replied Captain Cook. "Men," he continued, "this has been a hard day from the beginning with Cagle getting hit by that truck and us having to come on down here and set up on deadline. The whole damned ball of wax has been something I'd like to forget. So, what I have done is, this afternoon I sent Lieutenant Walton to town to talk with some women he knows at Carolina Fabrics. They agreed to meet us at the Beach House Bar at 1900 hours for a little dancing. Now I must remind all of you that they are nice young ladies, and I won't stand for anyone getting out of line." He looked directly at Charlie, paused until he had the young airman's complete attention and added, "That especially goes for you, Kesterman. You read me?"

Amid the guffaws, Charlie answered, "Yes, sir. You know me, Captain."

Cook replied solemnly, "Yeah, I know you, Kesterman. That's why I singled you out." Turning to Sergeant Jackson, he ordered, "Sergeant, please dismiss these misfits, and see that they are ready by about 1645 hours."

"Yes, sir." Jackson turned and roared, "Ten'hut!" Then as the troops snapped to attention, he followed with, "Dismissed!"

"Well, how about that," said Charlie, "looks like we gonna score our first night out."

"Don't count on it," JJ smirked.

CHAPTER 15

The Beach House Bar
7th Street, Downtown Myrtle Beach
Wednesday, 23 April 1952
1815 hours

The hole-in-the-wall dive, locally known as the Beach House Bar, was on the north side of 7th street where it meets the beach. A sea-weathered façade of rough gray boards gave it an undeserved aged look. During the tourist season, which lasted from about April through September, the front door was a pair of bat wings similar to those found in saloons of the old west. They swung inward or outward to accommodate the serious patrons, as well as the curious.

Inside, the floor was covered with sawdust. On the right, closest to the ocean, was a wooden bar fronting the length of the curio-cluttered wall with its array of relics from earlier days—marlin spikes, pieces of hawser, and a prominently displayed shiny brass wheel from a wrecked schooner. Scattered throughout the room in all available space were a number of rough wooden plank tables and crude chairs. The door to the men's room was through the back wall nearest the bar, and the ladies' room, unique in its own way, was a boxed-off corner to the left of the barroom.

One would not expect the ladies' room to be noticeable, and at first glance it was not out of the ordinary. A closer look, however, showed how it differed from any Charlie, Lucas, or JJ had ever seen or heard about. The doorknob was on the same side as the hinges, and when the unfortunate user did manage to gain entrance and subsequently perched on the commode, a bell rang, a siren sounded, and a red light flashed on the front of the door informing all within seeing and hearing distance.

Draft beer was the only alcoholic beverage served, and the method of service was as innovative as the ladies' room was unique. If more than a single mug was desired, it would be invariably served in a porcelain chamber pot.

Entertainment was provided by a two-man band, if the term "band" could conceivably be used in this context. Their musical instruments were a tinny piano and a bass consisting of a metal washtub to which a broom handle and a strip of automobile inner tube rubber were attached. The pair entertained by singing off-colored ditties and telling provocative jokes and behaving in a generally raucous manner.

As Charlie walked through the door followed closely by Lucas and JJ, he expostulated, "Holy crap, and then some! What have we been drug into now?"

"Beats the hell clean outta me," answered an awed Lucas. "Hell, I been around this old world twice and to at least one tail kicking, an' I ain't never seen nothing like this."

"Well, no matter, we're here, and I smell beer," Charlie broke in, refusing to allow his mood to turn sour, "and I got a bad craving for a cold one after all that's happened today. Need to settle my nerves after what that chicken-shit Cook said to me about being nice to women. Embarrassed me right to my bones."

1910 hours

The two barmaids were as different as individuals could possibly be. Leona was tall and slender, which alone would not have detracted much from her looks. However, her eyes were set close together and separated by an oversized nose. These features, coupled with a receding chin, gave her the appearance of a ferret. The other one, Mert, was short and possessed a prominent backside. Acting as a counterweight were her enormous breasts that at times interfered with her waitress duties. Her cropped curly red hair clung, reminiscent of a copper-scouring pad, close to her scalp.

The only women who had been in the place all evening were these two barmaids, and neither of them appeared either over-friendly or pretty. As the three young men continued to guzzle their green draft beer, Leona and Mert got prettier and prettier as the night wore on.

"You know what, men?" Charlie's speech was now slurred. "Give me about another gallon of that brew and them two womin gonna look downright beautiful. But right now, I'd have to take either one of 'em with me everywhur I went, was I married to either one of 'em. They're just too damned ugly to kiss goodbye. Matter of fact, they are both so ugly I wouldn't even ask either of you to make love to either one of 'em no matter whut and how much you owed me in favors." Charlie lifted the beer mug, took a long swig then continued philosophically, "I've seen some homely dogs in my life, but these two would win the prize for being the ugliest. They both remind me of an old gal back home in Mississippi. Used to take her squirrel hunting with me but had to quit."

After a pause, Lucas winked at JJ and asked, "Okay. Why did you have to do that, Charlie? That is, why did you have to quit taking her hunting?"

"Well," he replied solemnly, "I didn't have but one old single-shot shotgun and couldn't afford many shells, so I had her ugly them squirrels out of the trees."

"I don't understand. What do you mean uglied them out of the trees?" Lucas asked, pretending this was the first time Charlie had told the story.

"Just what I said: she'd let them see her face, and it was so ugly that they would fall out of the tree graveyard dead. Finally, it got to the point I had to leave her at home though."

"Why'd you do that?" asked JJ, knowing before he spoke that he should have kept his mouth shut.

Charlie giggled his drunken giggle. "Cause she was so damned ugly she was tearing 'em up too much."

"Charlie, besides being a prick, you're drunk," JJ stated emphatically. "In fact, I doubt you could find your own ass with both hands even with me and Lucas helping you." Drinking had just the opposite effect on JJ. He was enunciating with great precision. "But, as an expert on the more delicate sex, I would have to agree with you, Charles, that these old girls' looks have improved immensely since we entered this Mecca of opulence."

"What the crap you talking about? You cussin' me or something using words like that?" Charlie stood up, looming menacingly over JJ.

"You are indubitably an extremely ignorant, illegitimate result of a backstreet love affair, Charles. Don't you know anything?" replied JJ. "Lucas, please explain to him what I just said. Dumb ass, just an ignorant Mississippi turd and always will be."

Charlie reached across the table for JJ. "I'll whup your smart-assed ass right here and now 'less you apologize. I may be a turd, but I ain't dumb!"

JJ stood slowly and carefully, unlimbering his lanky frame, and raised his hands, palms out. "Hold on. Okay?" he said, grinning impishly. "I apologize, Charlie. I'm sorry that you're a dumb-assed, ignorant turd from Mississippi."

Up to that point Lucas had sat back enjoying the exchange, but now, seeing that things were fast getting out of hand, he jumped to his feet, upending his chair, and positioned himself between the antagonists before either could swing at the other. "Hey, you two, hold on! I thought we came here to have some fun and not to beat up on each other. So just sit back and take it easy. C'mon, shake hands and let's get back to some serious drinking. Them old gals probably would give you something you wouldn't want to take home anyway."

1950 hours

They had been in the saloon for nearly an hour and, between the three of them, had already consumed a pitcher and a half of draft beer. They were feeling a bit tipsy despite frequent trips to the latrine out back. From all indications the girls from the mill were not going to honor the date, obviously never intending to show up.

"You know? This whole deal seemed too damned easy all along to suit me," Charlie commented dejectedly, a little less drunk now after several trips to the men's room. "In all my vast experience with females of the opposite sex, I have always found that you got to spend a lot of time working them up before you can git them to say yes to anything. Now, tell me, just how long did Walton spend arranging this here little rendezvous? I'll tell you how long. He spent not over thirty minutes. An' that included the time to get there and back. I should know, I drove him out there to that mill, and sat in the jeep while he went in to talk to them. Seems to me we have been suckered into another of his and Cook's schemes."

JJ said, "Look, Charlie, it's not even 2000 hours yet. These women, if they're like any I ever knew, they just ain't gonna be on time. They ain't like you. You shower, run that dull razor over that peach fuzz you call a beard, slap on a little aftershave lotion, slick that greasy hair back, and you're ready to boogie. Why, men, it's a born natural fact, like farting, that girls just plain have to have more time for primping than men do."

"Well, I've known you ever since basic and I never knew you

was no philosopher, but we'll see, even though I ain't very optimistic that they'll show," responded Charlie. "Of course, they don't know I'm here waiting. But, to change the subject, it's Lucas's turn to buy." And with that he signaled the tall skinny waitress for a new pitcher.

By now the noisy, smoke-filled barroom, smelling of spilled beer and sweaty bodies, was crowded to capacity with most of the radar team and a scattering of locals. The girls still had not arrived.

An old man sat alone at the bar over in the corner, a half-finished beer before him. It sat in the film of water that had condensed from the once frosted mug. He slowly traced patterns in the moisture, his mind somewhere in days of long ago. His clothes were ragged, and the hat slouched on his head failed to adequately cover the graying hair that curled over a filthy collar.

Arnie, the bartender, was eyeing the man, wondering whether or not it would be worth the effort to throw him out. He could let him stay and hope that eventually the old bum would leave or that he would pass out, and then the police could be called to drag him off to the drunk tank to sleep it off. Then there were those damned GIs sucking up brew like it was their last day on earth. *Sure as a goat's rear-end shines in the moonlight and apes is ugly*, he thought, *this is gonna be a bad night. Why in hell can't I be at home with Lou tonight instead of being wet nurse to a bunch of underage soldiers and that damned old drunk? Hell, I might as well get that old cue ready for the fun because it's gonna start any time now.*

Arnie Alman had bartended at the Beach House for the past five years now and, in that time, had become adept at recognizing trouble in the making. This was one of those times. The essential elements were in place for a real humdinger tonight. The noise level was getting worse, the incidence of crude language had increased, and the old drunk provided a perfect foil for any one of those young fools inclined to cause a ruckus. Worse yet, no girls were present to keep those young studs' minds off of starting trouble.

The team's permanent KP was a little wiseguy from Brooklyn, New York named Pasanski. He had been in trouble from the moment he had reported for basic training at Lackland two years earlier. After finishing radar operator school, Airman Basic Pasanski, Salvadore J., A.F.18283380 had been assigned to the 707th but, once there, had discovered that he could volunteer to pull KP duty four days on and then have three days off. This arrangement not only suited Pasanski, but it also made Sergeant Jackson's task of finding someone for the other three days easier. In the long run, Pasanski stayed out of trouble and performed a vital duty for the team, which made everyone happy.

Pasanski had been wandering aimlessly around outside on the boardwalk since the team arrived and had just now come into the bar. He stopped at the swinging doors, pausing only long enough to locate Lucas and his friends. With his face lighting up like a well-fed puppy's, he walked over to their table and sat down without being invited.

Charlie frowned at Pasanski for the intrusion, winked at his two friends and asked, "Men, what was it that old drunk over there at the bar said about Yankee sons-a-bitches? You know, a couple minutes ago, just before Sal come in? Wasn't it something about people from New York City being so sorry they'd make love to their own sisters and then not even pay 'em for it?"

Lucas picked up on what Charlie had started and added in agreement, "Yeah, he said they considered mothers and sisters as part of the family and because they was kin folks, didn't deserve no pay. Seems like that old souse don't care at all for anybody from up that way. Come to think about it, he may very well have a point."

Pasanski looked in turn at the three men but couldn't make up his mind if they were serious or not. "Youse guys jerking me around ain't youse?" he whined.

Both Lucas and Charlie, looking aghast, spoke as one, "Naw, we wouldn't bullshit a real intelligent man like you, Sal. Why, you oughta know that, sharp as you are." Charlie continued, his eyes gleaming mischievously, "Man, you'd catch on to something like that right away should we try to mess with your mind. Why, we know there ain't no way we could pull something like that on you. We ever tried to bullshit you before, especially on something serious like this? Man, no way."

JJ sat there, grinning sardonically, and then joined Lucas and Charlie in ragging Sal when he saw Sal becoming angrier. "They're both telling you the gospel, Sal. That old coot said exactly that, and even more. We tried to get him to shut up but figured it was just booze talking. Why, he even said he bet there wasn't one in a hundred of you Yankees could tell your own father if you was to meet him on the street and he called you son!"

Pasanski exploded to his feet, kicking his chair over into the sawdust in his haste to rush the drunk.

"Oh sheeit!" said JJ, quickly getting up. "Now look what we done got started. Man, I didn't think that crazy fool would go ape like that."

"Well, hell, let's don't just sit here!" Lucas yelled, following JJ's example. We better stop that crazy bastard before he gets hurt, or worse yet, before he hurts that damned drunk."

Before they could reach him, the enraged Sal grabbed the old man and slammed him to the floor, trying to kick him in the face. Seeing that things were turning ugly, Arnie reached beneath the bar getting a firm grasp on the sawed-off pool cue he kept there for just such emergencies. As Pasanski drew his foot back to kick the drunk, Arnie whipped the larger end of the cue around in an arc, catching the young airman just above the right ear. The blow split Pasanski's scalp and crimson spurted as he dropped to the sawdust-covered floor like a pole-axed steer. Arnie immediately yelled for Leona to call the police. The words were scarcely out of his mouth when JJ, reaching across the bar, grabbed Arnie by the front of the shirt and dragged him onto the bar, sending several mugs crashing to the floor. As JJ pulled the outnumbered bartender toward him, Charlie snatched the old man's half-empty beer stein from the bar and whipped it across Arnie's jaw, sending him sideways along the wooden bar.

"Lucas, grab that crazy fool and let's get the hell outta here," yelled Charlie, pointing at the semiconscious Sal. "Cops will be swarming in here in a minute like gnats on a dead dog's butt."

Lucas pulled Sal upright by the right arm, hoisted the smaller man over his shoulder, and then raced for the back door. By then the rest of the team had managed to crowd either through the front door and spill out onto 7th Street and Beach Drive or had charged out through the rear emergency exit. Almost within the time it had taken for the first blow to be struck until the drunk dropped to the floor, the entire barroom had cleared, leaving only the barmaids, a bleeding Arnie, and the unconscious drunk. Even the two-man band had disappeared during the ruckus, leaving behind the washtub bass.

Running as fast as they could with Sal's dead weight, the airmen managed to get three blocks south along the beach when the sound of sirens brought them to a winded halt. Charlie and JJ pitched flat onto the sand, panting with exertion. Lucas caught up with them and, dropping Sal's limp body into the edge of the surf, flopped down beside them, sucking in great gasps of cool sea air, willing his pounding heart to slow.

"Charlie, you crazy bastard! Look what you got us into now! Godammit, I don't know why I hang around with a crud like you! Or you either, JJ," Lucas hissed, still breathing hard from the effort of carrying Sal and livid at having his evening ruined.

"JJ, you know it's just like always. Our boy, Lucas, is the picture of pure innocence. Never done nothing wrong in his whole life. He don't remember egging Pasanski on to bust up that drunk same as me and you, does he?"

"Yeah, Charlie, old Mr. Pious hisself. Makes me want to puke," JJ sneered, his face flat on the wet sand.

"Awright. Awright. I give up, but what we gonna do with that pile of crap laying there soaking up the Atlantic?" Lucas asked, then more calmly said, "More to the point, Charlie, was it necessary for you to damn near kill that bartender? Sometimes, Charlie, you can just be one mean son of a bitch."

"Yeah. Ain't that a fact," responded Kesterman, unconcerned.

"Had my way," JJ responded to Lucas's inquiry about Sal, "I'd let him wash out to sea and float to France."

"I agree, but don't reckon we can do that, JJ, you might have to take his place on KP." Charlie's mood had changed almost immediately from the anger of a few moments before. There was something about the quick transition that was unsettling to both Lucas and JJ.

"Yeah," said JJ, always the practical one, "drag his sorry Yankee ass out a ways and sober him up so we can head him back on his own feet. Don't want poor old broken down Lucas to have to carry him any further."

"Up yours. The both of you," was all that Lucas could think of to say, trying to rationalize the absurdity of it all.

Sal was more or less sober now but still had an aching head from the pool cue. He joined them as they trudged along the beach toward the bivouac until they deemed it safe to walk along the highway, hoping that one of the team carryalls would come by to pick up strays. But the trucks had already gone back to the site. Just their luck. By now, a fingernail moon hung high over the ocean to the east, leaving the bone weary airmen still only halfway to the bivouac.

CHAPTER 16

Shaw AFB, South Carolina, 707th AC&W Sq
Monday, 23 February 1953
0930 hours

Master Sergeant Jackson strode into the orderly room clad in his best command countenance. The clerk, Staff Sergeant Mickelson, looked up and pushed his glasses snug against the bridge of his nose, saying pleasantly, "Good morning, Sarge. What can I do for you?"

Jackson pointed to the file cabinets and grunted, "Get me a roster of Team I together while I'm reporting to Captain Cook. Okay? And I need it as soon as you can get it together."

Make a man top dog, and he's always in a hurry, thought Mickelson as he got up to comply with the order.

Without waiting for Mickelson to answer, Jackson marched over to the door marked *Radar Team 1, Captain K.M. Cook, Commanding* and knocked. Then, without waiting for an acknowledgement, he opened the door, stalked in and closed it behind him. Cook looked up and, ignoring protocol, merely touched his eyebrow with his right hand at Jackson's salute.

"At ease, Sergeant, and take a seat," he said indicating the metal folding chair to the side of his desk. When Jackson had seated himself, Cook continued, "Couple things we need to talk over. First off, the colonel notified me this morning that the team would be relocating for an indefinite time back at the beach. Apparently he was satisfied with our short maneuvers last spring and wants us to set up down there again—more or less permanently this time. Secondly, though, this will not only be for training purposes, but a part of our job will be to fill in some gaps in coverage along the coast for the Navy. And then thirdly, before we can do that, I need to know how our personnel stack up. In other words—do you think we're ready to take on the Navy's task? Oh, yeah, you did tell Mickelson to get me a roster, didn't you?"

"Yes, sir. He probably has it ready by now. Shall I have him bring it in?"

"Yes, in a minute, but first, do you think we're ready to do the job? I'll ask Walton the same thing when he comes in, but I want your answer first."

"Captain, in my opinion we can handle the job. The men have been training pretty hard since we had the shake-down run last year, and most of them have become fairly good at their work, good enough to have earned promotions."

"Good. If you will then, tell Mickelson to bring me that roster," ordered Cook, eager to get started. "We need to go over it pretty thoroughly. If I remember right, we're short a couple of operators and an automotive mechanic. We may also need to cut a deal with Team 2 for a radio operator."

"Yes, sir. That's about right, but I don't think that will be a problem. Word gets out where we're going, and we'll have more volunteers than we can handle." As Jackson was talking, he turned to the door and, opening it, called to Mickelson, "The Captain needs that roster if you have it handy."

Mickelson opened a drawer in his desk, removed a manila folder, and hurried into Cook's office. "Here's the list of personnel you wanted, sir. I also took the liberty of noting each man's MOS for your convenience."

Cook took the proffered folder, saying, "Thank you, Mickelson. If you will, have a seat in case Sergeant Jackson or I should have a question. Now, Sergeant," he turned to Jackson, "let's have a look at what we have to work with."

After Cook and Jackson had finished discussing the names and job qualifications on the roster, Cook said, "I guess we should get Walton in on this and get his opinion." Then nodding toward Mickelson, he asked, "Sergeant Mickelson, will you call Lieutenant Walton to join us?"

"Yes, sir. Right away," replied the clerk. "And, Captain, if you need a good clerk to go, I'm volunteering."

"See what I meant about there being no shortage of volunteers, Captain?" Jackson said, winking at Cook then at Mickelson. "Wish we could take you, Mickelson, but if we did it would have to be as KP."

"I would even consider that to get to go," Mickelson replied, grinning.

When Walton arrived, Cook reviewed the list of personnel he and the two sergeants had compiled. "Quinton, I think we should have little trouble filling the few empty slots for the team. With a bit of luck we should also be able to secure what equipment, parts, and supplies we'll need for an extended tour beginning on or around 1 July. Now based on what I've told you, what do you think?"

Walton considered for a moment, looked back to the list and finally said, "I see no problem, that is, if Sergeant Mickelson can get us the supplies we need."

"The supply situation will be a piece of cake," said Mickelson. "No disrespect intended, Captain, but I could do a much better job if I was going along with the team."

Cook laughed aloud. "Yeah, I know, but somebody has to do the dirt details. Getting back to business, though, there's one other thing, Lieutenant. Colonel Van Vleet has told me that we will be working closely with the Navy out of Charleston to monitor their air traffic along the Myrtle Beach area. Can we do it?"

"I knew there had to be a catch somewhere, Captain, but I can answer with confidence. I have been watching the men train, and they are as ready as they need to be. The responsibility of working with the Navy will make them even better."

"Thanks, Walton. Then it seems that we are agreed, that is, everyone except poor old Mickelson. But, Mickelson, I promise I'll have you transferred if I can swing it. Now, does anyone have any further comments?" He paused, letting the silence answer him. "Then I guess that's it."

CHAPTER 17

Myrtle Beach AFB, South Carolina, Radar Team I Quarters
Wednesday, 8 July 1953
1130 hours

During the Korea conflict, the mission of lightweight early warning radar teams was to move out a hundred miles or so from the primary unit to fill in those coverage areas inaccessible to the larger instrument. As such, personnel manning the portable equipment were often required to live in temporary quarters and be prepared to move at a moment's notice. Thus, these personnel were believed to benefit from some of the same types of training as those given to infantry. Among this training was the obstacle course at Fort Jackson, South Carolina.

The obstacle course there was laid out over a relatively flat area near the northeastern perimeter of the military reservation. Rows of coiled barbed wire were stretched strategically over the course. Interspersed among the rows were circular or rectangular berms, each containing light explosive charges set to go off randomly. Several machine guns located in fixed positions fired a constant barrage about four feet above the trainees but were also set so each could sweep left and right over the area. This was evident by the destruction of the tree line beyond the course. A four-foot deep trench located at the far end of the course parallel to the tree line served as a staging site for entering the course. A second trench behind the machine guns marked the end of the live fire area. Once the trainees had successfully reached the second trench, they were required to fix bayonets and charge a series of practice dummies. Each infantry trainee was required to go through the course in full battle gear; Air Force personnel needed only to wear fatigues, a web belt, canteen, first aid packets, and a steel helmet. Should a trainee falter in fear, or for other reasons, and be unable to finish, he had to remain in position waiting until all other personnel were clear of the course. Then, after what seemed an interminable time to the frightened man, one or more of the instructors would help him from the field to get his inevitable chewing out.

The team arrived at the obstacle course at 1231 hours, disembarked from the team duce and half truck, then sat around anxiously waiting their turn. Lucas, looking out over the field where several scores of cocky young infantrymen in full battle gear crawled and squirmed the long way under the wire past the exploding charges, nervously watched the drill hoping that he wouldn't freeze up going through the course. Machine guns clattered while explosive charges boomed giving the realism of battle to the crawling men.

His eye was drawn to one soldier lying about halfway through the course near one of the explosive pits. Several other men snaking past the motionless soldier paused momentarily before moving on, eager to finish and unconcerned with the weak-stomached laggard. With his hands on his hips, Mackley watched as the dwindling numbers of soldiers crawled across the field, looking back at the fear-stricken one.

"Men, look out yonder," Mackley said, shaking his head and turning to Phelps and Kesterman with a mask of false bravado. "See that fat boy about a hundred yards out, layin' there scared outta his mind? That's gonna be old Charlie out there in a few minutes." As he spoke he looked at his watch. "First one of them charges goes off anywhere near Charlie, it'll take him just about a week to clean out his drawers."

"Betcha sweet ass it ain't gonna be me," Charlie sneered, faking calmness. "I just might stand up out there, hunker over real low, and run that little course in record time. I doubt them guns is shooting much lower than four feet or so anyway."

"Sure, go ahead. Show off, and if Jackson don't eat you out, you'll forget and either get your tail blown off by that C-4 or shot by one of them machine guns by acting stupid and standing up too tall and gawking around like one of your Mississippi redneck buddies," Lucas continued ribbing Charlie.

"Won't be me. I ain't that tall, but now take JJ, even if he humped over he'd still be up there in the line of fire," he responded, trying to divert the ridicule toward Phelps. "Was I him, I think I might suddenly get the shits or something to get out of doing this little Boy Scout drill."

"Charlie," JJ replied angrily, "I can get through there crawling backwards before you can even get out of that trench. So don't gimme no more of your crap."

"Awright! Awright!" yelled Jackson at the waiting men. "You ladies get over here, and listen up to what I gotta say."

"Yessir, Sergeant Jackson, sir!" they chorused. "We'll give you our undivided attention."

"Then when I give the order, you three hotshots lead off—that's you Kesterman, Mackley and Phelps. Head down that trench over there, climb over the side and start crawling. When you get to the wire, roll over on your back, and scoot under on your butts. One of those charges goes off close to you, squeeze your eyes shut until the dust and dirt settles then keep on moving. And dammit, don't get stupid and stand up like an officer. Especially you, Phelps."

Charlie laughed at that and then yelled, "Come on, men! You heard Sarge, and JJ, don't forgit to keep your skinny tail down."

Lucas lunged over the lip of the trench, hugging the ground and deciding quickly the shortest and easiest route was to go slightly left for about seventy yards, then veer back a couple of degrees to the right. Hesitating no longer, he snaked through the sand and dirt directly beneath the fire of one of the .30 cal. machine guns, confident this would put him comfortably well away from the explosive pits. The clattering of the machine guns seemed louder out there under the rounds whining overhead. Even knowing they were several feet above his prone body, Lucas hugged the ground a little closer. Ten yards off to the right, a charge exploded, showering him with dirt and debris.

"Crap," he grumbled, seeing his route was not that far removed from the explosions after all.

Charlie inched beside him, grumbling, "Get a move on, Mackley, or get out of my way so I can get the hell through this Girl Scout joke."

Turning his head to face Charlie, Lucas spit, then said bitingly through gritty lips, "Thought you was gonna stand up and run this course, hero."

"Aw, the hell with you, and that damned Jackson too," Charlie replied, annoyed. "Now, dammit, get outta my way."

While they were mouthing at each other, JJ caught up, waiting only long enough for Charlie to crawl on and, without saying anything, moved past.

Lucas inhaled deeply, pulled himself forward using elbows and toes, eager to finish. Sand and dirt, tainted by the thousands of sweating men before him, filtered into the open collar of his fatigue jacket and mixed with the sweat soaking his faded fatigues. Helmet low on his head, vision obscured, Lucas aimed for the finish of the course, relying solely on instinct.

Suddenly he bumped into someone and, rolling to his side, looked into the staring eyes of the frightened G.I. they had seen earlier, still cowering, hugging the ground, waiting for someone to come for him. The terror-stricken man reached pleadingly toward Lucas. Tear streaks furrowed the dirt and camouflage grease on the man's face. His lips moved soundlessly.

"C'mon, follow me. You can make it," Lucas coaxed. "Just crawl over behind me, and keep my feet in sight."

The soldier shook his head and cried harder. *Poor bastard*, Lucas thought and squirmed on past the next explosive pit.

Later, when they had reached the end of the course, they stood shaking the sand and dirt from their fatigues and out of their boots, while cursing Jackson in particular and the Air Force in general. Their labored breathing, exacerbated from the long crawl across the course, underlined nights of easy living, drinking, and chasing girls. Once on the course, muscle tone quickly deserted them, leaving three exhausted, out-of-shape airmen. With dirt mixed with the sweat caking their hands and faces, they looked at one another, shaking their heads at what they had gone through.

Lucas looked out across the field and saw the rabbit-scared soldier still huddled fetal-like as two NCOs strolled nonchalantly out to help him. *Guess there goes an ass-chewing for that old boy*, he thought, thankful it wasn't him lying out there in his own crap.

Phelps's voice interrupted his thoughts. "Damnation!" he harped. "Had I known I'd be doing this sorta stuff, I believe I'd have joined the Navy. Least in the water I wouldn't have all this damned dirt up my backside."

"Aw, JJ," Lucas said, shaking the sight of the soldier from his mind, "don't look at it like that. Remember, it's been a month or so since you had a shower, so this gives you a good excuse now to wash your dirty rear-end when we get back to the base."

"Crap on you, Mackley...and you too, Kesterman. I know you're gonna say something smart-assed, too," JJ retorted disgustedly, pulling his boot off and shaking the sand out of it.

Back at the barracks, Jackson called the men together, giving them the rest of the day off to shower, wash their clothes and rest. After getting cleaned up, they lazed around alternately cursing the obstacle course and Jackson and talking about cars and girls, but not necessarily in that order.

"Lucas, I heard you mention to JJ the other day that you was interested in buying yourself a car. That right?" Charlie called.

"Yeah. But that was idle talk, Charlie. Right now I can't afford to go into debt. And I sure can't afford to pay cash," he replied disinterested, wondering what new deal Charlie was plotting.

"Tell you what," responded Charlie. "I'm thinking seriously about trading mine in on a new one. So, instead of going through some crooked car salesman, I'd be willing to sell it outright to you. Figure I could make you a good offer you couldn't turn down, and, like I said, I wouldn't hafta trade with no salesman."

"Like I told you, Charlie, I'm busted," said Mackley, feigning lack of interest and feeling Charlie out. Hoping to get him to commit himself first.

"But you ain't heard my offer yet," Charlie replied thinking how to handle him just right. "I'll tell you what I'm willing to do. I'll be losing money, but since you're my best buddy, I'll let you have it for…say about twelve hundred bucks."

"Charlie, that pile of junk ain't worth half that amount," Lucas responded, faking irritation.

Charlie jumped up and strode purposefully over to where Lucas sat on his bunk, hooked his thumbs in the back of his belt, and stared hard into Lucas's face. The muted talk in the barracks stopped as if on command, the talkers waiting to see what would happen next.

Melting the stern look, Charlie grinned his crooked grin and laughingly said, "That's a good one, Mackley. For a minute, I thought you was serious. Now, I tell you what, you can have her for an even thousand"

Off to the side, Phelps snorted, and Charlie turned toward him, frowning.

"Tell you what, Charlie," Lucas responded. "I ain't in no mood to dicker around with you. You make it nine hundred, and it's a deal. Otherwise, forget it."

Charlie scratched his head, silently figuring whether or not Lucas was conning him. Then, grinning sheepishly, he replied, "Okay, you got me by the balls, Mackley." Holding out his hand to shake on the deal, he said, "You give me fifty dollars down and pay the rest out at forty a month."

Three days after their handshake, Lucas accepted a bill of sale for a once maroon 1947 Chevrolet sedan, which was now the ugliest pea-green color he had ever seen, and Charlie Kesterman had Lucas's note for $850 payable at a rate of forty a month.

It didn't take Lucas long to realize that he had been taken in by Charlie. The car burned oil, the radiator leaked and the front end was in bad need of realignment. To Charlie's credit, though, he recruited one of the team's motor pool mechanics, and the three of them completely overhauled the Chevy.

Radar Team 1 Barracks
Wednesday 23 April 1953
0830 hours

After working the midnight to 0800 shift, Phelps had finished eating breakfast and was now getting ready to enjoy the rest of the day as he lay on his bunk. He would catch a short nap and then roam the beach near the boardwalk downtown. By then, there should be a few tourists around and, hopefully, maybe a girl or two sunning on the beach. If luck held, one might even have the straps of her swimming suit untied to get that extra ray of sunshine. If the action on the beach was slow, a trip to the pool hall off the boardwalk or a beer in one of the downtown bars might be in order. His girlfriend, Amy, wouldn't be out of school until late afternoon, but he would find some way to kill time until he was to meet her.

He didn't really mind the early shift since he was somewhat of a night owl anyway, and there were advantages to be had. It gave him the opportunity to sleep in during the day as much as he wished, and moreover, it left the evenings free to roam the bars and hangouts in Myrtle Beach. The freedom to move about during the day and early evening provided ample opportunities to meet a number of local girls. He had not been in town long before meeting one from the town's high school. Her name was Amy Lentz, and now most of his free time was spent with her instead of sleeping his life away.

Amy had lied to him. She hadn't meant to lie, but infatuated by Phelps from the first time he smiled her way, she set about maneuvering him into asking for a date. When he asked how old she was, Amy had said seventeen, soon to be eighteen, and a senior at Myrtle Beach High School. She was really only sixteen—San Quentin quail to a man as old as Phelps. He couldn't be blamed entirely, however, because this cute little girl looked older than most sixteen-year-old girls. A short, petite five-feet-four inches, she weighed about 105 pounds. To look at her, one would incorrectly assume that she was perhaps as old as she claimed, or maybe even a little older. Her figure was a trim 34-22-34. She had discovered the art of applying makeup and properly selecting clothing. When she wore no makeup, her real age was evident, but once all the lipstick and other cosmetics were applied, Amy transformed into the sophisticated older woman. After that first date with her, JJ swore to Lucas and Charlie that he was in love at last, that the ideal woman had been found, and that girl was Amy.

Soon after he reached Lackland for basic training, JJ knew that the Air Force was what he had been looking for, and this fact was confirmed once he was selected to go to radar maintenance school. Since his arrival at Myrtle Beach, and after meeting Amy, he had no doubt about what the future promised. Despite his generally lazy attitude, JJ took genuine interest in electronics, and was fast becoming an expert repairman. Cook had already suggested that he go TDY to Keesler and enroll in one of the advanced courses.

"I enjoy electronics and figure I can make a go of it," he'd confided to Charlie and Lucas. "But I'll tell you what else, that chicken-shit CO tries to send me back to Keesler, the Air Force is gonna have a fulltime AWOL on their hands. I ain't about to go back to that hellhole and put up with all that bullshit agin. He can court-martial me if he wants to, but by damn, I ain't goin'."

"What's the matter, JJ, you scared of our old buddy, Sergeant Webber?" asked Lucas scornfully, remembering all their troubles with their nemesis. "Man, all he can do to you is make your life miserable. Big boy like you should be able to handle that."

"Hell, Lucas, that ain't why he don't want to go back. If he's back there busting his ass in school then ain't no way he could git into Amy's pants. That means the road is wide open for this old stud," said Charlie, eyes daring JJ to respond.

Quickly obliging, JJ lunged toward Charlie and shouted, "Why, you son of a bitch! Haul your no good ass up off that cot, you sorry bastard. I'm gonna beat the living crap right outta you!"

Charlie jumped up laughing and dodged to the other side of the bunk out of JJ's reach. Taken aback at the flare-up, Lucas stepped out of the way of the two posturing men. JJ continued advancing while Charlie nimbly kept the bunk between them. Charlie's taunting laughter only added to Phelps's seething anger.

"I mean it, Kesterman, I'm damned serious about Amy, and I won't let you say things like that about her. You do—I'll whip your ass. You read me? And if I can't do it barehanded, I'll find an equalizer and break your goddamn face real good. Whatever it takes. Just remember this—you too, Lucas—I ain't standing pat for no kinda talk like that."

The laughter left Kesterman's face, and his dark eyes glinted in the subdued light of the barracks. "Phelps, to begin with, you ain't man enough to take me, but if it'll make you happy, I was only funning you," replied Charlie, sullenly. "But let me warn you, don't you ever threaten me again."

"Yeah, JJ, I apologize, too, if I was out of line," said Lucas, chastened by the outburst. "Now, come on you two. Shake hands an' let's go down to the site and take a quick swim and cool off. JJ, Charlie didn't mean nothing. He was just pulling your chain to get you riled up. "

CHAPTER 18

Myrtle Beach AFB, South Carolina
Team 1 Quarters
Friday, 10 July 1953

Charlie scanned quickly through the letter, frowning a time or two, and then put it back in the envelope and crammed it into a fatigue jacket pocket. Subdued, he walked across the barracks bay where Lucas and JJ sat talking and said, "Men, I got a letter from Mom this morning. Said that my brother James and my no good stepfather's guard unit had been activated, and they was gonna be stationed over at Fort Jackson for a few weeks before shipping out to Japan."

JJ looked up absently and commented, "I didn't know your brother and step-dad was in the Guard. When did they join?"

"Mel's been in for nearly fifteen years—long enough to make master sergeant. He talked James into joining about a year or so ago. Figured it would keep him out of Korea, but it sure don't look like it now. Pisses me off. I wouldn't mind going myself, but it's gonna be James instead."

"That's tough, Charlie," Lucas responded, wondering if Charlie was really serious about wanting to go overseas. "Guess you'll be heading over to Columbia before long to visit them."

"Yeah, that's right. Gonna go tomorrow, and if you guys want to go with me instead of hanging around this barracks sleeping your lives away, I'd be glad to have you tag along. We could stay with James at Jackson."

Both men readily agreed, knowing how boring weekends were lolling around the makeshift quarters. Their quarters, crowded as they were, provided little in the way of privacy and creature comforts. The old guardhouse barracks they now called home was a one-story clapboard structure at the edge of the base near Highway 17. The team, under the guidance of Jackson, had spruced the building up as best they could to make it livable. Whitewashed rocks delineated the gravel walk leading to the wooden steps at the front entrance. Austere furnishings of thin mattresses, metal cots, and individual footlockers barely interrupted the dullness of the interior of the building. As a concession to the smokers, half-gallon fruit cans nailed to support posts served as cigarette butt cans. To make it less confining, security bars were removed from the windows. In deference to the drab environment of the barracks, the friends used any excuse to be absent. Even the lure of the beach with its promise of beautiful suntanned, swimsuit-clad vacationing girls had diminished. To the three buddies a change of scenery was welcomed.

Fort Jackson, South Carolina
Saturday, 11 July 1953

"Pleased to meet you men. Charlie has talked about you often," James responded kid-brother-like when introduced to Lucas and JJ.

James, a younger version of Charlie, showed the same physical features but, unlike Charlie, seemed more mature in many respects. In temperament, he was the more easy-going, the more laid back of the two brothers.

"Mom and Mel won't be home tonight, but if you men want to, we can run out to their apartment for a few minutes this afternoon," said James, watching closely for Charlie's reaction.

Deftly diverting the conversation, Charlie replied, "Naw, James, you know how I feel about Mel. Wouldn't mind seeing Mom, but not him. Truth is we came over to see you and hit some of them joints around Columbia we been hearing about."

Expecting Charlie's reaction, James grinned disarmingly, saying, "Sounds good to me if it's okay with you men?" He looked at Lucas and JJ, lifting his eyebrows and waiting for their answer.

"If you're waiting on us, you're losing time," replied Lucas, eagerly. "Lead the way, and we'll be right behind you."

Near Lake City, South Carolina
The Pines Lounge
1900 hours

James stopped short of the turnoff leading to the Pines Lounge and said, "There it is, fellows."

"How in hell did you ever find such a trashy dump as this, James?" Charlie responded, eyeing the dilapidated building. "Hell, I ain't never in my short life seen anything like this. If it's as crummy inside as it is outside," Charlie continued, having seen the piles of beer cans and trash as they slowed within sight of the backwoods beer joint, "then I ain't so sure I want to go in. Where the hell are we, anyway—about a hundred miles from nowhere?"

"You're right, Charlie. It is a mite different I'll have to agree, but you gotta admit it sure has character and that's something a man just can't find anywhere. I mean, men, you gotta look real hard to find a paradise like what you see right here," James said, spreading his hands toward the honkytonk. "Bet Myrtle Beach can't compare with this place for style. And, yeah," he continued, "we're not too far out of Columbia, probably no more than a couple of miles from Lake City, but we took the longer scenic route—wanted you to see some of the country. Just figure I was plain lucky to stumble onto such a beautiful place as this," James proudly bragged, beaming like a schoolboy.

The Pines was a little farther south of Lake City than James had indicated at about fifteen miles, and almost seven from the nearest black-topped highway. The low, rough, weathered pine lumber building stood about a hundred feet off the gravel road among several large randomly situated pines against a background of equally large but thicker mixture of hardwoods and pine trees. A high board fence behind the building separated the lounge property from the woods. Visible from the road, mounds of empty beer cans and bottles piled against it behind the lounge, attested to the many nights of hard drinking by hard living men and women at the backwoods honkytonk. To the side of the piles of debris, a broken down shed struggled to remain erect. To the left, an old John Deere tractor had been abandoned with one of its rear wheels missing, its axle resting on a rotting block of wood. Across the road from the dusty parking lot, a large tract of thickly vegetated woodland, again dominated by virgin pine, gave the area an aura of remoteness.

They pulled into the parking area in front of the building and got out, looking around in awe. A gaudy broken neon sign, already lit up, blinked out the redundant message, "cold beer inside." From inside, a jukebox blared out a song about broken hearts and unrequited love. The plank door stood open, a dark maw beckoning them in by the siren lure of the music and promise of titillating pleasures.

"James, are you sure this is the right place?" asked a somewhat skeptical Phelps. "You sure we ain't taking our lives into our hands going in there? Looks like some of them crumby joints I know about across the river in Illinois from where I lived in Missouri, where they issue you a gun or knife at the door or at least ask about your next of kin."

"Yeah. This is it all right," he proudly answered. "I've been out here once or twice. Usually by about 2100 to 2200 hours things really start to roll. We're maybe a little bit early, and that may be why it's so quiet," he answered. "And it ain't nearly as rough as you think. Why, JJ, I ain't seen but a half dozen fights and only two killings—naw, three—in the last two weeks I've been coming out here. Remember this, a man's gotta have some excitement, and us ground-pounders ain't nice and well-bred young gentlemen like you bus-driving fly boys."

JJ let the jibe slide and said with a grin, "Don't know about Charlie and Lucas, but you done persuaded me, and I ain't easily persuaded." Shoving his hands deep into his hip pockets, he studied the building and said, "Now that we're here, might as well go take a look inside." Starting for the door, he called over his shoulder, "James, you can brag about you and your ground-pounding buddies being bad, but you ain't seen tough. Why, I'm so tough my crap's got muscles. Ain't that right, Lucas?"

"Yeah, sure, you're so tough you scare yourself," Charlie responded, laughing, before Lucas could reply.

Lucas had been waiting quietly, listening to the exchange between James and JJ. Lucas was scared but did not want to show it in front of his buddies. He looked at James and asked, "You sure about this place? I'd hate for my momma to get a telegram saying I got killed not in the line of duty."

"Trust me, men," James replied. "Trust me"

It was well on after dark, and the place was rapidly filling with the regular Saturday night crowd. Several rough-looking, hard-muscled men, obviously from one of the mills around Lake City, came in talking loudly, letting their arrival be noticed. Phelps glanced over at James with worry in his eyes. James looked back at Phelps and grinned just as a couple in their mid-twenties paused at the door, scanned the room, and slowly made their way over to an empty table. The crew-cut man wore blue jeans and a T-shirt, its left sleeve turned up with a pack of cigarettes bulging from the fold. She had on a skirt that was barely to her knees and a flimsy blouse, unbuttoned at the top showing considerable cleavage, a feat facilitated by a well-endowed body. Several heads turned, the men staring enviously and the women looking down their noses, showing transparent disdain for the girl. Charlie motioned toward them with a nod of the head and grinned his trademark crooked grin.

Couples, dancing to the loud jukebox sounds of Hank Williams and Les Paul, moved with the frenzy of a snake-handling church revival. Others sat around the tables surrounding the dance floor, talking and drinking the crowd favorites, Pabst Blue Ribbon and Jax beer, with the din becoming louder with each drained bottle. Over at a table near the wall, an animate drunk car salesman was telling how his wife was running around on him. The overly rouged, dark-eyed woman with him sat there quietly sipping on a watered-down Tom Collins. A man about the same age as the drunk eased over, sat down at the table and, after a while, rested his right hand on the woman's exposed thigh. Paying scant attention, the drunk continued ranting about his wife cheating on him.

Until now the evening had been pleasant even though it was not as exciting as Lucas figured it would be, or how James had described it, or how Charlie had hoped it would be, but now things were looking up. The smells of beer and whiskey and sweat and cigarette smoke hung heavily in the stifling air. The neon flashing jukebox got louder with each swig of tepid beer Lucas swallowed.

Charlie, bragging as usual, was trying to get JJ's attention over the noise, while JJ sat slouching in boredom and faced the bar across the busy dance floor. James held up an empty bottle at arm's length to catch the waitress's attention, indicating the need for another round. His arm suddenly dropped, plopping the bottle back onto the table. At the sound, Lucas looked up and stared, mouth agape, toward the door.

A woman of about thirty-two or three was coming in on the arm of a man several years her junior. He wore Levi jeans, a western style shirt and boots, while she had on a tight-fitting black dress short enough to emphasize long, shapely legs. Her breasts, jiggling as she moved across the room, seemed to be struggling to escape the confines of the scanty dress. Unlike her companion, she had eschewed boots and walked haughtily in shiny red high heels outrageously out of place in the honkytonk. Their different styles of attire, his faded jeans and her dinner dress, seemed as incongruous as their ages. Pausing momentarily at various tables to visit with acquaintances, they made their way to a table at the rear of the lounge. At first glance, Lucas sat mesmerized, but there was something hard about the woman's eyes that caught his attention—a hardness that heavy makeup couldn't quite conceal.

While his companions stared at the woman, Charlie, like a boisterous child wanting attention, excitedly signaled the waitress. When she came over to their table, he lowered his voice conspiratorially and asked, "Would you bring us another round? But more to the point, the real reason I called you over was to see if you could tell me who that sexy woman in them red high heels is?"

"I could," she replied, quietly studying the airmen, "but let me give you boys a little advice. She ain't for you. I've known her for several years and she's a wild one. Everybody thought that she had grown up and settled down when she got married a few years ago, but then her husband got killed. Since then, she's really gone off the deep end. Way she uses people you best steer clear of her. She's a hussy, that one!"

"How about introducing me to her anyway when you get the chance?" Charlie persisted ignoring the waitress's advice.

The waitress cut him off short, "No way, buddy. You want to meet her you go introduce yourself. I don't intend to be a party to you getting yourself messed up with her. Like I said, she's nothing but trouble."

"Ain't none of my business, but how did her husband die to make her turn bad again?" JJ asked, trying to ease the tension.

"I shouldn't tell you this, but I guess you won't let it alone unless I do," the waitress said reluctantly, considering her next words. "He was burned to death when his pickup truck crashed into an Air Force convoy west of Lake City a few months ago."

"Oh shit!" blurted Lucas.

Ignoring Lucas and raising her eyebrows questioningly, she asked suddenly, "Say! Ain't you guys soldiers?" Then before they could reply, she continued, "Your haircuts sure say so."

"James is," Lucas admitted, indicating the younger Kesterman, "but the rest of us is from Shaw," Lucas said. "Guess we may as well tell you. We was in that convoy when the wreck happened. It was one of them things that nobody ever dreamed would happen. It just did. When one of our people stepped off of his truck fender, that pickup hit him, and then skidded into a couple of our other trucks and into the ditch. Feller burned up before anyone could do anything—not that there was anything anyone could do."

"Then, you boys take my advice and drop it. And don't mention you were involved. People around here wouldn't take too kindly to you if they found out."

After their drinks were served, they more or less pretended to drink them, but by then the luster had worn off the evening. James got up and stretched, saying, "I got a feeling we better haul ass out of here. I don't think that waitress was bullshitting us about these folks."

"Awright," Charlie replied, surprisingly agreeable, "but I got me a stronger feeling I'm gonna be coming back over here sometime pretty soon."

"Yeah, Charlie, and I got just as strong a feeling you're either gonna get the crap kicked out of you or get yourself killed," his wiser younger brother told him.

"Awright, James, we'll leave, but watch it," he responded sharply. "You know I don't like to be told what I can or can't do. Especially by you, little brother. So, best you go easy."

Across the room the car salesman was still complaining about his wife cheating on him. The bored woman with him sat there quietly nursing the Tom Collins. The man who had joined them earlier still had his right hand on the woman's thigh. Suddenly he reached over with his left hand and pinched the woman's breast. The scathing look he received caused him to quickly remove his hand from her thigh, get up unsteadily, and stumble off to the men's room at the back of the lounge. JJ looked at them, then at Lucas, and shook his head at the primal state of the human species.

CHAPTER 19

Myrtle Beach AFB, South Carolina, Radar Team I Quarters
Saturday, 29 August 1953

Within days after Lucas bought his old Chevy sedan, Charlie had gone to Columbia and purchased a new 1953 gold-colored Chevrolet convertible. Besides its heavy chrome, the car was equipped with the latest style AM radio and came with whitewall tires as standard equipment. The newest innovation was its Power-glide transmission which did away with the need to shift through several gears to reach cruising speed and left Charlie's right arm free for more important things like snuggling his latest girlfriend close as he drove.

He was careful with the car, constantly washing and polishing it. Lucas and JJ kidded him about carrying a rag around all the time to wipe any stray spot or squashed bug off of it. He allowed no one to get into the car with dirty shoes, not even his current favorite girlfriend. The extreme care he showed for the car went as far as his selecting a parking spot well away from the other vehicles around the team quarters.

"You know, Lucas, since Charlie bought that car he seems a lit-tle easier to get along with," said JJ, as he was getting ready to go on duty. "I don't know how he could afford it, but I'm glad things are going better. For awhile there, I thought him and me was gonna tangle."

"Know what you mean," replied Lucas, nodding his agreement. "You don't know about what happened to him before he joined up, I guess?"

"Whatta you mean? You mean something happened that makes him act like a bad ass? I thought he was always that way. Ever since I met him seems like it don't take much to set him off."

Lucas paused then, assuming confidentiality from JJ, said, "Don't you ever let on I told you. I said I wouldn't tell nobody, but you and me are friends, so I guess it's okay to tell you."

Lucas then related what he had heard mostly from others about Charlie and Maggie Debreau and of how Maggie's mother had broken them up, even getting Charlie fired from his towboat job. He recounted the little that Charlie had confided and emphasized his promise to Charlie not to tell. He finished by saying, "I'd heard a little about what happened before Charlie and I talked, but never knew the whole story until recently. Got to talking with a guy from Vicksburg who knew both Charlie and Maggie and he said when she dropped Charlie, he took it pretty hard. Matter of fact, old lady Debreau was supposed to have gotten him fired, but Charlie told me a different story, that he got canned over some deck hand getting killed. I ain't sure what really happened, except he lost his job. After that he got to drinking heavy and started showing a mean side. Said at one time he almost went to jail for beating the hell out of a guy who insulted her. Only thing kept him from it was that he agreed to join the Air Force."

"Well, I feel sorry for him in a way, but hell Lucas, we all have our troubles. Difference is, most of us git over them. Ain't no need for him to treat me and you like dirt. I won't let on that you told me, but I'll still have to admit, I kinda wish there was someway he could know I found out. Might tone him down some."

Charlie had been avoiding Lucas and JJ, not wanting to be bothered with either of them. His mood had been sour for several days now. He had seen them talking confidentially earlier and, suspecting he was the subject of their conversation, had slipped quietly away.

Sitting quietly in the team quarters, Charlie stared at the smudged, crumpled letter, trying to divine its contents. It had arrived in yesterday's mail. He recognized the handwriting and, without even noting the return address, crammed it into his fatigue jacket pocket. Something in the recesses of his mind told him the letter bore bad news.

He was sitting on his footlocker in the room shared with Lucas and Wilson Anderson, staring into space and shutting out the world. Anderson, who had been napping on his bunk, rolled over, grumbled at Charlie, then left the room. Now that he was alone, Charlie took the crumpled letter from his pocket, smoothed it as best he could and tore off the end of the envelope. He blew into the envelope, ballooning it, and then removed the single sheet of thin paper. The letter written in delicate, feminine script smelled lightly of lilacs.

> Dear Charlie,
>
> I scarcely know how to tell you about what must be said. One can delay the inevitable only so long. We had some good times when you were stationed here in Biloxi. I know that I did. But, Charlie, I'm afraid the old saying that distance makes the heart grow fonder just doesn't hold true. In fact, our being so far apart has had the opposite effect. I hope you know what I mean. I don't want to hurt you, but one has to be honest. I have met someone…

Charlie wadded the letter and threw it at the tin cigarette butt can nailed to the door facing. Thinning his mouth in anger, he muttered "Damn," through clinched teeth as Lucas came into the room.

Lucas saw him sitting alone and asked, "Huh? What did you say?"

"Nothing. Just talking to myself," he replied softly.

"Maybe so. But you don't look too happy, so what's ailing you, buddy? You look like your dog died just after your girlfriend told you she was pregnant."

"You didn't miss by far," Charlie studied Lucas's eyes before replying. "Remember Mona Emerson—you know, that girl I knew in Waveland? Well, she just sent me a Class A Dear John letter. Dropped me like I was a bug in her hand."

"Hell, Charlie, way you been chasin' them girls around here no one woulda ever known you an' Mona was still serious." Lucas's effort at trying to cheer Charlie up fell flat.

"Lot of things you don't know about me, Mackley," he responded with bitterness in his voice.

"Yeah, I guess. Tell you what. Let's find JJ and get a few brews in you, and you won't even remember what old what's-her-name's face looks like. Hell, Charlie, I didn't know you were still interested in her after the way you talked about some of them other girls you been dogging, especially that little blond from Arkansas. What was her name? Lila? Yeah, that's it." *Old buddy, I know a helluva a lot more about you than you think,* thought Mackley, trying not to let his face reveal his feelings.

"That didn't last long, and besides, I was never very serious about that one anyway. Really had a thing going with Mona, though. At least I thought I did. Only time I been real serious since Maggie. So I guess I was trying to forget Maggie when I was with Mona." Shrugging, Charlie continued, "But you may be right, Lucas. Maybe we should go have a few drinks later on, but right now I want to be alone. I gotta think some things out."

"Okay, if that's what you want. See you later." Lucas replied, glancing at his watch and seeing it was almost noon. He had gone to the room to see if either of his roommates was ready to go to the mess tent for chow. Charlie's letter had made him forget why he dropped by in the first place.

"You gonna stand there all day, Mackley?" asked the mess sergeant, Willie Armistead, irritation surfacing. "I got a whole team to feed and don't need you holdin' the line up."

"Sorry, Sarge, I guess I was daydreamin'"

"Hell, Lucas, you wasn't daydreamin'. You wasn't even in this world," admonished Armistead with a smirk, while slopping some spam and a spoonful of corn on the airman's kit.

Once through the serving line, Lucas took his mess kit outside and sat with his back against a tree in the compound. While dabbling at the food, he considered how much Kesterman, and maybe even himself, had changed since Biloxi. Charlie was a good radar repairman and pulled his weight as a valuable member of the team. Lately though, he often seemed moody and sullen. One could never judge just how he would react in any circumstance with him taking offense for the slightest reason. Lately he seemed to be overly testy with everyone, especially with Phelps. He hadn't been that way when they were in school at Keesler.

Lucas looked at his uneaten food, his appetite blunted. He drained the coffee, now cold, from the canteen cup then walked over and dumped the unfinished meal into the garbage pit, his mind still on Kesterman.

CHAPTER 20

Toddville, South Carolina
East Bank of the Pee Dee River near the Bridge Approach
Saturday, September 12, 1953
8:15 P.M.

Two young people sat in a pickup truck on the sandy bank of the Pee Dee River near the bridge west of Toddville watching stars reflecting from the water's surface as the river flowed endlessly to the ocean. The gurgling sound of the water swirling beneath the bridge muted out background sounds of night creatures just emerging as the moon rose startlingly red through swaying trees on the Pee Dee's eastern bank. The woman fragrance of the girl prowled through suppressed feelings, stirring emotions in him as they sat cuddled in the old pickup. Off toward Toddville a dog bayed, and downstream from where the couple embraced, an owl hooted. In an overgrown field across the river, the lonesome sound of a whippoorwill momentarily saddened the girl, catching unspoken words in her throat as she snuggled closer to her lover.

Feeling her move closer, the boy whispered with soft concern, reluctant to break the magic of the night, "You okay?"

She huddled closer against his chest murmuring, "Yeah. I was listening to that old whippoorwill, and…and I don't know. I couldn't help it. I thought I was gonna cry."

He held her away for a moment then looked intently into the girl's youthful face where fathomless eyes returned his gaze. The hint of a smile touched her lips as he traced the contour of her face with a trembling finger. Impulsively, he kissed the tip of her nose and then, pulling her close again, nuzzled the girl's neck savoring the slight scent of jasmine in her hair. The full moon, now a sliver disc, continued its unrelenting trip across the crisp autumn sky hurrying their night away.

They had been there by the Pee Dee for nearly three hours, vibrantly alive in their own small corner of the world when the girl, becoming uneasy about getting home late, took a furtive peek at the tiny gold watch on her wrist. It was Saturday night, and she was allowed to remain out a bit longer on weekends. Nevertheless, she had promised that she would be in by no later than ten o'clock, although her curfew was ten-thirty.

Seeing her glancing at her watch, the boy unwrapped his long arms from about her, stretched, and yawned widely, murmuring quietly, "Time to go?"

"Yeah, guess we'd better. I promised my folks I'd be in pretty soon," she answered, frowning, not wanting the magic of the moment to dissolve pushing them back to reality.

Both jumped involuntarily as a branch snapped loudly just outside the truck near the driver's side.

"Did you hear that?" she asked, fright showing in her quivering voice.

Not quite sure of what it was, the young man reassured her, saying, "Probably it was a limb falling out of a tree, or maybe some kind of animal sneaking around out there. It's nothing but night sounds, or maybe this old truck settling down."

She looked past her companion, a sudden look of horror on her young face, screaming as the gun exploded, its muzzle flash temporarily blinding her. The boy slumped, propelled to the right against her, blood spraying from the mortal passage of the bullet where it angled through his chest burying itself deep in the padding of the back of the seat. Before she could react, the intruder rushed around to her side of the truck, jerked the door open and pulled the terrified girl out. Screaming, she fell to her knees and struggled to get up as the assailant kicked her hard in the side. Prone on the litter-covered ground, with her breath knocked out, the girl curled fetal-like, covering her face. Another vicious kick sent her rolling onto her back where she lay sobbing.

"Awright, bitch! Shut up that caterwauling, or you'll get what I gave your boyfriend after I finish with you. Now me and you're gonna have us some fun. So lie back and enjoy it," he snarled cruelly as his eyes glinted evilly in the faint nightlight. He stood over her slowly unbuckling his belt.

Ten minutes later, whimpering, she lay defiled and cowering beside the truck, trying to cover herself with the torn clothing that had been ripped as she was assaulted. Numbed mind unwilling to function in her terror, the frightened girl clamped her eyes shut and tried to blot out the despicable perversion that had occurred. The boyfriend's hand dangled lifelessly from the seat where he had slumped. She knew without looking that the he was dead, and that whatever help she got would have to be on her own initiative.

Cautiously, she chanced a glance around, careful to move only enough to see. Movement drew her attention to the other side of the truck. Dark clad legs moved back and forth on the other side of the truck near the door. Shoes that appeared to be heavy work boots crunched the scattering of sandy gravel by the pickup. Breathing heavily, the man jerked her dead companion from the driver's seat, causing him to tumble from the truck. She watched, spellbound, as the man dragged the body to the back of the pickup and, with a curse, shoved it over the tailgate to let it plop heavily into the truck bed. Stifling a sob, she got shakily to her hands and knees and then slowly stood, careful not to lean against the truck, sensing her weight would draw the killer's attention. Hesitating momentarily she ran, panic-stricken, toward the bridge leaving the false security of the truck.

"Whoa right there, bitch! Where the hell you think you're going?" the harsh voice commanded.

Her leaden legs refused to move, held immobile by sheer terror. Frozen in place, the girl silently pleaded, *Oh, God! Help me!*

His measured footsteps approached, and she could sense the hand reaching out. Darting suddenly away, she raced, terror stricken, toward the scattering of trees and underbrush bordering the river, with her only thought to reach the relative safety of the Pee Dee. Tripping over a broken branch, she fell, sprawling, then frantically scrambling up, unmindful of scrapes and cuts, and clawed through the brush and vines as the remnants of her clothing fell away. Again she stumbled and then lay panting like a wounded doe, unable to flee any longer from the determined hunter, too spent to go on.

The sadistic assailant, now stalking slowly, relentlessly, was almost upon her, his raspy breathing audible in the crisp night. Terrified eyes darted about, frantically searching for something with which to fend him off. Feeling around in the half-light of the dimming moon, her hand brushed against the neck of a broken beer bottle that had been carelessly thrown aside. A shadow suddenly blocked out what little moonlight filtered through the brush where she was hidden. He stood, feet widespread over the trapped girl, his cruel eyes staring ominously into her face. Recognition surfaced in her eyes as he dropped to a knee, watching, waiting. Terrified she opened her mouth to say his name, but no words came.

"So you know me, do you? You want more, huh? Well, sweetheart, I guess you know I'll have to…"

Desperately she jabbed the broken bottle into his face and rolled to her knees. Screaming curses, he pawed at the jagged cut on his cheek, wiping the blood away. Taking advantage of the opportunity, the girl raced for the Pee Dee, hoping for the security it offered. The noise of pursuit emphasized the only chance of escape.

"Oh no! Please! No!" she begged, defeated. The grasping hand raked past her shoulder as she desperately struggled through the weeds and underbrush. One terrified glance over the shoulder and her life quickly drained away as the machete struck the hairline at the base of her neck.

CHAPTER 21

Toddville, South Carolina
Saturday, September 12, 1953
11:45 P.M.

Jane Marie Wallace failed to return home by curfew on Saturday night, September 12, 1953. Her parents had imposed a 9:30 nightly time limit on how late the pretty high school junior cheerleader could remain out on weekday evenings but allowed some leeway for Saturday nights. Even then she was expected to be home by 10:30 at the latest.

Jane Marie was, for the most part, dependable but had recently shown typical teenage rebelliousness, a condition tied to coping with the rigors of growing into adulthood. It was not that she was disobedient, but with changes in body chemistry, there were physical and mental signs of her becoming a woman. She didn't mean to be outright defiant. Her actions were more annoying to her parents, Jack and Martha, than her indifference to their wishes. They knew that with tough love Jane Marie would eventually outgrow the snits and tantrums and develop into a sensible, mature young lady.

The most recent incident causing them worry involved Joey

Whitworth. Joey came from a family of indigent tobacco farmers living a short distance outside the small rural community of Toddville. Before dropping out of high school, Joey had been on the varsity football team where he starred in the backfield as arguably one of the most promising running backs in South Carolina high school sports history. His athletic abilities, however, failed to keep him in good standing. Problems with the coach arising from too many absences from practice resulted in Joey's dismissal from the team and his abrupt dropping out of school.

Joey's mother had died soon after the family came to Toddville in the summer of 1950 from North Carolina. The old man, a natural born failure, took to alcohol after losing his wife, and was only able to eke out the sparsest living toiling in the tobacco fields for Joey and his older sister Velma. Tired of the hand to mouth living, Velma ran off with a man from Wilmington. In a rage the old man tried to find her, but as with all his other failures, soon gave up, sinking even deeper into despondency. Joey was left with a chip on his shoulder to cope as best he could. But after meeting Jane Marie, seeds of hope had been planted in him, and now Joey could see his life turning around.

Joey and Jane Marie knew each other casually, mostly because they ran with different crowds and frequented different teen hangouts. She associated with the town elite and, until recently, gave Jack and Martha no valid reason to be concerned. Partly to assert her independence and partly to fulfill the thrill of that which was forbidden, Jane Marie began occasionally dating Joey. The relationship took on a serious turn soon after the young couple ran into one another at the local Frost Top drive-in. Joey tooled in one evening in his beat-up old Ford pickup, deliberately skidding to a sideways, sliding stop next to the sleek convertible where three of his former teammates and their dates sat talking. Jane Marie was with Geno Dantley, star quarterback of the team.

When the dust from his sudden arrival settled down, Joey swung open the pickup door, deliberately banging the side of Geno's convertible. Irate, Geno immediately confronted Joey over the incident. By then Joey had recognized Jane Marie and, ignoring Geno, leaned over, grinning wickedly at the girl saying, "Jane Marie, I'll be by to take you to the movie Saturday 'bout seven." And with that, he got back into the old pickup and, leaving Geno and Jane Marie speechless, spun out onto the road and roared off into the night.

"I'll whip his red-necked, tobacco grubbing ass," fumed Geno, reaching across and grabbing Jane Marie by the arm. Then, venting his anger at the girl, he snarled, "What the hell's going on, Jane Marie? You been two-timin' me?"

Calmly, she pulled his hand from her arm, feeling hurt by his outburst. Then inhaling deeply, she replied with calm bravado, "No, Geno. You should know me better than that. Now, please take me home."

Later that night alone in her room Jane Marie lay sleepless, disturbed by what had occurred that evening and at not knowing what to do about it. The outburst by Geno had destroyed their budding relationship. But, more disturbing was the brashness with which Joey had behaved. Still there was something about the way he had asserted himself that attracted Jane Marie.

As he had promised, Joey showed up promptly at seven o'clock on the dot, knocked on the door and, when Mr. Wallace opened the door, introduced himself. Skirting around his background, Joey, by omission, allowed the Wallaces to think that he was currently one of Jane Marie's classmates and still a member of the football team. By the same movement, he also failed to mention that he lived with his out-of-work father in a tenant shack on a rundown tobacco farm.

Still not comfortable, Wallace soon asked around about the boy and, when the truth of his background came out, tried to break up the relationship. Jane Marie continued seeing Joey, usually by slipping around and meeting him at the movies or the Frost Top drive-in downtown where the high school crowd hung out. This of

course, with its obvious ramifications, heightened the tension between Jane Marie and her parents. At that point her parents were
stalemated over what to do, and were seriously considering shipping her off to an exclusive girls' school down state in Charleston.

When Jane Marie had not come home by a few minutes past
midnight, a thoroughly alarmed Jack Wallace called the Toddville
Police Department office to report her disappearance. The deputy
on duty assured Jack and Martha that the girl had probably just lost
track of the time. He suggested to the anxious father that they were
more than likely parked down by the Pee Dee River or some other
secluded place and would be home shortly. He assured Jack that it
was routine for kids her age to frequent such places. But, under
Martha's prodding, Jack drove out to the Whitworth place to see if,
by chance, old man Whitworth might know where the teenagers
were.

Fifteen minutes later at around 2:00 on September 13, 1953,
Jack drove up to the old farmhouse and got out of his car to be
met by a crescendo of sounds from beneath the plank front porch.
When he approached, several scrawny, tick-infested hounds
charged, snarling and growling, toward the front gate of the picket
fence. Aroused by the commotion, old man Jeb Whitworth cracked
the front door slightly and peered out. Recognizing Jack, he
stepped out onto the porch clad only in his longjohns.

"That you, Jack?" he inquired, wondering what someone like
Jack Wallace would be doing out there at that time of night. Shrugging momentary apprehension away, he repeated, "Jack?"

"That's right, Mr. Whitworth. I apologize for having to awaken
you at this hour of the night, but I need your help," Wallace replied, his voice giving away the worry that nagged at him.

"Wal, you damned well better need it bad," he responded testi-
ly, his old-man growl mimicked the snarling dogs.

Ignoring Whitworth, Wallace continued, choosing his words
carefully, "Jane Marie didn't come home when she was supposed

to, and she knows that her mother and I always expect her home by 10:00 to 10:30 on Saturdays."

Realizing what Wallace was leading to and immediately jumping to the defensive, Whitworth retorted sharply, "What the hell's that got to do with me?"

"Whitworth, you know as well as I do that Jane Marie and your boy, Joey, have been slipping around together," replied Wallace, dropping his facade of politeness. "Now, I'm not blaming either him or you. All I'm interested in right now is if Joey is here and if he can help me find her."

Whitworth threw his hands up, saying, "For Christ's sake. Okay. Okay. I didn't hear him come in, but let me check to see if he's in bed."

The old man then backed through the door and left Wallace standing by the gate. The dogs, whimpering and growling, stared from beneath the porch, their eyes glowing embers in the darkness. Wallace waited impatiently for the old man to return.

When he did a few moments later, he had on his work pants and shoes. "Jack, Joey ain't here. I don't understand it. Don't understand it at all. He knowed we was due to take a load of cotton over to Florence today. Tell you the truth, Wallace, I jist don't know where his young ass might be."

Trying to remain calm, Jack said evenly, "I'm going back to town to talk to the police again. That don't work, I'm calling over to Conway and talk to Earl Lee." As he turned back to his car, he asked, "You want to go? I'll wait on you."

Dawn came with no hint of the whereabouts of the two teenagers. Horry County Sheriff, Earl Lee Tait, worked alongside Toddville Chief of Police, Jim Weldon, in the former's sparsely furnished office, trying to come up with a thread of information or anything to lead to Jane Marie and Joey's location. Unable to verify any immediate explanation for the disappearances, both lawmen were inclined to think that the couple had eloped. They were well aware that neither Wallace nor his wife approved of the relationship and had done everything possible to discourage it, but hormonal influences always overshadow common sense when teenagers think they are in love. They were equally aware that old man Whitworth didn't care one way or the other. Joey was a good boy, but in the small town of Toddville it was common knowledge that he didn't fit as a suitable mate for the daughter of one of the leading families.

"I got a feeling," offered the chief, leaning forward to tap his fingers anxiously on the desk, "that if we can hold off for a few days this problem is gonna solve itself."

"I agree, Jim. But how in hell do you plan on keeping Martha Wallace pacified until then?" Tait said, already wondering how they could stall Mrs. Wallace until the two youngsters decided to come home.

"I don't rightly know," responded Weldon, grimacing as he shifted, easing the pressure on his right hip. Then, seeing Tait's right eyebrow arch, he added, "Damned gun stickin' in my ass." Tait grinned while Weldon continued. "I do know this, Earl Lee, we better at least go through routine motions of some sort of investigation, or neither of us will git re-elected for another term. Not even for dog catcher."

"Tell you what, Chief. I'll put a man on it soon as I git back to Conway. And you do what you can at this end."

"Thanks, Sheriff, I appreciate that."

CHAPTER 22

Pee Dee River Bridge West of Toddville
Thursday, September 17, 1953
6:30 A.M.

On the early, wet morning of September 17, 1953, two local squirrel hunters stumbled upon the nude body of a young woman. Even in South Carolina's cool September weather, partial decomposition had already begun, but more grisly was the fact that the young victim's head had been hacked free with either a large machete-type knife or hand axe. A quick glance around told them it was missing. They immediately notified authorities in Conway, quickly leading them back to the spot where they had discovered her forest litter-covered body.

Both Sheriff Earl Lee Tait and Chief Jim Weldon knew at once that the body was probably Jane Marie's, and all doubts were dispelled when a comparison of physical features and fingerprints were analyzed. But beyond the discovery, troubling questions lingered: Why was the girl decapitated? Where was her head? And more importantly, where was Joey Whitworth?

A methodical search of the area failed to turn up much evidence except that the murder apparently occurred there at the river. Closer examination of the damp ground around the site revealed several sets of tire tracks, one of which probably belonged to Joey's pickup truck. Tait immediately dispatched Deputy Gene Varner to see if there were tire tracks at the Whitworth farm matching those at the murder scene. This proved to be fruitful, but beyond that, there were no other leads. It was as if Joey Whitworth, now a suspect, had dropped off the face of the earth.

As sheriff of Horry County, Tait assumed all responsibility for investigating the horrifying murder since the location of the body fell outside the city limits of Toddville and within his jurisdiction.

With that obligation, he ordered the Pee Dee River be searched and grapples be used if necessary to determine if Joey's body had been dumped into the stream. Tait recognized this was probably unlikely since neither he nor his fellow lawmen had found evidence of disturbances along the banks of the river where a body could have been dragged or rolled into the water. No matter, it was not in his nature to overlook any possible hint of what specific events had taken place to result in such a slaying as Jane Marie's. He would, he swore, find that girl's killer or killers if it took him the rest of his life.

A nagging thought kept creeping into Earl Lee's mind; *did Joey kill Jane Marie and then flee from the county?* He simply could not, deep down inside, believe Joey Whitworth was that kind of young man. There had to be some other explanation. Spurred on by the uncertainty surrounding the fate of Joey Whitworth, Tait vowed again to get to the bottom of the killing of Jane Marie Wallace.

On September 20, 1953, Tait's chief deputy received an anonymous telephone call from an unidentified male suggesting that a search should be made on an abandoned farm some two or three miles to the northeast of the murder site. Converging on the farm, Tait and his men found a densely overgrown rundown homestead. Weeds had grown up entirely around the place, and shrubs and small trees had already encroached onto what at one time had apparently been a prosperous farm-home complete with barns and outbuildings. It was immediately obvious from the mashed weeds and grass in the tire tracks that a vehicle had recently been driven into the front yard. Vegetation where the vehicle had stopped was flattened, indicating some type of recent activity.

The lawmen, under Tait's direction spread out and began the meticulous search through the buildings. Having had no success, the men returned by ones and twos to the cars parked at the front of the house with disappointment showing on their faces.

"Men, looks like I got you out here for nothing," Tait, disgruntled at their failure to turn up a single clue, told the dusty and sweating men.

"Guess that's what we're paid for, Earl Lee," responded Deputy Sheriff Gene Varner as he dragged a sleeve across his sweat-covered face.

"Yeah, I guess so," answered Tait, reluctantly accepting their failure. "Ain't doing no good here, so might as well…"

Before he could finish, South Carolina State Patrolman Bud White, who had been checking one of the sheds farther out back called excitedly, "Sheriff! You better come here! I think I just might have something."

Tait's heart skipped a beat. The dread of not knowing was now being replaced with the greater fear of feeling that their search was over. When he arrived where White was standing in the waist-high weeds, Tait realized they had overlooked an abandoned well. It had long since been boarded over to prevent the former residents from accidentally tumbling in.

As Earl Lee neared the well, the odor of decay permeated the air that escaped the opening where White had removed one of the boards. By now White was gagging, unable to do more than point toward the well before turning and falling to his knees in the weeds to vomit.

Steeling himself against what he knew would be in the well, Tait removed the remaining boards and anxiously peered into its depths. The former owners had used the well for the disposal of trash and cans and, along with years of neglect, had left the well nearly filled with assorted debris.

The horror he saw in the trash-filled well grabbed at Tait's very soul. Staring in death, Jane Marie seemed to chastise Earl Lee for waiting so long to find her. The girl's once long, full blond hair, now dank and soiled, hung obscenely from a skull from which the flesh had begun to fall away. Teeth that once graced a young girl's shy smile now grinned grotesquely at Earl Lee.

Equally horrifying was the arrangement of the gruesome evidence. The head was lodged between the knees of a corpse the killer or killers had dropped headfirst into the well. A closer look was not needed for Tait to tell whose it was.

As dreadful as the scene before him was, even more painful was the thought that fleeted across Tait's mind; *was that boy dead when he was dumped in there?*

"Goddammit to hell!" Tait expostulated vehemently. Then, remembering the other men were present, he regained his composure and, once again in control, said, "Gene, get things organized and look around here and see what you can find that we mighta missed. Probably done messed things up, but try anyway. You need me, I'll be back at the car calling Doc Cochran to come out and take over." Tait knew he was putting quite a burden on Varner, but there was no way he could stay there much longer.

"Goddammit to hell! What kinda crazy son of a bitch coulda done that?"

Friday, September 25, 1953
9:49 A.M.

"Kate, would you git Doc on the line for me?" Earl Lee asked his long-time secretary, Kate Garner. "I need to know what he's been able to find out about when them two kids was killed, and especially I need to know when the boy died."

150

Kate picked up the phone and dialed, letting her mind imagine the electrons speeding along the wire to the coroner's office across the street and down the block. Three rings indicated the connections were made before the click that prompted the feminine voice on the other end of the line to say, "Horry County Coroner's Office. May I help you?"

"Yes, Ethel, how're things going this morning?" Kate answered pleasantly. "Earl Lee wants to speak to Dr. Cochran if he's in this morning."

"Oh, hello, Kate. Doing just fine. Hang on, and I'll put Doc on."

There was a pause and then Kate heard Cochran's voice on the extension, saying, "What can I do for you, Kate?" as Ethel replaced the receiver in its cradle. *As if he didn't know*, Kate thought as she smoothly transferred the call, saying only, "The boss wants to talk to you."

"I'll git right to the point, Doc," said Earl Lee. "I know you ain't had much time, but if you could give me a rough estimate on the time of death on both them kids, I would appreciate it. And since we already know that Jane Marie was raped, I guess we can assume she was killed right afterwards. Guess the thing that is really bothering me is how and when Whitworth was killed."

"It's all in the report I sent you, but let me run through it again. I'll start by reviewing the girl's case, Sheriff," Cochran responded impatiently. Earl Lee sensed the irritation in his voice at having to go over the case again. He resented the seeming coldness of referring to Jane Marie as the girl. He didn't know what made him resent it, but he did. He knew that Cochran didn't mean to sound so cold, but had simply grown callous in his job.

"She was beaten and then sexually assaulted probably not more than an hour before she died. I would put the time of her death at about 10:00 to maybe 10:30 p.m., September 12. That would have been on a Saturday. The condition of her body makes this subject to some conjecture though. Now for the boy. From what I can tell, and keep in mind that I'll be looking further into both cases, he probably died before the girl."

"Why do you figure that?" asked Earl Lee, curious now, wondering if there was some significance, something he had missed earlier.

"I would think that the murderer would have wanted him out of the way while he ravaged Miss Wallace, and that may well be speculation on my part. One thing that makes me believe he died first was the fact that the path of the bullet that killed him entered just below the left clavicle then angled downward and to the right and exited the body above the right kidney. That would suggest that he—that is the boy—was sitting in the driver's seat of the truck. I suspect that the killer approached that side of the vehicle and fired through the window. There was evidence that the bullet cut into the great aorta. In a word, death was almost instantaneous."

"Well, that gives me a little more information to work with, but quite honestly, Doc, I'm out of suspects. At least since they was both murdered, I'm thankful Whitworth's death was fast and he didn't suffer. Just wish I could do something about Jane Marie. She shouldn't have had to die out there alone and scared. Why do some people have to be so cruel? She shouldn't have been hurt like that."

"Yeah, know what you mean," Cochran replied less clinically this time. "And by the way, have you found the pickup truck yet?"

CHAPTER 23

Myrtle Beach
Friday, September 24, 1953

Her eyes were leaden, and old lady Fulton droned on incessantly. Emily Johnson had been out late last night and, after nearly a day of dull classes, had reached the point where it was almost impossible to stay awake. Emily knew that if she even briefly nodded, Mrs. Fulton would tap her desk with that ever-present pencil, loudly clear her throat and call on her to answer some inane question. *Good Lord, won't she ever shut up?* The history class was only fifty minutes long, but each minute dragged on ever so slowly. Her eyes, already heavy from lack of sleep and Mrs. Fulton's monotone, were slowly closing despite Emily's best efforts to stay awake.

The sudden clanging of the bell resounding in a sleep-drugged mind startled her into awareness. Gathering her books, Emily hurried to catch the bus, suddenly more invigorated now that the school day was over. The last on board, she took the only seat left, one near the front of the bus.

Emily Johnson was a seventeen-year old junior at Myrtle Beach High School. She and her mother, Eula, lived alone in a small house not far from the ocean at 210 Oceanview. Em, as she preferred to be called, was the youngest of four children. Her older brother and two sisters were in their late teens when Emily was born and now, over seventeen years later, were married and living with their families in Alabama.

One day in 1938 when she was two years old, her father came home after work, strode into the bedroom, and packed his clothes into a suitcase. Without saying a word to either Em or Eula, he set the suitcase down by the front door, laid his endorsed paycheck on the dining table, and walked out of their lives. Eula never heard from him again, and Em grew up never knowing her father.

At seventeen, Em had already developed into a pretty young woman at five-seven and a trim 117 pounds. Penetrating dark azure eyes complemented honey-blond hair worn loosely about her shoulders. Clothes were a problem, but Eula was good with her hands and kept what few dresses and skirts Em had in good condition. To her advantage, Em could wear almost anything and look stunning.

She had met Joel and Betty Norman soon after they came to Myrtle Beach where Joel was one of the radar operators at the radar station. Emily often baby-sat some of the local children and, through the recommendation of one of Betty's friends, had agreed to sit with the Normans' baby on rare occasions when the couple were able to afford a night out. She and Betty soon became friends, so Em often visited the Norman house.

One Saturday night a couple of weeks later, Lucas and some of the other airmen from the radar unit dropped by for dinner. Following dinner that evening, Em had stopped by for a moment and was introduced to Lucas. She later confided to Betty that she intended to get Lucas to notice her and set her mind on how she might go about attracting him.

That night at the Norman's, Lucas scarcely appeared to notice the quiet, shy girl. Later on, when Em asked Lucas if he noticed her that night, he admitted that he had. But what he didn't mention was that she had left a lasting impression on him. He had to admit, after he had fallen in love with her that it was one of the best things that had ever happened to him.

CHAPTER 24

Myrtle Beach, South Carolina
Monday, 28 September 1953
1925 hours

Claude Beck's place, located about halfway between Myrtle Beach and Team 1 compound, had quickly become a favorite hangout for Lucas and his buddies. This was because after only a few days upon their arrival at Myrtle Beach, most of them had heard from the locals that Claude Beck's place was where the night action was.

While cruising the highway looking for girls, Charlie spotted a young woman turning into Beck's parking lot and, slowing up, had watched as she got out of her car, smoothing the tight fitting dress over shapely hips, and then disappeared into the café. He wheeled in, parked next to the girl's car and followed her in, choosing a seat at the counter where he could study her. Later, back at the site, he bragged about how she couldn't take her eyes off him and how it was a matter of time until they hooked up. Lucas found out later that it was Charlie doing the eying and that when she objected to his unwanted crude advances. Claude Beck intervened, threatening to throw him out to prevent trouble.

The small café became a favorite spot because of its excellent sliced barbeque served along with cold beer in long-necked bottles. Additionally, Claude allowed his customers credit on their purchases so long as they paid up each month on payday. Claude and his wife, Ellie, had operated the small business for several years as a simple mom and pop operation until one night at closing time when Ellie suddenly dropped dead of a heart attack. After her unexpected death, Claude, with the help of his youngest daughter, Beth, continued the business, although his heart was not in it anymore.

The girl had been in Claude's before, and after the encounter with Charlie, she was usually escorted by a muscular technical sergeant from the local South Carolina National Guard unit. However, this evening, several weeks later, she was oddly alone. As was her custom, she was dressed in a thin print dress that clung seductively to her body. It was easy to see why the national guardsman and Charlie were attracted to her. She was about five feet-eight inches tall, weighed about 120 pounds, and looked like a Vogue fashion model. She was, unlike many models, not cadaverous and hollow-eyed but had curves in all the right places. Each of those pounds was properly placed, adding to her gracefully slender body. Even if she had not possessed natural beauty, her poise and carriage would have no doubt attracted attention. It was evident from the confidence reflected in the way she conducted herself that she was vainly aware of her beauty and, without self-consciousness, used all of her physical attributes to her best advantage.

On entering the rustic café, she surveyed its interior, her eyes pausing on each of Claude's male customers before moving on. Her gaze lingered slightly longer at the table where JJ, Lucas and Charlie sat drinking beer. A slight upturn of her lips suggested the hint of a smile as her violet eyes swept past the beguiled airmen. Long raven hair swirled, reflecting deep purple as she moved purposefully to one of the booths mid-way down the north side of the room.

"Hot diddle-dee-damn!" Charlie exclaimed. "Did you see the look she gave me?"

JJ reminded him sardonically, "Charlie, she looked at every man in this here entire café including old Claude over there. Likely it was Lucas or me she was eying with that there 'I want your body' look."

"Yeah, Charlie, any girl that gits a bit of sand in her eye and blinks, you think she's putting a move on you," added Lucas, bitingly. "Man, I never seen anyone as struck on himself as you."

"Well, I know what I seen," blustered Charlie in response, and, with that, he got up from the table and swaggered over to the girl's booth.

"Well I'll be dipped," Lucas shook his head in disbelief. "I guess he was right about her after all."

Unimpressed JJ added, "Looks like it, don't it?"

The two finished their beers then Lucas stood, saying, "You care for another one, or are you ready to get outta here?" Before JJ could respond, Lucas held up his hand to stop him then, sitting back down, replied, "I do believe our lover boy struck out after all, JJ. Just look at that hang-dog look on the poor boy's ugly face. Maybe he ain't as good with the girls as he thinks."

Charlie came back over to their table and flopped down, shaking his head. "Dammit, don't either one of you say a damned word. Yeah, you're both right. I didn't get to first base with the bitch but," he paused, "just give me time. I'll have her in the back seat of my car before you know it. That little ol' gal just don't recognize quality even when she sees me hanging around bums like you two."

Lucas and JJ laughed, finished the last of their beers and left money on the table to cover their tabs. As they were leaving, JJ asked, "You coming with us, Romeo? Or do you plan to stay here and git drunk?"

"Naw, I ain't," Charlie replied, miffed. Then, with a malicious gleam in his eyes, he added, "I think I'll run down to the VFW where people are appreciated."

Horry County Hospital
Myrtle Beach
Tuesday, September 29, 1953
10:37 A.M.

Evelyn Ruth Dendy lay propped up in the hospital bed, her head resting on two pillows. The young woman's battered face was visible evidence of the brutal beating she had endured. The flesh around her left eye was bruised and livid, her lips split as a result of the onslaught. Barely conscious, her confused eyes followed Earl Lee as he paced at the foot of her bed.

On the night before, two late night strollers found the young woman lying in the surf about two miles north of North Myrtle Beach. Quick action on the part of the couple had prevented her from being pulled into the foaming surf by the powerful undertow of the incoming tide. Whoever had beaten the girl had fully expected her to be washed out to sea and drown.

Tait paused in his pacing, looking sympathetically at the girl and, seeing that she was now somewhat awake, gently asked, "Miss, are you feeling up to talking. I'm Sheriff Earl Lee Tait. I'm gonna need your help, if you're up to it, to find out who did this to you."

Evelyn attempted to speak, but could only manage a hoarse croak. Carefully, with her left hand she motioned Earl Lee to come closer.

Earl Lee pulled a chair up close to the girl's bed, sat, and looked into her eyes, wondering if he should question her now or later. Deciding he needed to know some answers right away, he inhaled deeply and asked, "Can you talk? I need to know what happened to you, but if you ain't up to it, I'll come back later."

Her eyes darkened and, with a cracking voice, she struggled to say, "No, please stay. If you would, please give me a drink of water. My mouth is so dry."

Tait poured a half glass of cool water from the pitcher on the bedside table and held it to the girl's bruised lips. She flinched but managed to sip a few drops of the cooling liquid before motioning the sheriff's hand away.

"Now, miss, do you remember what happened to you last night?" Tait asked. "You were found on the beach a good ways north of here, but right now, that's all we know."

Before the sheriff could continue, she whispered, "No, I don't remember."

"Miss, what I'm gonna say is gonna be painful for you, but we need to talk about it. But first, let me call a nurse to help me." Earl Lee didn't wait for a response before stepping to the door to ask Nurse Jennie Lee to come in.

Jennie Lee entered, looking questioningly at the sheriff. Tait said evenly, "Thanks, Jennie Lee." Then, nodding toward Evelyn, he continued. "I've got to ask Miss Dendy some delicate, uh, rather personal questions, and I would like for you to be here to help me. Okay?"

In response, Jennie Lee pulled the other of the two chairs in the room over to the girl's bed and indicated with a nod that he should begin his questions.

Earl Lee took a deep breath and, looking intently at the two women, quietly asked, "Miss Dendy, when you were brought in last night you were examined by the doctor on duty. I don't know how to say this any other way, except straight out." Ill at ease, he paused, eyes lowered, and mulled over his next words. Then, as unemotionally as he could, he said slowly, "He found that you'd been sexually assaulted as well as almost beat to death."

The girl started to say something, but Tait hurried along before she could interrupt, afraid that if he stopped now he would lose his nerve. Again looking into her eyes, he reached over and gently took her hand. "Now, Evelyn…do you mind if I call you Evelyn?"

A brief smile touched her torn lips. "No," she whispered.

"Well, Evelyn, do you remember what happened last night? We know from Claude Beck that you were in his place sometime around 7:30 or 8:00 last night, but he couldn't remember when you left or if you left with anybody. So, if you can, try to remember anything at all that might help us catch the man who did this to you. I've got a feelin' whoever you left Claude's with, if you were with someone, was the bastard—excuse me—the man who hurt you."

Evelyn, sobbing by now, squeezed Earl Lee's rough hand. "Mr. Earl," she barely whispered. "Everything is a blank. I don't even remember going to Claude's last night. I must have from what's been said, but I don't remember anything."

The sheriff gently extracted his hand from her grasp, brushed a stray tress back against her head and then, getting up, paused to look down again at the girl's battered face. *I'll git the sick son of a bitch who done this.* Motioning for Jennie Lee to follow, Tait strode purposefully out into the corridor of the hospital. Once out of Evelyn's hearing, he touched the nurse's arm and said quietly, "Jennie Lee, you'd be doing me a big personal favor if you would see that young woman gits special treatment."

Without waiting for a reply, Earl Lee turned and walked rapidly down the corridor, leaving Jennie Lee shaking her head in amazement and murmuring, "I'll be damned. I never woulda thought in a million years that old Earl Lee had a kind bone in his body."

CHAPTER 25

Myrtle Beach AFB, South Carolina, Team I Quarters
Monday, 28 September 1953
0920 hours

Military life is an existence of predictable, mostly dull events. The old adage of "hurry up and wait" has governed the lives of enlisted men from the first time rugged cavemen formed a loose team and then, with assorted clubs, set out to raid their neighbor's camp out of sheer boredom. It was true then, as now, these low men on the totem pole were prodded to hurry up but were then required to sit around and impatiently wait for action.

Several off-duty men with nothing to do and no money to do it with were hanging around the barracks, hoping Sergeant Jackson would spend a few more minutes down at his favorite donut shop before returning to assign some useless tasks for them, for no other reason than they were lying around doing nothing despite being off duty. They didn't worry about Captain Hill or Lieutenant Walton since Hill was probably still shacked up with his latest girlfriend, and the lieutenant, being a family man, seldom came in anyway.

Kesterman was lying on Willie Armistead's bed with his hands clasped behind his head, looking past crossed shoes toward JJ and Lucas. Three or four other bored airmen were sitting around playing poker and using Willie's blanket-covered footlocker for the card table. Willie, the team's entrepreneur, had managed to keep the game running for two days straight and was steadily winning. As various players tired or went on duty, usually broke, others took their place. Willie took time out from running the card game and his money lending business only long enough to see that his cooks were preparing meals for the team. Except for those small business interruptions, he could be found hustling his fellow airmen.

Glancing over toward Charlie, Willie slammed the deck of cards down noisily and growled, "Kesterman, git yo' sorry ass off mah bunk. I don't wanta sleep where your white trashy ass been. Stink mah fart sack up, you layin' on it lak dat."

"Hell, Willie, you don't sleep in it anyway. Every minute you have your black ass off, you're over in North Myrtle Beach sleeping with one of them women of yours or setting on your butt cheating us at cards. Bet you ain't slept in this bunk more than once or twice since we been here," Charlie replied, irritated.

"I ain't gonna argue wid you, white boy. You don't move it, I'm gonna mess up the other side uv dat ugly face uv yours," he warned, picking the deck up and shuffling the cards. Indicating Charlie's cheek with a card, he asked grinning, "Whur you git dat cut der on yo face enyway, Charlie. Dat ol' ho Betty you been jivin' scratch it up?"

Charlie touched the still healing wound, then jerked his hand away and growled, "Yeah. You could say that."

"Hey, men, did you hear about that boy and girl over there at Toddville?" JJ, seeing Charlie's eyes flash in anger, asked quickly trying to change the subject. The topic around the barracks had centered for several days about the discovery of their bodies and speculation about who could be responsible for such a cruel killing. From what little information the police had released, there were no suspects for the grisly crime, and apparently, very few clues existed for the authorities to work with to solve the slayings.

"Yeah," someone said, "seems like that's about all I been hearing about now for days. Damn shame, too. And you know I been thinking about the whole deal. Seems to me like I ought to know that girl. Yeah. Didn't Charlie try to date her once or twice not long ago?"

Looking over at Charlie Kesterman, Lucas watched his reaction then replied carefully, "I think he was hanging out over that way a couple months ago. As a matter of fact, I heard ol' JJ was chasin' after her, too."

JJ started to speak then stopped abruptly. With venom showing briefly in his voice he retorted, "Leave me out of this mess, Mackley. I ain't involved in any of this. And then smiling weakly, he continued, "but you know, I believe that's right about Charlie. I remember she sorta ignored Charlie. Fact is, she cut him right off at the knees. Treated him like a scumbag, didn't she? Ain't that about right, Charlie?"

Charlie's face grew dark. "Naw, that ain't true, and you bastards damned well know it ain't. Sure I been around over there, but I ain't never seen either one of them people before."

"Hell, Charlie," responded Lucas, smiling benignly, "don't get your butt in the air, JJ was just asking. For that matter, I've been over there chasing around a few times myself. Come to think of it, I think I seen her a time or two. Even tried to pick her up one time. Wouldn't even look my way, though."

Charlie replied, his voice modulated, more restrained, "Well, I don't think we should be making light of something like that. Two people been killed, and we're hanging around jawing almost like it was an everyday common thing. Just bothers me is all."

Taking advantage of Charlie's more moderate response, JJ looked him face-to-face and, in a taunting voice, responded, "Charlie, I frankly don't give a happy rat's rear end if what I've said bothers you or not. You've been acting like a sore-tailed cat for weeks now, and it's time you realized it."

A tight smile spread across Charlie's face, the aftermath of JJ's rebuff. But instead of reacting belligerently, he pinched the bridge of his nose as if trying to blot out something distasteful. He realized JJ was staring, and jerked his hand away, deflecting JJ's comment, and asked, "Have you noticed that everywhere we go there seems to be somebody dying?"

"How's that?" Lucas asked, wondering what Charlie was leading to.

"Well, think back. Seems like I heard that Sergeant Webber got killed." Both Lucas and JJ, now attentive, started to respond but stopped short as Charlie continued. "Then there was that farmer over at Lake City a couple years ago. And now, there's them two kids over at Toddville. Then there was that…" He looked for a moment at Lucas and JJ as if he wanted to say something more, but instead got up and left the room, leaving the others wondering.

Lucas watched Charlie's back as he hurried purposely through the door and thought, *Webber killed? What the hell is this all about?*

Radar 1 Installation
Tuesday 29 September 1953
1623 hours

Even though Lucas was on duty, his uniform indicated otherwise. He'd taken a rare opportunity to relax and wore his physical training shorts while lying back against one of the maintenance van's front wheels to soak up some late afternoon sunshine. With his eyelids heavy, he let the steady hum of the Buddha power generator lull him to sleep.

A noticeable movement down the empty beach about two hundred yards away momentarily caught his attention, causing him to sit up straight for a closer look.

Shading his eyes against the shimmering glare along the curving beach, he recognized Phelps, similarly clad in khaki shorts and loping loose-legged along the surf's edge toward the radar site. Within hailing distance, JJ slowed to a trot and called, "Hey, Mackley, c'mon. I got us a really good deal worked out with some fishermen up thata way, and I need your help." Without breaking stride, he pointed back up the beach, still closing toward Lucas.

He looked up the shore to the north about a quarter of a mile, then back to a slowing JJ, then back up the beach. From where he stood, Lucas could see a dory being rowed out into the rolling surf swells beyond cresting whitecaps, and from the looks of it, a long net was being fed out over the boat's transom by a gesturing man in the stern. On shore, three more men held the free end of the net and leaned against the increasing weight of the seine.

In the fall, almost like clockwork, schools of mullet migrate just off shore along the Carolina coast. During such movements, local fishermen harvest thousands of pounds of these delectable fish. Mackley had seen schools churning the sea's surface before but had paid little more than passing attention to them.

"So? What about it?" Lucas asked, curious.

"Git Charlie, if he's around, and maybe a couple more men to help us. I'll tell you what we're gonna do while we run back up yonder where them people are," JJ shouted back excitedly, gesturing toward the fishermen. "C'mon! They ain't gonna wait on us all day."

Getting reluctantly to his feet, Lucas fell in behind JJ and turned back only long enough to yell at one of the radar operators to relay JJ's message to Charlie to meet them on the beach. Turning, JJ paused to wait for Lucas to catch up and as they ran plodding heavily along the sandy strand, explained why he was so excited. The fishermen had found an unusually large school of mullet then needing a few more strong backs to haul the seine to shore, had enlisted JJ.

As he approached the busy fishermen, Mackley saw that the school was indeed huge and thought more muscle help would be needed. But what was in it for him and JJ?

Already, the dory had reached shore. Literally hundreds of fish were thrashing about, leaping into the air, attempting to escape the confines of the net. Many more were being crowded together in the silty waters near the bottom.

"All they want are the mullet," JJ said, excitedly. "Said we could have all the bluefish we wanted and even agreed to throw in a mullet or two."

The men, fishermen and airmen alike, bent to the task of hauling the fish-laden net to shore. Initially, the seine moved easily through the surf, but once the fish were herded into the decreasing confines of the net and the lead line began dragging on the sandy bottom, more physical effort was required to pull the net onto the beach. By now Lucas, with his arms straining against the weight and sweat pouring, wondered if the whole deal was worth the effort. *Damn JJ for spoiling his woolgathering.*

 Sea birds appeared drawn by some primal instinct toward the school of panicked mullet. One gray herring gull swooped low over JJ's head, the air currents from its wings ruffling his hair. Sensing the bird's approach, JJ looked up just as the gull empted most of the contents of its stomach. Dodging agilely aside, JJ shouted at the circling bird, "You sorry little son of a gun! You tried to shit on my head!"

The man in the dory laughed uproariously and opined solemnly, "Boy, you just learned the first rule of catching mullet—don't ever look up."

Kesterman sauntered over, followed closely by Anderson. "Okay. Git outta the way you weaklings an' let a real man do this child's work," Kesterman said arrogantly. One of the fishermen spat toward the surf, eyed Charlie and started to respond but then thought better. Instead he simply pulled harder on the line, giving no more response than an indifferent shrug.

"If there was a real man around, we just might consider doing that," replied JJ, feigning displeasure. "But then, on the other hand, I'm danged if I see one around here right now. What about it?" He pretended to look about. "Do you see one, Lucas?"

Lucas, Anderson, JJ, and the fishermen laughed and turned back to the job of pulling the fish-laden net toward the shore.

"That the way you guys feel, then you sure as hell don't need me," growled Charlie with a sneer. "Haul the damned net in by yourselves." The still tender, jagged cut on his cheek reddened as belligerence built up.

"Talk about touchy," JJ commented. "Don't you know I was only riding you? Wouldn't have asked you out here if I didn't want you. So simmer down and lend a hand."

His mood changing, Charlie grabbed one of the net's ropes and began pulling earnestly, challenging them. "Well, c'mon. Let's drag this net in before them fish get away."

Letting excitement override exhaustion, the airmen helped the fishermen load their catches, holding out a sizable pile of blue fish. The airmen looked at the flopping fish. Then all eyes went to JJ.

Hands on hips, JJ glanced out to sea, then back at the bluefish, then cautiously upward at the thinning flock of sea birds, remembering the old fisherman's advice. A breaker rolled in, almost reaching the pile of fish. JJ again stared at the pile of flopping fish and asked seriously, "Now we got 'em, what're we gonna do with 'em?"

"Beats the hell outta me," Lucas, replied. "It was your idea not ours."

"Yeah," Anderson said, sardonically. "Seems to me you coulda traded our sweat for a dollar or two or even maybe a case of beer instead of all them stinking fish."

"Awright. Awright. That the way you feel, tell you what. I'll clean a bunch of the best ones and git Claude to fry 'em up for us and meet you here later—say around 1900 hours. We can chip in and get a case or two of brew and have us one more whing ding. Oh, yeah. If you losers can round up dates this late, bring 'em along."

On the Beach
1947 hours

A yellow half moon had risen over the eastern horizon, its beams dancing off the incoming tide like golden glitter. A brisk breeze was blowing in from the ocean, setting just the right mood, while on the beach a driftwood bonfire blazed skyward to cast exaggerated shadows from the group of young people. Charlie and Betty Hutchins had wandered idly hand-in-hand down the beach until out of sight. Several of the others relaxed, lying on the cool, damp sand. Others were on G.I. blankets, talking low and gazing into the glowing embers of the fire, mesmerized by the moment.

JJ and Amy Lentz sat near Lucas by the fire discussing how their lives were changing since he came to South Carolina. Amy snuggled closer to him, pulling a beach towel over her bare legs. JJ grinned and reached down and patted her bottom, pulling her closer. Lucas, watching the couple, suddenly felt a pang of loneliness, wishing he was back in Arkansas.

"You know, Mackley," JJ said, interrupting Lucas's thoughts, "I believe our boy, Charlie, has really changed since our days back at Keesler. Used to be he was fun to be around. Seems like now all he does is bitch about everything and lose his temper when things don't go his way, like this afternoon."

Wondering how to respond without saying the wrong thing, Lucas replied, "Yeah, I've noticed that, too, JJ. If you try to be friendly, the next thing you know he's jumping down your throat. Sometimes it seems like he enjoys being a bastard."

"Well, I've about had it with his lip at times, but the hell of it is I still kinda like him. Thing is, I always thought until lately he was an okay guy," JJ said, a touch of bitterness in his voice.

Lucas glanced at Phelps, mulling over what he had said then decided not to follow up. *I wonder if JJ's really concerned about the change in ol' Charlie. Was there something in his voice I missed? Maybe he knows more about that girl and boy in Toddville than he's lettin' on.*

Seeing that Lucas wasn't going to respond, JJ turned his attention back to Amy, letting the matter drop. After a bit, he and Amy got up, both looking quizzically at Lucas, then strolled silently hand-in-hand toward the water's edge, leaving Lucas to his thoughts. Lucas continued sitting on the sand and staring into the fire as other couples broke away from the party and either left the beach or ventured along the shore.

Lucas didn't know how long he had been sitting after the couple left. His head snapped up as JJ demanded loudly, "Dammit, Amy. What's wrong with you now? I only asked if you wanted to walk down yonder along the water."

Even over the sound of the surf and wind, Lucas could hear the girl say, "Please, JJ, I don't...You're hurting me!" Then a bit louder, "No! I know what you want!"

Well, ol' JJ ain't havin' a helluva lot of luck with ol' Amy tonight, Lucas idly thought. Then, aware that he was staring at them, he ducked his head, embarrassed to be eavesdropping. They realized he was listening and looked in his direction then quickly away. Pretending that he had not overheard them, Lucas got up, stretched, and headed for his car.

The party broke up shortly after the brief exchange between Amy and JJ, and as Lucas drove back alone to the compound, what JJ had said about Charlie crept into his mind. Whatever the exchange between Amy and JJ had been about, it made him wonder what was happening. Seemed to him that not only had Charlie changed, but also, over the past few months, so had JJ. *Guess I have, too,* he thought.

During the drive back to the barracks, Lucas reflected on the deteriorating friendship that Charlie, JJ, and he had enjoyed during those days in Biloxi. Back then, it was three pals against the world, sharing the fun and consequences. The devil with everything else. Now, those times were in the past. *Maybe this is how it is as you get older, or maybe the friendship was only a fleeting thing anyway*, he brooded.

The three still frequented Claude's, but the old camaraderie was gone. Charlie seemed to be away from Myrtle Beach more often than before. He would get into his convertible without saying anything and drive off, never bothering to look back. More often than not, it was late at night before he returned, and even more oddly, he would go straight to bed without speaking. And then there was Phelps. He had dated Amy Lentz almost every night since early summer, but now however, they were seeing each other less frequently. *What was it Amy had said tonight at the picnic—something about him hurting her—or was it just a lover's spat? There's a hardness about Charlie but it looks like ol' JJ's got a mean streak, too. I'm sure he slapped Amy.*

Lucas had a deep-seeded feeling that both men were no longer the same easygoing buddies he once enjoyed being around. Then, feeling the hurt of broken friendship, he silently repeated, *I guess all three of us have changed. It's not like it used to be. And, I feel it never will be again.*

CHAPTER 26

Conway, South Carolina, Horry County Sheriff's Office
Wednesday, October 14, 1953
9:31 A.M.

Kate Garner, secretary in the Horry County sheriff's office, tapped lightly on Earl Lee's door and then, after a brief pause, pushed it open. Earl Lee looked up from the pile of papers, a dark frown on his face telling Kate that she had interrupted him at an inopportune time.

"Yeah, Kate. What you need?" he grumbled, irritated.

"I know you're busy, Earl Lee, but I think this is important, or I wouldn't have bothered you." Then without giving him a chance to stop her, Kate said curtly, "There's a Mr. Fred Dendy in the outer office wanting to see you. Sounds like he's the father of that Dendy girl that was assaulted over at Myrtle Beach about a month ago. Said he needed to see you real bad."

Earl Lee sighed, saying apologetically, "Okay, Kate. Thanks." Coddling his half-asleep foot, he rose and followed her to the outer office where a gray-haired man of about sixty stood nervously waiting.

"Mr. Dendy? I'm Sheriff Tait. What can I do for you?" Tait said formally, extending his right hand to the haggard, worried man.

"Sheriff," he responded, giving Earl Lee's offered hand a quick nervous shake. "I'll get right to the point. I ain't heard nuthin' from my daughter, Evelyn, in over two weeks, and that ain't like her. She always lets either her mother or me know where she is. Her mother and me are divorced, but she always keeps in touch with one or the other of us. Didn't think too much about it until Audra called me this morning upset and asked if I would see if I could find her."

"Well, Mr. Dendy, did you try her place?" asked Tait, already knowing the answer.

"Yessir, I did," replied Dendy, worry creasing the corners of his eyes. "And that's what's got me concerned. Got the landlady to let me in, and I swear, Sheriff, I don't think anybody's been in that place for days."

"What do you mean? How could you tell?"

"Well. First off, the place had that closed-up smell about it. Know what I mean—kind of stuffy and musty. I thought that was probably reasonable, though, since Evelyn does sometimes visit friends for a week or so at a time, except that this time dirty dishes were in the sink. And they'd been there a long time. Long enough for mold to grow. It's just not like her to leave her place dirty like that."

A chill crept over Earl Lee, and he shivered despite the warmth of the office.

Seeing Tait's reaction, Dendy hesitated momentarily with his own concern growing. Then he continued, hoping the sheriff would make his fear go away. "Mrs. Warren, she's Evelyn's landlady, also told me she hadn't seen Evelyn around lately either. And, Sheriff, I just…"

"Tell you what, Dendy," Tait interrupted, trying to allay his own fears, "I got to run over there this morning, so I'll drop by and talk with Mrs. Warren and take a look around. Now I don't think you need to worry none, but tell Kate here how I can reach you, and I'll get back with you soon as I can."

Earl Lee was standing staring out the office window at nothing in particular when Kate came in. Reading his look correctly, she said, "You got that same feeling I have about this, don't you, Earl Lee?"

"Yeah, Kate," he reluctantly admitted, "that girl's lying out there somewhere dead just like that little Wallace girl."

Horry County Sheriff's Office
10:20 A.M.

"Sheriff's Office. This is Miss Gardner. What can I do for you?"

"Kate, this is Ira Prewit down here in Lake City. How are you doing this mornin'?" the tinny voice at the other end of the line responded.

Recognizing Prewit, she replied, "Good to hear your voice, Ira. Guess we're staying busy like you. Now tell me, what can we do for you?"

Sheriff Ira Prewit had been in the office nearly as long as Earl Lee Tait, and both men were longtime lawmen as well as good friends, each holding considerable respect for the other. Even though she asked Prewit what he was calling for, Kate knew that he wouldn't be calling unless it was important. Prewit was the type who shunned modern conveniences when possible and used the telephone only when necessary.

"Is Earl Lee in?" asked Prewit, speaking a little too loud into the telephone. "I need to talk to him real urgent."

"No, he's not, Ira. You just missed him," Kate explained, then added, "With that double murder at Toddville and now a missing girl over at Myrtle Beach he's been pretty busy. Matter of fact, he's gone over to Myrtle Beach this morning. Got a call from one of the local officers that a girl's body had washed up near North Myrtle Beach sometime last night."

"I have to tell you, Kate, I hate to load more problems on him, but don't have any choice," he said, still speaking loud. "I've been keeping up with the killing of them two kids from Toddville. Can you tell me if he's making any headway on finding out who done it?"

Kate answered candidly, "Not a whole lot, Ira. And it's really bothering him."

"Well, like whut I was getting around to, I got me a similar case," Ira cut her short. "Happened right out of Lake City. Woman was nearly beat to death then had her head pert near cut off. Matter of fact, she might of survived the beating, but the slashing finished her off for sure. Might not be any connection at all, but the way this killing happened sure looks a whole lot like them ones over at Toddville, 'specially with that little girl."

Kate was familiar with the details of the Toddville slayings, and Ira's description of what happened at Lake City proved the similarities were chilling. There were questions that needed answering before actual connections could even be surmised. Best let Earl Lee handle this. "Ira," she said, considering what to say, "give me a little more information on what happened, and I'll have Earl Lee call as soon as he gets back."

Horry County Sheriff's Office
10:45 A.M.

After fielding Prewit's disturbing call, Kate returned to her cluttered desk, quickly finishing off the accumulated paperwork. Grabbing the opportunity to relax for a few minutes, she leaned back in her chair, pressing her fingers against her temples to try to ease the tension of the past couple of days. Her eyes had no more than closed when the ringing of the telephone jolted her back to the present. Reaching groggily for the receiver, Kate answered, "Hello, sheriff's office. How may I help you?"

The voice on the other end of the line sounded distant. "Hi Kate. Jim Weldon here. Earl Lee in?"

"No, sorry, Jim," she replied, now fully alert. "Can I take a message and have him get back to you?"

"Yeah, let him know we found Joey Whitworth's pickup about half a mile from where we found his body. It was hidden in a patch of bushes in an old field. Whoever left it there had placed some brush over it so it couldn't be seen very easily. Tell him we'll process it an' get back to him soon as we can."

Horry County Sheriff's Office
3:23 P.M.

When Earl Lee walked in later that afternoon, Kate knew by the look on his face that something had deeply disturbed the sheriff. Hurrying past, he went straight into his office and closed the door behind him. As the door swung shut, Kate heard Earl Lee's chair give as he settled into it. In a moment, he sighed deeply and then was silent. A few minutes later, she heard him stirring behind the closed door. Then, the doorknob turned, and Kate braced herself.

Earl Lee opened the door, looked sheepishly at Kate, and motioned for her to come to his office. Studying his face, she saw a man she had not seen before; a sadness had aged him. His tormented eyes momentarily held hers as she walked toward the chair he had indicated. Kate sat waiting, but Earl Lee turned away, slowly going over to the window and solemnly staring out into the mid-afternoon busy town square of Conway.

Turning back to her, his mouth working, Earl Lee gestured with his hands and said with emotion cracking his voice, "Kate, I'm sorry I was so rude a few minutes ago. I hope you'll understand an' forgive me when I tell you what happened."

Kate's hands flew involuntarily to her mouth. "Oh no! Earl Lee! Don't tell me Evelyn Dendy's dead?"

Earl Lee's shoulders slumped as he sighed dejectedly and confirmed, "Yeah. She was found late last night, and we just got a positive I.D. this morning. Apparently, she'd been stabbed several times around the face and upper body and then dragged into one of those small creeks near the beach. Her body was found where the creek empties into the ocean."

"Have you notified her folks yet? If you want, I'll go with you."

Spreading his hands in resignation, Earl Lee responded quietly, "I appreciate that, Kate, but this is something I have to do alone." Starting toward the door, he stopped short, asking, "By the way, before I go see Dendy, did anything happen while I was gone?"

"Yes, Jim called. Said to tell you they had found Joey's truck and he would call when they finish checking it out. Ira Prewit also called this morning soon after you left the office. Seems he has a murder that is a whole lot like the Wallace-Whitworth case. Told him you'd call him back as soon as you got in."

"He say who the victim was and when it happened?" Tait, again the professional lawman, wanted to know.

Searching her mind for details, Kate responded "Yes, he gave some information, but I got the impression he would tell you more when you called him back. Anyway, the victim was a woman, Sarah Moorland, about thirty or so. Lived just out of Lake City. I really didn't get much more except for the way she was mutilated—cut up pretty badly."

CHAPTER 27

Lake City, South Carolina, Sheriff Ira Prewit's Office
Monday, October 19, 1953
10:15 A.M.

Sheriff Ira Prewit got up from his well-worn desk in the small office and enthusiastically shook Earl Lee's hand. "Good to see you again, Earl Lee, even under these circumstances."

Where Tait was tall and raw-boned, Prewit was scarcely five-feet-five inches tall, a cocky little rooster of a man, and could not have weighed more than 130 pounds soaking wet. His physical appearance was deceiving though. He had been known to walk up to some of the worst troublemakers in Florence County and, without using his gun, place them under arrest. In fact, it was rumored that Prewit did not even carry a gun, but so far, no one had had the courage to challenge him to find out.

"Good to see you, too, Ira, but I'd rather we was out looking over that no good old bird dog of yours than working on a case," answered Tait congenially. "I gather from the little information that Kate gave me that you been about as busy as me."

"That's a real understatement, Earl Lee," agreed Prewit. Then getting right to the point, he said, "Don't know if you've heard about that tobacco farmer, Roscoe Moorland, and his widow or not, but that's what I wanted to hash over with you."

Tait didn't interrupt but merely shook his head, acknowledging that he was only vaguely familiar with what Ira was talking about.

Prewit continued, reiterating the details of the death of Moorland as well as the subsequent events that may be related. Nodding, Earl Lee said, "Yeah, I remember that now, but what's this Kate was saying about his widow. I don't unnerstand the connection."

Ira held his hand up saying, "This is where it gits beyond the normal, Earl Lee. Roscoe was a pretty much of a boozer until him and Sarah got hitched, then he more or less quit his drinking and settled down. They still liked to hang out at some of our local honkytonks, especially the Pines Lounge. Limited their drinking to a couple of beers but loved to make them honkytonks and dance."

"Tell me this, Ira, did they have any kids?" Tait asked, but then realized he didn't know why he thought it relevant.

Prewit frowned at being interrupted. "Naw. And that probably caused Sarah to take up her old ways. After Roscoe got hisself killed she took to going out near ever night, drinking heavy and generally raising hell. Had to go out to the Pines two or three times myself and take her home."

"You still ain't got to what all this has to do with me," Tait reminded him patiently.

"Well, like I said," Prewit responded evenly, "back last summer—I think mid-August or there about—her body was found in the bedroom of the trailer where her and Roscoe lived before he died. She had been beaten up pretty bad and was cut bad about the head and shoulders. Coroner said the slashing and stabbing was what probably killed her, although he couldn't be completely sure. Estimated she'd been dead for nearly a week before a cousin found the body and called me."

"Maybe I'm missin' something, Ira, but what makes you think there's a connection between my murders over at Toddville and this one?"

"Just look at the facts, Earl Lee. I don't know much about the condition that boy was in, but from whut I understand about the

Wallace girl, she was hacked up pretty bad with a knife or axe."

Earl Lee shuddered as the image of Jane Marie's accusing face crept back into his mind. Shaking his head, trying to make the image go away, he said, "I don't know, Ira. What you say may be coincidence." When Prewit didn't respond immediately, Tait modified the comment. "But, you may have something."

"I know you gonna think this is farfetched, Tait, but that same bunch of Air Force folks that come through here in that convoy are the same ones you got over at Myrtle Beach."

"Whoa! Hold on! That is gittin way out, Ira. That ain't even close to being farfetched. What you're saying is farther out than that," Tait said, having a hard time grasping Ira's reasoning.

"You didn't let me finish, Earl Lee. What I was gonna tell you was that some of them same boys has been hanging out at that same honkytonk where Sarah Moorland hung out."

Tait protested, still unable to accept Ira's reasoning, "But, Ira, that don't prove a damned thing, and you know it. Must be half the young men in this area out there some time or the other."

"Awright, Earl Lee, I'll drop this on you then. It's rumored that some of them men may be involved in another killing in Mississippi. Fact is, a major from the air base over at Sumter was over here nosing around asking questions not long ago. Didn't talk to him myself, but was I you, Earl Lee, I just might ask myself if any of them boys has been hanging around in the vicinity where them two kids from Toddville was murdered."

Tait sat in deep thought for a few moments considering whether or not to tell Prewit about the latest murder at Myrtle Beach. Finally, deciding to hold off for now, he stood and thanked his fellow lawman. "I appreciate what you told me, Ira. Let me think on it a while. Call me if anything else turns up, and I'll do the same."

By the time he reached Conway later that evening, Earl Lee was no closer to putting the pieces of the murders together than before. His talk with Prewit only added new questions he would have to find answers for.

CHAPTER 28

Norman House
Myrtle Beach
October 21, 1953
8:30 P.M.

Lucas arrived at the Normans' shortly after going off duty at 1600 hours. Already, there was a hint of an early winter coming to the Carolina coast. Near the radar installation this morning he had noticed a light frost painting the sparse sere grasses with a silvery sheen, and now in the late afternoon, dusk was muting the chilly harshness of the now deserted streets of the resort town.

A few days before Joel Norman had casually mentioned that Lucas might enjoy stopping by for a home-cooked meal. Concerned that the young couple were barely making ends meet on Joel's meager pay as an airman second class, he had begged off a couple times. This time though, both Joel and Betty had insisted, and, with reservations, Lucas had eventually accepted, determined to repay their kindness.

Lucas pulled to the curb in front of the modest rental house, switched the engine off and got out. Sergeant Jackson's old Ford coupe was parked in the drive behind Joel's battered Nash. So, apparently, he was not the only guest invited tonight. *Well,* he mused, *with others there, maybe this would give me an excuse to leave early.* Socializing was never one of his strong points. He had never been one to enjoy such occasions, but if others had been invited, maybe the pressure would be off him. With that reassuring thought in mind, he strolled onto the front porch and knocked lightly on the door.

Soon after, the door opened, and Emily Johnson stood there smiling. "Hi, there," she said cheerfully. "Please come on in. Joel and Betty are in the kitchen, and Sergeant Jackson is already here."

Lucas sensed a slight, involuntary arch of his left eyebrow. *What was Jackson doing here? Was he here with Emily? Naw, he's too old for her. Guess old Joel's getting in a few brownie points.* A quick glance at Emily's twinkling eyes told him she had noted his confusion.

"No, he's not with me," she whispered. "I was babysitting with little Joel, and Betty asked me to stay for dinner, if you're wondering what's going on."

I knew that, he thought. Joel had mentioned several times that Emily watched their baby on the few occasions that he and Betty were able to go out or when Betty had to be away running errands. Embarrassed, Lucas blurted, "I knew that." Then grinning foolishly to cover up, he said, "Go change the kid's diaper or something."

Emily giggled impishly, then patted his arm and wiggled off to the kitchen. Shortly afterward he heard laughing and, shaking his head, walked over to where Jackson sat and said to him, "Good to see you, Sarge."

They ate the simple but well prepared meal, steering all conversation away from the military activity and job functions. Joel and Betty described how they had grown up in a small town in Tennessee and had been high school sweethearts. Married right out of high school, Joel had knocked around east Tennessee working odd jobs, while Betty had found part-time work as a waitress in one of the local greasy-spoon cafés. In order to avoid the draft when the Korean War broke out, Joel had volunteered for a tour in the Air

Force. Once he was transferred to Myrtle Beach, Betty and the newly arrived Joel, Jr. had joined him.

After dinner, they sat around making small talk. Jackson excused himself, explaining that some matters back at the installation required his attention. Lucas felt obligated to stay a little longer, so while Joel and he talked, Betty and Emily washed the dishes and put away the leftovers, rejoining the two men when they had finished.

Lucas glanced at his watch and, realizing that it was almost 9:30, got up saying, "It's late, and I gotta be going."

Before he could thank Betty for the dinner, she interrupted, "Lucas, I have a favor to ask of you. Would you mind dropping Em off on your way? It'd save Joel a trip."

Taken aback at the boldness of Betty's request, Lucas struggled for the right response. Then, after an endless pause, he managed to stammer, "Sure. Okay, be glad to."

Emily sat with lowered eyes, uncomfortable with Betty's abrupt approach. She had confided that it would be nice if she could get the young airman to notice her and had even gone so far as to say she intended to wrangle him into asking for a date. That had all been woman talk, though. But now, her feelings were about to be exposed.

Delighted at their discomfort, Betty laughingly said, "It won't be that bad. It's only a short drive, and I really don't think he'll bite you, Emily."

Lucas smiled at Emily, walked over to where she was sitting and took her hand, saying, "Don't pay any attention to her, Em. I really would like to take you. Now, if you're ready, let's get outta here before they think of something else."

Grateful, she let him help her into her coat, and after thanking their hosts, the couple hurried to the door.

Joel snorted in the background, and Betty giggled, satisfied that she had pushed them together.

"I really am glad I'm taking you home," Lucas told Emily in the car. "Old Betty did me a big favor by asking." He reached over and touched her arm.

She had been sitting crowded against the car door since they had left, ill at ease and staring at the Carolina winter night. With that small gesture of his touch, she turned and smiled uneasily. "Thanks," she stammered. "I hope you won't feel angry with me if Betty embarrassed you."

"Of course, I'm not embarrassed. Shook up a bit but not embarrassed. Now then, move over this way." When she complied, he put his arm around her shoulder, saying, "Gotta have my arm like this or else I can't drive right."

CHAPTER 29

Veterans Hospital
Biloxi, Mississippi
2004

Marty Judson glanced out the window of her small cubicle office in the administration building and saw Chief Master Sergeant Lucas Mackley slowly making his way across the lush lawn, headed for his favorite spot. She had observed before that he preferred the tarnished iron bench beneath the boughs of the huge live oak over more comfortable seats closer to the building. Smiling at the thought, she recalled the time she had seen him sitting half asleep in that very same spot. The smile lingered as she remembered the confused look on his face. Marty hadn't intended to startle him; only the fact that he had been sitting there for so long had caused her to break away from the pathway and approach him. He had reacted unexpectedly, calling her "Em," then, trying to hide his embarrassment, he had mumbled something about dozing off. Eventually, she had determined she would get the truth about the girl called Em.

Since that encounter, Marty had made it routine to drop by his room or to make some excuse to go over to the old tree to visit for a few minutes. She had really wanted this job with the Veterans Hospital but was now having second thoughts. The sight of so many old men, nearly all carrying the mental and physical wounds of countless campaigns, was taking its toll. It was sad to see most of them had been dumped on the trash heap of unwanted human flotsam, whose only purpose now, since they had honorably served their country, was to wait patiently to die with dignity. The sadness engraved in Chief Master Sergeant Mackley's face especially preyed on her mind. During the past few weeks, she had gleaned only part of the story about Em from the taciturn old man.

Lucas eased over to his favorite bench, slowly looking about and seated himself facing the open Gulf to gaze pensively at an occasional fishing boat going by and heading for the barrier islands. Except for the encroachment of gaudy casinos and neon-lit motels, the strip alongside U.S. 90 was much the same as back in 1950 when Charlie, JJ, and he were naïve young airmen. Suddenly the poignant memory of Em gripped his innermost thoughts, and he was being carried back to those days at Myrtle Beach, where his innocent world had come crashing down.

Forcing his muddled mind to dwell on more pleasant times with Em, his thoughts once again turned back to one cold, moonlit night many years ago at Claude's.

Claude's Place
Myrtle Beach, South Carolina
Thursday, 5 November 1953
2153 hours

An unusually early November cold snap had plummeted the temperature to hover around freezing when Lucas paid his tab and walked unhurriedly from Claude's barbeque place. The full moon was a bright orb in the autumn night, the air was crisp, and although there was little wind, a coldness cut through his thin fatigue jacket, chilling him. Shivering, he casually walked to the '47 Chevy, his feet crunching the nearly frozen ground. Ice crystals were already forming in the puddles of water in the parking lot as he pulled away from Claude's and turned south onto the highway. The beer and barbecue had been a pleasant respite from the usual fare offered up by the mess sergeant Willie Armistead. On his salary as a staff sergeant, though, such treats were not often possible. Such was not the case back at Keesler, but here at Myrtle Beach things were looking up. As he drove through the winter night, it felt good to be alive.

The team had been stationed at Myrtle Beach now for slightly over six months—long enough for the men to begin to function as a well-trained unit and for several promotions to have been made. In fact, he had just recently been upped to his present rank of staff sergeant and was now the NCOIC for radar maintenance. Other things had also changed, some of a more subtle nature, and not necessarily for the good. Lately, Charlie had been drinking more than usual, at times seemingly distantly remorseful. When Lucas had tried to get him to open up and talk, Charlie often cut their conversation short or changed the subject entirely. He would become evasive or mumble something about personal family problems. Even JJ seemed less friendly than when they were students at Keesler.

A nagging half-remembered thought slipped into Lucas's mind. JJ had always seemed solidly in control, never letting anger show, at least until lately. Since he'd started dating Amy Lentz, he'd become more testy and, like Charlie, allowed suppressed feelings to erupt. Maybe, Lucas considered, they were just a bit jealous of his sergeant rank.

A mile farther down Highway 17, he turned right into the team compound, parking his Chevy in one of the spaces reserved for NCOs near the barracks. Sergeant Anderson was alone in the room already asleep. Trying not to awaken him, Lucas slipped out of his shoes and outer clothing and crawled into a sleeping bag on his cot, hoping that he could make it through the night without having to get up to relieve himself of all the beer he'd consumed at Claude's joint.

Not even a couple hours later, Lucas was awakened by a nasty jolt. Forced from his deep, alcohol-induced sleep, Lucas recognized Charlie's giggling, half-drunken voice. "C'mon, turkey. Wake up! There's a good-looking woman outside who wants to see you."

Still more asleep than awake, Lucas struggled to enter the living world. Had he heard right? Did Charlie actually say, *There's a girl who wants to see you?*

"What the hell, Charlie? You crazy or drunk?" Lucas mumbled still trying to collect his wits.

"I ain't kidding, Lucas, Emily Johnson is out there in my car waiting for you to come out. I don't know why, but she's there waiting."

Fully awake now but still not comprehending, Lucas asked, "You're telling me she wants to see me? Now?"

"Yeah. Like I said, I don't know why in hell she would, but get your sorry backside up and get out there before I have to go do your job for you," Charlie said, laughing.

Lucas pulled on his fatigues and slipped into his shoes as he made his way past the snoring airmen in the main bay of the barracks and eased quickly out the door into the parking lot, still expecting to find no one there. Knowing Charlie, he would not have been the least bit surprised had he been snookered and played for the fool. But sure enough, when he got there, Emily stepped out of the car and stood shivering in the bone-breaking November coldness of the night, waiting for him.

Lucas had taken Emily home a couple of weeks before after having dinner with the Normans'. After walking her to her door that evening, he hadn't lingered long, sensing that she was uncomfortable being with him. He had given only a quick peck on Em's cheek and she had backed off, mumbling a word of thanks, then slipped quickly inside and closed the door in his face. He remembered standing there confused, wondering what had upset her. Shaking his head at the turn of events, Lucas moseyed back to the Chevy, driving away without even looking back.

Struck by her little-girl, innocent charm, he had wanted to ask her out for a regular date, but her abruptness didn't allow him the chance. He had shrugged the idea off, rationalizing that she was probably too young anyway. She seemed to be just a kid of seventeen but, in experience, seemed much older than her tender years indicated. She was tall and willowy and only beginning to show signs of womanhood. Even then she was quite capable of turning heads. Her hair was honey blond and long, hanging just below her shoulders, and when she walked there was just a hint of seductive wiggle to her hips, designed no doubt to tease and tantalize.

As he approached, seeing her in the winter moonlight, he wondered why he hadn't been more persistent in getting her interest.

"Hi, Lucas," she spoke softly, watching with a lowered chin, a little embarrassed as he came closer. "I hope you don't think too badly of me for leaving you standing there the other night. I guess I was embarrassed over Betty pushing you on me. Anyway, I cried and couldn't sleep after what I had done. I'm sorry," she whispered. "I know it's my fault, but I was hoping to see you again. I know we've met only a time or two, and I acted so silly, and you haven't been around, or even asked me out. I…"

"Hey now, just a minute," he cut her off, partly to prevent her from being embarrassed and partly because it was true that he hadn't called her. "I can explain," he offered limply. "I've been pulling some extra duty but meant to drop by," he lied glibly. "Really wanted to, but anyway I'm glad you're here. Thought ol' Charlie was pulling one when he said you were out here."

Showing relief, Emily let out a long-held breath and looked up to meet his gaze before continuing. "I was afraid you weren't interested in me any longer. I was at Claude's, hoping I'd see you, but you had already left. Then Charlie came in, and while we were talking, I mentioned I'd like to see you—that I'd just missed you. And he said he'd bring me out here to the compound—that you were here. I thought he was leading me on. I didn't realize he meant now when I told him okay, but before I could stop him, we were in his car driving here."

Taken aback by Emily's boldness, Lucas unconsciously kicked at the frozen ground with his unlaced boot searching for something to say. Then, realizing what he was doing, moved closer to the girl, his mind in a whirl. "I'm glad you didn't stop him," he said, trying to cover his hesitation.

Before he could say more, she ducked her head in embarrassment at the boldness of what she was about to say. "I've wanted to be with you since you took me home from the Normans' that night."

"Yeah, me, too. Sorry I didn't call."

"Now that that's settled, I want to ask you to do something, but you don't have to if you don't want to. Okay?"

"Sure, whatever you want," he replied, wondering what was happening.

She hesitated momentarily then blurted, "Would...would you get us a couple of beers and then let's go down to the beach and drink them and listen to the ocean and watch the moon and listen to music?"

Hot damn almighty! Lucas's mind shouted almost loud enough for her to hear. *I done died and gone to Heaven! Did I just hear what I thought I just heard?*

Before he could savor the thought, she jerked him right off his cloud and back to earth. "Lucas, I'm scared, and I know I'm doing something good girls are not supposed to do. So promise that you won't let anything happen."

Hell, under the circumstances, I might even agree to marry the girl, and of course I do have my fingers crossed, he thought.

They drove back toward Myrtle Beach with Emily snuggling against his right side, his arm holding her tight around the shoulders. While she waited, Lucas left the car idling and hurried into Claude's to buy a half dozen long-necked bottles of Pabst Blue Ribbon beer. In his haste to get back to the patiently waiting girl, he slipped on the scattered patches of ice, nearly falling. Grabbing the rain channel above the car door to steady himself, he strived to regain his footing on the slippery ice. Opening the door, he placed five of the bottles on the back seat, opened the sixth and handed it to Emily. She fidgeted, uneasy, as he settled behind the steering wheel and closed the driver's side door. Tentatively lifting the cold bottle shakily to her lips, she licked a tiny fluff of foam from the opening of the bottle and then sipped a small taste of the beer, grimacing as the malted flavor of the liquid coursed along her tongue to her throat.

Lucas shifted the car into reverse and backed carefully out of the parking space for the second time that night. Changing to low, he depressed the accelerator, and the car moved smoothly out onto Highway 17. A hundred yards down the road, they were cruising along near the speed limit.

The compound that housed the radar team was west of the highway and separated from the beach where the radar installation was located by a narrow strip of woods. At intervals, lateral roads paved with crushed oyster shells led to the beach from the main highway. They turned onto the road nearest the radar site, then onto a narrow winding dirt road angling off, which emerged near the radar installation. About halfway down the road was a small clearing. Lucas slowly drove to it, parked the car, turned off the ignition, and doused the lights hoping that this late at night no one else would be using the lane.

The full moon cast an ethereal glow that muted its cold harsh countenance. Once their eyes adjusted, they saw the woodland glade assumed an almost daylight aura. Shadows pirouetted, dancing in a moonlight ballet driven by invisible breezes softly through the brittle winter trees. Emily, sipping from the bottle, snuggled closer to the nervous, young airman. The music softly wafted like a summer breeze from the car radio as the moonlit-cast shadows danced among the wind-stirred trees girdling the clearing. The couple whispered in soft tones and stole occasional kisses.

"One dead soldier," Lucas muttered, tossing an empty bottle out the window, then, reaching back, felt around in the back seat for another beer. More romantic music, more whispers, sighs, heavy breathing, more sips of now warm beer, more kisses. Lucas pulled Emily closer and felt his heart racing as if it would burst. He could feel her firm young breasts through the thin blouse she was wearing. Blood pounded in his ears as he felt himself grow more and more excited. She moved closer, panting, her lips hungrily seeking his. With his heart threatening to explode, he held her tightly.

They kissed. His tongue sought hers. He felt the ache in his groin and remembered the promise to her earlier as his erection grew. His hand slipped beneath her blouse, deftly undoing the clasp of her bra. With his left hand he took his time unbuttoning each button on her blouse, gently slipping it slowly from her thin shoulders. She shrugged, causing the flimsy bra to fall away, exposing white young breasts.

With a kiss, more like a brotherly buss than that of a passionate lover, he gently pushed her away. Not understanding the sudden change of what she thought was a rebuff, her lip quivered, and a tear, a pearl in the moonlight, trailed down her cheek. Blinking back the tears, she then giggled when she saw what Lucas was really doing. Removing his fatigue jacket and tossing it onto the backseat with the beer. More comfortable now, he once again pulled her close, kissing her full on the lips.

Easing away once again, he unbuckled his belt, undid the buttons on his pants and pushed them along with his shorts down to his ankles. The moon seemed to beam brighter as they made love. Music drifting softly from the radio was never sweeter.

Later, exhausted, they lay entwined, savoring the moment, the first time for each. Neither wanted to move. The moonlight danced on Emily's wan face. At the realization of what had happened, tears of joy slowly welled up and slid down her cheek following the course of sadder earlier ones.

Lucas said nothing but kissed her and allowed her to move from beneath him. At that moment, he knew he had found the girl he would spend the rest of his life with.

She nestled, snuggling against his warm and trembling body, shivering as he encircled her in his arms. Neither spoke. Each retreated into their own thoughts, neither harboring any regrets. Lucas felt her body slowly relaxing in his arms, and then, there was the soft sigh as Emily slept. He looked at her asleep in the stillness of the moonlight, awed at her little-girl beauty.

She was a little girl, yet moments before had been a woman. Did he seduce her or did she seduce him? Or was their lovemaking a matter of fate, destined to happen, an event over which neither had control? Regardless of the reason, Lucas fell in love at that moment, falling asleep as he held her.

Emily shifted, awakening him. She shivered, and Lucas realized they had been sleeping long enough for the cold night air to seep into the car. Gently easing her out of the way, he switched on the ignition and stepped on the starter. As the car coughed to life, cool air from the heater blew over Em's naked body. She stirred and, eyes opening, smiled in the light of the dashboard and gazed lovingly at Lucas.

"I love you, Lucas Mackley," she murmured softly. Doubts disappeared in that smile and those words. She brushed a kiss on his cheek and began to dress.

CHAPTER 30

Shaw AFB, South Carolina, 707th AC&W Sq
Saturday, 21 November 1953
1320 hours

Sergeant George Mickelson looked up frowning as Major C. W. Cummins, followed by two burly Air Policemen clad in perfectly tailored Class A blue uniforms, swaggered arrogantly into the orderly room outer office. The APs removed their white helmet liners in unison and placed them under their left arms leaving their right hands free as they stepped to the side standing at ease, their alert eyes straight ahead. Major Cummins strutted importantly to the sergeant's desk as Mickelson got up, standing at attention.

What the hell is this? "May I help you, sir?" Mickelson asked, holding his voice neutral.

"Sergeant," the officer demanded, trying to intimidate, "please tell Colonel Van Vleet that Major C. W. Cummins of the Judge Advocate Office wishes to see him immediately on an extremely urgent matter."

Yeah, thought Mickelson, *that's what they all say, prancing in here so high and mighty. Guess somebody parked in the general's space again.* The noncom responded, refusing to change expression. "Yes, sir. I'll see if he can see you." With anger flushing his already ruddy face, Cummins wheeled away from Mickelson's desk and, followed by the APs, opened the colonel's door without knocking. Starting to protest, Mickelson followed them into the colonel's office, unsure of what to do. "Sergeant, please wait outside," Cummins ordered. Mickelson looked at Van Vleet for guidance and, at the colonel's nod, left the room while one of the APs closed the office door.

Mickelson, unhappy at the major's gaffe, returned to his desk allowing the trace of a smile to touch his face. "Now, there's one half-witted officer if he thinks he can barge into the colonel's office like that. He's just about to get reamed out, but good," he muttered half aloud. Seated at his desk, the smile spread across Mickelson's face as he reached over and flipped the intercom on. Leaning back and plopping his feet on the desk with clasped hands behind his head, he waited for the fireworks to start.

The nameplate on Van Vleet's desk read, Lieutenant Colonel Harold G. Van Vleet, Commanding, 707th AC&W Sq. The American flag and squadron banner stood proudly displayed to the right of the colonel's desk. The office was Spartan, a reflection of the colonel's austere personality. Other than the colonel's desk and unpadded swivel chair, two Government Issue straight back chairs completed the furnishings. Prominently displayed on the wall behind Van Vleet's desk was a portrait of President Dwight D. Eisenhower. The only other nonmilitary concession was a small framed photo of the colonel's wife and two children.

"Colonel, I am Major C. W. Cummins on special orders from the Judge Advocate General's office," Cummins stated, trying to get inside the colonel's head. "We have a serious matter to discuss concerning one or more men in your squadron. In fact, I might add, it is a matter of the utmost importance, or else I would not have presumed to burst into your office unannounced."

Van Vleet stood up, deliberately letting Cummins wait while he studied the younger officer, letting him squirm. The two APs remained at attention staring stone-faced at Truman's portrait. *Let the over-bearing jerk sweat,* thought Van Vleet, turning deliberately away, determined that the major's arrogance wouldn't be ignored. Suddenly wheeling around, Van Vleet pinned him with cold eyes and cut the major short, saying abruptly, "Major, I don't care what your orders are or, for that matter, where you came from or who the hell issued your orders or what the hell ever it was you presumed. You will observe military courtesy, or I will personally put you under arrest after I bodily throw your pompous carcass out of this office. Now, get the hell out of here, leave those goons outside, and enter this office properly and report to me in the correct military manner. Do you read me, Major?"

"Y-yes, sir!" Cummins, cowed by Van Vleet's outburst, meekly replied. Then, he and his men retreated to the outer office, closing the door quietly behind them with humility. Once in the outer office, his voice betraying embarrassment, Cummins instructed the two APs to wait in the jeep. Cummins approached the CO's door once again and rapped lightly. Staff Sergeant Mickelson, scarcely able to hide his pleasure as he watched the officer wait patiently for the old man's permission to enter, smothered his glee by pretending to search through a stack of folders.

"Come!" roared Van Vleet, still quite visibly agitated by the junior officer's breach of military etiquette.

Cummins opened the door so that it was slightly ajar, tentatively peered past it, and then marched stiffly to face the colonel's desk where he remained standing ram-rod straight at attention, his right hand in proper position above the right brow in the correct military salute. His left hand hung along the outside seam of his trousers with the thumb hugging the seam. His eyes focused on a spot just above the colonel's head. Van Vleet allowed Cummins to remain at attention while he ostensibly finished glancing over some papers. Carefully, he then laid the papers face down on his desk, a deliberate move to prevent Cummins from seeing their contents. Straightening them into a neat stack, he then allowed his eyes to focus on the major, beginning at Cummin's belt buckle and continuing upward until he had pinned the man like a bug in a museum display case with his icy stare.

Picking up a pencil with his left hand, Van Vleet casually flipped a return salute with the right hand, asking snappishly, "Now, Major, what may I do for you?"

"Sir, as I tried to explain before…"

Again Van Vleet cut him off, growling,. "Major, I don't give a good crap about before. I asked you a question. Now get to what you want, then get your insolent ass out of my office." Unconsciously, the colonel began tapping the pencil eraser on the desk while glaring angrily at Cummins.

Out of his league, and well aware of it, Cummins stood straighter, stammering by rote, "Yes! Sir! Two years ago a Staff Sergeant Wilbert B. Webber from the 3384th Radar Training Squadron at Keesler AFB was murdered. Webber was not exactly popular as duty sergeant for the squadron and had caused a large number of airmen to receive squadron punishment. In fact, Webber himself had been on the verge of being court-martialed at least once on a charge of brutality but, due to some technicality, managed to escape punishment. He was brutally beaten to death and, even though our leads have been thin, it seems that the killer may be one of your men."

Van Vleet's eyebrows lifted slightly, the only indication of interest.

Cummins, on seeing the almost imperceptible movement pressed on. "In fact, we have some evidence that there may have been either one, or as many as three, airmen involved and all of whom have been in your command for most of the time since."

Van Vleet asked, "And, Major, just how can you be so sure? There's bound to be thousands of men on that base at any one time, and any one of them could have killed that sergeant."

Cummins, sensing the change in the colonel's attitude, proceeded carefully, "Well, we can't be entirely sure, but on the night the sergeant died, three of your people—the ones we're interested in—signed out at about the time the body was discovered. Actually, that was about an hour before." Then consulting a notebook, correcting himself, he continued, "As a matter of fact, the squadron XO was notified at 0052 hours, about half an hour after the men under suspicion had signed out. We didn't connect the killing with the three right away, but after a number of interviews with men from the squadron, we determined that all three had had words with Webber at one time or another and had received squadron punishment at least once each because of him. One of the men, the one named Lucas Mackley, was reported to have waited at the top of the barracks fire escape one night and beat the hell out of Webber for some reason or the other. Of course, Mackley denied involvement, and no one could prove otherwise."

"To be candid, Major, I can't say as I blame Mackley if what you say about the sergeant is true. I'd probably have kicked his tail, too. But hell, man, just because men have arguments or one kicks the crap out of the other doesn't mean they're killers," the senior officer reminded Cummins.

"That's right, sir, but a master sergeant named Iwo, the squadron top sergeant, thinks he remembers that one of the three was unusually quiet the night they left Keesler, like something was weighing heavy on his mind. Only thing is he couldn't recall which one it was. He did remember, however, that the three had several hours before being allowed to sign out, partly at the duty sergeant's insistence, and also that they apparently had spent a good bit of that time at the base airman's club. That indicates that they had time to have done the killing."

"So what you're saying is you suspect one of my men of a serious crime, but in all reality, you don't have anything of substance for evidence? All you can say is that one man wasn't quite himself. He may've had any number of reasons for his behavior. He may've been feeling the effects of his drinking while he and the other two were waiting to leave. It is also possible he had a girlfriend he didn't want to leave. Who knows? So, Major, have you stopped to think just how flimsy that is? Now, what are you proposing I do?"

Cummins shrugged. "Well, sir, with your permission I'd like to plant a man in those mens' team and see what floats to the top. I'll admit I don't have much to go on other than a gut feeling, but that is all I can think of to do," Cummins said, almost pleading.

"It's been two years, so a few more days aren't going to hurt, I guess." Van Vleet formed a steeple with his fingers, staring off above the major's head, considering Cummin's request, then said, "Tell you what, Major, I'll talk with your boss and see if we can't work something out."

En route to Myrtle Beach AFB, South Carolina
Monday, 23 November 1953
1330 hours

Airman Third Class Issac Lieberman, riding back to Myrtle Beach with JJ and Charlie as a radar operator replacement for Airman Robert Smith, tried to engage them in conversation, but neither seemed interested. Charlie was driving, and JJ was content to lean back in the passenger seat and doze. Smith had been asking for a transfer for some time, and that had given Van Vleet the opportunity to replace him with Lieberman. He actually was First Lieutenant John W. Hendrix, working directly for Major Cummins and at that point, not even Captain Cook was aware of Hendrix's true identity and mission. The lieutenant had been given a crash course on how to read a radarscope, plot courses, and radio target information to the center at Shaw. Lieberman was sure that should the need occur, he could pick up additional help by observation and discreet questions.

The Beach House Bar
Myrtle Beach, South Carolina
Tuesday, 24 November 1953
1930 hours

"You hear the latest?" Charlie shot the question at Lucas who was sitting at a crude table in a far corner of the bar sucking up his draft.

Lucas swallowed lukewarm beer with a grimace and responded sullenly, "Naw, and I ain't no mind reader neither."

"I'll tell you anyway, good buddy, just so you won't have to go through life in total ignorance."

"I ain't begging. So speak up or drink up. I don't care which," Lucas answered caustically, irritated at Charlie's constant badgering. After over three years, he knew that Charlie would eventually get around to telling him anyway.

"Well, if you insist. You recall that no good horse's ass, Webber, back at Keesler? Well, he got hisself killed," Charlie said, dropping the news on Lucas.

"So?" Lucas didn't know if Kesterman really wanted to know if he knew anything about what happened to Webber, or if he was just commenting about Webber's death. In all reality, Lucas could care less about what happened to the late NCO. Since leaving Keesler, Lucas had given no thought to him one way or the other.

"Well, the kicker in the deck, for your information, good buddy, is that he cashed in the night we shipped out from down there. Seems like someone took a baseball bat and did a little batting practice with his head," Charlie snickered smugly.

"Charlie, you are a sadistic bastard, ain't you?" responded Lucas, shaking his head.

Something in his tone caught Mackley's attention as Charlie responded scathingly, "No good chickenshit son of a bitch got exactly what he deserved if you ask me."

Lucas said, eying Charlie closely, "So he got his come-uppance. Now who told you about this?"

Charlie replied, more calmly, "I was shooting the breeze with Mickelson back at Shaw yesterday, and he told me that some officer, an AP major named Cummins, busted into Van Vleet's office and the colonel kicked his butt out. After he let him back in, they discussed the situation. Mickelson said he wouldn't have thought too much about it except Van Vleet ate Cummins a new one for not waiting to be invited in. Naturally, Mickelson did a little eavesdropping. Said our names got mentioned."

A chill ran up Lucas's spine, causing him to shiver. "You sure it was us? What did they say about us?" he asked, voice sounding hollow in the barroom, even over the raucous din of the jukebox.

This was what Kesterman had been waiting for. "Bet your sweet ass it was us!" Charlie replied seriously, knowing he had gotten under Lucas's skin. "Two remembered us signing out that night and told them that one of us sure acted a bit agitated. Said even though we was kidding around a little, there was one of us acting not quite right. Said he 'specially noticed because men shipping out usually are in high spirits. Said one of us, though, was jist not behaving like a man leaving Keesler should act. Only thing was he couldn't recall which of us it was."

Lucas cut him off, trying to think, "Hell, Charlie, Phelps was nervous as a cat passing peach pits just before we left. I recall he didn't even show at the beer garden until almost time to check out." He then remembered he had whipped Webber out on the fire escape that night. *God!* he thought, *surely they don't think I killed him.* Fear like deadly venom coursing through the veins of a snake-bitten rodent surged through his body despite any efforts to remain calm.

At the time that it had happened, Lucas had pulled four consecutive days of KP duty. He had arrived at the barracks at about 1900 hours that night, finished showering, tossed his filthy fatigues aside, intending to wash them later, and laid down to rest for a moment. The darkened solitude of the bay, disturbed only by the snoring of JJ and the occasional creaking of cot springs as someone turned, familiar sounds, flooded over the barracks, soothing Lucas's exhausted body. A scraping noise out on the fire escape at the end of the barracks bay drew his attention, and dragging himself up, Lucas went over to see what was happening. Webber, staggering drunk, was fumbling at the door, apparently confused as to where he was.

Recognizing the sergeant and not wanting to get involved, Lucas started to turn but felt the heavy hand grab at his arm. Webber, trying to focus his whiskey-dimmed eyes, pulled himself toward the tired airman with unconcealed hatred on his face. Again, Lucas turned, only to have Webber spin him back around. Raging past the breaking point, Mackley had clubbed the sergeant across the temple with all the force he could muster. The drunken NCO fell against the wooden railing of the fire escape, splitting a three-inch gash in the back of his pig-like head. Massaging his hand, Lucas spat contemptuously at the unconscious Webber and stomped back to his bunk, seething with anger. Lucas lay there in the stifling bay, fuming, and didn't know that Charlie had witnessed the entire episode and made no effort to help his friend.

Charlie interrupted his thoughts, saying defensively, "You're right, Lucas, but as I remember, you was gone for a while too. As a matter of fact, I guess I was, too."

Mackley replied sharply, "You know goddamned well that I was with you damned near all the time that night, Kesterman. Looks to me like you may be trying to pin this on me saying things like that. You know better than that. Maybe we better get together with JJ and talk about this."

"Well, I'll tell you for certain, Lucas, I didn't do it, so I don't see what good talking would do. Way you're acting sure makes me wonder about you," he responded sharply.

Angry, Lucas shouted, "Why you sorry son of a bitch, you know damned well I was with you the whole time before we shipped out."

"All of the time?" Charlie reminded him again.

Lucas opened his mouth to respond but then clamped his lips closed, knowing arguing was futile. He had to admit, at least to himself, that he had indeed been gone for about an hour, but Charlie had also supposedly gone to make telephone calls to a couple of his girl friends. JJ was the unanswered question. Phelps's actions and demeanor that night stirred Lucas's imagination, even though he knew he could very well be accusing the man unjustly. *Oh, no! That sorry Kesterman knew before now that Webber was dead. He said something about him a couple of weeks or so ago when we was talkin' about them kids being killed. How did he know about Webber then?*

Myrtle Beach AFB, South Carolina, Radar Team 1 Quarters
Tuesday, 24 November 1953
2120 hours

The hot shower did little to alleviate the tautness in Lucas's body and mind. A shadow he could not shake had filled his entire being since Charlie had told him about Webber. Now it was clear Charlie had known about the killing at least two weeks or more before, and had said nothing. And, even more disturbing, Lucas had a bad feeling that Charlie was attempting to shift blame for Webber's death onto him. All afternoon he had searched his mind to see if he could remember exactly what had happened that evening in Biloxi two years ago. He knew he had done nothing wrong. What about Charlie and JJ? Especially JJ. Phelps had joined them at the beer garden only a short time before signing out that evening. And then, also, hadn't Charlie been gone a part of the time while they were waiting to sign out? Wrestle with it as he may, he could not get a grip on exactly when or how long Kesterman had been out of sight.

He recalled Charlie, saying something about telephoning some girl from a place west of Biloxi. *What was her name? Let's see. Mona something or the other. Yeah! That was it.* Mona Emerson. Hell, Kesterman didn't know her that well, but he claimed to be in love with every girl he ever met. Now, didn't he get a Dear John letter from her a little while ago?

Oh horse crap! He had gone back to the barracks to see if he could collect twenty dollars that Sam Nevels had borrowed. It hit him then. *I don't think I was even able to find Sam. If it comes down to it, I can't prove I was there all the time.*

Of course, he continued rationalizing, trying to reconstruct what happened that night. *JJ was out of pocket longer than either Charlie or me. And holy crap! I remember now how strange he acted. He's gotta be the one old Iwo was talking about! That's it! They're checking JJ out! Charlie and me are in the clear! But then, why is Charlie still trying to hang it on me? Or is he? Or is my imagination working overtime? On the other hand, maybe he's running scared like me.*

When Lucas left his quarters and entered the larger bay of the old guardhouse barracks, several men were sitting around talking about the murder. Even the usual card games had slowed since the new radar operator Lieberman transferred from Shaw. As Lucas continued on toward the door, he heard Lieberman speaking about what had happened in 1951 in Biloxi like he had been there.

"You know I'm the new man in this here outfit, so I don't know much about what's been going on. What I'd like to know is what you guys think about this whole mess. Now, don't get me wrong, I'm not prying. Just interested is all." Hendrix had deliberately cultivated Sal and Willie. Both men, he thought, would likely have had several opportunities to talk with members of the team or overhear interesting information. So far, however, he had drawn a blank. Either no one knew, or no one was telling what he knew or what he might suspect. Hendrix was finding that when the topic was mentioned, especially around him, the subject was quickly changed.

"I've known Lucas, JJ, and Charlie since I been at Shaw," Sal answered. "And I ain't never heard them say anything about no guy named Webber. Don't mean they don't know him. Means they ain't said anything to me."

"What about you other guys?" Hendrix continued, leading them. "Have any of you heard any of them saying anything at all about knowing Webber? Like, maybe what he was like? Ya know, stuff like that?"

Spinning abruptly around at the door, Lucas stomped back toward Hendrix, his eyes flashing. Jabbing a finger into Hendrix's face, he hissed angrily, "You feel like nosing into my life, you worthless crud, then ask me. You best just bug-off about that Webber crap. I don't like you one damn bit and don't..."

"I didn't mean..." Hendrix tried to interrupt, his face reddening and contracting with anger as he started to stand.

Lucas didn't let him finish but instead shoved him roughly back into his chair, shaking with rage. "Like I said, Lieberman, I don't like you, and with the mood I'm in, I'd as soon as not kick the crap out of you right here and now. So drop it." Daring him to respond, Lucas stared with disgust for a long moment then turned away and, without looking back, stalked through the open door.

"Holy crap! What brought that on?" asked Hendrix, feigning surprise. "Why, fellows, I didn't mean to get him so upset. I was just talking."

Willie, looking straight at Hendrix, paused a few seconds before answering. "Tell you whut, Lieberman. Was I Lucas, I'd uh whupped your smart ass all over this here barracks."

Shaw AFB
Major C. W. Cummin's Office
Wednesday, 25 November 1953
0930 hours

"Major, I've looked around, asked around, and listened to every one of those no good punks, and so far, all I've drawn is a blank," Hendrix said. "I get the impression that people clam up when I come near any of them. Makes me suspicious that they may know why I'm there. Anyway, I haven't found anything solid enough yet to make a case."

Cummins sat at his desk going through a never-ending shuffle of worthless paperwork and thought, *Knowing the type of punk you are, why am I not surprised that you were shunned?* "You're telling me that you don't know whether or not we're on the right track, Lieutenant?"

"Yessir, that's right. Like I said, Major, all I have is a gut feeling that our man is there, but that's all. Deep down I know he's one of those radar mechanics, but I can't prove it."

Shifting to a more comfortable position in the swivel chair, Cummins propped an elbow on the desk and, letting a hint of displeasure show, asked, "In that case, what would you suggest we try now in order to smoke him out?"

Without hesitation, Hendrix grinned confidently and said, "Let's ask Van Vleet to call each of them in for one-on-one questioning. We put a little pressure on—like suggesting a long stay at Leavenworth—then maybe somebody will slip up. Put some fear into them. Facing that colonel would even get the Pope to confess to the killing."

Cummins considered what Hendrix had proposed and, unable to think of a better alternative, reluctantly said, "Alright, Lieutenant, I'll go talk with him and see if he's willing to do it. He'll have a fit, but we have little choice." *I have to believe Hendrix is way off base,* he reflected. *Van Vleet looks after his men, and he's not about to throw one of them to the dogs. I guess we have to try something.*

Deep in thought, Cummins failed to see the sly look on Hendrix's face as the lieutenant left. *Get that smart-mouthed Mackley before that old bastard Van Vleet, and we'll see how well he holds up. Just wish I could be there. Mackley, your ass has had it.*

Chuckling aloud, he climbed into the jeep and started the long drive back to Myrtle Beach.

CHAPTER 31

"Sir, Staff Sergeant Mackley, Lucas A. AF 18283381 reporting as ordered." Lucas held his salute until Colonel Van Vlcct acknowledged. Snapping his hand down, Lucas remained standing at rigid attention.

"At ease, Sergeant Mackley. Do you know why you are here?" the colonel asked, his piercing eyes reading Lucas's mind.

Lucas replied, "No, sir." Instantly regretting the lie, he quickly added, "I have no idea, sir. Captain Cook told me to report immediately to you, and that's what I did." He could feel the sweat begin to trickle down his back along the channel formed by the muscles alongside his spine. He could not remember ever being so scared. All week long, since he and Charlie had talked, he had worried about this very moment. Being the ranking man of the trio of JJ, Charlie, and himself, he had expected to be the first to be questioned, and now, here he stood, wishing the ordeal would end. Nerves on edge, Mackley's entire body tensed as fear slipped in despite his efforts to remain calm. And the unknown of being first only added to his plight.

Was the colonel deliberately making him sweat, hoping that he would get flustered and say something he shouldn't say? Lucas felt a tingling, like needles stabbing randomly into his spine, along his hairline, at the nape of his neck. *Why doesn't that old coot say something? He knows I'm lying. I should have told the truth that I do know why I'm here.*

Van Vleet got up and, with his hands clasped behind his back, walked deliberately over to the only window in the room to stand gazing out across the quadrangle where several men were halfheartedly policing the grounds. A young airman first class in charge of the detail, bracing one of the men, could be heard yelling at the man as his arms flailed animatedly. Shrugging, the man sauntered away, flipping the airman in charge a derogatory gesture and deliberately kicking a cigarette butt to the side. Smiling resignedly, the colonel shook his head, wondering how to proceed with Mackley's interrogation.

Fighting panic, Lucas jumped involuntarily as the colonel abruptly turned and said, "All right, Sergeant, let's get this over with." He picked up the telephone, waited a moment, then spoke into it. "Sergeant Mickelson, bring your notepad and come in, please."

Immediately the door opened, and Mickelson came in and seated himself over to one side of the room without acknowledging Lucas. Van Vleet looked intently at Lucas for several moments as if deciding how to go about the unpleasant task. After a minute or so he sighed and proceeded, saying, "About two years ago, a Staff Sergeant Wilbert B. Webber was murdered at Keesler by a person or persons unknown. Until now, the investigation has been more or less stalemated, but recently, a master sergeant, I believe his name is Iwo, who was top NCO in your old outfit, the 3384th, remembered some things that happened that night and reported what he had recalled."

Unable to contain himself any longer, Lucas interrupted, "Sir, I don't understand what that has to do with me."

"Sergeant, please do not interrupt. I'll do the talking for now," Van

Vleet snapped, frowning. "Now, do you remember Sergeant Iwo?"

"Yes sir. He was top sergeant in my squadron. Well respected, I might add."

"Did you know Sergeant Webber?"

"Yessir. Everyone who's ever been in that outfit during the past five or six years knew that son of a, uh, Sergeant Webber. Most of them have had a run-in or two with him." Mackley corrected himself, gesturing uneasily with his hand. "I mean, before he was killed. Far as I know, though, there never was nothing serious. He was quick to get riled up, usually at things that didn't amount to much."

Overlooking Mackley's use of a disrespectful term in reference to Webber, Van Vleet probed further with a challenging tone in his voice, "Like what, Sergeant?"

"Well, Colonel, things like being slow falling out for school formation or having your bunk area not exactly up to his standards, all sorts of things. Rinky-dink stuff mostly, sir. Even the brown-nosers hated him because he was one pissed-off-at-the-world individual."

"Sergeant, did you know about his murder before today?" Van Vleet asked pointedly, catching Lucas off guard.

Mackley hesitated, trying to think before answering. Inhaling deeply, he lied, regretting it no sooner than the words passed his lips, "No, sir, I didn't know, sir."

Appearing to ignore Lucas's answer, Van Vleet continued describing the night of the murder. "The killing occurred late on the night of 3 March 1951, or maybe a little after midnight, the night you and several other members of your class shipped out." He paused, gauging Lucas's reaction, studying the younger man's eyes.

The pause was endless. *Oh no, that old fart's readin' my mind!*

"Now, Sergeant, think carefully before you answer." Van Vleet's voice broke like thunder into Lucas's mind. "Did you have anything to do with what happened?"

Lucas felt his heart racing and sucked in an involuntary breath. Before he could reply, the colonel looked directly into his eyes and said, "Tell me as best you can exactly what you remember about that night." Turning to Mickelson, he curtly instructed, "Be sure to get all of this down, Sergeant Mickelson."

Lucas swallowed the bile building up and replied, "Yes, sir." In a hesitant, barely audible voice, he related his recollection of the events that night, feeling that he was getting in over his head. It was crazy, but that old saying kept coming to him: When you find yourself in a hole, quit digging. The irony was he couldn't stop digging. "Well, sir, Charlie Kesterman, JJ Phelps, and me was in the same barracks and class all through radar school. When we graduated, all three of us got assigned to Pope, and since we had a delay en route in the same general area of Arkansas and Missouri, and Charlie was the only one with a car, we decided to drive to Pope together when our leaves was over." Lucas paused to catch his breath. "Me and Charlie loaded JJ's and our stuff in Charlie's car that night. We had about four or five hours to kill before we could sign out," he paused again before proceeding, "but while we were waiting, me and him, that is Charlie, went over to the Airman Club beer garden to drink beer. JJ had said he'd meet us there later."

"Did Airman Phelps, meet you later?" the colonel asked, his right eyebrow slightly raised, the only change of expression.

"Yessir, but I don't remember how long after we got to the club before he showed."

"Did either you or Sergeant Kesterman leave the other alone after the two of you arrived at the club, or were you in each other's company all the time that night?"

"No, sir, I don't think so. Charlie or JJ was there most of the time, and one or the other of them should have seen me all the time," stated Lucas emphatically.

"Now, Sergeant Mackley," Van Vleet continued, "think carefully. Try to remember. This happened over two years ago, and remember also, memory can be quite tricky," Van Vleet prompted, studying Mackley's reaction.

Lucas was thoroughly frightened. By now he could feel himself trembling all over. He was praying that the colonel didn't notice. Was he really with either Charlie or JJ during that time or was there a time when he left? He had gone back to see Nevels! But for how long, and did anyone see him?

"Now, Sergeant," Van Vleet reminded him, "as I understand it, you were in the presence of either Kesterman or Phelps at all times that night. Right?"

"Yessir, that's the way it was. But, sir, I can't remember exactly back two years ago."

"What about Kesterman then? Did he ever leave by himself during the time you were at the club?" Van Vleet asked, raising that questioning right eyebrow again, unnerving Lucas.

Hesitating longer than he intended, Lucas tried to force his muddled mind to remember what he had already told Colonel Van Vleet, but his mind refused to function. After what seemed forever he decided, *I'm not gonna cover for Kesterman or Phelps or anybody. I got a bad feeling that I'm in deep already, and I ain't getting in any deeper.* Unable to remember, he finally decided to tell the truth. "Yessir, I think he did leave once for about forty-five minutes or so to make a phone call to some girl. Charlie is a womanizer, that's a known fact, uh, sir."

Lucas watched the officer's face and eyes. No reaction. Nothing. No change of expression at all. *Stony-faced old bastard.*

"Do you know the girl's name, Sergeant?"

Lucas jumped as if he had been poked in the ribs. "Yessir, I think her name is, uh was Mona Emerson," Lucas stammered.

"Sergeant, before I dismiss you, I must remind you that due to the seriousness of this matter that you are to talk to no one about what transpired between us today. Especially, you are not to discuss this with Phelps or Kesterman. Do you understand?"

"Yessir, Colonel," Lucas responded, meekly.

Outside a few minutes later, a thoroughly shaken Mackley sat in the jeep, trying to collect his thoughts. Finally, the trembling in his legs subsided enough for him to start the vehicle and begin the long trip back to Myrtle Beach.

CHAPTER 32

Myrtle Beach AFB, South Carolina, Team I Quarters
Sunday, 20 December 1953
1923 hours

"One of us is in a heap of trouble!" Lucas said with his hands jammed into his back pockets and wrinkled concern written all over his darkened face. "Colonel Van Vleet ordered me not to talk about Webber's killing, and I guess he told each of you the same thing, but there're some things we need to get straight. I danged well didn't kill Webber. Didn't like the no good bastard no more than either of you, but I didn't touch him. Well, at least not that time. He got his sorry ass beaten to death, but I didn't do it."

"Whatta you mean—not that time?" asked Charlie accusingly.

Lucas answered acidly, "Just exactly that. Him and me had a few words once or twice, but that was all. Kicked his ass, but I ain't killed no one."

Leaping to his feet, Charlie stabbed a defensive finger at Lucas and shouted, "Then you must still think I'm the one who killed him, don't you?"

"I'll say it agin. That ain't what I meant, Charlie. All I said was, I ain't done nothing like kill a man."

Kesterman leaned back on the edge of his bunk, shouting angrily at Lucas, "Seems to me you done got either me or JJ guilty and already in the hot seat, you low life son of a bitch!"

Several men playing cards across the room looked up and one of them, annoyed, yelled, "Shut the hell up, Kesterman. Can't you see we're in a serious poker game?" Willie stepped from his room, glancing at Charlie, and shook his head, then went back inside and slammed the door behind him, grinning.

"Naw, that ain't what I said at all! And you know it. I said I ain't done anything, so if it was one of us, which I ain't saying it was, then it's got to be one or the other of you," Lucas repeated, his anger rising.

Until now, JJ had remained quietly listening to the exchange, but now, looking from one to the other of the two men, he growled, "Well, I sure as hell ain't guilty either, so don't go accusing me. If either of you are, let's step outside right now and settle this man to man."

Jumping quickly to his feet again, Charlie shouted vehemently, "If you're feeling froggy, c'mon and start hopping. We can get this settled between us right now. I've about had enough of both of you."

Lucas tempered his comments and threw his hands up in disgust. "Well, Van Vleet has had all three of us on the carpet, and I guess he asked you the same things as me. I got the idea when I was questioned that they knew a whole lot more than they was letting on. I'll admit I was scared and would have told him about anything he asked. Only thing is I didn't know anything to tell. So, it seems to me like our problem now is, what do we do? Do we keep our mouths shut and see what happens? Or just what do we do?" With his voice cracking with emotion and worry, Lucas finished, saying, "I damned well don't want to spend the rest of my life in Leavenworth or, worse yet, end up in the electric chair."

"Well, I'm for keeping quiet," said Kesterman, "and waiting to see what happens. Let 'em try to get something on us if they can. Ain't any need to give them anything they don't already know."

"Yeah, I feel like Charlie, I guess," JJ added, worry etching his face. "They had anything on one of us, or even thought they had anything, that sorry jerk would be in the stockade by now." He continued, half believing what he was saying. "There's something wrong here, though, that bothers me. I keep worrying about this new guy Lieberman asking so many questions. Somehow, that jist ain't quite right. Wouldn't be a bit surprised if he turns out to be a mole."

But before he could finish, Charlie interrupted, "What's that you're saying about Lieberman? What's he got to do with all this? You really think he's got something to do with all this crap?"

"Like I was about to say, he's cornered me a couple times, always trying to pump me on what Van Vleet asked me and what I knew about Biloxi."

"And, what did you tell him, dumbass?" asked Charlie, sneering. "I guess you spilled your goddamn guts to him."

JJ breathed in deeply and let his breath out slowly as he considered his response. "I'll let that pass, Charlie," he finally said, "and blame what you said on the fact that you are as worried as Lucas and me. No, I didn't tell him anything he didn't already know."

"Damn right. He's been nosing around asking people questions about me, too. Tried to pump me once or twice, but I ain't told him a damn thing either," echoed Lucas. "So? What about it, Charlie, you going along with me and JJ and keep your flapping mouth shut?"

"Yeah, I guess so. What other choice I got?" replied Charlie, shrugging.

"And there's one more thing, Kesterman. This has been bothering me for several days, so tell us straight," said Lucas. He looked hard at Kesterman and asked pointblank, "How did you say you found out about Webber?"

Kesterman swallowed hard, then hesitated before answering, "Like I told you, I got it from Mickelson."

Lying jerk, thought Lucas, looking disdainfully at his buddy. Big trouble was brewing, but there was no way to put the toothpaste back in the tube.

CHAPTER 33

U.S. Veterans Administration Hospital
Gulfport, Mississippi
The Present

"Sergeant Mackley, you called me 'Em' the other day. I don't want to pry, but I've heard you say her name several times and wondered who she is. The way you said her name, I gathered that she is someone special." Marty had seen him sitting on the bench under the old tree, apparently in deep thought, unaware of the rest of the world around him. Age lines furrowed his brow, and despair seemed to hover like death's angel over the old man. She had hesitated at interrupting him but, seeing his sadness, felt a pang in her heart and hurried over to visit with him.

Steeling herself, she asked again, hoping she had not stepped out of bounds. "You have talked a little about what you did back when you were in the Air Force, especially about Myrtle Beach. I would really like to know about Em, so would you tell me more about her?"

Chief Master Sergeant Lucas Mackley stared silently at Marty, making her uncomfortable, frowning at being disturbed. The hint of a smile touched his thin lips on recognizing the vivacious young nurse. Finally, he realized that she had asked a question.

Seeing his confusion, Marty repeated the question.

His watery eyes turned soft at the mention of Em and, just as quickly, turned granite hard at the intrusion into his private world.

Seeing that she had upset the old man, Marty stammered apologetically, "Oh, Sergeant Mackley, I'm so sorry. It's…it's just…"

Then, taking her slender hand in his wrinkled, trembling one, Lucas smiled weakly and said, "That's all right, Marty. I know you meant no harm."

She waited for him to continue, but when he said nothing else, Marty inhaled deeply, let the breath out slowly, and replied, "But you called me Em the first time we met. Why? Do I remind you of her?"

The painful look he gave her caused Marty to pause and momentarily wonder if she should push the old man any further. Still, on other occasions, she had caught him staring pensively at her, staring as if he had known her before, maybe somewhere in another life. Reason told her that this was not possible. They had never met until that afternoon right here under this weathered old tree. Yet, he had seemed to want to tell her something but, when pressed, Lucas always went silent. She was beginning to remove her hand from his, but in a sudden move he pulled her down on the bench beside him, looking intently into her deep blue eyes.

In a voice that sounded suddenly vibrant, Lucas said evenly, "Miss Marty, I've partitioned that part of my life with Em away for all these years. When you came walking toward me that afternoon, I thought I was dreaming. I'm an old man now, and as with old men, sleep doesn't come easy. Many lonely nights since those days I've lain awake, finding myself back in Myrtle Beach, South Carolina, as a wild young airman. It was your image that dragged that elusive dream of foolish youth back to trouble me all over again. I don't fault you, uh, Marty, for wanting to know my story, and I guess maybe I owe it to you to tell you about that time in my life."

Marty sat silent, intrigued by the old man, knowing that he was going to reveal about what must have been a painful time. Unmindful of her other duties, she listened patiently, enthralled but disturbed as his poignant story unfolded.

"I've been thinking about those days often now and about my two best buddies, boys like me, Charlie Kesterman and JJ Phelps. We had gone through radar mechanics school right down the road there at the base," he said, pointing toward Keesler. "After we shipped out to a new assignment in the Carolinas, some terrible things happened that I've tried to repress but have had to live with all these long years."

Marty placed her free hand on his frail shoulder, feeling guilty at dragging up his past, and started to get up and leave. Pulling her gently back down, Lucas quietly chastised her, saying, "Em, uh, Marty, you wanted to know, so please indulge the whims of this old man. Now, let me take you back to Myrtle Beach in 1953."

In his rambling, sometimes animated, way he described to her the events that led up to when he met Emily Johnson. Sitting rapt beside Lucas, Marty pictured herself back in his earlier world as he talked.

Lucas related to Marty how he and Emily Johnson had met at Myrtle Beach and fell in love. Leaving nothing out, he detailed the events leading up to the deaths in Mississippi and South Carolina and how those dreadful events not only led him to gain the love of Em but, also, how those same moments destroyed his life. "Now that you know about the murders, let me describe for you how Em and I, in our naivety, tried to escape a situation from which there was no escape. Let me take you back there."

Myrtle Beach, South Carolina, Team 1 Radar Operation Site
Monday, 28 December 1953
1600 hours

Finishing the daytime shift at 1600 hours, Mackley didn't bother returning to the barracks but, instead, drove to the highway west of the tracking site and headed toward Myrtle Beach. All day his troubled mind could not shed the specter of Webber's killing. The death under other circumstances would have been only of passing interest. There had been confrontations with the late sergeant, but those dealings were in the past and, unpleasant as they were, hadn't mattered until now, because now he could be charged with murder. That possibility seemed more certain than ever, and if he was charged, the good life with Em here at Myrtle Beach would unravel.

The nagging thought of his being dragged into this mess, and more than likely being blamed for Webber's death, tore at his mind without respite. He could remember both Charlie and JJ having been gone a part of the time prior to their checking out and leaving the squadron area. There was no doubt about it: JJ hadn't gone down to the club with Charlie and him. He was also quite positive that Charlie had been away at least once for forty-five minutes, or maybe more, during the evening under the pretense of calling one of his girlfriends. He had known both men for over two years now. They had worked together, drank together, honkey-tonked together, tomcatted around together, and were the best of friends. Colonel Van Vleet had said there were suspicions that one of them may be a killer. That possibility seemed incomprehensible to Lucas, although mulling over what had happened during his time in Biloxi did plant seeds of doubt.

Mistrust had already stuck its face into their friendship, but were they being set up? Was the colonel playing mind games? After all, the question of guilt or innocence seemed to be based on Sergeant Iwo's vague recollection of the night they shipped out and that one of them had acted strange. With the passage of nearly two years, those recollections would have dimmed for something as inconsequential as someone's subtle behavior. The whole deal may be Colonel Van Vleet getting the monkey off his back, and after a few queries the entire thing would go away. To top it all off, there was Charlie's dishonesty about knowing Webber had been killed. This was the wedge that split the log wide open.

He had to talk to Emily. The question that gnawed at him now was how could he tell her that he was under suspicion of something like murder? Would she believe him? Old Lady Johnson would purely have a fit when she heard.

He was almost even with the street where he needed to turn before realizing it. With a quick glance in the rear view mirror, he hit the brakes hard and whipped the steering wheel to the right. "Crap, all I need now is some dumb cop sitting over there waiting for me to take out somebody's yard," he muttered, glancing guiltily around.

Slowing to a moderate twenty miles per hour, Lucas smelled the salty scent of seawater as the Chevy rolled down the side street toward the ocean. When the water with its white breaking surf came into view, he turned left at the next intersection, driving halfway down the second block to 210 Oceanview. The address was misleading since the ocean was still three blocks east with the beach obscured by several rows of houses and apartments closer to the water. The Johnson house was a small cottage set close to the street. A broken concrete walk led to the front porch, accessible by a low set of crumbling reddish brick steps. Climbing jasmine vines hung tenaciously to a crude trellis at the south end of the porch, providing partial privacy. Peeling faded white paint, accelerated by exposure to the ever-present salt air, gave the house a weathered grayish dismal look under the hazy winter sun.

Lucas pulled to the curb, got out, and hurried to the front door, trying to ignore the dilapidated condition of the Johnson house, anxious about what he must tell Emily. She must have been waiting for him because on the second knock she opened the door and stood there smiling and said, "Hey, Lover, you're early." The mischievous twinkle in her dancing eyes told him that she was not at all displeased.

"Yeah," Lucas reached out, giving her a quick hug. "Can we, uh, go somewhere and talk, Em? It's important."

"Sure." She turned, calling her mother, "Momma, I'll be back in a little while. I'm going out with Lucas. Okay?" Emily was not asking Mrs. Johnson's permission; she was only letting her know that she was leaving. Grabbing a sweater, she hurriedly pulled it on and, brushing back her hair with slender fingers, followed him out the door.

They walked to the car where Lucas opened the door, and Emily slid in. Going around to the driver's side, Lucas got behind the wheel and looked over at the young woman, who had now moved over by his side. He started to speak but stopped and instead touched Emily's cheek with the back of his right hand, unable to say anything. Finally, returning his gaze to the dash, he turned the switch on and stepped on the starter.

Back on the blacktop highway, they rode in silence for a while, watching the white line blurring past them, the Chevy's tires humming to the rhythm of the early evening wind. Impatience showing in her voice and tears welling up in her eyes, Emily asked, "Okay, Lucas, what's the matter? You haven't even kissed me, much less said a single word. All we've been doing is driving."

Lucas looked at the girl by his side and hugged her, saying, "Yeah, I know. I've been trying to work up the nerve to tell you what's on my mind."

As he spoke, he turned into one of the numerous sandy, palmetto-lined side roads that ended at the beach, and parked the car. "Come on, Em, let's walk down along the water."

"All right, Lucas, but you're scaring me," she replied, nervously picking at a loose thread on the sleeve of her sweater.

Seeing the confusion on her face, he quickly said, "Honey, I'm really sorry. I didn't realize I was doing that. I didn't mean to. You're my whole life, and I never want to hurt you."

They stopped a few feet short of the water and watched the surf roll in. Facing each other, he put his arms around her slender body, tenderly kissing her. He had known her for only about a month and a half now, but that time had been the happiest time of his life, and now he was afraid it would end.

They stood embracing. She was happy to be with him. He was dreading what he must ultimately reveal. The surf rolling up the beach and the wind rustling through the dry sea oats behind them were the only sounds.

"Lucas," she muttered, her voice breaking as she pushed away, "are you trying to tell me that we're through, that you no longer love me?" Tears glistened in her eyes.

Lucas realized what she was thinking. "Oh, no! Em, I love you more than you'll ever know. So, get that silly notion out of your head right now!" Embracing her, he continued hesitantly, "I've got to tell you. I gotta tell you something that's gonna be hard for you to believe, something that's gonna hurt. I'm in some pretty serious trouble that I don't see how I can git out of."

He then told how he had been called back to Shaw a few days ago and how Colonel Van Vleet had questioned Charlie, JJ, and him about the beating death of Webber, explaining in detail about the late sergeant. He pointed out that each of them had been out of sight of the others for some of the time before they were allowed to sign out on that night in Biloxi. He didn't tell her of his doubts about Charlie and JJ, fearing she wouldn't believe him. Even if he'd had the courage to reveal how he felt about them, the thought of losing his two best buddies kept him mute.

While he related these events, Emily stood statue still, looking into his eyes, hardly blinking and occasionally wiping a stray tear away. Numbed and dumbfounded by his confession to her, she made no response.

"Em, I swear, until the colonel called me in, I didn't even know for sure Webber was dead. I'll admit I hated his guts, but so did most of the men in the squadron. There was reason for me to beat him up, and I did once, but there was no reason for me to kill him."

A quiet Emily reached out, drawing Lucas close and whispering, "I believe you, Lucas, and you know I love you. Now, let's go back to the car where it's warm, and you can let me hold you and try to make things right."

CHAPTER 34

Conway, South Carolina, Horry County Sheriff's Office
Friday, January 8, 1954
1:25 P.M.

During the drive back from Lake City in a cold sleety storm after visiting with Ira Prewit, Tait worried over the murders, unable
to find even the flimsiest thread that might lead to a solution of the
killings. When it appeared some fact might shed some light, it invariably came to a dead end. Getting back to Conway after dinner, he
begged off his wife's offer to fix something to eat and, ignoring the
hurt look she gave him, drove back to the office.

Worrying over what Prewit had said and his own problems with
the murders at Toddville and Myrtle Beach, Tait suddenly reached
for the telephone and dialed a number from memory. He impatiently picked up a pencil and waited, tapping the eraser at the battered desktop and listening as connections clicked down the line.
Moments later, the sound of ringing alerted Tait.

Tait recognized Ira's voice at the other end in Lake City and
said, "Hoped I'd catch you, Ira. This is Earl Lee. Yeah, I know, but
I need to get you to run up in the morning, if you can. Think it's
time you and me and a couple others got together on them matters

we discussed today."

After the call to Prewit, Tait put through a second one to Lieutenant Hiram Rodgers at Shaw AFB, inviting him to attend the meeting. Then, satisfied he had done all that could be done, he leaned back in his chair and propped his booted feet on the desk. With his hands clasped behind his head, he closed weary eyes and tried to picture how to fit the little information available into something that made sense.

Awaking confused, he let his feet fall from the desk. The sun was already up. Its cadmium yellow beams flickered through the barren branches of the small tree just outside the office window. Tiny motes of dust, stirred up as Tait got up and crossed to the window, glittered like miniature snowflakes in the bright sunlight. A police cruiser with the Toddville logo on its doors pulled to the curb, and Chief Jim Weldon got out, hitched up his pants, and walked over to the front entrance.

Seeing Weldon, Tait opened the door before he could knock, saying wearily, "Jim, I ain't had a helluva lot of sleep lately. So if you don't mind, let's amble over to the Bluefish, and I'll buy the coffee. The others ain't due for another half hour or so, anyway."

Two cups of strong black café coffee later, they were back in the department office. Tait looked at the group gathered in the small room, reading the tension of the past few weeks on their faces. Attending were Chief Weldon of Toddville, Sheriff Ira Prewit, Lieutenant Hiram Rodgers of the USAF air police, and Kate Garner, Tait's secretary. Clearing his throat, he said, "I appreciate each of you taking time to help out in this rather difficult situation. I'm about at my wits end on this one. Thought if we got together and compared what we know, maybe we could make some headway."

Lieutenant Hiram Rodgers, assigned by Major Cummins to investigate for the Air Force, started to speak, but Tait held up his hand to stop him. "Let me put what I know on the table first and, I'll give everybody a chance to speak up and agree or shoot me down. Like I said, I need help."

Pausing for a moment, Earl Lee took a deep breath and began, "Among us we got a total of five murders. The lieutenant has to worry about that sergeant that got beat to death down in Mississippi in '51. Ira's got the Moorland woman from over near Lake City; me and Jim have got that pair of teenagers from Toddville. And, finally, I got to worry about what happened to Evelyn Dendy over north of Myrtle Beach. Now, I'm gonna ask each of you for your comments as you see fit."

Again before the others could interrupt, Earl Lee forged on. "I ain't had time to go over all the stuff we already have, but Kate," he indicated his secretary, "pointed out how similar the murders were. Seems all of them was vicious."

"I don't know about your cases," said Rodgers, seeing pictures of the dead airman in his mind, and I've probably told you all of this before, but that sergeant at Keesler was really worked over. His face was a bloody mess, and I believe he had a broken rib or two, and the left collarbone was shattered. Any one of a half dozen of the blows to his head could have killed him, even if he could have survived the other injuries. Probably didn't have a chance after the first lick. In my opinion, whoever did it had to be a maniac."

"That sounds a whole lot like what happened with Sarah Moorland," Prewit said, not waiting to see if Rodgers was finished. "She was beat up real bad, but she had also been slashed about her head and neck, too. The fact that she was cut up seems to me to make her murder different from that sergeant's. Also, he was a older man, and except for the Whitworth boy, them others was women and girls. In Moorland's case, I doubt there was a bone in her face left unbroken. I ain't never seen nothin' like it in all my life."

Rodgers stopped Ira with a raised hand, asking, "What was used to kill her, Sheriff?"

"I can't rightly say, Lieutenant," he responded, scratching his ear. "Condition her face was in, it hadda been some kinda heavy, blunt object like a sash weight from a winder. Jist don't know, though, since we never could find no weapon. She coulda died from the knife wounds or from the beating. Walter Franks, the coroner, was inclined to think she died from being stabbed so many times, but I don't think that he's really sure."

Weldon, looking intent, asked, "Ira, do you have any suspects yet?"

Prewit, shaking his head, replied, "No. We've looked into some leads, but none of them has panned out. I do have some suspicions, but I ain't told anybody except Earl Lee here because the evidence is so weak."

"Ira's right, Jim," interjected Earl Lee. "He's getting worked up over them Air Force boys, but like he admits, he ain't really got no real proof they was involved."

"Well, I still think they's some kinda connection between them and all these murders," insisted Ira indignantly.

After grinning at Ira, Earl Lee turned to Weldon and asked, "Jim, how about telling Prewit and Rodgers what we know about those two young folks over at Toddville and the young woman from Myrtle Beach? Figure we oughta lay everything on the table. Might jog our memories to make sense of the whole mess."

"Okay, Earl Lee." Weldon summarized what he, Tait, and Kate knew about the two kids' deaths. He finished with, "As in the Mississippi and Lake City murders, both victims were mutilated. And as you know, the girl, Jane Marie Wallace, was raped an…and decapitated."

Even though the others had heard about what had happened to the girl, the re-telling of the two slayings and of how Joey's body and Jane Marie's head were found in the shallow well, evoked renewed uneasiness in Weldon's audience. Kate bowed her head and dabbed at her eyes. The hardboiled Sheriff from Horry County wiped at his nose to cover his sadness. Ira pretended to look out the window while Rodgers doodled in his notebook, unwilling to look at the others.

Earl Lee coughed, breaking the silence, and cleared his throat before relating the details of the beating and ultimate murder of Evelyn Ruth Dendy at Myrtle Beach, again emphasizing the brutality of the slaying. With the horror of the deaths on their minds, no one immediately spoke.

Tait looked at Kate to catch her attention and said, "Kate, if you will, get all of what we'll be saying down during the remainder of this meeting and see that everybody gits a copy. Provide whatever details you can. Okay?"

Opening a notebook, she nodded to indicate she was ready.

Tait, again the dedicated lawman, forced his emotions aside and said, "I see one common thread that Kate reminded me of the other day, so I'll pass it on to you. Every one of these killings has been of the most merciless kind I have ever seen or heard of. Usually when someone kills somebody, they do it quick and clean so they can get away before they're seen. In these cases, though, it looks like the bodies was cut up or beat up after they was dead, and doing that would take some time. So, whoever it was acted slow and deliberate. And, if nothing else fits, that alone seems to say one man—one man working alone."

Ira then added, "You're right about that, Earl Lee, but there's a difference between the murders and the victims. Four of them was young people, and three of them was fairly young girls or young women. All of them, I'd say, was from about seventeen to thirty. That soldier from Biloxi was well over thirty-five, which don't seem to fit at all, but I'm convinced there is a connection somewhere."

"Look, Sheriff Tait," Rodgers said, "I don't know many of the details of your cases, but from what has been said this morning, I can see a definite tie-in with the female victims. They were young, well-known and apparently well-liked, and—I think this is significant—they all were a bit flirtatious."

"Well, I'll be damned!" blurted Ira. "Sorry, Kate," he apologized, realizing what he had said. "I think what the lieutenant jist said is right. So, the question now is how do we tie in the Whitworth boy and that soldier?"

Earl Lee sat back the swivel chair, letting Jim field the question. Jim quickly responded, "I suspect that Whitworth happened to be in the wrong place with the wrong girl. I can imagine that the killer was after the girl, and killed the boy to keep him out of the way. So, it appears we may be dealing with a sex crime, and it's beginning to look like the killer knew all those girls. I still can't tie that sergeant's murder into this. This is pure guess work on my part, but it's looking more and more like one of them airmen is responsible."

"Are you saying you suspect one of them boys because they knew the girls?" Tait asked, thinking that Jim had hit on the missing thread.

Weldon quickly replied, "It sure looks that way to me."

"You may have something there, but I can't quite buy in yet. Can you shed some light on that, Lieutenant?" Tait asked, gesturing toward Rodgers.

"I'll have to admit that I can't. There is something that nags me, though, about this whole deal. We have what seems on the surface to be three or four separate incidents but, considering what we know and what you said, Sheriff Tait, about it being the work of one individual, there is still one thing we are leaving out. I have weak evidence, as you are aware, that some of the men at that radar site over at Myrtle Beach may, and I emphasize the may, be involved with Sergeant Webber's death. Now, consider this, and I'll leave it up to you people to decide for yourselves. Those men are within a reasonable distance of where the more recent murders have occurred. In my mind there has to be some sort of relationship. I just can't work it out, but Chief Weldon could be on the right track."

Then, almost challenging Tait to disagree, Prewit said emphatically "Earl Lee, I'm inclined to agree with the lieutenant on that one. We maybe ought to look close at the possibility that our killer is right out there at that base. Matter of fact, I'm leaning toward that Mackley boy bein' the one we want. Them other two ain't in the clear in my mind, though. Kesterman from what I can gather is a hard case. Phelps is low key—a loner—an' that makes me suspicious. Like I've said, I'm leanin' toward Mackley, but even if I think that boy is guilty, I would like to know more about Webber's background. It looks to me like there jist might be more to the case than what appears on the surface." Turning toward Rodgers, he continued. "Lieutenant, could you brief us on the Webber investigation in more detail?"

The lieutenant summarized what he knew about the case, covering the man's brutal nature, drinking excesses, and antisocial behavior. Other than the savage beating the sergeant had sustained, he could add little more toward solution of the crime. He did, however, review how the troops under Webber felt about him and, similarly, how his fellow NCOs in the squadron regarded Webber. Rodgers told of the death of Mattie Lou Simpson, the woman, found dead in Biloxi's Back Bay shortly before Webber's death, pointing out that some suspicion had been cast on the late sergeant. He emphasized that there were questions but that Webber was never charged, even though, in his opinion, there was evidence that might have tied Webber to the woman. He could not say why he was not charged, and as far as he knew, her death was still being considered a suicide. "From what I learned about that case, I am convinced that Webber was quite volatile and I suspect mentally disturbed," Rodgers added.

"I gather that the Simpson woman didn't have signs of mutilation like the female victims here in South Carolina," Tait commented.

"That's right," Rodgers agreed.

"Then, wouldn't that rule out any connection with these killings?" Tait asked.

"I don't think so," replied Weldon. "On the surface it appears that we got not one but two motives. With the girls, I would guess they were killed because they wouldn't have anything to do with the killer. And I'm assuming one killer at this time. We all seem pretty well agreed that the Whitworth kid just happened to be in the way. That leaves Webber, and as I recollect, Lieutenant Rodgers told us all three of them airmen had problems with him. So, it seems to me that one of them boys knocked him off to get even. Them girls was killed for an entirely different reason, but that still don't point to which of them boys did it," Weldon finished, spreading his hands, looking expectantly at the others.

"So, you're saying one of them coulda got old Webber, but maybe a different one killed them others?" Tait inquired, not quite accepting Weldon's argument. "I noticed you left out the woman in Biloxi. Why?"

"Aw, Earl Lee," Weldon responded. "Maybe I'm reading something into the whole mess that just ain't there. As far as the Simpson woman—maybe her death had nothing to do with the others. It's also possible that whoever killed her didn't have time to mess her up like the others."

"What about the rest of you? Anyone wanta respond to Jim?" Tait asked, and waited for someone to speak up.

No one in the group, gone suddenly quiet, seemed willing to stick their neck out. Mulling over what Weldon had said, they remained silent, refusing to meet Tait's gaze. Studying their faces and trying to divine their thoughts, Tait leaned forward, nervously tapping the top of his desk.

Weldon glanced up, suddenly aware of the irritating tapping. Shaking his head, he then turned to Prewit and asked, "What do you have that makes you so sure Mackley is our man, Ira? You hinted that you thought Mackley and his buddies might be involved, but you ain't told us why."

"Got to admit, Jim, it's only a gut feelin'," Ira reluctantly admitted, "but like I told Earl Lee, there's too many coincidences. Some of them boys has been seen around all them murder sites or at least in the general vicinity. That's something that sends up a red flag for me."

"Question is, Ira, how do we smoke him out, and if he is guilty, how do we get him to confess?" asked Tait. "Or for that matter, if one of them other two, or all three, is guilty, how do we prove it?"

Toddville, South Carolina
Monday, January 11, 1954
7:45 A.M.

The telephone was ringing as Jim Weldon unlocked his office door. Walking over to the desk, he picked up the receiver and said, "Jim Weldon."

"I'm real glad the law in Toddville is out early doing its job protecting all them good citizens over that way."

Weldon recognized Tait's gravelly voice as it came across the distance. "Mornin', Earl Lee. I almost hate to ask, but you calling this early, there's no doubt you want to tell me something I probably don't want to hear."

Tait answered, imagining the frown on Weldon's face, "You got that right, Jim. You gonna be around for the next little while? Afraid I may have us some more bad news."

"Well, I ain't had my morning coffee yet, so why don't you meet me at the Bluefish Café? I can be there in a few minutes."

"Like I said, Jim, I hesitated to call, but we need to discuss something important. It's something I don't feel comfortable talking about over the phone, though."

Exactly nineteen minutes later, the Horry County Sheriff's Office police cruiser pulled up in front of the Bluefish next to Weldon's cruiser, and Earl Lee got out. Moseying to the door, he adjusted his holster belt to a more comfortable position, pulled the door open, and entered the small dingy eatery. The odor of stale cigarette smoke and frying bacon assailed his nose as he looked around for Weldon. Tait approached the corner where he sat, pausing only long enough to mouth to the middle-aged waitress to bring him a cup of coffee. Extending his right hand to Weldon, he said, "Thanks for coming, Jim. You made good time from Todd-ville."

Weldon took the offered hand without getting up and said, "Mornin' again, Earl Lee. Now, take a seat and tell me what's on your mind."

"Well, Jim, like you may have guessed while we talked on the phone earlier, this may or may not be significant, but with all these other murders we've had, I can't help running scared over the least little thing."

"Okay, you got me interested," Jim responded, trying to read Earl Lee's face.

The waitress set the coffee mug before Earl Lee with one hand and topped off Weldon's cup from the coffee pot she was holding precariously in the other, sloshing some of the amber liquid on the oilcloth covered table. Daring either man to speak, she whirled around and, scurrying behind the counter, plopped the vessel noisi-ly on its base.

"She musta had about as lousy a night as me," Tait commented wryly. "Anyway, to git to the point of what I wanted to talk with you about, around 6:15 this morning Sheldon Lentz called me at home about his oldest girl, Amy. Said she didn't come home at all last night."

"Aw, crap," blurted Jim involuntarily. Then, trying to remember how old she was and thinking if she was an adult she might have a plausible reason for being out, he asked, "How old is she?"

"She's still in high school, so I figure she must be somewhere around sixteen or seventeen. Too danged young to be staying out all night, but let me finish what I had in mind. Before I called you this morning, I took Ira Prewit's advice and checked around out at that Air Force station. Went by and got a picture of her and showed it around. Couple of them airmen recognized her as a girl that's been running with the one called Phelps."

"But, Earl Lee, that don't necessarily mean anything, and we both know it," Weldon reminded him lamely.

Tait responded patiently, "I know that, Jim, but when I called Lentz back, he told me that he was not aware that the girl even knew any of that bunch."

"Uh, oh. So, what you're saying is that you suspect that she may not be just missing but may be our next murder victim! Shit fire, Earl Lee!"

"That's exactly what I think. If I'm right, it points right out there to them airmen. At this time, the likely one is Phelps."

"But like you've said before, it don't implicate them in those other deaths."

Weldon got up to leave, but Earl Lee motioned him to sit back down, saying, "Thanks for checking out the Whitworth boy's truck, Jim. I looked over what you sent and don't really see anything new. Pretty well verifies what we figured. The bullet hole was where you'd expect it to be if the killer shot Joey while he was sitting in the truck."

"Yeah. That fact, and the blood on the seat, leaves no doubt about it," Weldon agreed. "Thing now, Earl Lee, is to get who done it."

CHAPTER 35

Myrtle Beach AFB, South Carolina, Team I Orderly Room
Tuesday, 29 December 1953
1000 hours

Master Sergeant Jackson picked up the field phone connecting the orderly room with the radar maintenance van on the beach and gave the handle three cranks. At the other end of the line, A/3C Robert Turner picked up the field phone, thumbed the lever, and spoke. "Radar maintenance van, Turner," he said, then released the lever and waited.

"Turner, is Mackley there?" Jackson's gruff voice demanded.

"Yeah, Sergeant," Turner replied.

"Okay, put him on the line, will you?" Jackson ordered.

A couple seconds later, Lucas picked up. "Yeah, Sarge, what can I do for you?"

"You have your car with you? Yeah. All right, meet me downtown at the doughnut shop in about fifteen minutes. And don't be late. I need to talk with you."

Twelve minutes later, Lucas turned right into the Dixie Doughnut Shop parking lot and waited in his car. Shortly afterward, Jackson pulled into the space next to Lucas's car, killed his engine, and silently motioned for Lucas to follow him inside. Once there, Jackson led the way to a booth toward the rear in the corner and slid in facing the door. "Never did like to sit facing the corner," commented Jackson, dryly. "Makes me uneasy."

Mustering a thin grin at Jackson's attempt to break the ice, Lucas slipped into the seat opposite and waited, taking in the smells of frying donuts and fresh brewed coffee. "Yeah, you know, Sarge, ol' Wild Bill Hickok always sat with his back to the wall in card games. Messed up one time, and a guy walked up and shot him in the back of the head. Same thing with Jesse James."

Lucas clamped his mouth shut at Jackson's scowl, waiting for the sergeant's next move. At any other time, this would have been a pleasant break from routine duties, but the urgency of Jackson's call had warned him that this was no social visit. Jackson motioned to the white-uniformed waitress staring at them from behind the counter for coffee and indicated that she bring them each a doughnut as well. This done, he leaned back, calmly studying the young airman sitting nervously opposite him.

Master Sergeant James Jackson was in his early thirties, balding, and slightly overweight. He had served in the Pacific theater during World War II and, following cessation of hostilities in 1945, transferred over to the newly organized USAF in 1947 as a staff sergeant. He had married his high school sweetheart a few days before enlisting in 1942. The pressures of being in the service had ruined the relationship, and his wife left him for an Augusta, Georgia lawyer a year later. A confirmed bachelor following his wife's desertion, the sergeant swore off the myth of marital bliss, substituting instead the disciplined security of the Air Force, avowing that if he ever needed female companionship he could find it in some cathouse. That way, he maintained, there would be no permanent ties with accompanying heartaches.

Jackson had still not told Lucas why the pressing need to talk, and the fact they needed to meet privately off base had only added to the intrigue.

While Mackley fidgeted uneasily, the older man casually stirred a liberal amount of sugar into his coffee, took a large bite of his glazed sinker, and washed it down with some scalding coffee, grimacing as the amber liquid burned down an already smoke-irritated throat. Dragging a chubby hand across his mouth, the sergeant then reached into his fatigue pocket to pull out a crumpled pack of Camels. Shaking the pack, he mouthed one of the cigarettes before returning the rest to his pocket without offering one to Lucas. Remembering that he hadn't eaten the entire doughnut, Jackson balanced the cigarette on the rim of the half-filled ashtray and, eyeing Lucas, took another bite and chased it with coffee.

Dammit, thought Lucas. *I ain't gonna sit here watching him eating them damned doughnuts all day. Way he acted when he called me I thought he had something important to talk about.*

Jackson continued leisurely eating the doughnut and sipping the now cold coffee while Lucas squirmed. Finally, over the edge, Mackley blurted, "Dammit, Sarge! You didn't ask me out because you like my good looks. So out with it, what the devil do you want?"

Jackson, taking no offense at the outburst, picked up the cigarette and tapped it against the Formica table top, considering his words carefully before he said, "Mackley, word from Colonel Van Vleet is that either Kesterman, Phelps, or you," Jackson emphasized the you, "are prime suspects in the killing of that joker back at Keesler." Jackson paused to let his words sink in, trying to read the younger man's reaction.

Lucas gasped audibly, nearly choking on a bit of doughnut stuck halfway down his throat. Hurriedly, he washed it down with a drink of water. Coughing to clear his throat, he responded, "Sarge, you know I couldn't have had anything to do with that mess, but there ain't no way I can prove it. But then, JJ or Charlie can't prove they didn't do it either."

"Yeah, I know that, but I thought you ought to know how close that AP major is getting ready to haul you in," Jackson told him. "And now that I've messed your day up, let me drop this on you. Have you thought about old Tait might be trying to link you an' your two pals to Toddville."

"What? What did you say?" Lucas asked, refusing to believe his ears.

Jackson reached over and touched his arm, saying, "I'm sorry, but you needed to be told. If anybody should ask, I ain't told you nothing. Understand?"

Thoroughly shaken, Lucas was able only to mutter, "Thanks, Sarge. I need to get on back to the site and think on this. And the coffee and doughnuts are on me."

Jackson smiled, "Why, Mackley, I expected that. Now get out of here."

Back at the installation, Charlie Kesterman was waiting impatiently for Lucas, knowing something was amiss when Lucas had left so abruptly earlier. Hearing the car drive up and park, he walked out and waited idly for Mackley to approach.

"Turner told me where you been." He paused, then, not willing to wait any longer, demanded, "What did Jackson have to say? I guess all this secrecy was all about what's going on with the investigation of that son of a bitch Webber's killing."

When Lucas responded, aggravation reflected in his sharp answer. "Yeah, besides drinking coffee and having a couple doughnuts, the subject of Webber did come up casual-like."

Charlie's face became drawn, his mouth a narrow slit, and Lucas could almost hear his teeth grinding as he struggled to control his temper. "Look, Mackley, I don't know where in hell you think you're coming from, but you better start walking a bit lighter. I've already told you, don't try to shift any blame on JJ or me, especially on me. You understand what I'm saying?"

"Charlie, if you got nothing to hide, then you got nothing to worry about. You want to know what me and Jackson talked about, then you best go ask him," Lucas responded calmly. Brushing past Charlie without looking back, he went into the maintenance van.

Claude's
1900 hours

Lucas sat alone in one of the back booths nursing his fourth beer of the evening. He couldn't exactly say he was drunk, but on the other hand, there certainly was a feeling of lightheadedness. Ever since he had explained to Emily about Webber's death and his own fears of being involved, that was all that was on his mind. She had tried to assure him that since he was innocent of any wrongdoing there was nothing to worry about. But with his mind tormented as it was, no words of assurance could allay his fears of the future.

How he wished that Em's trust in him was true. He hadn't done anything wrong, but the whole affair was gnawing at him, driving him crazy. It would not let go of his jagged-edged mind. Was there any way he had not thought this whole mess could be laid on him? JJ just the same as blamed him, and now, it looked as if Kesterman was even more determined to place Lucas at fault. Mulling over the bad feelings with his buddies he assured himself, *I'll remember those bastards. Anyway, it was probably JJ who did it and was trying to shift the blame onto him. JJ didn't like Webber and had about as much trouble with him, if not more, than anyone else in the squadron. But what am I thinking? Here I'm blaming my best friends. I can't believe I'm doing that. Damn! What's the matter with me? I must be losing it?*

Just a few days ago, Lucas had the world by the tail in a downhill pull: a sweet little girl to love, a pretty good job as NCOIC for radar maintenance, and up for promotion to technical sergeant. And now, what a mess things had turned into.

"Dammit!" he muttered. "How could a man get himself into such a god-awful mess and not even know really what happened to get hisself into such a situation?" There in Claude's, he sat alone, blocking out the background noises, idly sipping the beer, its taste now bitter.

Startled, he looked up as Charlie walked in, heading in his direction and, without waiting to be invited, sat down across from him. Fresh air let in by the open door briefly cleared his mind, but Charlie's presence only darkened his already sour mood. "Have a seat," Lucas said with sarcasm dripping from his voice. He didn't really want to be disturbed now, especially by Charlie Kesterman. "Guess you made a special trip jist to mess with my mind, didn't you, Charlie?"

"Well, hell's bells, Mackley, if that's the way you feel, screw you." Charlie responded angrily, starting to get up.

"Aw hell, Charlie, don't mind me. Sit down and have a beer," Lucas said more civilly as Charlie settled back into the seat.

The two men sat staring each other down, trying to decide how to begin a discussion that both were reluctant to start. Finally, after some consideration of what Kesterman had said earlier about the three of them being suspects, Lucas said, "Rumor has it that the wheels back at Shaw are about ready to nail somebody for Webber's murder, and I also expect you can guess whose ass it is."

Kesterman started to respond, but Lucas held up a hand and cut him off. "And that's what's got me scared. The three of us all deny being involved with that killing. Maybe we're all innocent. I know I ain't done nothing, but that ain't likely to cut no slack with Van Vleet and that AP major, Cummins. With our luck, though, one or the other of us is gonna be blamed sure as you're sitting there. Matter of fact, I been warned that I head up their list."

Charlie's earlier belligerence suddenly changed as he carefully studied Lucas. Then just as suddenly as his changing mood, he chug-a-lugged his beer and carefully placed the empty bottle on the table, and slid it over against the wall. Then wiping his mouth with the back of his hand, he got up, saying, "Gotta go. Betty's waiting for me right now, so can't be late. But saw your car out front and thought I'd cheer you up with the latest news."

Like hell he wants to cheer me up. "All right. Thanks a lot, Charlie," said Lucas, refusing to be baited. "But let me ask you, don't you feel the least bit scared about all this stuff that's going on?"

"Naw," Charlie replied confidently. "Don't do much good to

worry. And besides, even if I was guilty, there ain't no way nobody's gonna pin it on me."

After Kesterman left, Lucas sat lost in deep thought, still nursing the remnants of brew in the amber bottle. It hit him then. Kesterman said that he had stopped to cheer him up with the latest news but really didn't tell him anything. Finally, he muttered, "Aw hell," slid out of the booth, pulled on his fatigue jacket, and walked out into the chilly night.

Mackley left Claude's, driving south along the ocean on Highway 17. The turmoil in his mind had bothered him for days. He had never in his life been in such a quandary and for the life of him could see no way out. The only time he seemed to be able to get his mind off his troubles was when he was with Em. Even then, he caught himself allowing his thoughts to go back, trying to figure a way out.

The sign said Murrells Inlet was five miles ahead. He didn't remember driving this far but obviously had because he was there. He looked at his watch. Almost 0145. "Better git myself back. If Jackson misses me this time of night, he'll figure I took off. Come to think of it, that might not be a bad idea at that," Lucas muttered half aloud. He turned off 17 at a closed gas station, circled back onto the highway and drove toward Myrtle Beach. "This is plain no good. Maybe I better go see Captain Cook and ask him what to do. Only thing is if I ain't careful what I say, I may mess myself up real good."

The drone of the car's wheels on the blacktop paced the miles as they ticked off on the speedometer. By the time he had reached the base, he was no closer to solving his problems than before. In fact, they seemed to have grown even more insurmountable with each revolution of the car's wheels. God, he needed Em with him.

He drove through the gate, switching the car's headlights off so no one would see him enter. Coasting into an empty space, he parked the Chevy and, closing the car door quietly, slipped silently into the barracks. Undressing to his shorts, Lucas lay on his back with his fingers interlaced behind his head, unable to fall asleep yet too exhausted to think clearly. The sounds of sleeping men in the main bay of the barracks pervaded the night. His roommates, Anderson and Kesterman, slept peacefully. Outside on Highway 17, the rumble of late-night trucks disrupted the usual night noises. Sleep still evaded him.

In the few short months since he and his two companions had been at Shaw some troubling changes occurred. Charlie's moodswings from overly friendly to almost extreme sullenness worried Lucas. Phelps had also changed, but his change was harder to see. To Lucas, Phelps's change was more ominous because it was so subtle. Both men had begun drinking more than ever before and appeared to be involved in fights more often as well.

Not long ago at one of the team beer parties, the two had nearly fought over JJ's date. He had invited Amy Lentz to the party, and Charlie had spent considerable time flirting with the young woman to the annoyance of Phelps. Beer and liquor intensified the increasingly bitter feelings they felt over Amy, and if it weren't for the timely intervention of Sergeant Jackson, they would have come to blows. Later they did shake hands, apologizing to each other. In retrospect, Lucas now wondered if the apologies were sincere.

The CQ announced 0600 hours over the bitch box. Lucas rolled over and, placing his bare feet on the rough floor, staggered upright. Shaking the cobwebs of weariness from his mind, he stumbled to the latrine and splashed icy water onto his face.

Bloodshot eyes stared back from the broken mirror above the basin. He brushed his teeth and then turned off the cold water, allowing the warm to reach a comfortable temperature. He rinsed the grime of yesterday from his face and added a bit of hot water to his shaving mug, whipping up lather with the brush. After applying the lather, he checked the blade in his razor, decided he could get one more shave out of it, and quickly scraped his face. Finished, he ran his comb through his hair, noting it would soon be time for a trim, but by then, he'd be in the guardhouse and wouldn't have to worry about it.

CHAPTER 36

The ringing of the field phone shocked Lucas back to his senses. In the confined space in the maintenance van there was little room to relax. He had talked the supply sergeant back at Shaw out of a well-used padded swivel chair and, in slack times on duty, had used the chair for catnapping. Only moments before he had dropped into the chair, hooked his left leg over the arm and dozed off.

Letting his feet hit the floor of the van, he reached over, pulled the phone from its leather case and then, keying it, said, "Radar maintenance, Sergeant Mackley."

As he released the butterfly lever, Charlie's voice came hollow over the line, "Lucas, Charlie here. Some APs and the local sheriff are on the way out there to haul your ass in! From what I could overhear when they was talking with Cook, looks like you gonna get charged with knocking Webber off."

Lucas heard the click of the butterfly lever release on the other end of the line. Stunned, he started to reply and guiltily looked to see if someone was listening. The blood drained from his face, and the contents of his stomach churned sickeningly. Panic took adamant residence in his mind.

Think! Dammit! Think! Don't panic! Dammit, git a hold on yourself!

The field phone hissed to life again, and Charlie spoke, more urgently this time. "Mackley! Did you hear whut I just said? They're coming out there to arrest your ass! So move it!"

Realizing Kesterman was repeating the warning, Lucas responded, covering panic with feigned bravado. "Yeah. Yeah. Thanks, Charlie. I gotta get off this phone and think."

"Well, you damn well better not spend too much time because they'll be on you in about ten minutes or less," Charlie warned, and before Lucas could say more, killed the line.

Breathing hard, Mackley stood, shaking uncontrollably for what seemed an eternity before dropping the phone back into its case. Forcing his taut nerves to calm down, he headed outside to his car, willing himself to walk slowly so as not to arouse suspicion.

Exaggeratingly cautious, he raised the hood and pretended to check the oil. Closing the hood, he then moved around the car, opened the door, and slid into the driver's seat and sat there momentarily. Then, apparently having made up his mind, he started the vehicle, backed out of the parking area and turned north along the beach road.

Knowing the sheriff and AP detail would be arriving soon, he sped up until the small dirt road that led off to the left of Beach Drive came into view. Turning onto the road, he continued to the clearing where he had taken Emily that first night. He stopped in the clearing and waited with the car idling with only the low rumble of the engine to give him away. Soon the sound of the jeep could be heard followed by the more sonorous sound of a civilian car. The vehicles slowed at the intersection, their engines winding downand then as they moved toward the radar site. Lucas sat quietly, well concealed in the woods, confident that the idling Chevy could not be heard over the regular highway traffic behind his hiding place. Counting off the seconds, he gave them ample time to reach the installation then drove on across the woods to Highway 17 and proceeded rapidly north toward the Johnson house.

A sour-faced Eula Johnson answered Lucas's knock. "Hello, Lucas," she greeted him coldly, thinking, *Sorry jerk, wonder what no good he's up to now?* "Emily ain't here right now. She ain't out of school yet."

Oh, hell! Lucas thought, glancing at his watch. It was only 1500 hours, at least fifteen or twenty minutes before she would be home. Looking blandly at Mrs. Johnson, he asked hopefully, "Would it be okay if I come in and wait for her? It's really important that I see her, Mrs. Johnson." The scathing look she gave him caused Lucas to back off. "On second thought, ma'am, I can wait in the car. Uh. Thanks, anyway."

"Suit yourself," she responded acidly, slamming the door in his face.

Lucas returned to his car, trying to look as casual as possible while watching the street behind in the rearview mirror. There was no question that once the authorities found him missing from the radar installation the first place they would look would be here and then the next would be Claude's. He had to run. *Please, Emily, hurry!* he silently begged.

Then, the sound of a heavy vehicle pierced the numbing afternoon quiet. Turning the corner a block behind his car was the familiar yellow of a school bus. It came to a stop just in front of his car, and its door opened. Emily emerged, immediately ran to the Chevy, and got into the passenger seat. She threw her books into the back, scooted over beside him, and kissed his cheek. It was then that she realized something was wrong, but before she could say anything, Lucas turned on the ignition and started the car.

As they drove away, Mrs. Johnson came to the door and sadly shook her head. "There goes my baby," she murmured, tears welling up. "Got a feeling something is bad wrong. Just can't seem to be able to control her no more." Turning, she re-entered the house.

When they were out of sight from the house, Lucas put his arm around Em's shoulder and said softly, "You know the problem with that guy in Biloxi that I told you about. Well, it has finally come to a head. Honey, I'm in real deep trouble now. More trouble than you could ever dream about in your whole life. An' to top it all off, Jackson hinted that they may be trying to tie me an' JJ and Charlie to them kids at Toddville. Both Sheriff Tait and the APs are hunting me right now. Hadn't been for Charlie warning me, I'd already be on the way to Shaw under arrest."

Stunned, Emily inhaled sharply when the impact of what Lucas was saying hit her. Before she could say anything, Lucas continued, "Emily, I've never lied to you, and I swear I'm not lying now. Like I told you the other day, I had nothing to do with killing that guy. I didn't like him one bit, but neither did most of the other men in the squadron, and right now I'm on the run, and I don't know where to run to. I only know that I had to see you once more before I took off."

"Lucas, of course I believe you. You should never think any other way. Don't you know that?" she assured him, trying to hold back the tears blinding her eyes.

"Yeah, I know. If there's anything I can count on in this crazy mixed up world, I know it's you," he replied, hurting inside. The break in his voice told her how desperately frightened and uncertain he was.

"Okay, now that that's settled," she grinned, trying to change the mood, "what do we do now?"

Taking his arm from around her shoulders, Lucas placed both hands on the steering wheel. "No! Em! I don't want you involved," he said more harshly than intended.

Hurt by his apparent lack of feeling but more angry because of his apparent rejection, she shot back hotly, "Look, Lucas Mackley,

I don't give a damn what you want. I am involved and have been ever since a certain night not long ago when we made love and you told me you loved me. So, don't you dare exclude me now! Do you hear me?"

Turning the steering wheel loose, Lucas raised his hands in mock surrender and, grinning sheepishly, quickly said, "Okay! Okay! I know when I'm whipped." He playfully cuffed her on her upturned chin with his right hand. "It's just that I'd die if I thought I ever caused you any hurt. What if they corner us somewhere and there's shooting? You could be in danger."

"No, Lucas, it's settled. I'm going with you. You run—I run. Now, let's drive while we decide what to do."

They left Myrtle Beach on a little used back road, one that eventually would take them to Conway, twenty-five miles west of the beach. As they drove, Lucas tried to force himself to think of their best course of action. Finally, he said to the girl snuggled quietly beside him. "Look, I have about $250 and some change, nearly a tank of gasoline, and the clothes I'm wearing. I think there's a sleeping bag and a couple of blankets in the trunk and that's it. You have the clothes you're wearing and what money you have in your purse."

She giggled, "You're right about my clothes, but wrong about the money in my purse. I may have three or four dollars left from my lunch money, but that's all."

"All right," he said, "when we get to Conway, I'll give you what money I have and let you out. You get me a shirt, what clothes you need and both of us toothbrushes. Let's see, get whatever personal stuff you need and us something to eat. I'll pick you up at the Bluefish Café in—say, an hour. Okay?" he continued, thinking aloud. "And don't be afraid. Even if they do stop you, they won't hurt you. Tell 'em I made you come along."

"Yeah, sure." She bent over and pecked a kiss on his cheek then got out as he momentarily pulled the car to the curb.

Myrtle Beach, South Carolina, Team I Operations Site
Monday, 11 January 1954
1438 hours

"Goddammit! You boys in your pretty Greyhound bus driver suits done messed up as usual!" exploded Tait. "You come down here where you don't belong to begin with, ask for help which I ought not give, then mess things up to hell and back! Couldn't catch your own asses with both hands, even, by damn, if somebody showed you where they was! Ought to walk off right now and leave this mess up to you." The irate man continued with blazing eyes, daring anyone to speak. "Would, too, except I can't let y'all go running around here loose. Might shoot some voter."

The AP officer, Lieutenant Hiram Rodgers, familiar with Tait's blunt manner, remained outwardly calm and waited until Earl Lee cooled off. "Sheriff, I can appreciate your feelings," he said, holding his hands out in a placating gesture, "but because the murder at Keesler took place on a military base, it is considered a federal concern. I'll admit we really don't have much on this man, so it was unreasonable to expect him to take off like he did. I guess it goes to show you, there's no telling what a man in that kind of bind will do. I also must admit that since this is now apparently in your jurisdiction, I must honor that."

Determined to get the last word in, Earl Lee rumbled, "Like I tried to tell you a while ago, Lieutenant, Mackley has too many friends, and they alerted him we was on our way out there the minute we left that compound. But, then, it ain't no skin off my back if you lose him. I'll admit he may be a suspect in a couple local murders, but so far, I ain't got a reason to bring him in. So, as long as he's gone and outta my jurisdiction, I ain't worrying."

Struggling to control his temper, Lieutenant Rodgers turned to his driver, a burly staff sergeant, and nodded toward the jeep, saying, "Sergeant Willis, get on the horn, call Shaw, and notify Major Cummins that our man has run. Let him know that we'll check around, and if nothing turns up, we'll be back at the base in about three hours."

Saluting, the sergeant turned to the jeep where he radioed the lieutenant's message.

Tait, unable to resist joshing the young officer a bit more, muttered tauntingly, "Yeah, Lieutenant, looks like your bird has flown the nest and is migrating south on you."

"Yes, Sheriff. It looks that way, but we'll get him sooner or later. We always do," he replied curtly.

Seeing that the officer was not going to rise to the bait, Tait said evenly, "I shouldn't do this, but I guess you do need some help. Was I you, I'd go as fast as my little old jeep could carry me over to Mackley's gal friend's house. I understand he's been running around with Eula Johnson's youngest daughter, and I'd bet a month's pay, you put a little pressure on that old lady, or for that matter the girl, and one or the other of them will tell you where he is. That don't pan out, check out Claude Beck over at Claude's barbeque and beer joint. All them Air Force people usually hang out there, drinking and raising hell."

"Thanks for the help and advice, Sheriff," Rodgers answered appreciatively.

Outside in the jeep, Rodgers ordered, "Let's check out that girl's place first, Sergeant. Where did that redneck sheriff say she lived?"

"Two-hundred-ten Oceanview, sir," the driver answered as he started the jeep and shifted into low.

Fifteen minutes later, the trio parked in front of 210 Oceanview, and Rodgers knocked while the two enlisted men waited at the foot of the porch steps. When no one answered, Rodgers waited a few seconds longer and knocked again, much harder this time.

From somewhere in the rear of the house the husky voice of a woman called loudly, "Hold on, I'm coming."

A moment later, Eula Johnson opened the door then, wiping

her hands on a dishtowel, growled, "Well, what do you want? I ain't got all day."

"Mrs. Johnson?" Rodgers inquired, studying her face.

"Yeah."

"I hate to bother you," Rodgers said, almost solicitously. "I can see you're awfully busy, but this is really important." Seeing that she wasn't eager to reply, he hurried on, asking more forcefully, "Would you happen to know a young airman named Lucas Mackley?"

Hesitating, she considered her words with the law. She didn't particularly care about Lucas, but she surely didn't want to get involved with no telling what, nor did she want Emily in trouble. "What do you want to know for?" she questioned, understanding now what the AP on their armbands meant and belatedly wishing that she had not asked.

"Now don't get me wrong, Mrs. Johnson. I'm not accusing him of anything. We just need to speak with him for a few minutes," he lied glibly, "until we get some misunderstandings cleared up. Nothing for you to be concerned with, ma'am."

Intimidated now by their stern demeanors, imposing uniforms, and the guns holstered on their hips, she glanced briefly at the men then lowered her eyes. "He was here a little while ago, but he left. You might try Claude Beck's place over on 17. He ain't there, then I don't know where you'd likely find him."

The faint roar of the ocean seemed louder, drowned out momentarily as a low, sleek black car glided past, slowing for its sole occupant to gawk at the unexpected presence of the Air Police.

Mrs. Johnson flinched as Rodger's voice invaded her confused thoughts.

"Very well. Thank you, ma'am. You have been of considerable help. I certainly appreciate that, and as I said, there's really nothing to worry about. This is just routine."

The three men wheeled about in synchrony, returning to the jeep, while Mrs. Johnson hurried into the house, closing and locking the door behind her. Leaning against the door, she worried for her daughter. "Lord, I hope they ain't at that café. I don't care about him, but Emily is with him. Why in Heaven's name didn't I keep my big mouth shut and just not say anything at all?"

Easing into the companionship of the old sofa, she wept for her child.

Conway, South Carolina
1735 hours

Lucas drove randomly around Conway, timing himself so he would be at the Bluefish Café when Emily finished in the store. While driving, it occurred to him that the APs would probably expect them to head west, eventually going to Arkansas to familiar surroundings. With this option ruled out, it now essentially became a choice of going north into North Carolina or possibly Virginia or south to Georgia or Florida. Since it was winter, heading south seemed best.

Emily was waiting impatiently on the sidewalk when he turned the corner. Quickly glancing cautiously up and down the street, he glided smoothly to a parking spot paralleling the curb. Even before the car had completely stopped, Emily opened the passenger door and slid in.

"Let's get out of here, Lucas, before I have a nervous breakdown," she giggled excitedly.

As they drove, Lucas explained what he was thinking they should do, dreading to tell her that it would be best for her to stay behind. Putting off the inevitable as long as possible, he finally tried again to convince her to stay.

"Em, please listen to me. You know I love you. I've told you over and over, but this is serious. I don't want you in trouble. Up till now you're not involved very much. They probably know you're with me, but that's all."

"Oh, be quiet, Lucas, and listen to me! I am involved. I've

helped you get away up to this point, and that makes me guilty of something, I suppose. And, like I told you before, you have me whether you like it or not."

"Yeah, but what if I have to leave the car and run for the woods, or suppose we git shot at?" Lucas argued, shaking his head. Seeing he was making little headway, he patted her knee and added, "You know, you are one stubborn woman."

"Honey, if it comes to you needing to run, then I'll give up and try to slow them up while you get away," she promised.

Overwhelmed by her show of love, Lucas could only counter her argument by reaching over and squeezing her hand.

Claude's
Myrtle Beach, South Carolina
Monday, 11 January 1954
1525 hours

"Mr. Beck, I'm Lieutenant Rodgers from Shaw Air Force Base over near Sumter. Sheriff Tait informed me that you may be able to help me," Rodgers said, extending his hand to Claude. When Claude refused to shake hands, the lieutenant dropped his and quickly reached into his jacket pocket to remove a picture of Mackley and shoved it in the restaurant owner's face. Disturbed by Beck's rude behavior, Rodgers dropped all remnant of politeness when he demanded, "Do you recognize this man?"

Claude reluctantly took the photo, turning it sideways, then back straight. Looking into Rodger's angry eyes, he turned the picture over, stalling. Rodgers waited patiently, letting Claude simmer. The two enlisted men stood at ease on either side of Rodgers, their faces emotionless. The airman in the photo, although younger, was no doubt Mackley.

Rodgers continued, "And before you answer, in case you are wondering why I'm asking, the man may be involved in a serious crime. In fact, it involves murder. So, again, do you know him?"

Rodgers's imperative was strongly emphasized.

Claude hesitated before answering, feeling sweat popping out on his bald head. He worried, *What am I gonna do now. I damn well don't wanta get my own tail in a sling.* He knew Mackley and had no intention of causing him any unnecessary trouble. On the other hand, he still had to consider himself. He would tell only what he had to about the boy. *That lieutenant looks like a mean son of a bitch, but hell, I'm a civilian and he can't touch me.* "No, I'm not sure if I know him or not," he lied, knowing Rodgers knew he was lying. "There're maybe twenty-five or thirty men out there at that old base. Hell, almost every last one of 'em comes in here at one time or the other, but in uniform they all look pretty much the same to me."

"I'll repeat my question, Mr. Beck. Do you know this man?" Rodgers demanded, staring the other man down and crowding his space.

Pushing aside his own fear of being involved, Beck, in no mood to be pushed around, blurted, "And what's it to you, soldier boy?"

"I'm just following orders," Rodgers remarked mildly, smiling benignly. "He's wanted for questioning concerning the death of a noncommissioned officer about two years ago at an Air Force base in Mississippi. We are following routine procedures, and when his name came up, it made us think he might know something about what happened."

"In a pig's rear end, sonny, I been around a bit. Served in the army in '44, so don't pull none of that—we're following orders—stuff on me. Thet stuff won't flush, and you know it."

"All right, Beck, I'll tell you what I know. There's fairly substantial evidence available that he may be tied in with the beating death of the man. It is possible that a witness may be able to place him at the scene. At least there is the possibility that Mackley can tell us something about the case. We simply don't know yet. On the other hand, he may have a foolproof alibi." Rodgers let Claude think on that before continuing, saying sternly, "And Mr. Beck, I am an officer in the United States Air Force on official duty. I am not a soldier boy as you are inclined to put it."

A slightly intimidated Claude Beck decided to be forthright and said, "Okay. His name is Lucas Mackley, but I guess you already know that. The last time I seen him was a couple nights ago. Him and Charlie Kesterman was here talking real serious and drinking beer in that there booth over there. Don't know what they was talking about, but Charlie didn't stay long before he left, looking a little pissed." Claude indicated the booth in the corner where Lucas and Charlie had sat that night two weeks earlier discussing Webber's murder. "As far as I know, though, he ain't been around since."

Seeing that he had wrung all the information from Beck that he was going to get, Rodgers ordered his men to follow him outside. Once there, he told them, "Men, we may as well head back to Shaw. Sergeant, call in and let them know we're on our way."

15 Minutes East of Conway
Highway 501
1746 hours

Sitting in the back seat of the jeep, Airman L. C. Blakely suddenly reached out to touch the lieutenant's shoulder and pointed back toward the car that they had passed moments before. "Sir, did you see that car?"

"Uh, uh, no," replied Rodgers, turning his head quickly.

"Yessir, that one that's headed back toward Myrtle Beach. One that just passed us." By then the car had disappeared around a curve. "It looked a helluva lot like the one described to us that Mackley owns and looked like there might have been two people in it."

"Sergeant Willis, wheel this vehicle around! See if you can catch them. Maybe we'll get lucky this time. After dealing with that sheriff and that fat assed Beck, we need to have something positive happen."

"Yes, sir, Lieutenant!" Willis replied enthusiastically, and slowing, pulled onto the shoulder of the highway and, without much more than a cursory look in both directions, twisted the wheel hard to the left and spun the jeep into a sharp U-turn. Once the vehicle straightened out, heading east along the highway, the sergeant jammed the accelerator to the floorboard. The tires shrieked in protest as the jeep sped after the fleeing automobile. In that short interval, the car had rounded a sharp curve and disappeared into the darkening night.

Highway 501
1750 hours

"Oh, my God! Lucas, did you see who we just passed?" shrieked Em, her eyes wide with fear.

"I sure did, but you know, Em, there ain't much they can do. They're off the base, and I don't think they can do more than follow us. But then, I guess they could radio Tait, but that would take a little time."

"But, Lucas," the girl was still insistent, "if they do follow us, we need to be ready to do something," she worried aloud, staring terrified back down the road into the darkness. A pinpoint of light bobbed in the distance, causing her to squeeze his arm. "Lucas, I think they just turned around and are coming after us."

"All right, Em, don't panic. If I remember right, there are several curves in this road, and every now and then there's a dirt road that turns off. If we can get out of their sight long enough, maybe we can take one of them side roads and wait till they go on by," he said, giving her a quick sidewise glance.

Almost as he spoke, the road entered a wide sweeping curve to the right, and as the Chevy moved into the arc, the lights of the jeep swung left, disappearing into the thick roadside trees behind them.

Gripping the wheel with both hands, Lucas stared intently at the road and cautioned, "Em, keep a close watch and let me know when you see their lights again. I gotta concentrate on looking for a place to turn off. We don't want one that looks too obvious, though. But we gotta have one they won't suspect."

While Emily scanned the highway behind them, Lucas searched the road ahead for a suitable overgrown area where they could hide out of sight from the highway. He drove through the curve and onto a straight stretch, still with no place for cover. Behind them the jeep's headlights entered the curve they had just traveled, silhouetting utility poles and roadside trees in their glare. Emily sat, fearful, by his side, her eyes staring unblinkingly back down the road at the approaching jeep.

"Take it easy, Em, they ain't caught us yet. We still got a good chance of outrunnin' them," he assured her, not fully believing it himself. "If I remember right, or at least it's true for our vehicles— military ones are supposed to have governors on them to limit their speed. Our luck, though, AP jeeps could probably outrun a danged jet."

Lucas pushed the gas pedal to the floor as they entered another straight stretch of highway, hurtling through the darkness with the speedometer climbing snail-slow past sixty-five to seventy. The jeep seemed not to be gaining, but neither were they able to gain any distance advantage on their pursuers. The Chevy, struggling to catch the headlight-lit space, raced down the highway, while behind them the jeep seemed to be keeping pace, a reminder of their desperate flight.

The jeep's headlights disappeared again as the Chevy moved into another slow sweeping curve. "Ho boy!" Lucas shouted, elated. "There it is, sticking right out there! Just perfect!" But before he could react, the car sped past the small obscure logging road that angled sharply back to the left on the left side of the highway. Almost hidden from view by several scrub pines and roadside weeds, only sharp or desperate eyes would have seen it. It had apparently not been used for some time and was now not much more than an overgrown trail.

Lucas pumped the brakes trying not to leave skid marks to give them away, simultaneously pushing the light switch to the off position, and pulled onto the right shoulder of the highway, executing a U-turn and reversing direction. Kicking the accelerator to the floorboard, he drove more by instinct than by sight about fifty feet up the dirt road and immediately killed the engine. Popping noises of the cooling engine, deafening in the sudden quietness, interrupted the otherwise stillness of the night. Disturbed weeds, pushed down by the passage of the car, sprang back, swaying mutely in the cold, windless South Carolina night.

Tightly gripping the steering wheel, he forced himself to calm down. Pent-up air exploded audibly from his lungs. For the first time since seeing the lane, he realized he had been holding his breath. As he gripped the steering wheel, Lucas sat there, eyes tightly closed, and forced his taut nerves to settle down. With racing hearts the young lovers listened intently for the sounds of the pursuing jeep. Em had not spoken. Lucas could almost hear their hearts pounding and the adrenaline racing through their trembling bodies.

Now in the distance, the drone of the jeep engine neared. The distinctive hum of mud-lugged tires vibrated in the otherwise stillness of the darkness. With their hearts beating faster, they clung tightly to each other, waiting for the jeep to slow, an indication they had been discovered. Em shivered, and Lucas heard the involuntary intake of her breathing. She shivered again, touching his arm for encouragement. Lucas patted her knee reassuringly.

Wondering aloud, Lucas asked, "Were they close enough to see us turn? Damn! When I went off on that shoulder, I forgot about dust."

The Doppler sound of the approaching jeep told them that it was getting near. Lucas opened his eyes and hugged the girl closer. Quietly sobbing, her slender body shook uncontrollably.

The jeep was almost even with their position just off the high-way. Was it slowing? Had one of them seen the dirt trail? "God, please don't let them see where we turned," pleaded Lucas. It came even with the logging road! Was there a change in its velocity? No! Now it was past the turnoff!

"Keep goin'! Please don't look back! Hot damn!" Lucas, shouted, then kissed Em fully on her mouth. "Let's get outta here while the gettin's good!"

Mackley switched on the car and stepped on the starter, hoping that nothing had torn loose on the wild careening ride over the logging road. A quick look at the gauges suggested that no major damage had been done. Revving the engine gave no unusual sounds. After backing the car onto the main highway, Lucas paused only long enough to look both ways for traffic then shifted into low gear to begin the return trip to Conway.

Logging Road off Highway 501
Between Conway and Myrtle Beach
Monday, 11 January 1954
1921 hours

"Well, men, that's either one lucky son of a bitch or one sharp son of a bitch, I don't know which. I would've given odds that we would've caught him by now," said Rodgers, letting his disap-pointment show.

Their scanning flashlights cast shadows over the broken terrain, as the three air policemen examined the broken brush and crushed grass where Lucas had driven onto the logging road. Tracks angling sharply back from the highway indicated where he had turned off the blacktop. The thin skin of ice, refrozen on the surfaces of pud-dles on the dirt road further informed the men that a vehicle had recently been driven there.

"Yessir. That was slicker than greased owl crap the way he got us around that curve, then cut back on this logging road. He got damn lucky and found it by chance or else he knew where it was all the time," Sergeant Willis offered, clearing his throat and spitting a glob of phlegm to the side. "Any way you look at it, he damn well snookered us."

The other AP, Airman First Class Cletus Blakely wished he was back at the base instead of out here hunting some wild kid. Looking around him in disgruntled frustration, he asked impatiently, "What now, Lieutenant? Do we go on back to Shaw? Or since he's got to be in this area close by, do we get help and try to flush him out?"

"Let me think," Rodgers answered, considering his options. He was reluctant to return empty-handed to Shaw. But then, on the other hand, beating the back roads for the rest of the night seemed even less warranted. When they'd first seen Mackley's car, it was going toward Myrtle Beach, but now its tracks indicated they were headed back to Conway. So, unless he had taken a different route along some backcountry road, there was a good chance he might still turn around and, once again, head on to Myrtle Beach. In Rodgers's way of thinking, Mackley was proving to be elusive as well as single-minded. He seemed to have definite goals in mind, but what Rodgers could not quite understand was why Mackley apparently felt compelled to return to Myrtle Beach. That is, if that was really his intention. And yet, it made some sense because the girl was from there. He had to be planning on taking her home and then running. But where?

What he had to do was either catch Mackley before the girl got home or enlist Tait to help in the search. Tait had the manpower, while he only had himself and two men. The choice was clear. Mind made up, the officer motioned to Willis, saying, "Sergeant, he's not going to like it one bit, but get on the horn and see if you can raise that hick sheriff."

"Yessir!" responded Willis, grinning broadly and trotting toward the jeep to make the call.

Conway, South Carolina
Sheriff Earl Lee Tait's Office
Monday, January 11, 1954
7:25 P.M.

Earl Lee had been sitting with his feet propped on his desk, deep in thought about that young airman Mackley. There was something about the whole deal that didn't seem to square with the facts. For all of his years in law enforcement, he had come across some difficult cases but none that troubled him like this one. He had known that Johnson girl all her life, and as far as he knew, she had never been in trouble. Old Lady Johnson was a sour tempered old biddy. But, maybe she had good reason to be down on society. Her no-good husband, Jake, had run off to Columbia with a nineteen-year-old girl, leaving her when Emily was just a baby, and there was no doubt that she'd had a pretty rough time. Furthermore, from the way Mackley's friends and commanding officer talked, he was beginning to think they also believed he hadn't being mixed up in this mess. Although he didn't personally know the boy, he was becoming more inclined to agree with them. He shook his head, grinning at the thought of Mackley making such fools of his pursuers.

Still, it looked as if one of those three airmen were involved in some way. Not only did it appear there was a link to the Mississippi killing, but since his talk with Ira Prewit, he was beginning to believe there could be some connection with the murder of Sarah Moorland, along with those of the three young people here in Horry County. His own gut feeling, though, told him that Mackley was not the one he should be after. There were too many pieces to this puzzle that still eluded him.

He let his feet slide off the desk, leaned forward in the padded swivel chair and, grabbing the half-full coffee mug, took a swig. Then, grimacing at its acrid taste, Tait spat in the general direction of the wastebasket and slammed the mug back on the desk. Placing his feet next to the mug, he again leaned back in the chair. The splitting headache he'd had since the whole mess started hit again. Clasping hands behind his aching head, Tait tried wearily to squeeze the pain away. Soon, the dulling effect of the warm office and the effort of attempting to make sense of a trying situation had the elderly sheriff dozing.

"Sheriff," said the voice, seeming to come from far away.

"Dammit, Pete! What the hell you want?"

Deputy George "Pete" Peterson had taken the radio call from Sergeant Willis of the air police and read the urgency in the NCO's voice. He reluctantly decided it was in his best interest to risk Tait's wrath and awaken the venerable lawman. Pete stood at a safe distance from the sleeping man then reached out and touched Tait's shoulder, gently shaking him. "Sheriff, them Air Force folks need help agin."

Slowly opening his eyes and yawning, Earl Lee asked, laconically, "What they got theirselves into now, Pete? They get lost finding their way home?"

Pete laughed, "Well, not quite. It's worse than that. They found their man and the girl, but before they could arrest him, they lost him agin."

"You ain't bullshitting me are you, Pete?" A rare grin split Earl Lee's craggy face. "Now, why don't that surprise me?"

Pete repeated what the AP sergeant had told him, concluding with, "They didn't even come close to apprehending him. Made them look downright stupid, way he slipped past 'em."

"You didn't wake me up jist to tell me that them three was stupid, now did you?" asked Tait, miffed.

"No, Sheriff, I didn't, but you ain't heard it all yet. Mackley caught 'em in a curve and cut back out of sight on a old logging road. Soon as they went by, he pulled out, and it looks like he headed back here to Conway."

"How do you know, Pete?" asked Tait, dropping his feet and sitting up straight.

"How do I know what?" asked Pete, confused.

"How the hell do you know Mackley headed back to Conway? Did it occur to you that he could have doubled back again on that bunch and could be in Myrtle Beach right now?" Tait asked, his temper flaring. He tried to divine what Mackley might be thinking.

"Aw, Earl Lee. He wouldn't do nothing dumb like that," mumbled Pete.

"Okay, maybe. Maybe not, but now what do they want from us?"

"The sergeant said that since they didn't really have jurisdiction, to ask could you give them a hand in running Mackley down."

"Aw, hell! Aw, double hell! I knew all along you was gonna say that! Hell, Pete, I wish them kids would git plumb away, but I guess we better git involved to watch out for them and them dumb air policemen as well. Put out a call for McKay, Tatum, and Simmons to report in immediately and call that dumb-assed lieutenant to let him know I'm on the way."

CHAPTER 37

Conway, South Carolina
Tuesday, January 12, 1954
5:30 A.M.

Emily sat quietly, looking pale and exhausted from the frantic events of the past several hours. They had successfully eluded the Air Police, but one question loomed at the forefront of their minds: How much longer could they hold out before the authorities were close again? No doubt the Air Police had already contacted Tait for help. There was also no question that with the distinctive pea green color of the '47 Chevy, every law enforcement officer in the entire state of South Carolina would recognize it. Ditching the car, however, would put them on foot, and that would leave them worse off. Lucas glanced at the gas gauge, noting the tank was slightly over half full. Based on the car's fuel economy, he could expect to go maybe another 150 miles and, by driving prudently, maybe as many as 175.

Their options were limited. Under the circumstances, Lucas concluded it was unlikely the authorities would expect them to return to Myrtle Beach. He was familiar enough with many of the back roads that he felt confident they could stay off the main highways and work their way to the vicinity of Murrells Inlet. From there it should be possible to travel generally southwest toward Waycross, Georgia. The problem of obtaining sufficient gasoline for that extended trip bothered him, though, and presented the most immediate problem. Unless they had some extremely good luck coming, chances were they would be recognized and captured.

Emily stirred and glanced back down the road in alarm, asking, "What're we gonna do now? They know about where we are, don't they?"

She made Lucas proud of the way she was holding up after the long frightening ordeal of running and hiding along the highway, but the flight was taking a heavy toll. He had to be straightforward with their future. "Yes, Em, I'm afraid it's only a matter of time now before they catch us. You are right. I think they know pretty well where we are," he told her frankly. "Them APs recognized us and know we can't get very far before they get help to hunt us. We ain't got very much time to figure how we're gonna get away."

They rode in silence for a few more miles before he could drum up the courage to admit what he was planning, being careful to solicit her input. As he explained, he could tell Emily was scared, probably more at that moment than she had ever been in her young life, but still gutsy enough to readily agree with his plans.

The moon, well above the horizon, had brushed the ebony of night away, lifting their spirits. Its light, dancing across the cold landscape, cast a surreal glow. Winter-barren trees, with their branches spread like ghost sailors on ghost ships reaching to some god in the cold January sky, swayed eerily as the Chevy steadily distanced them from Conway.

A fair distance south of Conway, the pair located a secondary road which appeared to run generally to the southeast and that, with luck, would take them closer to Murrells Inlet. If Lucas re-membered correctly, several such roads intersected with Highway 17 between Myrtle Beach and the Inlet. Now, if only they could choose the right ones to keep them away from Highway 17 until they were near Murrells Inlet, their chances of getting away would improve.

A quick glance at his watch indicated the time was 0700 hours. Lucas had not slept for over twenty-four hours; Emily napped fretfully off and on during the night, crying out, miserable and scared. Exhausted from the lack of rest, both fought the tension that held their bodies captive. Even though it was only hours ago since their desperate odyssey began, it seemed a lifetime. It was tempting to pull off the road into some secluded area, shut the rest of the world out, and fall asleep for an hour or two, but Lucas knew that at this time of the morning people would be up and stirring, increasing the odds of their discovery. The need to rest and sleep was overwhelming, but this was not the time for such luxury.

His eyes focused back on the road as the fuzzy image of a small country store and gas station came into view. Laying his hand on the sleeping Em, he asked softly, "Think we should risk stopping yonder and take a chance on gassing up?"

"How much we got now?" Em asked, shaking the burden of exhaustion away. Then, realizing this could be their last chance, added, "I would guess that we have a long way to go, so maybe we should."

Mackley pulled up to the gas pump, turned the engine off and got out. He turned, saying, "Why don't you go in and get us something for breakfast if they have anything, and I'll see to the car."

It was still dark, but even then Lucas could tell there were clouds streaking the sky to the west, high ominous ones, suggesting bad weather. He thought, *All we need now is for it not only to be cold, but for it to rain or snow. Likely freeze to death if it does.*

The attendant, a crabby old man of about sixty who Lucas guessed was also the owner, presently emerged from the store. "Whatcha need, buddy?" he asked, grumbling at having to leave the warmth of the store's pot-bellied stove.

"Better fill 'er up, I guess. Going over to the beach before driving on down the coast. My wife ain't never seen the ocean, so I want to make this a good trip for her."

Noticing Lucas's uniform for the first time and simultaneously spotting a pretty good sale, the attendant thawed, asking, "You from around these parts? Seems like the closest base I know of is over west of Sumter." While he talked, he slipped a pair of well-worn gloves on, pumped the reservoir to the mark, and reached for the filler hose.

"Yeah, that's right. Got enough of that place and decided to take myself a short leave," Lucas replied, trying to be friendly.

The attendant eyeballed the glass reservoir, removed the gas nozzle, returned it to its holder on the pump, and looked at the gauge before saying, "Looks like you got a little under twelve gallons, so that'll be exactly two dollars and a quarter."

Lucas reached into his fatigue pocket then, remembering he had given Em all his money, said, "My wife is looking for some cinnamon rolls and milk and other stuff, so tell her and she'll pay you."

The attendant cast a sidewise look at Lucas, shrugged, and went back inside the store. Grinning, Lucas slid behind the wheel and waited for Em.

Emily came out after a few minutes hugging a sack of food to her chest. As she got in the car, she whispered conspiratorially, "Lucas, let's get out of here. That man really looked me over. Made me feel a bit uneasy."

Lucas teased, "Girl, I don't blame him. Ever time I see you I do the same thing. You just do things to me."

"Smart alec. You know what I mean. He looked and acted like he knew who we were."

"Yeah. I know, Honey, and I'm sorry I kidded you, but I was just trying to make you feel better. Matter of fact, I even told him you was my wife."

She pulled his face toward her and kissed him. "You don't know how close to the truth that is. Now get us outta here."

Wondering at her comment, Lucas shrugged and turned back to their present dilemma. He knew that Em was right about being recognized, and as soon as they were out of sight, a telephone call would be made to the authorities. They had to make it to Murrells Inlet as quickly as possible and then, once there, he had to persuade Em to return home. He doubted that even alone he could run and hide very much longer. With Em along, capture was certain.

Since leaving the store, the Chevy had steadily eaten up the miles, putting distance behind them. The sun was well above the tree line, and most of the early morning fog had lifted, leaving a promise of a clear, cold day. The clouds that caused concern earlier were now faded away. Around a curve, the highway divided. Although he was not sure which way to go as he approached the junction, he steered to the right, hoping he had made the right choice.

Conway, South Carolina, Horry County Sheriff's Office
Tuesday, January 12, 1954
9:33 A.M.

"Sheriff, that green Chevy we been hunting was seen about an hour or so before daylight this morning leaving town on 544," the deputy informed Tait. "There's a whole network of back roads off in that direction, and no telling which one he's taken."

"Thanks, Pete." Earl Lee faced the Air Force lieutenant. "Well, Lieutenant, looks about like your man's done it to you again. That bird has flown. That sucker's either smarter than hell or one of the luckiest men you'll ever run into. He's outguessing all of us at ever turn. Sure never figured he'd head back toward Myrtle Beach, though. Gotta hand it to him, he's made us look foolish so far."

Feeling humiliated for the third time in twenty-four hours, Rodgers gritted his teeth and tried to gracefully accept the sheriff's needling. "Yes," he said mildly, "it looks that way, doesn't it? But right now my problem is how to prevent him from slipping away again."

"Was I you, which I ain't, Lieutenant, I'd get me a detailed map of the area from here back to Myrtle Beach, on down to about twenty miles past Murrells Inlet. And while I was doing that, I'd notify every law officer in that triangle to be on the lookout for a pukey pea green '47 Chevy four-door Fleetmaster sedan. After that, I'd call Fletch McQuail over south of Myrtle Beach, and ask him to stand by with his dogs—now that'll cost you, but it'll save you in the long run. Way I figure it, you corner that boy, he's gonna cut out on foot," Tait advised, "and when that happens, you gonna be glad you got them dogs."

Lieutenant Rodgers was turning away to instruct his men when Tait stopped him short and added, "Another thing, Rodgers, you better believe them two kids is way ahead of you. That boy knows there's a damn good chance that car will be stopped, so him and that gal have already made plans for what to do if that happens. An' it will happen."

Again interrupted from instructing his men, Rodgers spun as Pete addressed Tait. "Sheriff, just got a call from J.B. Henderson, you know, the feller who owns that store and gas station about fifteen miles down 544. Says our man was there not more'n an hour ago. The girl was with him, too. Described them to a tee. Greedy bastard wanted to know if there was a reward."

"Sounds like J.B., always thinking of how he can make a buck. There you have it, Lieutenant. It's up to you now," Tait said, smiling disarmingly and enjoying the officer's discomfort.

1:15 P.M.

Later, alone that afternoon in his office, Tait sat, eyes partially closed, trying to put the pieces together. The office was quiet with only the monotonous tapping of the keys on Kate's typewriter and the subtle noises filtering in from outside on the street to disturb him. Tait got up, stretched and rolled his left shoulder to loosen it then went over to the window, distracted by loud talk outside on the street.

Old man Zeb Whitworth stood nose to nose with Jim Weldon, arguing animatedly. With his mind momentarily off his problems, Tait watched, wondering what it was all about. Then, with a rare smile cracking his face, he suddenly turned and called to Kate's office, "Kate, would you get them files on the Wallace-Whitworth killings?" He hesitated a moment, then added, "And I guess you may as well bring me the ones on Evelyn Dendy and Amy Lentz, too."

The opening of the file drawer alerted Tait that his request was being carried out. Shortly afterward, the tall, slightly graying woman knocked lightly on the door and, without waiting, entered. "Here you go, Earl Lee," she said handing him three thick folders. "Something new come up, or am I being too nosy?"

Tait answered cautiously, "I don't really know, Kate, and no, you're not being nosy. Since I found out about that latest mess, that killing down in Mississippi, something's been nagging at my mind. Trouble is I just can't pin down what's bothering me. All those cases was brutal just like whoever done them was crazy. Ain't no ordinary killer gonna mess up his victims like these was. He will kill them but he ain't gonna take the time to mutilate them like this one done. There's something missing, but I just don't know what it is in this puzzle. Then I jist saw old man Whitworth jawing at Jim out the window, and something seemed to click. Lost the thought, though."

Looking at her boss quizzically, Kate asked, "And you think going over the files might bring it back? Earl Lee, you've read them a dozen times already." Then, fearing that she was nagging, she quickly amended, "Earl Lee, you know how those airmen are always chasing girls all over the country. Has it occurred to you that Mackley and the others may have messed around over at Toddville? Maybe you should ask around, especially ask some of Jane Marie's and Joey's friends. And didn't you also mention to me that Evelyn Dendy was quite often at old Claude Beck's place over at Myrtle Beach where those airmen are always hanging out? Also, you need to stop and consider what Ira and the others have been telling you about the Moorland killing at Lake City and how there seems to be some connections with all the other murders and with some of those same airmen—at least with those from around here."

"That's right, Kate. As I recall, I believe I did say that Miss Dendy was a regular at Claude's, and Ira is convinced there is a connection with the trouble at Lake City and what happened here. You know, Kate, like you jist said, them airmen seem to have been around where the murders happened and appear to know the victims. You know, we may be closer to solving this than we think. My problem is I'm having trouble tying all of this together. That Lieutenant Rodgers is sure he has his killer in Mackley. That is if he can catch him." Tait smiled. "But I'm jist not convinced that boy is guilty. Not convinced at all."

"Like I said, Earl Lee," Kate reminded him, "back off and look at the time frame and where each killing occurred and…"

Kate saw the hint of a smile on Tait's lips and the crease at the corner of his eye. The smile changed into a broad grin. "Thanks, Kate! You jist may have given me the thread I need. If I can show just one of them boys was anywhere near when each of them people was killed, I may be able to come up with something solid. And, Kate, I think I know who I'm after."

"I don't suppose you are willing to tell me who," she said.

Tait smiled knowingly and replied, "Not yet, Kate. Not yet."

Veterans Hospital
Gulfport, Mississippi
The Present

Compelled to hear Chief Master Sergeant Lucas Mackley out, Marty sat quietly listening, intrigued by his account of that part of his life in Myrtle Beach and of Em Johnson. He had taken Marty back to those days, detailing his first encounter with the pretty young girl, the story of how they became entangled in a web of murder and deceit, and their desperate flight.

They had been there under the ancient tree out of the devilish Mississippi sun for the better part of the afternoon. Checking her watch, Marty saw that the workday had ended over an hour ago, but she couldn't leave after hearing the intensity of his voice.

Late afternoon traffic on Highway 90 was picking up as people headed home, relieved to get away from the pressures of the workplace. Out across the Mississippi Sound, a shrimp boat cruised its route, its diesels straining with the weight of the trawls dragging from its booms. The discordant voice of a fish crow cawed in the pines behind them, fussing at some intruder.

Marty shifted her position on the metal bench to face Lucas more directly. With her mind full of question, she fidgeted, preparing to speak, but a gnarled hand silenced her. "You wanted to know about Em," he said evenly. "What I'll tell you now will show the steel in her, how she was willing to give everything for me. Young as we were, trying to get away, we had just about come to the end. Each time I thought about giving up, the thought of losing Em kept me going." More patient now, he paused briefly, gazing out across the Gulf waters. Looking back at Marty, he said, "I've let myself become distracted, so let me get back to what happened that afternoon at Murrells Inlet and in the days that followed. We were trying to make it to Murrells Inlet and then head south to Georgia."

Highway 32, Southeast of Conway
Wednesday, January 12, 1954
1058 hours

Leafless deciduous trees lining the road struggled against the encroachment of pines and palmettos near the coast. Even this far north, their starkly, barren branches hung eerily with shrouds of Spanish moss. Mistletoe growing symbiotically in dull green clusters on host trees only gave back a few luminous pearl berries to winter birds. Along the side of the road, red haw with its scarlet fruit dominated the under-story. Before long, ancient hardwoods gave way to thinner growths of spindly pines with clumps of saw palmetto covering the forest floor. Now and then, the faint aroma of salty sea air slipped into the car carried on wind currents generated out over the Atlantic.

"I think we may have given them the slip," Lucas said without conviction, trying to reassure Em. By then they were only a few miles from the Inlet and had to decide their next move. Mackley dreaded going on alone but, by the same token, feared for Em's safety. He was sure that no harm would come to her should they be stopped, but it never occurred to him that he would be in a predicament like this. Needing time to think and talk, he drove off the highway along a small side road winding its way into the taller and thicker vegetation.

Afraid to stop the engine should it become necessary to leave in a hurry, Lucas left it idling and explained to the girl beside him, "We both gotta rest and grab a few minutes of sleep, Em. I'm so beat, it's all I can do to keep my eyes open, and I know you're about as worn out, too. But before we rest, I gotta say this. I don't want to, but I have to."

Emily knew what was going to be said, dreading to hear it spoken aloud. She kept silent and gazed lovingly at the young man she would give her life for, and waited. A crease formed across her brow, and a slight quiver touched her lips. She had been considering something she should have told him days ago but had not had the courage to until now. Now the time had arrived for him to know the secret she had kept bottled up. She didn't want to use it to force her will on him, but considering his apparent decision to leave her, she felt she had no choice.

"Did you hear me, Em?" he asked, breaking into her worried thoughts.

She shook her head and said meekly, "No, I was thinking about something else."

He grinned and touched her arm. "Yeah. That was apparent.

Now listen to me. The law is gonna catch up with us sooner or later, and right now I think sooner. That means I got to leave you where it's safe and you can…"

Before he could finish Em took him by the shoulders and pulled him around to face her, blurting defiantly, "Dammit, Lucas, you dense or something? I have already told you. I am not gonna allow you to run off and leave me. Now or anytime! Can't you understand?" A tear slid out of the corner of a sad eye, her voice turned pleading.

Cupping her face with trembling hands, he looked deeply into deep blue eyes   and implored, "Let me finish. I'm not leavin' you. It's just that I know that I'm gonna have to git rid of this car. Damn thing sticks out too much with that crappy green color."

That brought a slight smile to Em's tortured face and a lingering pang to Lucas's heart. *Lord! I hate to let her go.*

"What I had in mind was to drop you off somewhere near the bus station in Murrells Inlet so you can get a bus back to Myrtle Beach. I'll…"

Again she stopped him. "No. I won't do it!"

Exasperated but equally proud of her grit, Lucas looked at her sternly. "You are one bull-headed woman. Now listen. Like I was saying, you go back home, and I'll ditch the car somewhere out of the way to throw 'em off. Then I'll head south and then circle back north. Give me about three or four days, and I should be back near the radar site. You may have to check our place out a couple times 'cause I can't be exactly sure when I can get there. Ask either Charlie or Sergeant Jackson to take you to the radar station. From there, you can slip over to the clearing. Don't trust JJ at all and Charlie very little—I got a bad feeling about both of them. Comes down to it, go to Jackson if you have any doubts about JJ or Charlie." Lucas didn't attempt to explain why he felt the way he did about either one of them. It was just a feeling that wouldn't go away. Maybe there was no substance to them, but the troubling doubts still lingered. Momentarily taking his eyes off Em's pale face, Lucas scanned the barren woods surrounding them trying to think through what to do.

This time Emily's soft voice interrupted his thoughts. "Lucas, you are my first and only love, and I wasn't gonna tell you this yet. With all the trouble, and everything, but you're forcing me to." She held his hands as she spoke. "I'm pregnant."

Lucas's head snapped around as he stared her in the face, trying to comprehend. His face went white. Then he grinned and stammered, "Did … did, I hear you right?"

"Yep, buddy, you sure did. We're gonna have a baby." All he could say was, "I'll be damned!"

CHAPTER 38

Murrells Inlet, South Carolina
Wednesday, 13 January 1954
1021 Hours

His mind in a whirlwind, Lucas wrestled with Emily's revelation back in the palmettos that she was carrying his child. Why had he let things get out of hand that night so long ago? Why did he let the moment of passion take over and irrevocably change their lives? They should have dated, enjoyed being together and eventually, when both were older, married and settled down. Instead, like a fool, he had gotten her pregnant. And now to top all their troubles off, she had been dragged into siding with a fugitive.

No, that wasn't entirely true. Em had insisted on coming along with him. This made it more imperative that she go home. There was no way he could let her or the baby be harmed, and the way things looked, sending her home was the only way he could protect them. With his mind torn apart, Lucas struggled for a way out. On the one hand, he was pleased, but on the other, he was scared for the girl and his unborn child. Since she had told him about her pregnancy, Emily had still insisted that she was not leaving him. Her loyalty only enforced her resolve.

The bus station came into view down the street, and Emily, silent until now, repeated stubbornly, "Lucas, you may as well not say it. I ain't getting out of this car. You try to make me, and people will see and hear and we'll be in trouble." Praying the bluff would work, she leaned close and touched a kiss to his cheek. If that didn't work maybe a little pouting or crying might.

"Aw crap!" Lucas blurted. "Look over yonder!"

Moments earlier they had parked on the west side of the bus station, lingering over what might be their last moments together. As they watched, two South Carolina State Police patrol cruisers pulled to either side of the street on the other side of the station. With his mind made up, Lucas turned to Emily and insisted, "Don't argue with me, Em. Get out now! You got no choice! I'll see you in a few days—three at the most. See if Charlie or Jackson will take you to the radar site, then slip over to that clearing—you know our place. Now do like I asked. I love you, Em." Cranking the car, Lucas reached across in front of her and opened the car door.

With a quick final whisper of love and a brief kiss, Em slipped out of the vehicle and began to walk dejectedly away, not looking back.

Hearing the blaring sirens, Lucas glanced quickly toward the cruisers and saw the flashing lights flare on. Aware that he had been spotted, he slammed the Chevy in gear, and as the tires squalled, looking for traction on the pavement, the Chevy raced from behind the station past three buses. Departing passengers paused, startled then puzzled at the disturbance, they shrugged and continued boarding. One man, hurrying to catch the Charleston bus, stepped aside and cursed under his breath as the first of the cruisers roared past.

Just as Lucas cleared the corner, the patrol cars sped by, skidding into the bus station lot where he and Em had been only moments before. Without bothering to look for traffic he downshifted to second, skidding the car onto the highway in the direction from which they had come. With the accelerator pedal jammed to the floor, the Chevy careened past the city limits sign on 544. Just ahead, the bridge spanning the Intracoastal Waterway loomed dangerously close. The Chevy, capable of easily outrunning the Air Police jeep, could not compete with the souped-up cruisers closing rapidly from behind. The only chance to get away was either to out drive them or abandon the Chevy. A glance in the rearview mirror showed the cruisers rapidly closing the distance, forcing Lucas to make a potentially perilous decision.

"Well, by damn! Let's see if you crapheads can drive or not," he said angrily, slamming the brake pedal and simultaneously putting the Chevy into a skid to the left. The car spun 180 degrees, sending gravel cascading as the rear tires fought for purchase on the shoulder of the road. With the direction reversed toward Murrells Inlet, Lucas eased up on the brake and floored the gas pedal, fishtailing the car as he fought for control. The pursuing cruisers whipped by in the opposite direction, narrowly avoiding a collision. Unable to turn around as Lucas had done, the heavier cruisers sped across the bridge dangerously close to crashing. In those few seconds Lucas had roared out of sight down Highway 17 south of town, free for the moment.

Beach houses flashed by on the left while Mackley searched the road, looking for a place where he could turn off out of sight until the lawmen passed by. A small bayou spanned by a narrow bridge appeared ahead. On both sides of the approach, steeply inclined graveled ramps gave access to the water's edge. Lucas slowed only enough to safely negotiate the ramp, then steered right, braking as he pulled underneath between the foot of the bridge and the sluggishly flowing stream. There, waiting anxiously among several parked vehicles and fishing boats, he released the steering wheel, forcing his taught nerves to relax.

Moments later, the sound of the pursuing vehicles rumbled ominously overhead. Dust and debris filtered from beneath the bridge with the heavier pieces plunking into the nearly calm surface of the bayou. After counting off what he estimated to be between thirty and forty seconds, Mackley drove on under the bridge and back up the ramp on the other side. Quickly looking down the road to his right in the direction of the disappearing police cruisers, he eased onto the pavement. Driving back through Murrells Inlet, he headed north toward Myrtle Beach until he found a shell-paved road leading to the beach. There, he turned onto the access road and drove partway to the ocean before pulling in among the scrub pines and palmettos.

Lucas sat trembling as he gripped the steering wheel for support and nervously jumped at the crackling of the cooling engine. The adrenaline pumping through his shaking body kept him on edge, refusing to let the excitement of escape dissipate. His tense muscles eventually relaxed, and his body slumped wearily behind the wheel. Slowly, his breathing returned to normal, and his mind cleared. That was the closest yet he had come to being caught.

Thank God, he thought looking skyward. Em had gotten to the bus station. He felt sure they had not seen her and that she would be able to make it home all right. His immediate concern was what he would need to do to continue eluding his pursuers. To leave in broad daylight was to invite inevitable discovery. The most promising option was to stay hidden in the trees until nightfall and hope he would remain undiscovered until then, so he could get on his way to meet Emily.

Time dragged by, tauntingly slow. For the hundredth time he looked at his watch. Fifteen-thirty hours, still several more before dark. Alone there in the palmetto thicket, he considered his chances. Better sleep. This may be the last time he could for a while. Another look at the watch. Fifteen-forty hours now. He could almost hear the ticking of the infernal thing mocking him.

Despite his efforts to remain alert, his eyes grew heavy from the monotony and he eventually dozed.

Later, a noise disturbed him, snapping him fully awake. Was it someone sneaking up on him or was it an animal prowling, searching for food? There it was. A raccoon, unaware of Lucas's presence, wandered by in front of the car, stopping now and then as something promising caught its eye, and then pausing to paw at some potential tidbit of food. The animal finally moved on, and all was silent again. Lucas sighed in relief. The watch showed only nineteen minutes had gone by.

Shadows lengthened as the day waned. *Please, God, let Em and the baby be safe*, he silently implored. Lucas estimated he was about eight or nine miles south of the base. He would have to travel slowly and probably stay clear of the beach, but he should be able to reach a place near the clearing where Emily would meet him in three days. Earlier that morning, it had looked as if bad weather might be coming in from the west. Now those clouds had dissipated and, as usual, late afternoon and early evening clouds were gathering to the east over the ocean. Tonight there should be plenty of darkness to hide his movements. He had told Emily to expect him in three or four days, but he could stay concealed in the woods surrounding their meeting place easily enough.

It was nearly dark now. The red winter sun finally gave up and sank into the western horizon, leaving the gloom between late afternoon and total darkness. Taking the small amount of food that remained from their supplies, he ate half a sweet roll and put the rest back in the sack. Slipping out of his fatigue shirt, he donned the checkered flannel shirt Em had bought for him. He hated to leave the military field jacket as cold as it would be tonight, but he would be too easily recognized with it. He tossed it into the back seat and retrieved his small bag of food. Hesitating momentarily, Lucas looked around uneasily then walked resolutely off through the palmettos toward Myrtle Beach.

He had gone perhaps three miles when he felt it was safe enough to halt for a few minutes to rest. He sat on a fallen log and massaged the cramped muscles in the calves of his legs. His labored breath, visible in the cold night air, betrayed his presence, but at this distance from the car he felt safe.

"Boy, just a couple of miles and my legs are locking up. Life has been too easy lately. I ever get out of this I'm gonna have to get back in better shape," Lucas grumbled half aloud.

Stars were visible now through occasional breaks in the wind-driven cloud cover, but even then, there was scarcely light enough to see. For the past half-hour he had spent most of the time stumbling around, falling over broken limbs and assorted forest debris, clawing forward, gaining little headway. After tripping headlong over a fallen log, he slowly struggled to his feet. Common sense told him to curl up there by the log, spend the night, and go on tomorrow. After all, there was plenty of time before he was to meet Em, yet something in his heart urged him onward to be with her.

It took a moment for the sound to penetrate his tired mind. Dogs. Baying loudly, they followed his trail in the distance.

"Dammit. They're on my tail for sure!" Lucas muttered. Grabbing up his food sack, he dogtrotted, stumbling in the general direction of his destination.

South of Myrtle Beach
Palmetto Woods
Wednesday, January 13, 1954
7:42 P.M.

"Looks like that ol' boy pulled another fast one on you fellers. Don't think you people will ever learn. He's making complete fools of you." This time Tait directed his sarcasm at the state patrolmen who had allowed Mackley to escape at the bus station.

"Hell's bells, Sheriff, you oughter seen that crazy fool drive. Whipped around that station and hauled ass back the way he come then once he got to that bridge, spun that damn Chevy around and damn near caused me and Tyler to hit one another. Skeered the pure crap outta me."

South Carolina Highway Patrolman W.C. Tyler spoke up, "He got a head start on us goin' south and just plumb disappeared. Last

I seen him was when he was headin' back toward town. Fast as we was goin' there was no way we could turn around and catch him. No way was I gonna risk breakin' my neck drivin' like he was."

"Say he was going south? Then tell me, W.C., if he disappeared going south, then how in hell do you explain how his car's setting right here jist eight miles outta Myrtle Beach?"

"Beats me, Sheriff," W.C. admitted sheepishly, "but with them dogs of McQuail's, I'll lay odds we'll have him by sunup."

"Yeah. Sure," Tait muttered. He was cold and tired, and his bad leg was acting up. He didn't know why he kept on running for office each term. None of those people in Horry County appreciated what he did anyway. "Awright, W.C., he may have messed up leaving that coat." Turning to old man Fletch McQuail who was holding the leashes of four eager bloodhounds, Tait ordered, "Fletch, let them dogs get a good whiff then turn 'em loose. And Lieutenant," Tait added turning to Rogers, "I realize the Air Force thinks this is a military matter. But since we're in my backyard, if you agree, I'll take charge of this here search."

Rogers quickly concurred, agreeing to place his men under Tait's direction.

Tait was sixty-seven years old; he had been in law enforcement for most of his life, and he had been sheriff of Horry County for the past twenty-six years. His first wife had left him soon after he was elected to his first term, ostensibly because she didn't want one of his deputies to come to the door late some night and tell her that Earl Lee had been shot or, worse yet, killed. He had not been shot, but had torn the ligaments in his knee wrestling a drunk into submission six months after taking office. She took that as proof that he was doomed to be killed on duty, and no amount of persuasion could convince her otherwise. She didn't seem to understand that leaving would not make any difference in the least whether he lived or died or in what manner death would eventually occur.

Ludeen, his second wife, was more tolerant of his job. It was not that she was any less concerned for his safety, but she had adopted an easygoing attitude toward things beyond her control. As a result, she simply lived each day as the good Lord dictated.

The years had mellowed Earl Lee. From the firebrand he had been as a young deputy, his attitude toward law enforcement and people had moderated to the point where the law was no longer black or white but, more accurately, some shade of gray in between. That philosophy had obviously worked well because he had been re-elected a number of times.

Three Miles North
2055 hours

The baying dogs spurred his flight, urging him on without regard to stealth. Lucas forged ahead in the inky darkness, stumbling and struggling through the tangle of brush and deadfalls, impervious to the frigid cold. He had covered the better part of three miles since he had left the car at dusk, although it was difficult to accurately estimate the distance of the circuitous route. The sound of the dogs appeared closer, but then, sounds carried exceptionally well on still winter nights such as this. Even dampened by the roar of the surf from the nearby sea, their baying allowed him to easily distinguish individual bugling hounds.

With their muzzles tight to the frozen ground, the bloodhounds moved easily through the brush, steadily gaining on Lucas. Tait's men, confident in their pursuit, trotted along more slowly, depending on the dogs to hold the fugitive at bay once he was treed.

"By damn," Lucas muttered to himself with false bravado, "they ain't caught up with me yet!" The copse of scrub woods he was fleeing through was probably no more than a quarter of a mile wide. Since he was about midway between the beach and Highway 17, he should be able to reach the highway well before the dogs were on him. Once across the highway, it should be only a short distance to the Intracoastal Waterway. He needed more space in which to maneuver if he was to get away from the dogs. The narrow band of scrubby woods where he now found himself was made for Tait and his men to easily run him to ground.

As best as he could remember, west of the waterway there were immense, wild, and uninhabited tracts that were populated with thick vegetation, sprinkled throughout with expansive bogs and marshes. Once beyond the road, the inhospitable terrain would favor his ability to evade capture, and with a modicum of luck, he should be able to hide out for a day or so and then double back to near where he was now.

"Them damned dogs! Can't be more than a couple hundred yards behind me now. Damn you, Tait!"

Lucas stumbled from the woods into the partially water-filled ditch along Highway 17 and paused, orienting himself. *Now where the hell was that waterway?* Crossing the road, he raced across a small field to the west, his legs protesting each crucial stride. The baying of the dogs seemed to momentarily fade, or was it his imagination? No matter, he was getting his second wind. With terror surging through his body, he sprinted toward the waterway, a marathoner at the finish line. There! Ahead the glinting of light on water broke the darkness. Mackley skidded to a halt just short of the water and quickly scanned the shoreline along the canal but could see no bridges.

"Well, why should I be disappointed?" he grumbled. "With the kind of luck I been having even if there was a bridge, the damn thing woulda fell down the minute I stepped on it."

Looking over his shoulder, he saw the dogs loping across the road, their bodies silhouetted by the headlights of an approaching automobile and their shadows exaggerated in the glaring lights. With their bodies close to the ground, the hounds' baying spurred Lucas into action.

He looked fearfully at the forbidding murky waters of the canal then back at the racing dogs. Waiting no longer, he leaped as far as he could out into the waterway. The icy waters sucked the breath from his ravaged body as his feet touched the silt-layered bottom.

Tilting his body forward, he pushed upward and broke the surface of the dirty water a good twenty feet from the edge of the waterway. Spewing brackish water, he gratefully sucked in icy air. Slowing only long enough to find the opposite shore, Mackley swam noisily across the canal, driven by abject fear.

He crawled up the frozen bank and fell, rolling onto his back unable to go on. Wisps of mist curled from the canal's surface, the only betrayal of Lucas's passage. Overhead, a feathered cloud slipped across the moon, momentarily plunging the riverbank into darkness before sailing on its aimless journey across the winter sky, allowing the moon's ephemeral glow to return, pushing back his fears.

On the other side of the waterway, the lead hound reached the canal and stopped short, uncertain. The other dogs crowded around the leader whimpering impatiently for the men to arrive. "Bark, you no good bastards!" Mackley chastised the dogs. "Go ahead and jump in and freeze your goddamned asses off! Go ahead you danged fools!"

A thought struck him then. *Hey, I can't be more than a couple miles from that bridge near Murrells Inlet. Man! All I gotta do is head west, hit as much water as I can, throw them dogs off, then get back to that bridge and if I get lucky, back to my car.*

Waiting no longer, Mackley slogged ahead through the freezing, stagnant lowland waters. In his need to put as much distance between himself and the dogs, Lucas didn't bother to avoid any of the deeper pools, but plunged on single-mindedly due west as nearly as possible.

Was it exhaustion affecting his mind or were his pursuers falling farther behind?

9:31 P.M.

Deputy Sheriff Houston Babb commented, "Them dogs done got on his tail, Earl Lee! Man, just listen to 'em!"

Gene Varner added, "Better'n a good coon hunt, ain't it, boys?"

Tait sharply cut them off, saying, "This ain't no coon hunt, so all of you shut your mouths." Jabbing a finger at one of the men, he said, "You there, Houston, go over there on that beach, and Gene you get over to the highway. Rest of us will follow along behind them dogs. Now, get moving. I want this over before morning."

A change in the dogs' voices broadcasted that they were on a hot trail, indicating that it was only a matter of time before they ran their quarry to ground.

Suddenly pulling up short, Tait ordered the men to stop. "Hold the noise so I can hear!" he cautioned. Then, cocking his head to one side, he listened. The dogs were quiet and no longer running straight. Having lost the scent, they became confused and now were casting about, trying to relocate a mark.

"Hell fire! That boy has hit that danged river, and them stupid dogs of yours don't know what the hell to do." Tait growled, turning furiously to old man Fletch McQuail.

"Dang it, Sheriff, I didn't hire 'em out to track fish. They'll track anything on land to hell and back, but thet boy of yours done took to the water," Fletch retorted, defending his dogs. "Onl'est way we gonna pick him up agin is to git on the other side and try to find where he come outta the water."

"Goddammit, Fletch, I know that!" yelled Earl Lee, exasperated. "What I wanta know now is what has Gene been doing all this time. He shoulda seen Mackley when he crossed the highway. Guess there ain't no need to tramp through this damn jungle any longer. Let's git over to the highway and git down there where them dogs is."

Waccamaw River, South Carolina
Near Murrells Inlet
Wednesday, 13 January 1954
2205 hours

The Intracoastal Waterway, or as a portion of it is known, the Waccamaw River, extends along the coast of the Carolinas and Florida, along the Gulf States, sometimes flowing through existing streams and rivers. It is, therefore, a series of man-made canals connecting convenient streams. Slightly southwest of Myrtle Beach, the waterway and the Waccamaw River, a tributary of the Pee Dee, are the same. The Waccamaw flows entirely within the coastal plain between the larger Pee Dee and the Atlantic Ocean.

Westward from the Waccamaw to the Pee Dee and beyond, much of the area is low marshy land of the coastal plain, populated by alligators, water moccasins, and a variety of aquatic plants and animals. Huge bald cypress trees rise to magnificent heights of well over a hundred feet into the sky where they overshadow smaller tupelo gums and lowland hardwoods. Over the years, button bushes, willows, and other thick rooted bushes, small trees, and shrubs have trapped sediments to form hammocks isolated as small islands in the marshy fen. Roots of the cypresses protrude through the stagnant waters in the form of knees to obtain air denied them by the decaying vegetation of the bottom mud. It was this tenebrous area that drew Lucas.

"If I can fool ol' man Tait into thinking I'm gonna head on out into them swamps all the way to the Pee Dee, I may have a chance to turn toward Murrells Inlet. And if I do, I should be able to get my car back and skedaddle outta here before they know I'm gone. Gotta make him think I'm running at random," Lucas said through chattering teeth, trying to convince himself that escape was possible.

The cold had penetrated to the innermost core of his energy-sapped body, which was soaked from the long frigid swim across the Waccamaw. What little remained in his ravaged body was rapidly playing out as the night grew colder. Each slogging movement was agony to Lucas's spent muscles. Crawling from the muck onto one of the hammocks, he lay prone in the mud and debris, too far gone to continue. His hands ached from the cold, and every breath of the stagnant air tore at his raw throat.

Lying there, he forced his mind back to the image of Em dejectedly walking away, head bowed, toward the bus station only hours ago. "Please, God, let her be safe at home."

Pushing self-pity aside, he struggled to a sitting position. The air he exhaled hung like a shroud around his head, a sure indication of his position. Reaching into his pocket, he withdrew the remnants of the cinnamon roll he had saved. Although it was soggy from being immersed in the river, he crammed as much of the mushy mess into his mouth as he could, savoring the sodden morsels.

Temporarily refreshed, he muttered, "Gotta move. That old man's gonna be on my butt any minute now. Gotta get to the car before he figures out which way I'm going. I'm freezing. I gotta get to the car and warm up."

Laboriously, he got to his knees and, using a small willow as support, pulled himself up to stand on numb feet. Looking toward the sky, he projected the best direction by using the big dipper and North Star as guides. Choosing a heading, Lucas stepped back into the dank water and began the tortuous trek toward Murrells Inlet.

The clouds that were forming over the sea earlier now moved inland and closed up, enveloping Lucas in a darker night. The chilling misty rain that held off earlier now filtered through to the earth, making Lucas's progress through the morass even more difficult.

Time was lost. Only the instinct of the hunted had kept him moving. By now, his body and mind were nearing complete breakdown. *Oh just to lie down for a few moments*, he thought. Even the cold seemed more tolerable now. His hands were numb, but they no longer ached as before. Standing there in the vastness of the swamp, he sensed something was different. What was it? There was only silence.

The dogs were no longer baying!

The only sounds were muted dripping of the drizzle through trees and his tortured passage to Murrells Inlet. "Well, how about that? When did they stop?"

Unable to go any farther, Lucas sat on a rotting, fungus-covered log, laughing hysterically. "Thank you, Lord! Thank you!" he shouted. Tears of utter exhaustion ran down his mud-stained cheeks.

After a short respite, Lucas struggled to his feet and looked at his watch. "Twenty-two-thirty-nine hours. Ain't sure how much further I gotta go, or even how much longer I can last, but I sure can't stay here much longer, or they'll figure out what I'm trying to do."

East Bank of the Waccamaw River
Wednesday, January 13, 1954
9:53 P.M.

"Gene, take them men there, double time back, get them vehicles and bring 'em here. McQuail, give your truck keys to Gene. You wait here with them dogs," Tait directed, gesturing.

Twenty minutes later they pulled up at the Waccamaw River Bridge. Crossing over the bridge, the men quickly unloaded the dogs while Tait instructed McQuail to track down stream while the rest of the posse waited. A half-hour later, a scent was struck some 150 feet below where Mackley had crawled from the river.

While McQuail's dogs tracked along the stream nosing out Mackley's trail, Tait paced impatiently, fuming at the delay. A sudden change in the dogs' excited bugling signaled that a scent had been found. "Awright, men! Get after him, and dammit, don't lose him this time," Tait growled, aggravated by the multiple delays.

Within two hundred yards from where Mackley's spoor was recovered, the hounds stopped short, casting about unable to pick up the scent again.

"Double dammit!" shouted old man McQuail. "Them damned

dogs has lost him agin. They wasn't mine, I'd shoot every danged one uv 'em right through their worthless carcasses."

The sheriff looked at the waiting men. With their hands jammed in their pockets, they stomped around trying to coax a little feeling back into their extremities. They were wet, dirty, and tired.

Seeing their misery, Tait shrugged and said, "Hell, he'll still be around in this area come daylight. He sure ain't gonna git much rest, so we should be able to run him down then. All of you go on home and report back here at daylight in the morning. And, Lieutenant, we'll need you and your men here, too. Fletch, you bring them no-good dogs again. We probably gonna need 'em. Yeah, we got us one smart son out there."

Almost hope he gets away, thought Tait as the others loaded up and left.

Waccamaw River North of Murrells Inlet
Thursday, 14 January 1954
0245 hours

Lucas crouched quietly in the bushes near the bank of the Waccamaw River to wait and listen. The drizzly rain had slacked off, extinguishing the agonizing bite of its chill, and overhead the clouds were breaking up. Lucas had been there for about fifteen minutes without moving, patiently biding the time when he would attempt to cross back over the murky river. Finally, deciding it was safe to make his move, he slid down the steeply sloping clay bank and into the frigid waters. Gasping as the icy waters immersed his already chilled-to-the-bone body to the shoulders, he cautiously pushed away from the shore and dogpaddled into the mild current. Angling across, he aimed at a point near a large river birch about a hundred yards downstream.

As he swam sluggishly, the last remnants of strength rapidly dwindled, and his leaden arms and legs refused to function. Pausing for a moment he treaded water, attempting to estimate how much further it was to the other shore. A quick glance told him that he had not yet gained the midpoint of the waterway. Panicked now, he regretted having slowed at all. Better to continue until he gave out and drowned than to waste time in self-pity treading water.

A long fifteen minutes later, he painfully crawled from the river and, using the gnarled birch's exposed roots, climbed higher onto the riverbank. Sucking the winter air deep into his aching lungs and shaking uncontrollably from the cold, he continued, knowing that if he didn't keep moving he would either freeze to death or be quickly captured.

He removed his shoes and poured the muddy water from them. Placing them upside down where they could further drain, he then peeled his sodden socks from his numbed feet. Wringing the water from them, Lucas then put them back on and slipped into the wet brogans.

After carefully looking around for any lawmen Tait may have left behind, he moved east, trying to stay close to the more densely overgrown areas. With no early morning traffic yet to warn him, Lucas reached the highway before realizing where he was. Hunkered by the roadside, he blended in with the brush and shadows. From this vantage, he searched, trying to pick out some familiar landmark. Dawn was not far off.

Taking the chance that he was somewhere south of the beach road where the car had been left, he struggled to his feet, still not sure of where he was.

Bellying down on the shoulder of the road, Lucas snaked his way across the highway to the opposite side and into the ditch. Smiling, he thought, *I never dreamed that when I went through that obstacle course at Jackson I'd ever need or use the experience. Oh, Christ! I woulda been up that well-known creek if one of them big-assed trucks hadda come by while I was out there in the middle of that road. I can jist see me smashed flat like a snake in the summertime.* Again he smiled. *Too late to worry now, though, I guess.*

Overhead the sound of approaching airplanes broke the silence of the early dawn. Red navigation lights of what appeared to be a pair of single engine planes blinked, tracking the flight south along the coast. *Must be a couple of navy pilots heading for Charleston,* he mused. *Hope the boys at the site are on the ball an' picked them up. Funny I should be thinking about things like that. Hell, I ought to be worrying about finding my car and getting out of here.*

He loped along the edge of the woods for a quarter of a mile before finding the small road he was searching for. Dropping carefully to his hands and knees, he tried to determine if it had had travelers recently. There appeared to be several sets of tire tracks, but on second thought, that was to be expected. After all, the Air Force and half the lawmen in Horry County, South Carolina, had been out since late yesterday afternoon and night looking for him.

"Well, here goes nothing." For the first time he was feeling optimistic about his chances of escaping. "Now if that peckerwood sheriff forgot to leave a guard at the car, I'll have it made. I'm not taking any chances, though," he told himself.

When he figured that he was within 150 feet or so from where he remembered driving off into the palmettos, he slowed and cautiously crept closer through the underbrush.

He froze. Somewhere ahead someone coughed. "Dumb ass. Just told me what I needed to know."

Crawling ever so slowly now, Lucas homed in on the guard. There! The glow of a cigarette as the guard greedily sucked smoke into his lungs and then blew it out in a long contented sigh. Lucas could smell the pungent exhaled smoke drifting to where he lay prone, scanning ahead. "Yep, there was the old Chevy. And yeah, I can make that dumb guard out now."

The deputy was leaning against the left front fender of the vehicle, appearing to gaze leisurely off toward Highway 17, lost in the narcotizing effects of the cigarette. Lucas lay motionless until he could get his bearings, then, worming toward the beach road, he eased along its edge toward the ocean well beyond the car, hoping the roar of the surf would muffle the sounds of his movements.

Once past the point where the car had been driven into the brush, Lucas snaked north, parallel to the shore until he was even with the right side of the car. He approached from the ocean, moving short distances at a time before stopping to listen. Satisfied that he had gone undetected, he slowly went to a crouching position and remained stationary, watching for any hint of discovery. The guard was still there, lost in his own little world. Lucas crept almost imperceptibly toward the rear of the car.

A sudden noise stopped him dead still. The guard had shifted his weight on the fender with the vehicle groaning in protest.

Lucas was now less than five feet from the unsuspecting deputy, hidden against the darkness of the undergrowth. *If he turns now, I'm screwed*, thought Lucas, grinning.

Slowly. Four feet. Three feet.

"Hey," Lucas softly whispered.

Startled, Deputy Gene Varner whirled, dropping the cigarette, and grabbed for his gun. "Whut th …"

Lucas hit him hard on the point of the chin before he could finish, and Varner dropped to the ground, stunned. Lucas was on him in an instant, flipping the addled deputy on his belly, pulling the pistol from its holster and tossing it to one side.

"Just keep your drawers outta your crack and behave yourself and I won't hurt you," Lucas told him. "Understand?"

"The hell with you, you bastard," Gene responded, resentfully. "Just you wait till the sheriff gets a hold of you."

"Yeah, yeah, you're scaring me to death. Now, like I told you. Shut up!"

Lucas removed the deputy's handcuffs from his belt and dragged him to a small pine tree then forced him to reach around it. After snapping the cuffs on so the deputy was securely bound to the tree, Lucas stepped back with his hands on his hips to survey his handiwork.

Varner continued cursing and elicited a stern warning.

Lucas held him off. "One more word outta you, and not only

am I gonna kick some ass, but I'm gonna gag you with one of my dirty socks. Now, what'll it be? Your choice," the exhausted airman growled sharply.

Varmer's only response was a glower in Lucas's direction.

Stripping the wet shirt off, Lucas replaced it with the fatigue shirt left behind the afternoon before. Then sliding behind the wheel, he reached to switch the ignition on.

"Goddamn you, Tait!" he exploded, seeing the ignition key was gone. "You bastard! You no good bastard!"

Jumping out of the car, Lucas hurried to the shackled deputy and grabbed him by the front of the shirt, snarling, "You lie to me and I'm gonna kick your balls so far up you, you'll talk soprano for the rest of your natural life. I'm tired, and cold, an' I'm pissed, so damn you, don't try me! Where the hell are my keys? Tell me and damn you, don't you lie to me!"

The intimidated Varner considered Lucas's rage and mumbled, "I swear to God, Tait took 'em. Figured you might sneak back here, so he took your keys and left me on guard. I'm telling the truth, I swear to God."

Lucas patted the man's pockets and, pushing him against the sapling, replied with satisfaction, "Awright, I guess you're telling me straight. But if you ain't, I'll get my chance at you eventually, and you can bank on it."

Getting back into the car, Lucas reached under the dash, felt around and pulled two wires loose. Twisting the ends together he stepped on the starter. The engine turned over a couple of times, sputtered, caught, and died. He pulled the choke all the way out, pumped the gas pedal, and depressed the starter again. A pall of blue smoke erupted from the tailpipe as the car coughed to life, finally settling down to a purring, throaty rumble.

Pleased with the turn of events, Lucas smiled and backed out then turned to pull onto Highway 17.

South of Myrtle Beach

Palmetto Woods
Thursday, January 14, 1954
5:30 A.M.

"You stupid idiot!" Tait raged. "I ought to leave you hand-cuffed to that tree 'til hell freezes over! I told you to stay awake and watch out for that slick son of a bitch, and here you let him sneak right up on you and knock you on your tail, take your gun away from you and handcuff you to a tree with your own cuffs."

Varner ducked his head and whined pleadingly, "But Sheriff, I was, uh, watching and he slipped up on me from the beach, and..."

"Goddammit! Varner, don't you have any sense at all in that rock you call a head? You think he was gonna walk right up to you and introduce hisself? He knew you'd be too damned dumb to be watching in all directions. You dumb turd, I hope you enjoyed them cigarettes because one more foul-up and you're out! You understand me?" His anger spent, Earl Lee turned away from Gene, having the good sense to humble a man only so much.

"Now what do we know?" The sheriff answered his own question, "He left here in his car after apparently hot wiring it." Tait held up Lucas's car keys. "And dumbass over there don't know which way in hell he went when he got to the highway. That right, Gene?"

"Yeah. Guess I was too busy trying to git loose from that tree," the hangdog deputy mumbled.

Tait ignored his response and said instead, "Guessing as to the time it woulda taken for him to slog three miles or so south through that mud and water, swim the river and then slip upon Varner here, I figure he has about two to three hours on us. Question is which way did he go? My guess is he's somewhere in the Myrtle Beach area. He ain't gonna leave that little ol' gal of his without telling her goodbye. Agreed?"

Each deputy nodded his assent. After listening to the berating Tait gave Varner, none of the others were going to dare to dispute the sheriff's deductions.

CHAPTER 39

Radar Team 1 Quarters
Friday, 15 January 1954
1017 hours

Several airmen, among them Charlie and JJ, lazed around in the main bay of the stockade barracks playing cards, napping, or discussing the latest events concerning the hunt for Lucas Mackley. Although rumors had floated around for several days, few of the men figured things would have gotten out of hand enough for him to run. When the news broke, no one believed any of the three airmen was guilty of such a heinous crime, but then Mackley ran, planting seeds of doubt and leaving the team split on the question of guilt.

Pretending to show concern, Charlie asked, "Has anyone heard if the law's caught his ass yet?"

One of the poker players looked hard at Charlie before replying. "Don't think so, at least not yet. Heard though, that Emily Johnson was seen getting off the bus downtown late in the afternoon a few days ago. Somebody said they took her to Conway to Tait's office and questioned her. Kept her there until Miz Johnson went over and took her home. Said she was crying and looked pretty worn out."

"Man I don't doubt that a bit," someone added, shaking his head negatively. I guess them two been through a hell of a time at that. Can't imagine Lucas running through those swamps out there, especially in the winter. Wonder that he ain't frozen to death by now."

Phelps was sprawled on his bunk with his eyes closed. Rising up to lean on one elbow, he commented, "Don't know if I coulda held out this long myself running like he had to do. I been down in some of that country, and let me tell you that's some mean territory out there, grown over in bushes and vines like it is."

"JJ, dumb as you are, they woulda caught you the first day, and you know it," said Charlie acrimoniously. "Matter of fact you woulda been too scared to run in the first place, so that woulda ended that."

Ignoring the sarcasm, Phelps said, "Well, I feel sorry for old Lucas, but him taking off like he did makes me wonder if he ain't guilty after all." The others failed to see the thin smile touching JJ's lips.

"Well, it's just a matter of time now before he gets caught anyway. Fool's gotta be guilty or he wouldn't run like he done," offered one of the other airmen. "Ask me, I think it was a damned fool thing to do."

"Hell, from what you told him, Kesterman, you probably scared him into taking off like he did. Any one of us woulda done the same thing," countered JJ, glowering at Charlie.

"You got that right," Anderson agreed. "Nobody in his right mind would have let them rednecks take him in. Best thing old Mackley can do is slip back, if he can and turn himself into Captain Cook."

"I doubt he could do that," the team medic, George Williams, said. "Bet they got this place locked up tight as Betty Hutchin's underpants. Ain't that about right, Charlie?"

"Ain't what right?" asked Charlie.

"Ol' Betty's drawers," replied Williams.

"Look, you useless bastard," responded Charlie, eyes flashing angrily. "Keep your mouth shut and don't smart off about my girl."

Williams laughed and shot an obscene gesture toward Kesterman.

Sal Pasanski looked in at that moment. His fatigue sleeves were rolled up past the elbows, and soapsuds covered his hands from washing the cook's pots and pans. "Kesterman, that girl Mackley been messing with sent word she wants to see youse."

"Yeah? Why'd she go to you instead of coming directly to me?"

Stung by Kesterman's comment, Pasanski acidly replied, "Don't make no difference now, does it? Long as youse got the word. But for your information, I seen her at Claude's last night and told her I would tell youse she needed to see you right away—that it was very important. Now youse has been told," he replied stalking out without waiting for a response.

"Looks like everybody is sore-assed over what's happening," observed Anderson. "Even ol' Sal ain't his usual cheerful, annoying self tonight."

Charlie and JJ exchanged looks, neither wanting to be the first to leave. Finally, both got up and went outside.

Shaw AFB, South Carolina, 707th AC&W Sq
Friday, 15 January 1954
1110 hours

Lieutenant Colonel Van Vleet, Captain Cook, Lieutenant Rodgers, and Master Sergeant Jackson were discussing how the progress of the search for the fugitive airman, Staff Sergeant Lucas Mackley, was proceeding. Sheriff Earl Lee Tait had been asked to participate but declined, offering the excuse that he was out of his jurisdiction, when in reality he didn't want to be hampered by the red tape of military protocol. His method was to get right to the crux of the problem as quickly as possible, hunt for leads where he could find them, and get on with the search.

Colonel Van Vleet looked at the AP officer. "Lieutenant, since you are apparently in charge of this manhunt, just exactly what are your plans for apprehending Mackley? And be detailed and specific."

Lieutenant Rodgers knew he was on the spot for failing to capture Mackley. The earlier bravado he had shown when dealing with Mrs. Johnson and Sheriff Tait faltered as he stammered, "Well..., sir, I...I guess my men and I'll go back to Myrtle Beach and check with the sheriff then play it by ear from there. As you know, Colonel, I have to be careful since this is essentially a civilian matter now with these local murders tied in. We can help but really only with their permission. And also, sir, before I do anything, it'll be necessary to report to my CO."

Scared jerk, afraid of his shadow, thought Van Vleet. "Cook, Mackley is your man. You got anything to say?"

Cook considered for a moment how to respond before replying, then carefully phrasing his answer, he said, "Yes, sir. I sure do. First off, I don't think for a minute the man is guilty of anything except for running away and possibly being AWOL. In the second place, that ass of a six-week wonder," he indicated Rodgers, "comes..."

"That's enough of that kind of talk, Captain!" Van Vleet cautioned, even though he held the same opinion.

"Yessir," Cook continued. "As I was saying, Lieutenant Rodgers was largely responsible for scaring Sergeant Mackley into running in the first place. This wouldn't have happened had he handled the situation more carefully."

Lieutenant Rodgers opened his mouth to protest, but Van Vleet held his hand up to indicate it would be wise for him to remain silent.

"Proceed, Captain Cook. You got me curious now."

Cook continued, "Lieutenant Rodgers came to my orderly room, and in the presence of several of my personnel proceeded to demand the where-abouts of Mackley and stated what he wanted him for. Old Sheriff Tait was with him and did attempt to ameliorate things but with little success. It was necessary, obviously, that I tell the lieutenant where Sergeant Mackley was. However, because it was known well in advance that he was wanted, Mackley was gone by the time the sheriff and APs arrived at the radar site. This could have been avoided had the lieutenant contacted me first, and I would have had Sergeant Mackley available. Lieutenant Rodgers could have then discretely arrested him."

"That the way it happened, Lieutenant?" Van Vleet's eyes pierced Rodgers.

Regaining some composure, Rogers answered in a quavering voice, "Yes, sir."

"And now, Captain, comes the big question." The colonel turned his attention back to Cook.

Although he pretty well knew the question, Cook had to ask anyway. "Sir, what would that question be?"

"Don't try to con an old pro, Captain. You know damned well what question. Who the hell warned Mackley?"

"Colonel, that I truly don't know. I have a feeling, though, that almost any one of the men would have done it if given the opportunity. That includes everyone from our permanent KP all the way to the Top here." Motioning to Jackson, he continued, "That about right, Sergeant?"

The NCO nodded, "Yes, sir. I'd say so, Captain."

"So you see, Colonel, I doubt we'd be able to find out who it was even if we looked the rest of the year. That doesn't seem to me to be a very high priority now. The arrest of Mackley does."

"Guess you're probably right, Captain," agreed the colonel. "Sergeant Jackson, you got anything to add before we break this little confab up and let the lieutenant get back to the beach?"

"No, sir, except to suggest that, since he has already been working with the sheriff, Lieutenant Rodgers leave at once and report to Sheriff Tait when he gets to Conway. It might be helpful also, sir, if you would call Tait and assure him that the lieutenant will be most happy to cooperate with him in every way."

"Good idea, Sergeant. Now, if there is nothing else…" Van Vleet paused, letting the unasked question hang. Then, hearing no responses, he curtly snapped, "Thank you, gentlemen. Dismissed!"

Outside in the team jeep, Sergeant Jackson turned to Cook as he cranked the vehicle. "Captain, you sorta pushed the colonel just a bit in there, didn't you?"

Cook spat onto the pavement beside the jeep. "Yeah, the old codger needed to be shoved just a little. This whole mess needs clearing up before it gets any farther out of hand. That bunch of crazies ever catches up with Mackley, they may well panic and kill him, or he may end up killing one of them. Just hope old Tait can keep things in hand."

CHAPTER 40

Horry County Sheriff's Office
Conway, South Carolina
Thursday, January 14, 1954
6:15 P.M.

"I got me a strong feeling in my gut that there boy's gonna show up either close around that radar site, that old guard house where them men are staying, that Johnson girl's place, or maybe here around Conway. I ain't so positive about Conway, though, because I don't think he has any ties or reasons to be here. I believe he was here before only by chance. I believe them two was only passing through, maybe on the way to Arkansas. I understand that's where he comes from," Sheriff Tait told his deputies. "Our job then is to try to outguess him or, with our thin forces, try to cover all likely places where he is apt to show."

"But look, Sheriff, there ain't but four or five of us available to help, not counting you. You're talking about at least three possible places, maybe four he could show. So agin, how do we cover all them places twenty-four hours a day for no telling how long?" Varner asked, his whiney voice betraying his misgivings.

Under Sheriff Birdie Cox added in agreement, "Gene's right,

Earl Lee. We have to spend that much time hunting for him, ain't no way we gonna be able to do it and take care of our other duties at the same time. What happens if we have to investigate a wreck or work a fire or all sorts of things that might happen? We ain't got the men to spare to hunt that boy."

Wishing he hadn't overstepped his place, Gene said, "Tell you what, Sheriff, I need the job and I do respect you, but I gotta question why we have to do this. Mackley was supposed to have killed that feller in Mississippi, so why do we have to string ourselves out so thin? Seems to me them folks in the Air Force oughta be huntin' him, not us."

"Gene, you know good and well they don't have jurisdiction in this unless we give it to them. And I damned well ain't gonna do that. Hell, men, that lieutenant and them two flunkies of his are liable to shoot that boy, if by some miracle they do stumble onto him. And I just can't let that happen."

Gene continued fruitlessly arguing with Tait. "No matter, Earl Lee, to me they're the ones oughta get the crappy details in this hunt. We could give support, but catching him is their job as I see it."

"You're more than likely right there, Gene," responded Tait. "But I still got to see one of us is with them so they don't mess things up. Now, Birdie, work me out a schedule, I'll look it over and we'll git on with catching this guy." As Tait rose to leave, he added, "I want that list when I get back in about an hour and a half."

Before he could leave, though, Kate called from the outer office, saying, "Earl Lee. Sheldon Lentz is on the phone. Can you take it?"

6:25 P.M.

Tait left his office and drove directly to Emily's house. Arriving about twenty-five minutes later, he parked his unmarked patrol car and walked purposefully to the front door. Instead of punching the bell, Tait rapped on the weathered door facing. Movement within the house told him someone was home.

Emily came to the door and opened it, waiting for Tait to speak. Tait saw the weariness in the girl's eyes and in the way she tried to appear unafraid. *That girl is jist about done in,* he thought, *so I better make this as easy as I can.*

As kindly as the gruff old sheriff could, he said to the girl, "Emily, I don't want to do this, but believe me, this is something I gotta do. You want to, you can have your momma here with us."

The concern building in the girl's eyes disturbed Tait, and he quickly set about allaying her fears, saying soothingly, "Now, girl, it ain't what you're thinking. Far as I know, that boy is safe. Doubt, though, that he's exactly happy right about now. Matter of fact, way he's been running, he's gotta be about to the end of his endurance."

Giving the sheriff a sad little smile, Emily responded, "Thank you, Mr. Tait. I've been worried to death about him. So much I just don't know what to do any more. All I can think about is him out there cold and hungry and hiding."

Tait stopped her. "That's what we need to talk about. What can we do to git him outta this situation?" Tait didn't intend this to be a question. He was telling the girl gently he intended to eventually capture Lucas but that his job would be easier and that the outcome would be better for Lucas if she helped them.

"Mr. Tait, I know what you want. You want me to tell you where he is, but I don't know. I imagine you already know the last time I saw him was a couple days ago at the bus station in Murrells Inlet." Emily deliberately omitted telling him of her plan to meet Lucas later. So, in her mind she was not actually lying to Tait because at the moment, she really didn't know where he was.

"Okay, Em, I'll take your word that you don't know, but it would help that boy if you find out and let me know," said Earl Lee. "Now, if you'll excuse me, I gotta get going. Tell your momma I asked about her."

Once outside in his car, Tait sat for a few minutes worrying over all of the things that had occurred over the past few days. Had this been a routine day, Earl Lee would have been at the Bluefish tanking up on coffee, listening to Varner or one of the other deputies grousing, or just plain taking it easy. This day, though, had caught him up in a mood as dreary as the cold winter day outside. The facts necessary to clear up the crime were elusive as a willow-o-the-wisp while the threads tying them to the killer or killers remained nebulous, much like a forgotten name on the tip of one's tongue. The dots in the puzzle were there begging to be joined, but so far, Tait had been unsuccessful in drawing the finished lines.

Emily's tortured, hollow eyes tore at his mind. *That little gal probably don't know exactly where that boy is*, he thought. *But one thing's for sure: Her and him got somethin' in mind where she'll git up with him sooner or later. And I'd bet my left nut it'll be pretty soon now.*

Tait sat a moment longer, pondering over the puzzle then, taking the radio mike from its holder on the dash, keyed it. When Kate responded, he said, "I need you to do me a favor. See if you can git up with Weldon, and ask him if he can meet me in the office. I know it's past his working hours, but I need to talk with him."

Kate replied, "I'll see what I can do for you, Earl Lee. When do you expect to be back, and do you need me to stay here?"

"I should be there in about another twenty minutes or so, and no, there ain't no need for you to stay. If you can't find Jim, just leave me a note."

Tait arrived back at the office just after Kate had left. Her neatly printed note indicated she was unsuccessful in locating Chief Weldon. Tait sighed and reached for the telephone.

8:45 P.M.

"Dammit, Earl Lee, you sly old rascal, I guess you know I wouldn't do this for just anybody."

Weldon grinned and accepted Tait's outstretched hand. "I guess you know I could've been home with Momma enjoying a good steak and all the trimmings right now if I hadn't answered that danged phone."

Jim had pushed the stack of overdue reports to the side of his desk, got up, yawned and then reached for his keys. As his hand encircled the door knob, the telephone rang, startling him into a nervous jump. Retracing his steps, Weldon knew before picking up the receiver that Earl Lee was calling him. Hunting for an excuse not to answer, he paused sighing, then resignedly answered, "Jim Weldon."

After dialing, Tait held the phone and listened for the ring at the other end of the line, imagining Weldon sitting at his desk, leaning back and longing to go home for the day. Weldon's voice sounded distant, reluctant, and Tait hesitated before speaking, hoping Jim had not noticed. Finally, in response to Tait's unusual request, Weldon replied, "Give me about twenty minutes to get over there," and without waiting for a response, dropped the receiver with a click in its cradle.

"I know, I know, Jim, and I appreciate you coming. Now c'mon and we'll go down to the Bluefish and I'll buy your supper, on Horry County of course, but you know I can't take Momma's place." Tait laughed, feigning contriteness.

After they'd finished eating, Earl Lee ordered more coffee and waited while the tired waitress brought the pot over, sloshing the strong black liquid into their half-empty mugs. As she sauntered away, Jim followed her with his eyes, eliciting a tired comment from Tait, "Now, now, Jim, keep your mind on business. You know that worn out ol' gal ain't Momma."

"Piss on you, Earl Lee," Weldon responded jovially as he reached for his coffee mug. Taking a healthy slug of the hot coffee, he grimaced at the bitter taste and plopped the mug back down.

Seeing Jim's reaction, Tait shoved his own mug aside and said,

"Now that I just broke my budget feeding your tapeworm, I'll tell you why I wanted to see you. First off, I put a twenty-four-hour surveillance out for Mackley, and also, I just got back from Myrtle Beach where I talked to the Johnson girl. I hope that by keeping an eye on her and watching out for Mackley and putting a tail on them two friends of his, we can wind this mess up for both of us before too much longer."

"Know what you mean, Earl Lee. Except for that one running, don't look like there's been any breaks at all in these killings."

"Well, there is one bit of news, Jim."

"What's that?" Weldon asked, hoping it was for once good news.

"You remember the Lentz girl from Myrtle Beach?"

"Yeah, that the one that was going out with that airman, Phelps? What about her? Oh hell! You didn't find her dead, did you? Damn! That's all we need," Weldon grumbled, slamming his fist on the table. From behind the cash register, the tired waitress looked up, shrugged, and went back to her daydreaming.

"Naw. This is good news for once. Got a call from her father jist before I went to see the Johnson girl this afternoon. Said Amy had a fight with Phelps and run off to Orangeburg with an old boyfriend. Apparently got to thinking what she had done and got scared and after a few days took off from him and hitchhiked home. Lentz was somewhat pissed at her but seemed damned happy that she was back home safe and sound. Apologized for the trouble she caused everybody."

"I'm glad to hear that, Earl Lee. Figured she would surely turn up like them others," Weldon responded, visibly relieved.

"I will tell you this, Jim. I got some strong suspicions of who killed that Moorland woman down at Lake City, but I can't quite put everything together no matter how much I gnaw on it. I don't want to prejudice your thinking, but I still believe all of them killings are related," said Tait, hoping he was finally on the right track. "I still can't rule out Kesterman and Phelps even though that crazy kid, Mackley, took off like he done."

"I think you're right about them being tied together, but I'll not mess with your reasoning by asking who you think killed Sarah Moorland."

Claude's
Friday, January 15, 1954
6:57 P.M.

Emily had been in Claude's since shortly after she'd gotten home from school earlier that afternoon. Mrs. Johnson hadn't been very pleased that she was gone but gave in as a last resort when she realized the young woman intended to defy her and go anyway. Emily didn't want to disobey her mother, but she knew that it was necessary to see Charlie to get his help if she was going to be able to go to Lucas on time.

Noticing that Claude eyed her suspiciously, she asked for a coke and nursed it uneasily, knowing that she, a seventeen-year-old, should not be in a beer joint. No matter, she had to see Charlie, and this was the only way she could. So, the lonely girl waited there for Charlie to show.

Every now and then Claude would look over at the girl and was once or twice tempted to say something to her but each time looked away when Emily returned his stare. Finally, Claude breathed in deeply and exhaled audibly before purposefully coming from around the counter to the booth where Em sat forlornly.

"Emily, can I sit down here with you for a minute?" he asked, uncharacteristically meek. "I know it's none of my business, but it looks like you could use a friend."

Emily looked up at Claude's weathered face and then silently bowed her head again as though the weight of the world rested on her shoulders.

"Look, I've heard some of whut's going on with you and that boy Lucas, so you wanta talk about it?" he asked, placing a beefy hand on her frail shoulder.

Emily raised her head and stared unseeingly, on the verge of tears. "No, Mr. Claude. There's nothing to talk about," she replied, her heart breaking.

Claude persisted. "Now look, little girl, there's something going on with that boy and you. I've heard plenty of talk about how he's supposed to be messed up in them deaths around here and even that one back there in Mississippi. I'll tell you this much, I ain't knowed Mackley very long. But I know this for certain. He ain't never killed nobody, no matter what that lieutenant from Shaw said the other day. I don't know why he felt he had to take off like that, but it happened and that can't be helped now."

Emily looked up and murmured softly, "Thank you, Mr. Claude. You're about the only one, except me, that thinks he's not done anything. Why, Mr. Claude, even Momma is convinced he's guilty. Seems like the whole world's against him."

"Now, now, honey. Take it easy. Things will work out awright. What we gotta do is figure out how we can help him." Claude paused, thinking. "Now I ain't gonna ask you where he is. I bet you know, but I won't put you on the spot to where you have to lie. But if you could, git word to him, then let him know I'll do what I can to help him git outta this mess."

Tears flooded down Emily's cheeks. Claude slipped out of his side of the booth and moved to sit next to her, placing his arm around her shoulder. "Please don't cry, Em. I promise, we're gonna git him outta this. I promise you. Okay?"

A middle-aged couple came in accompanied by a blast of cold air and sat at a nearby table. The man was not tall but appeared to dominate the room. His graying hair, cut short, emphasized the dark blotches that covered his swarthy face. The large hands resting nervously on the table supported short stubby fingers that made the hands seem fat and out of proportion to his short forearms. The woman, in contrast, small and mousy, had hair falling limply against a drawn face. She wore no makeup. The man grew increasingly impatient as they waited, staring toward Claude and

Em. His patience exhausted, the man started to speak, but the woman shushed him. Ignoring them, Claude continued holding Em and spoke softly to her as she sobbed her heart out.

The man finally lost all semblance of patience and called gruffly, "Hey, You! You over there! You in the restaurant business, or are you gonna sit over there all night putting the make on that there little girl."

Claude's 210-pound body exploded from the booth, his demeanor changing from a solicitous, fatherly figure to one of rage. Grabbing the man by the front of the jacket, he dragged him from the table. Getting a firmer grip on the back of the man's collar and belt, Beck propelled him toward the door.

Charlie Kesterman, arriving seconds earlier in his gold Chevy convertible, pulled the door outward and agilely stepped aside in time to narrowly avoid colliding with the man hurtling toward him. The man hit face-first, skidding on the frozen gravel. Rolling over, he painfully sat up with a baffled look on his bloody face.

Jabbing a meaty finger in his direction, Claude said matter-of-factly, "I don't think I need your business."

The man's terrified wife stood transfixed, mouth agape. Turning toward the awe-struck woman, Claude spoke gently, "Ma'am, I expect it's best that you join that slob out there." Claude indicated her husband sprawled in the parking lot.

Equally astonished, Charlie looked at Claude. "What the devil did you do that for? Man, if I hadn't opened that door when I did, you would have throwed that fellow clean through it."

"Damned right I woulda!" said Claude and then, turning toward Emily, he gentled his voice again and said, "Pardon me, Em. He opened his dirty mouth at the wrong time. Now. Whatcha need, Charlie?"

"Gimme a regular barbeque and a long neck Pabst. I'll be over there with Emily. That is, if she don't mind." Going over to where Em was sitting, Charlie slid into the booth across from her and asked, "How you doing, kid? Or is that a stupid question under the circumstances?"

"I think you can guess, Charlie," she quietly replied. "How about you? You doing all right?"

"Yeah, guess so." Without further preamble Charlie got right to the reason he was there. "Pasanski said you told him you needed to see me. So, here I am."

"Thanks, Charlie. Lucas said that I should get in touch with you and that you'd help me get to the radar station so I could go to the place where I'm gonna meet him."

"Whoa! Now wait a minute! I don't know about that. Ol' Lucas done got hisself in deep doodoo, and I ain't so sure I want in there with him. If he's gonna be anywhere near the station, I don't want to know about it. I don't want to be connected with him in any way while the law's after him."

"But, Charlie, you're his best friend, and if it was you needing help, you know he'd do what he could for you. He wouldn't even think twice if you was in his place."

"Well, hell, Em, that's just it, I ain't in his place."

Distraught, Emily pleaded, "You won't be in any trouble. All you need to do is take me near the radar site and let me out where I tell you. If you see anyone following us, you can bring me right back home. Please?" Em had thought she never would beg, but now she was pleading with Charlie with all her heart.

They sat without talking, studying each other. Em was sure he would refuse to help her. Charlie, methodically chewing the sandwich, wondered if he was getting himself into trouble.

They sat there, two uncomfortable people, waiting for the other to speak. Charlie mulled over what Emily had asked, washed the last of his barbeque sandwich down with a swig of beer, and licked his fingers. "Okay, okay," he finally said. "But the minute things start to go sour, I'm outta there. I ain't gonna get my tail in no sling for nobody. You understand?"

Relief flooded Em's face. "Yes, I understand. You won't get into any trouble, I promise," she assured him. "And thanks, Charlie."

Radar Team 1 Quarters
2043 hours

The brand new, gold Chevrolet convertible cruised smoothly into the turn that led to the parking lot of the compound. Charlie Kesterman selected a spot near the entrance of the building but far enough away that the chance of someone bumping his car with a carelessly opened door would be less likely. He sat there pondering the events that had occurred over the past few hours. The Air Police, Sheriff's Department of Horry County, and most of the local authorities were hunting Lucas Mackley down, and he didn't want to get involved in any way that might implicate him in any of the trouble surrounding Mackley.

His present concern, however, was that he'd stupidly promised Emily he would help her get to Mackley. For the life of him, he didn't understand why he had agreed to do such a dumb thing and get involved with her problems. He wanted to stay as far removed from that mess as possible. He rubbed his palm against the scar on his cheek in deep thought. *Damn*, he wondered, *why didn't the silly little bitch hook JJ into taking her wherever in hell she wanted to go? I guess I could back out. Don't a man ever learn?*

Still grumbling to himself, Kesterman entered the makeshift barracks and went immediately to the room he shared with Mackley and Anderson. He sat on his bunk, removed his shoes, then lay back with hands beneath his head to stare at the unpainted wooden ceiling. *I got no choice,* he considered. *I guess I can dump her off at the site, then get out of there as quick as I can, and then hope no one sees me with her.*

His mind made up, Charlie rolled over on his side and, within a few minutes, was snoring loudly.

210 Oceanview
Myrtle Beach, South Carolina
Saturday, January 16, 1954

8:16 P.M.

"Momma, I've gotta talk with you."

Eula Johnson had been dreading this moment for days. Every waking moment she worried about it, and at night after she went to bed, sleep eluded her. She knew the life she now lived was about to change, and the change was certain to be one she didn't want. She also rationalized that time didn't stand still and whether or not things were good, one had to accept them and go on living as best they could. She had prayed that when that time came, she would be strong enough to handle whatever happened.

"Come here, baby. I know you've had something on your mind lately. Just don't know for sure what it is. You been out late at night, and a couple nights ago you didn't even bother coming home at all. I was worried to death about you, child." Eula Johnson didn't mean to fuss, but her words were cutting through Em's heart nevertheless. Sensing that Emily was begging for help, she softened her tone, saying, "Honey, I'm sorry. It's just I been worried sick about you."

"I'm sorry, too, Momma. I don't mean to hurt you and make you worry, but you're the only one I can turn to. Please, Momma, please help me," she implored, barely able to speak.

"Oh, honey, come here. Of course I'll help you if I can. You should know that."

"I know, Momma." Em sniffled the words, fighting to keep from crying. "It's about Lucas. He's in trouble. Real bad trouble."

"I know all about it, Em. Earl Lee Tait come by when you didn't come home the other night and told me about Lucas. Now, tell me how you're mixed up in this. I know you're into something. I don't know what it is, but to help you I have to know what it is. Before you do though, Em, I want you to know that I don't believe that boy killed that fellow down there in Mississippi either."

"Momma, I love you. You don't know how much I wanted you to say that," the girl smiled, "but it's worse than that."

Really concerned now, Mrs. Johnson frowned and interrupted. "What do you mean, Em? What can be worse than this? Ain't what trouble Lucas is in about as bad as things can get?"

Emily shook her head, breathed in deeply and, drawing herself upright, said haltingly, "Momma, this is hard for me to say, and it'll be hard for you to hear. I don't want to hurt you, but you gotta know, and sooner or later you will. There's more than just me and Lucas involved. Me and him are gonna have a baby."

Eula Johnson slowly got up from the couch and wrapped her arms about her daughter, holding her closely as she had done when Em was an infant. Both women were crying, one in relief that the secret had been revealed and the other in the love held for her child.

Finally, Eula released Emily and held her at arm's length. Smiling tenderly for the first time in a long time, she said, "Em, we'll see this through together. And, honey, things have a way of working out. And they will for you and Lucas, you'll see."

CHAPTER 41

Horry County, South Carolina
Highway 501 Outside of Conway
Thursday, 14 January 1954
0743 hours

One would have had to be looking for the car to see it since it was well hidden just off the highway, blending with a stand of low scrub trees and brush.

Lucas retraced the route he and Em had taken a few days earlier on their way back to Myrtle Beach. He'd had little difficulty finding the logging road where the two had slipped away from the APs that night before returning to Conway. It was risky to hide in the same place as before, but on the other hand, it seemed neither the military nor the local authorities would think to look there. It was a calculated risk he was willing to take for the chance of a few more hours of freedom, of the opportunity to get back to Em and, if luck held, to get out of South Carolina. He also didn't believe they would think him stupid enough to hide in the same place twice in such a short period of time. Anyway, he had just about gone as far as possible. Rest and sleep, at least a couple of hours, before going on had become necessary.

Walking back to the main highway, he attempted to replace the bent over brush and shrubs to their original positions, and to scatter pine needles over his tire tracks. He looked at his handiwork and, once satisfied, returned to the car and climbed in.

Dame Fortune had smiled on him, allowing his narrow escape from almost certain capture near Murrells Inlet, and not only that; through the negligence of the deputy sheriff, he was able to recover the Chevy. Now, getting back to the woods near the radar site undetected to meet Em presented the next obstacle. A lot depended on whether or not Em could persuade Charlie or JJ to help her get to the planned rendezvous site, or if one of them was unwilling to take her, would Sergeant Jackson? No matter how careful they were it would be a close call. He knew he and Emily would have to depend on one of the three, but deep inside he was worried about being forced to rely on either JJ or Charlie to help her. *I wish I had told her to go to Jackson first*, he thought.

The biggest worry he had now though, aside from the pressing need for rest and sleep, was Tait. *He may be an old codger, but he's a damned smart old codger,* Lucas admitted. *I've probably got maybe a couple hours or so before he figures out that I've been doubling back on him. Don't think that dumb-assed lieutenant has it figured out or ever will, but bet my stripes old Tait is getting real close. Matter of fact, almost seems like I can feel him breathing down my neck right this minute. Old bastard.*

The sound of early morning traffic racing by on the nearby highway lulled him to sleep after a bit. Off and on he would stir, but his exhaustion didn't allow him to fully awaken until well into the late afternoon. The sun moved lower in the west, elongating the shadows closing in on the thicket. As it continued its westward journey, light slipped through the windshield, falling full across his face. Involuntarily, Lucas snorted, turning away from the brightness and pawing irritably at sleepy eyes.

Awakening with a start, he looked about confused, unable to remember where he was. Once his mind cleared, he realized sleep had stolen away most of the day. Panicked, he snatched a quick glance at the dashboard clock. It was almost 1700 hours, time to go.

Hunger pangs, reminding him of the missed meals spread over the past day and a half, gnawed incessantly. He searched among the few things in the back seat and finally found the remains of a few cookies Em bought at the country store where they had stopped for gas the other morning. The stale crumbs did little to satisfy his hunger but instead aggravated his thirst. The water in the roadside ditch tempted him, but the thought of drinking water fouled by no telling what temporarily slaked the need. "By damned if I'll do that, not after drinking half the water in the Waccamaw when I couldn't help it," he groused, "but I ain't in no mood to drink outta no danged ditch on purpose."

What I gotta do now is think out how I can git back to meet Em. We got to figure out what to do. No matter, I have to see that she and the baby are okay. Why did this have to happen to us? He let his mind dwell on Em before forcing himself to think of how he could get to see her. *I could wait until tonight, then drive back to Murrells Inlet and make my way back through the woods like I was going to do before, I guess. Sure as I do though, if Tait has me figured out, I've had it. Hellfire, what's the matter with me? Them figuring on me doubling back so much, it makes sense for me to try to drive somewhere north of Myrtle Beach, hide this car and sneak down along the shore.*

North Myrtle Beach, South Carolina
Friday, 15 January 1954
2113 hours

Mackley wheeled the car into one of the several vacant public parking areas near the ocean midway between Myrtle Beach and North Myrtle Beach and parked it in the shadows.

Taking a moment, he debated whether or not to change back into his civilian shirt or to still wear the fatigue shirt and jacket. Considering the season, he opted for the latter. The olive drab fatigue uniform would also allow camouflage more effectively in the woods near the installation. It would be necessary to hide out in the woods for several hours, or possibly even a couple of days, before Emily was due to show up, so concealment and stealth were necessary to avoid discovery.

On first thought, he considered walking along the edge of the water but decided that should anyone be up and about, he would more than likely be seen. With the moon due to rise soon, he would also be silhouetted against the sea. Even with few tourists this time of the year, the chances of being seen and recognized were too great out on the beach alone in the dead of winter.

Since most of the summer homes fronting the highway were now empty, he decided to casually stroll along the sidewalk between the houses and the road. Perhaps boldness would be his best ally. Getting out of the car, he reached into the back, found the fatigue jacket and put it on then, pulling his cap down low, began walking southward. Several yards away, Lucas stopped and looked back at the car. For a moment, he was suddenly sad. This would be the last time he would ever see the green Chevy, but there was nothing else he could do but leave it. He turned back toward Myrtle Beach and, with eyes downcast, plodded south.

Two hours later, Mackley was near the north end of the boardwalk in downtown Myrtle Beach. At that point, Lucas turned left behind the Beach House Bar to the beach and walked to the boardwalk as unobtrusively as possible, hoping all the while that one of the men in his unit would not see and recognize him. Every step toward his destination was agonizing because of the fear of discovery. The closer Lucas got to his rendezvous with Em, the more frightened he became. To come so close to being with her again and then be captured before he could hold her in his arms once more would be almost more than he could bear. The promise of a new life with Em and the baby forced him on.

The boardwalk bent at a slight angle back to the right as the beach veered a bit westward. As he passed the angle, the south end of the walk came into view a hundred yards farther on. Finally, he stepped down the five steps onto the sandy beach, momentarily hidden from view.

Whether the tension in his body was from fear or from sheer exhaustion, he couldn't tell. But whatever the cause, Mackley had to pause for a breather. His legs were rubbery from fatigue, and he was shaking from hunger.

Bleary-eyed, Lucas Mackley had come as far as he could without rest. If Tait should be standing right there in front of him holding a pair of handcuffs, ready to snap them on, he would have to accept his fate. He had to stop and rest both mind and body or risk complete collapse.

Looking back along the walk, he saw no one approaching from behind. Quickly glancing shoreward he saw no one in that direction either. The inland streets also appeared deserted. In a quick movement, he ducked low and crept into the shadows beneath the boardwalk, again pausing to carefully peer from beneath the walk's concealment. Finally satisfied that he had not been observed, he crawled farther back into the recesses beneath the boardwalk. A restless sea continued its endless roar as its breaking waves tried to breach the narrow strand. Huddled in the sand Lucas slept, lulled by soothing sea noises and sheer exhaustion.

Footpads creaking on the salt-soaked boards above him accompanied by the sound of voices startled Mackley into full alertness. "Damn!" He crept near the steps and silently cursed, "Why didn't I keep going? I coulda been to them danged woods by now."

He heard the lilting feminine laughter and the murmured words. "Hon, keep your hands where they belong."

More laughter, then silence. Lucas held his breath, fearing imminent discovery.

"Baby, that's exactly where I'm putting 'em, where they belong," hissed a husky male voice.

Realizing the interlopers were unaware of him under the

boardwalk, Lucas quietly exhaled. That voice sounded familiar. *No, I'm imagining things*, he thought. He was embarrassed by being in the uncomfortable position of eavesdropping on the couple engrossed with one another and apparently unaware of his presence. Even more disturbing was the thought they just might decide to join him under the walk for privacy to carry on their lovemaking. Things were turning serious, and he was trapped there with no way out. From above he could hear deep breathing from the man and woman.

"Lowell," the girl panted, "please stop. We can't do this. Suppose you knock me up. Would you be willing to marry me?"

"You know I would, Lucy. Girl, I love you so much I don't think I can do without you."

"And just how many other girls have you told that old bull to?"

"But, Lucy, I ain't gonna let nothing happen. I promise."

"Well, one…I don't know. Did you bring a rubber?"

"Aw hell, woman. We don't need one. I told you I wouldn't let you get pregnant."

Lucas almost laughed out loud. That was the same line he had fed Emily. And now look. She was nearly a couple months along. *For two cents I'd crawl out of this hiding place and kick some ass. Lying dog.*

"Aw, Lucy. Come on now, me and you could crawl under the boardwalk and lie on the sand and make mad, passionate love."

Lucas nearly choked. *Holy crap! They come under here an' I'm dead!*

He heard Lucy say in no uncertain terms. "No way, Lowell. I ain't going under that boardwalk or any other place with you."

Lowell's voice became agitated. "All right, if that's how you feel about me then maybe we ought to just call it quits right here and now. You tell me how much you care for me, but that's just a lie. You don't trust me when I say ain't nothing gonna happen. Just irks the crap outta me you won't believe me. Plain pisses me off is what it does."

Lucy showed her true grit. "No, Lowell, it ain't a matter of me trusting you. It's a matter of you not respecting me, and right now, it seems like you think of me as nothing more than a whore. I know my way home, so you can haul your backside outta my sight. Okay?"

Mackley felt like calling out to the girl, *Good for you. That's telling the sorry bastard!*

He heard steps retreating back down the boardwalk. Lowell stood above Lucas, grumbling for a few minutes more. "Damn teaser. Shoulda knowed I wasn't gonna make it with her."

Lucas heard the disappointed man walk over to the boardwalk railing.

Oh hell! That son of a gun is taking a leak. Lucas rolled to the side in time to avoid being splattered.

Myrtle Beach, South Carolina
Near Team 1 Operation Site
Thursday, 15 January 1954
0249 hours

Mackley walked stealthily the last half-mile through the woods to the small clearing for his meeting with Em. Snaking along the damp, frigid forest litter for the last hundred yards, he located a small depression, partially surrounded by brush, and wormed deep among the broken limbs against the trunk of a fallen tree. From that position, he found a relatively unobstructed view that allowed him surveillance of the entire woodland opening. His rumbling stomach reminded him that he hadn't eaten in several hours, and even then the fare was Spartan. The thought of walking on over to the radar station and giving up was tempting, but what would that accomplish? To give up now would concede guilt and, despite knowing the outcome of that, his own stubbornness wouldn't let him give in. It was certain he would be in even more trouble. Not only would he be charged with killing Webber, but there were surely charges of being absent without leave, escaping arrest, assaulting an officer of the law, and no telling how many more charges Tait might conjure up.

He lay with his back against the rough bark of the decaying log, staring off into the darkness and re-living the past few weeks. He and Em had parked there an age ago. No, it had been only a month or two.

Hell, I ain't been able to think straight since Em left. You sorry jerk. You shouldn't have drug that girl into this mess. You could have stopped her. Woulda made her mad, but that woulda been better'n throwin' in with the likes of you.

He began feeling a sadness that would not go away. The desperation of running had erased any hope of life ever returning to how it was. The plans they had for going to Waycross now seemed in the distant past. When Em left him at Murrells Inlet something seemed to die within him. Sure, Em was carrying his kid, but how fair was it for either of them to be burdened by his mistakes?

Boy, that was some night. Lucas's mind wandered back to when he and Emily loved in the secluded spot he was now staring at. *Never in my life would I have thought I'd meet a girl like her. On top of that, she actually looked me up. Here I was busting my butt chasing women, and there she was right there waiting for me all the time. If I ever git out of this trouble I'm in, I'll spend the rest of my life making it up to her.*

The sun, a bright red cadmium ball in the crisp early January dawn, crept through the trees from the ocean and awakened Mackley. He carefully searched in all directions, moving as little as possible before slowly standing, avoiding sudden movement that could give him away. Assured he was alone, he again searched carefully for anything unusual or out of place. Finally satisfied that he was alone, he stepped away from the hiding place and urinated at the base of a small pine tree.

Once relieved, he returned to the deadfall and checked his watch—0722 hours. Em would not be there for several hours yet. He had a long wait ahead, but that could not be helped. He had been fortunate so far in being able to get here unobserved. Now, if that luck held, he would be with Em. *Boy! That couple on the boardwalk last night scared half my life away. I bet I look ten years older jist from that one thing,* he thought, smiling. *Tell you what, Lucas, my boy,* he laughed silently, *that old boy danged near peed right square in your face.*

He reversed his position along the log, this time with his head toward the ocean. By squirming against the log, he managed to wallow out a relatively comfortable place to lie. Even tired and cold, sleep would not come to shut out the misery of hiding and waiting. He looked at his watch for the tenth time. Nine-thirteen hours. Time snailed along.

On Highway 17, sounds of traffic increased to a steady pace, announcing that the day was well into its prime. Every now and then one of the team's vehicles turned right from 17 onto the shell-covered road, and soon after, the sound of it slowing to turn right onto the beach road could be heard as it headed toward the installation. The unmistakable hum of a jeep passed along the beach road and stopped at the radar site. Lucas wondered who it was. Probably Jackson returning from picking up the mail downtown and of course, having his morning coffee and doughnut. Jackson's routine never varied; he always drove to town, leaving the compound at exactly the same time each morning. He always stopped at the doughnut shop for his one doughnut and single cup of over-sweetened coffee. *Man, I'd enlist for another tour for one of them greasy things right now.*

The sun was at its apex off in the southern sky when Mackley fell asleep, and all afternoon he dozed off and on before finally giving in to sleep soundly near dusk. Natural night sounds awakened him to an ebony night awaiting the moon to push back the darkness. Again peering about cautiously before standing, he stretched his cold-stiffened legs and hugged himself trying to restore circulation to his battered and shivering body. The voice of the man on the boardwalk ran familiar through his mind, but he still could not place it. His watch showed the time was just shy of 2000 hours. He would be holding Em close again in a few more minutes.

Myrtle Beach, South Carolina
Friday, January 15, 1954
7:10 P.M.

Emily waited impatiently for Charlie to come for her. When she had approached him about taking her to meet with Lucas she sensed hesitancy, maybe even fear. Perhaps it was simply the fact that Lucas was in trouble with the authorities and Charlie just really didn't want to get involved, as he had told her. People were funny about associating themselves with someone in trouble. Adversity was a great indicator of true loyalty.

At this late hour, however, Emily would have to trust Charlie if she was going to get to Lucas. JJ might take her to where she needed to go, or maybe Sergeant Jackson, but she had committed to Charlie, and even though she was frightened she had to go through with the commitment.

Time dragged slowly on as she waited, the second hand on the watch took an eternity in its circuit around the dial. She had gone back to school after returning from Murrells Inlet, but her mind was on Lucas. Looking back she could scarcely remember what had happened during the days since returning to Myrtle Beach. Again Em looked at the watch. The hands had scarcely moved. Charlie should be coming soon.

She pushed the window curtain aside and looked hopefully toward the street. It was quiet with the street devoid of traffic at this hour. It was still fairly early in the night, but this late in January, darkness came near 5:30, some two hours ago. The worried girl let the curtain fall back into place and turned from the window.

Her mother, watching with a questioning look on her face, tentatively said, "Em, you need to quit worrying so. Lucas is gonna be all right."

"I know, Momma, but I can't help being afraid for him. He's been out there in the cold running from all those folks for so long.

Seems like a lifetime. Momma, he's my life now, and if something bad happened to him, I don't know what I'd do."

Eula pulled her daughter close and hugged her. Both women jumped at the knock on the door.

Mrs. Johnson guessed that the person knocking had come for Emily. She looked into Emily's face and said, "Emily, I know you're up to something, but I also know there ain't a thing I can do one way or the other to get you to let the law handle this. So I won't try. Now, honey, run along and do what you gotta do, and remember I love you."

"Thanks, Momma. Love you, too."

U.S. Highway 17 South
2110 hours

Charlie and Emily drove south on Highway 17. The road to the radar installation was still about a mile away. Both had ridden in silence since leaving the Johnson house ten minutes earlier. Em stared straight ahead into the darkness beyond the reach of the car's headlights, feeling an ominous uneasiness. Was it wise to trust Charlie? Well, it was too late to worry now. She would let him take her only to the radar site, then walk from there.

Kesterman drove without speaking, wondering where the girl would direct him next, suspecting it would be the radar site.

They passed a familiar landmark, and she turned to face Charlie, saying, "We're almost to where we should turn off, Charlie. If you would, please turn left right up yonder a ways and take me to the radar station."

Kesterman's dark eyebrows rose, but he remained silent. Slowing as the oyster shell-paved side road came into view, he braked the car and turned smoothly onto the smaller road. When it ended at the beach, a right turn placed them only a short distance from the site. As they approached, the rotating antenna told them the radar set was operating. When he parked the car and they got out, the rumble of the smelly diesel generators drowned out the noisy sound of the nearby surf.

"Now what?" Charlie asked, stone-faced.

Em appeared not to hear.

"Now what?" Charlie repeated impatiently, massaging the scar on his cheek.

Em dismissed the question. "Thanks Charlie, for bringing me out here. You can go now. I'll be all right. So, you can go on back to the compound if you want to. I won't keep you any longer." Emily tried not to let him see how eager she was for him to leave, so that she could continue on to meet Lucas.

"You sure?" he inquired, reluctant to go, staring at her with dark piercing eyes.

"Yes. Yes, I'm sure. Thanks again. You've been a big help," Em replied dismissively, trying to evade the sinister look he was giving her.

"No problem, Emily. I could hang around a bit longer if you want." Charlie didn't appear in a hurry to leave.

Emily looked at her watch and glanced around nervously. Finally, she turned back to Kesterman and repeated, "Thanks for bringing me out here, Charlie. I'll wait here to see if Lucas comes for me."

"And if he don't? You know that boy's in a heap of trouble. You need a real man to git you out of this, Em."

Irritated, she replied, "Then I'll find somebody to take me back home." Em moved away from him as she looked out over the dark ocean.

Scattered clouds scudded northward across the face of the full moon, briefly blotting out its silver light with their passing. The evening tide crashed against the sandy beach, roaring as each wave crested and broke, creating whitecaps just before falling to the sand then surging foamingly forward to break like pearls on a golden platter. When each wave retreated, bubbles issuing from the water-soaked sands marked the hideouts of the myriads of sand fleas and other small crustaceans. Tiny shore birds raced back and forth, dodging the incoming waves, seeking out the minute organisms.

"Oh God, Lucas. Seems that even nature has told on you just like those waves are telling on those little animals in the sand out there on that beach. I pray for you to be safe, my darling, but I'm so afraid." Em softly wept for Lucas as Charlie reluctantly returned sullenly to his car and drove away into the dreary winter night.

It was time to go. Emily looked around to see if anyone was watching, and when she felt the men at the site were busy with their duties or simply not paying attention to her, she casually walked to the edge of the surf then strolled north along the deserted beach. Some distance from the site, hidden by the night shadows, she made her way through a narrow row of sea oats and grasses to the beach road. There she paused and, seeing no one, turned left onto the lane and hurried to the open glade. Stepping into the familiar clearing, Em whispered in a barely audible voice, "Lucas?"

Lucas was standing behind a large pine tree at the edge of the clearing when Emily came out of the shadows into view, softly calling his name. Caution, honed to a fine edge from hours of running and hiding, caused him to hesitate momentarily before stepping into the open. Em sensed movement and, whirling about, saw him emerge from the woods.

She gasped, and her face brightened as a smile touched her lips. "Oh, Lucas!" She threw herself at him, crying, "I've missed you so! Oh, my love, you'll never know how much."

All Lucas could do was to stand there and stare longingly at the girl, his mouth dry and unable to speak. Loving her more than ever.

"Boy, seems like I always have to ask you. You gonna stand there all night? Or are you gonna kiss me?"

That snapped him out of his trance, and he tenderly enfolded her in his arms. "Girl, you better believe I'm gonna hold you and kiss you. After what we been through, I ain't never gonna let you go again."

CHAPTER 42

Myrtle Beach, South Carolina
Woods near the Team 1 Operations Site
Friday, 15 January 1954
2113 hours

"Well, now, ain't that a real sweet scene. You two slobbering over each other like two sick kittens on a hot brick. Makes a man want to throw up."

The young couple turned to stare in the direction of the voice. Silhouetted by the rising full moon, the intruder stood threateningly close, glaring at them. The barrel of a revolver gleamed in the faint light as he purposefully stepped from the shadows into the clearing where Lucas and Em stood in shocked silence. Hard, glinting eyes pinned them to the background of darkness, his face obscured in the dim moonlight. An aura of pent-up malfeasance from those eyes made Lucas shudder as he stared at death. Had that evil always been there? Had he just been unable to see or unwilling to accept it?

"Lucas, my boy, you had your chance. You just simply wouldn't run when you could, would you? You had to come back for your dear little Emily and mess things up for everybody. Ever since we left Biloxi, I been having to play the clown, act the fool, hoping that no one would come here looking. But no, that ain't the way things worked out. Believe me, I tried to steer the law away from you, Lucas, but you was too dumb to understand what was going on!" The timbre of the demented voice rose to a spine-chillingly high pitch.

"I got no choice now, Lucas! I'd save your ass if I could but not if it means losing mine. And you git arrested, the law's gonna question you and sweat things outta you that you don't even remember that are bound to point right smack dab at me."

Em and Lucas stared, frozen in time, unable to either speak or move, transfixed by the madman before them.

"Damned right I hated that bastard Webber same as you. Only difference is I seen my chance and done something about it. I swear, Lucas, I didn't mean to actually kill him. Only wanted to rough him up a little, but when he come at me there in that rec room like a mad dog, I grabbed that bat and went at him. When I left there he was alive, I swear he was." The voice was pleading for understanding. Pleading that was lost in insanity.

Lucas found his voice and, with Em beside him trembling, said with a calm not felt, "What I don't understand is that you woulda had to have had blood all over you. From what I've heard about Webber he was pretty messed up, and there was a lot of blood splattered around. When you came back to the club, I don't remember seeing any on you." Swallowing the fear that rose in his throat, he thought frantically, trying to stall for time. "How did you manage that?"

"Yeah, that did worry me then and some since. You was just too drunk to notice, but no matter. I stopped by the car, grabbed a clean pair of fatigues, and changed in the latrine. Stuck the bloody ones under the front seat of the car. If you had looked you'd seen I had on newer ones when I got back."

Lucas's mind raced as he continued stalling, trying to think of a way to escape. He was too close for them to run. They could get no more than a step or two before…

"I'll tell you something else, good buddy," the strident voice interrupted Lucas's deliberations. "You thought you was so smart getting on my case about that little bitch over at Toddville, and that one that was always hanging out at Claude's. Little teasers treated me like dirt, but I showed both of 'em. Gave 'em what they deserved. Then, that damned whore over at Lake City thought she could just drop me cold and get away with it. Even tried to blame me for her husband's death. Showed her, too."

"You mean it was you killed them girls? Man, I don't believe you."

"Damn right I killed 'em. Had my way I mighta got me a couple more, too. That whore Amy Lentz that JJ was messin' with. Shoulda got her, too. May git her yet, she don't watch out."

Still playing for time, desperately trying to think, Lucas asked, "Why did you kill that guy from Toddville? He wasn't a girl."

"I'll tell you why, Lucas. He just plain got in my way. That's all. Plus, she chose him instead of me. Couldn't let old Jane Marie git away with that, now, could I? No siree. No way could I let that happen."

"There's still something I don't understand," Lucas said, puzzled.

"Yeah, what?" he asked, relishing the power he held over the terrified couple.

Lucas replied, "You remember that woman back there in Biloxi, that got herself killed, and we thought it was Webber? Well, I gotta know—was it him?"

The deranged laugh sent a deathly chill through Lucas. "Yeah, my man, ain't that a pisser. You always thought it was him. Hell, I'll tell you exactly what happened," he said, talking matter of fact as if he was relating a favorite story. "I was cruising along Back Bay—just killing time, and when I drove past Gallataine's, I seen her come out of the building and walk down toward one of them joints along the bay. Figured I'd follow her, maybe even get lucky and pick her up. Damned bitch wouldn't have nothing to do with me, though."

Disgusted, Lucas said sneeringly, "So?"

With his eyes flashing angrily, the maniac growled, "You wanted to hear this, so shut the hell up and listen. Like I said, the bitch wouldn't even look at me but just kept walking, flipping her tail. Finally, I drove off. Matter of fact, I drove around for an hour or so and was about to go in the Bayside Bar when she came up drunker than ol' Cooter Brown. Saw her go in and decided to wait and get her when she come out. I was about to give up, when about an hour later that fat bastard Webber comes strutting out like he owned the world and got in his car. Instead of leaving, bastard just sat there waiting. Wouldn't you know a few minutes later she comes out and gets in the car with him. Figured he was gonna take her out to the bushes and knock a little off, but that son of a bitch musta been queer 'cause he drove straight to a rundown apartment down the street where she got out, yelling something nasty at him. He yelled back and scratched out, heading toward the base."

Stunned, Lucas asked, "Are you telling me…?"

"You better believe it! Dragged her into my car and taught her a lesson!"

"Oh God!" screamed Em, clinging to Lucas.

Turning on her, letting his dark piercing eyes hold them at bay, the crazed man snarled, "That's right, Maggie, you dumped me back there in Vicksburg. I wasn't good enough for your high society momma. Not good enough for you…"

"Oh my God!" Lucas cried, shoving Em behind him. "He's crazy! He thinks you're Maggie Debreau!"

"That right, good buddy, she's good old Maggie all right, and I'm gonna fix her real good!"

Forcing himself to remain calm, Lucas pleaded, "No, Charlie, she's not Maggie. This is Em."

"No! No, you're trying to screw me over." Charlie advanced

crowding them back across the clearing.

The two men were face to face, standing no more than a couple of feet apart. The revolver gleamed, a lethal instrument ready to perform its ultimate act. The unmistakable metallic sound of it being cocked overrode the sounds of their hearts pounding.

"Goodbye, Maggie!" his voice snarled evilly.

Lucas lunged, simultaneously shoving Emily aside. "You sorry bastard!" he managed before dual shots split the night, one from the assailant's gun and the other from the edge of the clearing.

Charlie Kesterman fell to the ground, mortally wounded, his life ebbing rapidly from the gaping wound in his side.

Emily moaned, and as Lucas turned he saw her slump to the leaf-littered ground. Dropping to his knees, the dreadful truth hit him. He sat there with Em's head cradled in his lap, tears falling unashamedly from his eyes, as he held her hand and watched her life fade.

"Oh no! God! Not Em!" he cried.

Em squeezed Lucas's hand and smiled up at his grief-stricken face. "I love you, Lucas," she whispered and then closed her eyes.

CHAPTER 43

Radar 1 Orderly Room
Friday, 22 January 1954
1300 hours

Staff Sergeant Lucas Mackley emerged from Captain Cook's office as Sheriff Earl Lee Tait entered the orderly room.

"Good luck on your new assignment, Mackley. You're a good man and I hate to lose you, but I understand you wanting to transfer."

Lucas nodded. "Thank you, sir. I appreciate that." He saluted and then turned toward Tait. "Sheriff," he acknowledged.

"Son, I know that there ain't anything that I can say that'll make things easy for you. I won't even try, except to say I'm sorry I couldn't stop Kesterman in time. I do want you to know that I'd give my life if it would bring that little girl back."

Not really knowing what to say, Lucas replied, "Yessir, I guess we both would. Right now, though, Sheriff, I need some time to be alone."

"Boy, that ain't likely to solve anything. Em would be mighty disappointed in you. I expect she's up there," Tait pointed skyward, "ready to tell you to remember her but to get on with living your life."

"I know, Mr. Tait, but it sure does hurt something awful," Lucas answered, his sad eyes glistening with tears.

"I understand, son," Earl Lee said, looking the young man in the eyes. "It'll make me feel better if you knew whut happened in this whole mess. You up to listening to an old fool?"

"I guess so," replied Lucas, holding out his hands in resignation.

"Thank you, Lucas. As you probably know, several of us including Lieutenant Rodgers, Sheriff Prewit, Jim Weldon, Kate Garner, and me got together to try to piece together the puzzle of what was goin' on. It looked after a time that you, Kesterman, and Phelps was the most likely ones, and when you ran, it put you at the top of the list.

Mackley nodded, "Yeah, I guess I messed up good."

"That's right, Lucas, but actually your taking off like you did allowed me to concentrate on who I really suspected. Let me give you sort of a history of what we had. Remember that girl, Evelyn Dendy, who got raped last September then later killed, and that young couple from Toddville last fall?"

Lucas nodded again.

"Well, we found enough bits and pieces of information to make us a little more than suspicious of Kesterman, but we still didn't have enough to pull him in. When the mess with that sergeant's killing in Mississippi got us to thinking straight, things began to fall in place. Still couldn't nail him, though. All the time, I expected we'd find the Lentz girl dead somewhere. Things got muddied up when she disappeared and then reappeared. That seemed to point to Phelps, but she showed up after she'd run off to Orangeburg for a few days. So, that put Kesterman back at the top of the list."

"Whut really pinned it all down was the murder of the Moorland woman over at Lake City. You remember? She was that truck driver's widder. You know, the one that was killed in the wreck with that convoy you was in a couple years ago? Anyway, after he was killed, she went wild. Out honky-tonkin' about every night.

Seems Kesterman was over there tom-cattin' around and took up with her. Anyway, she apparently got tired of him after awhile and dropped him, and soon after she came up dead. Ira Prewit pointed out to me how her death was similar to the others. Things just fell into place then. Knowing that Kesterman was the only one of the three of you ever seen with her made him the obvious suspect."

"Like I said, Sheriff, I messed up by running. Had I not, things would have been different."

"Maybe so, Mackley," Earl Lee replied, knowing what Lucas was implying, "but can't no one tell what the future holds. Anyone in your situation would have done the same thing, so don't be too hard on yourself. Anyway," Tait continued, "that let me concentrate on Kesterman despite what Lieutenant Rodgers thought. There was just too many things aginst 'im. For example, we found out that besides dating the Moorland woman, he had been snubbed by both the Wallace girl and Evelyn Dendy. What really convinced me, though, was what that Emerson girl he was stuck on down in Mississippi told me. Seems he beat her up pretty bad a couple times. Anyway, we still didn't have enough on him to make the charges stick. Figured all I could do was to keep an eye on him."

When Lucas did not respond, Tait continued, "In your case, Gene was on you from the time you left North Myrtle Beach. We got lucky there when someone saw you park your car and start walking toward town. Me and Babb was watching Kesterman. Only thing was he got a little ahead of us, and before we could git to that clearing, he already had you covered. I shot soon as I could, but just not in time to keep him from shooting first."

Tait stopped talking, then nervously shifted and looked away. Lucas could see that he was having a difficult time explaining what happened and why it happened. After a moment, he looked at Lucas, sadness evident in his eyes. Tait's voice faltered as he placed his hand on Lucas's shoulder. "Son, I truly am sorry."

CHAPTER 44

U.S. Veterans Hospital
Gulfport, Mississippi
The Present

"Marty, you're the only one I've ever told about Emily. It's always been too painful for me to speak openly of her death. I remember that dreadful night. The moon was full and alive much the same as it was on the night Em and I made love in the wooded glade. When she died in my arms, the moon dulled. My life ended with her last breath," Chief Master Sergeant Mackley murmured sadly, his old-man voice breaking. "I suppose," he said finally, "when I look back more objectively, those dreams we had were never to be." Closing his eyes, he retreated back into his private hell.

Marty watched helplessly as a tear slid silently down his age-creased face. "Sergeant, I'm so sorry that I nagged you into telling me about something that I now realize hurt you so much," Marty murmured, placing an arm around his frail shoulders.

Opening his eyes, he saw silent tears slide down her cheek. Reaching over, he brushed one away in an old-man clumsy way. She smiled at him, tightening her arm about his shoulders.

"You know, Marty," he said, "I should thank you. I've held all of this back, feeling lowdown and sorry for myself. Well, it's time I quit wallowing in self-pity, and I'm glad it was you who made me finally turn those old memories loose. No, to answer the question I know you want to ask, I won't ever forget those times, but you made me finally realize what old Sheriff Tait meant about Em wanting me to go on living. At that point, not wanting to accept that she was gone, all I could think about was losing her."

Marty reached into her uniform pocket to search for a tissue. Not finding one, she wiped the back of her hand across her nose then, sniffing self-consciously, said, "Didn't mean to cry, but couldn't help it. And you know, from the first day I met you and you called me Em, I've wanted to know what happened. Something told me that something terrible had happened to the two of you. And now, at the risk of hurting you more, I would like for you to tell me what happened afterward. I gather that you transferred right away from Myrtle Beach, but what did you do after that?"

"There's not a great deal to tell," he said, shrugging as if his life had been trivial after Em's death. "JJ Phelps and I never were friends again. He didn't even come to her funeral, and I suppose it bothered me for a while. I suppose our friendship wasn't real after all. Anyway, after I left Myrtle Beach, a mutual acquaintance told me Phelps finished his tour of duty and went back to Missouri. After a few years, I thought a time or two about trying to contact him, but it was best that I didn't. The old camaraderie was gone, destroyed back there at Myrtle Beach."

"What about Sergeant Jackson and the others? Did you ever see any of them again?" she asked.

Lucas stared out over the smooth waters of the Gulf, trying to remember. Looking back at Marty, he answered slowly, "I really didn't want to see any of them because I didn't want to be reminded. There was one time, during the war in Vietnam, when I was in the PX on a stop-over at a base in Japan. Jackson was there, and, had he not recognized me and spoke, I doubt I would have noticed him. He had finagled a direct commission and, at the time, was a major working in the JAG office at Langley, Virginia. He'd gotten fatter and balder but otherwise, was the same old Jackson. After a brief, awkward visit I excused myself, telling him I had to catch a plane."

"I hesitate to ask," Marty said tentatively, "but did you ever go back to Myrtle Beach?"

"No," he answered, letting sadness once again slip into his voice. "I guess there were too many bad memories. Sometimes, since I've been here at Gulfport, I've thought about what it would have been like to return and, even now, the idea of going back has crossed my mind. But," he added smiling, "it may be better not to go and just remember the good times and those dreams Em and I had."

"You still haven't told me what you did after you left Myrtle Beach? I know that you remained in the Air Force, but did you ever find anyone else and marry?" The hurt look told Marty that she should not have asked, and quickly she said, "Oh, I'm so sorry."

Patting her hand, he responded, "That's all right, Marty. No, I never found anyone else. I did make a career of the Air Force. After my first hitch was up, I left the service and went back to Arkansas where I worked at several lackluster jobs for four years, all the time drinking heavily and feeling sorry for myself. Finally, recognizing I didn't want to continue living like that, I re-enlisted and spent the next twenty-five years or so going all over the world. I retired in 1985, spent the next four or five years in Arkansas then came down here to Gulfport."

His eyes seeming to sparkle a little more as Sergeant Mackley smiled and rose stiffly from the bench. "I thank you, Miss Marty, for letting me tell you about Em and me. Now, I feel a little tired, so if you don't mind, I'll go back to my room."

Veterans Hospital

Gulfport, Mississippi
The Following Morning

Marty Judson, RN, arrived early the next day, intending to visit Chief Master Sergeant Lucas Mackley before starting her regular duties. Turning off Highway 90 onto the complex grounds, she didn't see him seated on his favorite bench under the graceful old live oak and wondered where he might be. Driving on around the administration building and parking in the staff lot, she quickly checked her hair in the rearview mirror, got out and, after locking the car, hurried inside. Pausing at the desk long enough to sign in, she called to the nurse on duty.

"Be back in a minute. I want to stop in and visit with Sergeant Mackley for a moment." The look on the nurse's face stopped her as dread swept over her.

In a halting voice choked with emotion, the nurse said, "I'm terribly sorry, Marty. He died in his sleep last night."

Military Jargon

AC&W Sq: Aircraft Control and Warning Squadron
AFB: Air Force Base
AP: Air Police
AWOL: absent without official leave
A/3C: airman third class, formerly rank of private first class
azimuth: a direction expressed as an angle measured clockwise
from a reference point
bitch box: externally mounted loudspeaker for general announce-
ments within squadron area
bivouac: temporary encampment
B-4 bag: canvas traveling bag, suitcase equipped with zippered side
pockets
BOQ: bachelor officer's quarters
C-4: plastic, putty textured explosive
C-47: Douglas C-47 Sky Train, also "Goony Bird;" twin engine
prop-driven transport aircraft
CO: commanding officer
CQ: charge of quarters, non-commissioned officer responsible for
installation after normal working hours
delay en route: leave en route, leave taken in addition to allowed
travel time between duty assignments
deuce and a half: common two and one half ton utility truck; also,
six by six

Electronics Tng Sq: Electronics Training Squadron
GI: government issue, enlisted person
fart sack:: mattress cover
fatigues: coarse, durable uniforms for field, fatigue duty
F-16: multi-role jet fighter aircraft, also Fighting Falcon
F-80: early jet fighter aircraft, also Shooting Star
ground pounder: infantryman, grunt
JAG: USAF Judge Advocate General; responsible for judicial and legal functions
KP: kitchen police, mess hall helper
latrine: toilet facility
lifer: career military person
mess: meal
mess tent: field facility for food service
MOS: military occupation specialty
NCO: noncommissioned officer
NCOIC: noncommissioned officer in charge
obstacle course: training exercise to simulate combat situation
OCS: Officer Candidate School
OD: officer of the day with responsibility for squadron after normal duty hours
OJT: on the job training
old man: CO, commanding officer
orderly room: squadron administrative office
P-51: single engine, propeller driven fighter airplane, "Mustang"
PFC: Private first class, later designated airman third class, A3/C
PPI scope: radar visual indicator showing direction and distance of a target
PX: post exchange, multipurpose on base store
Radar: radio detecting and ranging, target location system
Sq: Squadron, basic administrative unit
TDY: temporary duty
Top: first sergeant, top ranking NCO
USAF: United States Air Force

VFW: Veterans of Foreign Wars
XO: executive officer; second in command of squadron

Military time is a twenty-four-hour system with each hour expressed with four digits.

Example: 0316

Civilian or conventional time from midnight to noon may be converted to military time by deleting the colon separating hours from minutes and formatting to four digits.

Examples: 3:16 A.M. = 0316 hours
11:29 A.M. = 1129 hours

To convert civilian time from noon to midnight delete the colon and add 1200.

Example: 2:43 P.M. = 1443 hours
(243 + 1200 = 1443)

The designations A.M. and P.M. are not used in military time.

Acknowledgments

The author wishes to acknowledge Franklin D. Rast who unselfishly gave of his time to preliminary editing of the manuscript and for valuable suggestions for its improvement. My appreciation goes to the late Ann Bigham for her editorial contributions and proofreading. Monica Ussery Enlow and Kathy Worley are recognized for proofreading the manuscript.

Special appreciation is given to Laura Fortune of American Book Publishing for her editing skills, and especially for her patience and guidance in making this book a reality. And to Nathan Fitzgearl and the folks at American Book Publishing, my thanks to you for taking a chance on me.

Finally, thanks to my family and friends for having faith in me. Their support is acknowledged and appreciated.

About the Author

Luther A. Knight, Jr. is a native of Clarendon, Arkansas. Following a four-year tour in the United States Air Force he earned a BSE degree from Arkansas State College and Master's and PhD degrees from the University of Mississippi. He joined the faculty of the University of Mississippi in 1968 and retired as professor emeritus of biology, devoting over twenty years to environmental and science education and research at Ole Miss. In recognition of his contributions to environmental biology, he was named "Mississippi Soil, Air and Water Conservationist of the Year" in 1995 by the Mississippi Wildlife Federation.

He married Janis M. King of Malden, Missouri, in 1955. They have two sons, Scott and Charles. Scott and his wife, Kathy, have two children, Brad and Anna, and live in Oxford, Mississippi. Charles has a son, Samuel, and lives in Jackson, Mississippi. Luther Knight and his wife, Janis, now live in Oxford, Mississippi.